BY THE SEA
REVISED EDITION

A modern comic adult fairy tale with an ensemble cast of Cinderellas.

Instead of a kingdom by the sea, our story takes place in and around a residential hotel by the sea. The architecturally eclectic Briers Hotel is situated on Leech Beach, a not particularly inviting beach, being often fog-bound and always scruffy. But it's the perfect setting for our Cinderellas, male and female, who put up with the scruffiness of life while striving to make it through their various personal seaside fogs. Theater; art; antiques; old movies; sex; more sex; death; fast and slow cars, chicken shit and cow poop; military bearing and erotic emissions—not to mention the wicked witch, the sea serpent by the seashore, the village ogre, the village idiot, and several Prince Charmings—all figure into this merry tale with a multitude of happy endings.

PRAISE FOR
BY THE SEA

"Steven Paul Leiva has written an engaging, thoughtful, and kind book. In this era of unlikeable characters and the idea that a "good" book is one in which horrible things happen to horrible people, Leiva has turned that entirely on its head. Even when people act badly, he has told their story with sympathy and grace, with complete kindness for even the most outwardly difficult characters. By the Sea is long, but it's not fat. It's all muscle. And what a satisfying book it is! Leiva has built his small world perfectly, and each character is so complete and well thought out that what at first seems disparate pieces fit together perfectly by the end. It's a hat trick in perfect proportions!" — **Jo Graham, author of Black Ships, Hand of Isis, and Stealing Fire.**

"Leiva writes the story with a great deal of depth and perception as he explores the lives, thoughts, and ambitions of each main character...the book's ending plays upon the they-all-lived-happily-ever-after angle in a quite satisfying but not wholly exaggerated manner. Oh, and by the way, the book is filled with plenty of salty language and sex scenes that are blushingly frank and explicit." — **Stuart Nulman, Montreal Times.**

By the Sea is a delightfully engaging story about an eccentric community that resides in the foggy environs of Leech Beach...Leiva deftly interweaves characters' past and present to create a vibrant ensemble that is immediately engaging...an appealing comic treatise on small-town politics where sexual liaisons abound, on a collection of individuals who live cheek-by-jowl but find to the hysterical effect that they know each other, not at all. By the Sea is a light-hearted, clever read. — **Literary Fiction Book Review.**

By the Sea is part of Steven Paul Leiva's thematic trilogy: **The Love, Sex, and Pursuit of Happiness Novels.** All three novels look at these essential aspects of the human condition, with each novel focusing on one of the three. By the Sea: A Comic Novel looks at our unease when unhappy. Bully 4 Love: A Rather Odd Love Story takes a skewed view of this most revered emotion. And The Reluctant Heterosexual: A Tragicomedy In Four Movements A Prelude And An Interlude, as the title predicts, concerns sex, which is not always the same as love, nor is it always a happy situation.

BULLY 4 LOVE
A Rather Odd Love Story

NAMED A "FAVORITE BOOK OF 2021" BY THE MONTREAL TIMES!

Adolphus Seruya is a happy, middle-aged, unambitious bachelor and History professor at a prominent community college. Then suddenly, SHE walks into his classroom. Lavinia Carson is beautiful in a unique yet compelling way. And radiant almost beyond description.

Thus begins a rather odd story of love rejected, love ignored, love found—and cuttlefish pizza.

THE RELUCTANT HETEROSEXUAL
A Tragicomedy In Four Movements A Prelude And An Interlude

Robert and Sandy are intelligent, creative, not unattractive, wealthy, married to each other, and in love. And yet their procreating bodies might as well be standing naked on a savanna in Africa in the late Pliocene Era. It's the sometimes-comic conflict between ancient bodies and modern culture. Can there possibly be a happy ending?

CAVEAT EMPTOR: As The Reluctant Heterosexual concerns sex, it is at times explicit in language, situations, and attitudes. Readers who are offended by such explicitness should not read this book.

By the sea

By the Sea

By the beautiful sea

You and I

You and I

Oh how happy

We'll be

By the sea

By the Sea

By the beautiful sea
You and I
You and I
Oh how happy
We'll be

A COMIC NOVEL
(Revised Edition)

STEVEN PAUL LEIVA

Magpie

Press

Cover design by Clarissa Yeo

ISBN-13: 978-1-7352985-5-9
Library of Congress Control Number: 2022916763

DEDICATION

For Amanda

Whether by the sea or inland,
Whether then or now or in the future,
All my love

CONTENTS

ACKNOWLEDGMENTS

The author would like to acknowledge that in the pursuit of happiness you never know when a prince or princess charming might come along.

BY THE SEA (I)

The Briers was a hotel by the sea. It was an architecturally diverse building of four stories, twenty-seven rooms, an antique store, and an elevator that had recently been added onto the outside of the building and was, oddly, for the exclusive use of the owners. The Briers catered to full-time residents but was not averse to the occasional transient guest, usually someone in sales. Despite the hotel's beach location, it was not a destination for vacationers, for Leech Beach, on which The Briers sat, was not an inviting beach being a bit scruffy and often fogbound. Nevertheless, the hotel thrived for love was at the center of its management, and mean-spiritedness was discouraged.

Early in the morning on the day this story begins, in the kitchen of the hotel's dining room—which no one had ever thought to give a catchy name, so everyone just called it "the dining room"—three Hispanics (as the U.S. Census Bureau insisted on calling them), each from a different country south of our own, were going about tasks they knew well. Maria sliced fruit to serve as a garnish on plates of eggs and stirred a large pot of oatmeal. Julio checked the refrigerator for their supply of ham, bacon, and eggs and heated the large stove and its long, well-used griddle. And Adelpha filled little vases with water, popping in little cut flowers that one of them had picked up at MacKay's Florist on their way in, shouting "Hola!" to MacKay, MacKay responding with "Ho-lot of shaking going on!"

Into the middle of this early morning busy kitchen and its sounds of jobs repeatedly done—the opening of doors; the opening of cans;

the kick start and rush of gas flames; slicing, rinsing, chopping; the cold, held breath of the freezer expelling when retrieval was at hand— came Frank, the morning head waiter. He stopped and surveyed the kitchen, then went up to Maria, who was just finishing preparing turkey salad for their lunch menu.

"Maria, my angel of the morning!" he greeted her, opening his arms to encase her short roundness in a hug.

"Frankie, my loove," she responded, taking the hug but not hugging back, her hands still encased in turkey salad-smeared plastic gloves.

"Have you seen Trudy? Tardy Trudy, I think we'll have to call her."

"No," Maria stated, smiling, knowing this was not the first time Frank had had to ask this question.

Then the back door opened and gave a more satisfying answer. Trudy, nineteen, bunched up, arm enfolding arm, head down, a peek of her cheeks revealing the rush of warm blood trying to do a job, walked in. "Gosh, it's cold out there," she said as hands started to rub arms, and she did a little dance which gave noticeable movement to her tightly restricted, blouse-covered breasts.

Frank looked at her with a condemning, if interested, eye, noting the tight blouse cut short, exposing much of her midriff and her low-riding jeans that extended south the exposure. "A jacket might have helped."

"I know. But I was in such a hurry, and it was really clear outside— did you see, it's beautiful—I thought it would be warmer."

"Trudy, my tardy miss, it is still winter, even without a cloud in the sky or fog rolling in. It's early morning; the sun hardly has time to do its job. And 'cold and clear,' is a common term."

"I know, but the only jacket I've got is that really bulky blue one, and I didn't want to have to carry it around after work because I figured it's going to warm up..."

"'fraid not; cold all day. Those of us who listen to weather reports knew that."

"Well..."

"Well, that's a lovely new blouse you've got. Wanted to take it for a promenade along the boardwalk after work?"

"Well..."

"See where vanity will get you."

"But that jacket's such a hassle."

"I understand. Like the hassle which you cause us when you're late."

2

Her eyes shot down in shame of a sort. "Sorry."

It was a lovely shame, and Frank allowed himself a moment to enjoy it.

"I still need to get off at two, please, Frank, please, please, please!"

"You were twenty minutes late; you can't work an extra twenty minutes?"

"Noooo!" Trudy made it the longest word in the English language. "I've got an audition," she announced, gracing "audition" with a reverence she wanted you to share.

"An audition?"

"For the new theater that they're starting. They're looking for company members. You get training and experience and everything."

"For a price, I assume."

"You pay dues, but my parents said they would pay if that's what I really want. If I make it, I don't have to go to college; I can become a famous actress."

"Is that guaranteed?"

"The head of the company has trained a lot of famous actors. On Broadway! Then they do movies."

"Oh. The Big Apple and the Big Orange. And now he's here to grace our Little Sand Pile?"

"Don't be sarcastic. And don't kill my dreams!"

"Dreamicide! I wouldn't think of it."

"What?"

"It was a joke, of a sort."

"Oh. You're too funny, Frank."

Mrs. Briers walked into the kitchen, room service breakfast orders in her hand. Trudy ran over to her.

"Mrs. Briers, I was twenty minutes late, and I'm very sorry my alarm didn't go off, but can I still leave at two? I have a very important appointment."

After this brief but intense assault, not unexpected and not surprising, Mrs. Briers turned to Frank. "Frank?"

"It's always slow around that time. Joe should have no problems with it."

Mrs. Briers turned to Trudy. "Can you come in twenty minutes early tomorrow?"

"Ah, well, I guess..."

"Otherwise, I have to dock your pay, and that's more accounting than I like to do."

"Oh, okay," Trudy said as she moved towards the employee restroom to change into her waitress uniform.

"Trudy." Mrs. Briers stopped her. "Make it thirty minutes early. You've just spent ten minutes talking about the twenty minutes you were late, right?"

Trudy smiled and stood up straight like a little soldier, but in no way ironically, and agreed with a cheery, "Okay!" Then she turned and entered the restroom.

Mrs. Briers turned to Frank. "How are thirty minutes early better than twenty minutes early?"

"Trudy has a very fluid perspective on life. It always flows to the positive."

"That could be a gift or a curse."

"Most likely a bastard hybrid of the two."

"You're too philosophical sometimes, Frank."

"Can you be too philosophical?"

"When guests are in rooms waiting for service, I would think so." She handed him the orders and left.

Some minutes before, upstairs in room number four, Allison Carr had looked at her clock and saw that it was 6:12 when dawn would arrive this day. She switched off the lamp she had been reading by, and the room became dark save for the leakage of rose light from the edges of the tall drapes covering her tall window. Using this subtle illumination, she left her bed nude, worked her way to the drawstrings, and opened the drapes. And there was the sea, vast in its reach, tinted rose from catching the first light coming around the bend. She opened her arms to greet the sea as it waved at her from its shore. "Morning, my old friend," she said aloud, but not loudly, hearing her voice for the first time that day.

There was no one below on the boardwalk in front of The Briers. Even if there had been, Allison probably would not have stepped her nude self away from the window. People out at dawn were either enjoying it and nothing else or rushing off to work, head down, disbelieving that they were awake at this early time. If anyone was viewing her, it could only have been a worker on one of the oil platforms that dotted the horizon, and only if he was looking through a powerful pair of binoculars. If such a worker existed, and if he wanted to take valuable time from his early morning duties on the platform to look landward and view the nude fifty-four-year-old body of a woman, then, Allison felt, he was more than welcome.

It was a small body. Even compared to no other body, its essence was slight. It had never grown beyond five foot two, and now, she supposed, it was losing height, although she had no intention of checking her supposition. Five foot two, eyes of blue, would continue to do very nicely as her response to any question about her height, a question she was not often asked anymore. Compact. A compact little thing, she thought of her body as taking up very little space, causing minimal impact. Good things: little packages, her mother had muttered whenever the subject came up during her childhood, in the days of longing for pure and perfect love, adventures on the road, and an inch or two more, maybe three, just that, and then she would be happy.

At least her eyes were blue. Faded? No, still bright. She believed that. Still the cause of comment—such incredible blue eyes!—and pride; pride as if it were she who had mixed the color after a long period of trial and error and had applied it with the most delicate perfection not just once but twice. A girl needs something to be vain about, her father had kidded, although she had always considered vanity to be the least of her faults.

Her breasts were small and always had been from when they suddenly popped out sometime between her twelfth and thirteenth birthdays. Her mother had not prepared her; her dad had made them a joke—Are you wearing your training bra? You know, the one with the little wheels. But she had always liked her breasts. They had widened the eyes of several adolescent boys and had felt the passionate touch, then warm affection of her husband, but sadly she supposed, had never suckled an infant. They had, though, felt the pinch of her self-love on those once rare occasions, now often moments of collapsing the universe to within the perimeter of her skin. And being small, there was less to sag—good things, little packages.

Her "room" at the Briers was two rooms. A bedroom, very spacious, with an arrangement of a wingback chair and a low table where she could sit and read and have her nighttime tea, along with the delicious pastries Mrs. Briers herself often baked. There was an armoire, a massive thing with diamond point panels on the doors, and a top so high it was where dust went to retire, as she kidded the cleaning staff whenever she needed to gently remind them to do their required duty to the fullest. Here she kept her clothes with no crowding, as she had very few. Not out of want, out of simplicity. Clothes once were nothing but confusion in her life, constantly needing to be brought to order through manipulation, culling the herd, and exciting new acquisitions. Now she had one of each, maintaining them with dedicated care, lamenting when one finally faded or frayed beyond care. Then she had to take it out of the armoire for the last time and go through the irritation of finding its replacement. The room also featured a built-in closet, but this was for storing things, things she just could not abandon after she had abandoned so much. They were in boxes, well packed, and labeled in detail. Small things, delicate things, some expensive, some frivolously cheap, that she had collected throughout her life. She liked to glance at them with passing views, just to know they were there, or to give intimate, hand-held looks, visually traveling the minutiae of shape, texture, reason, and sometimes the memories of when they became possessed, having possessed, and where and why. She had more small things packed in boxes than the top of the small mahogany dresser in the room could display with any sense of proper presentation. So, she rotated them, like changing exhibitions in a museum, every week, always on Monday. She always looked forward to Monday. It was a pleasure to take one last view of the treasures she packed, followed by a fresh re-acquaintance with the treasures she unpacked. Sarah, one of the cleaning staff, also looked forward to these changes. It broke the routine of cleaning other people's unchanging, dust-collecting lives, giving her a moment to share—tell me about this one, Mrs. Carr—if Allison was in a sharing mood, which she almost always was. If Allison was the curator, Sarah considered herself the caretaker and proud to be so. She dusted each small thing with concentrated care.

There was a large bed in this bedroom, an antique four-poster wherein Allison could get lost. And there was the sizeable floor-length window looking out to the sea. Sometimes she grunted as she pushed the heavy wingback chair to the window; other times, she grunted as she pushed it away.

The other room was a small sitting room with no window at all, a quirk from the conversion, seventy years ago, of a mansion by the sea into a residential hotel, now in the hands of its second generation of family owners. The room was furnished with a couch, chairs, a small writing desk, and most importantly, a bookcase, five feet tall and three feet wide. When Allison had negotiated with Mrs. Briers, this was the last of her requirements, which had included a window overlooking the sea. A bookcase, she had said, five feet tall, three feet wide with five shelves. Mrs. Briers had just the thing in her antique store and was more than happy to put it in the room for Allison's use. She had never had a resident willing to pay ten years' rent in advance. It meant, of course, locking in the rate, but the large infusion of cash was quite welcomed and was immediately put to use.

As the morning light went from red to a gentle yellow, Allison stroked the brittle hairs of her pubis, noting the long, gray wires that shot from the field. She remembered when the blonde patch had been soft, downy, and how her husband had loved to just stroke the very surface of the patch, like a breeze through a field of grass, never descending lower, depth not being a thing he was comfortable with. She remembered the gentle sensation it caused; she remembered being tickled by it.

While Mrs. Briers was downstairs overseeing the quiet stretch that was the waking up of their hotel, Mr. Briers was in their apartment on the top floor of the four-story building enjoying the early morning light filtering in through thin gauze curtains while he lay in bed waiting for Dmitri to come and take him out of it. He was a man who knew where his luck lay: in bed with him. For he was a man—for many years now and, he hoped, for many years to come—who never had to bound out of bed late for work or church or an early morning appointment of any kind. He stretched—his upper body, at least—and enjoyed a yawn while he listened to a wave crash. Using his two very strong arms, he pushed himself back towards the head of the bed and up the backboard coming to an elevated rest. He then gathered pillows and tucked them behind his back. Settled and happy, he reached for the TV remote and used it to command life to jump loudly into the room. He scanned the early morning talk shows, cable news, and the two classic movie channels. If he found nothing of interest, he would turn on the VCR or the DVD and continue whatever movie he had programmed last night for the last half hour before sleep. But the day before George Leslie had died, all the shows were reporting the fact, and the two movie channels were each running one of his eighty-seven films in tribute. Mr. Briers was immediately sad, expelling a mourning breath: Aww. He jumped from one show to another, back and in-between, catching as many of the expressions of sadness, words of tribute, displays of respect, and tiny celebrations of George Leslie's life as he could. And the clips, of course, the clips that flashed Leslie as a young man, so all-American handsome—open, with pleasing, good looks, nothing too fine, chiseled, refined, sophisticated, dark, or sensual— fighting the good fight for those who could not fight it on their own. There he was as the bumbling professor caught in a whirlwind adventure with the blonde Broadway bombshell babe, then as Daniel Boone blazing trails, and as Wilber Wright, who, with his brother, blazed higher trails. And there he was in strong, steady maturity as the President of the United States, calming the nation during a time of trial; as the cruel, insane rancher ordering the death of his son (what a departure, triumph, and Oscar-winning role!), and, finally, as the lovable old coot who turned a depressed urban neighborhood into a Garden of Eden, finding his own grey-haired Eve in the process. George Leslie—dead at the age of eighty-six.

There was a knock at the door, and Dmitri entered. Mr. Briers turned to him with two tears rolling past his cheekbones. "George Leslie died," he said.

"Who?"

"George Leslie!"

"Who?"

"George Leslie! The actor. One of America's greatest movie stars!"

"Mr. Briers, I was born in Russia," Dmitri whined, his chosen form of communication.

"He was an international star, Dmitri! World-renowned! One of the greatest! And you came here when you were eighteen months old; so, don't give me this stupid immigrant shit! It's not your place of birth; it's your time of birth. That's your problem, you seventeen-year-old git!"

"What's a git?"

"An idiot."

"What's an idiot?"

"See that mirror?"

"Yes."

"Look into it."

"You're funny, Mr. Briers."

"That's right, laugh at the invalid."

"I meant funny weird, not funny ha-ha."

"That's right, put down the invalid."

"You could drive if you wanted to."

"What?"

"You could drive a car."

"Who changed the subject?"

"See, they've got cars you can steer with one hand and accelerate and brake with another."

"I thought you were supposed to have both hands on the wheel?"

"You didn't, the night you crashed."

"How do you know?"

"I don't know, I just know. Everybody knows."

"Well, the problem was not how many hands I had on the wheel; the problem was I was dead, stinking drunk! So let that be a lesson to you."

"I hate school."

"I don't doubt that for a minute."

Dmitri was tall and skinny and sharply defined, full of endpoints that protruded irritatingly like quills that prick—elbows, fingers that seemed too long even for him, and his nose, a baby hawk nose. But he was surprisingly strong as he picked Mr. Briers up out of bed and took him into the bathroom and set him on the toilet, where Mr. Briers immediately started to urinate and defecate.

"Mr. Briers, can't you wait until I leave?" Dmitri whined in disgust.

"Hey, you're lucky I still have control of my functions. Otherwise, you'd be changing my Depends every morning."

"I wouldn't have taken the job then."

"Sure, you would have. You want that fast car you're saving up for, don't you? Who else would have hired you?"

"Can you hurry up; I've got to get to school."

"What for? So you can take a nap?"

"Come on, Mr. Briers,"

"All right, then, get out of here so I can wipe my delicate anus, then you can come in and put me in the bath."

Dmitri returned to the bedroom and sat at the edge of the bed, his back curving as he relaxed his upper torso, taking all possible strain off it. He waited not with the virtue of patience but the inertia of boredom.

"All right, Dmitri, my anus is as clean as a whistle. Now I would like to get the rest of me clean."

With a sigh edged with a whine, Dmitri stood up and entered the bathroom. He started the bath water, checked the tray with Mr. Briers' shaving gear, putting a fresh blade in the razor. All the while, Mr. Briers told Dmitri about his favorite George Leslie film, none of the particulars of which Dmitri would ever remember as he paid no attention to what Mr. Briers said, ten percent of his attention being on his duties and ninety percent being somewhere in the open county in a fast car accelerating beyond one hundred miles an hour. The bath water ready, he picked Mr. Briers up off the toilet and placed him in the tub. Mr. Briers was ready to complain that Dmitri had made the water too cold or too hot, but he was surprised to be greeted by mother-warmth, so soothing he fell instantly in love with Dmitri even though he knew Dmitri got it right by pure chance alone.

"Do you want your rubber ducky and battleships?"

Mr. Briers looked over at his bath toys with some desire. The Battle of Midway was tempting, but:

"No, I'll just get so engrossed in playing I'll make you late for school."

This was fine with Dmitri, and he returned to the bedroom, sat on the edge of the bed, and dreamed of fast cars.

The lobby of The Briers was originally the foyer of the mansion built, then abandoned, by a man the Great Depression had not destroyed, but the death of his wife had. It had been built for her and completed on the day of her death, or so the tale—the tale everyone preferred—went. The front desk was small and unobtrusive, and easily manned by one person. Other than that aspect of commerce, the rest of the lobby was a surprisingly intimate and cozy great room stocked with an eclectic mix of furniture, some of which rotated in and out of Fletcher's, Mrs. Briers' antique store, and were for sale; some of which had first been placed there by Mr. Briers' parents, who had bought and converted the abandoned mansion into a residential hotel; and some, while nice, which were simply utilitarian and so arranged to receive the most use.

Tom was manning the front desk. He was a tall, balding young man who had studied accounting and business at the local college, got fair grades, had a pleasant, if shy, personality, little desire to expand horizons, and an amateur interest in the stars. Mrs. Briers was hoping to make him manager one day, taking over some of her duties, giving her more time to pursue the search and sale of antiques, the side business she had started three years ago that was becoming the engine of this enterprise. Or Enterprise, for she did, indeed, think of the hotel as a ship, as a "she." As a living, breathing entity, she oversaw and commanded

"Tom," she said as she walked up to the desk. Tom looked up from paperwork, smiling, ready and happy to listen. "Remember that Mr. and Mrs. Comstock are checking in today. I've got several pieces they want to look at, expensive ones, so let's make their stay very pleasant."

"They're the decorators from Atlanta?"

"Yes, and I'd love to have them for steady customers."

"Well, I've got them in twelve, and I made sure the curtains are open. So, when they walk in, they should get hit with the view."

"Good boy."

"Good morning."

Philip McFadden walked up, arm extended. Tom, graceful in a movement almost automatic, reached under the front desk and retrieved the morning paper and slipped it into the hand at the end of that extended arm. It was not the local paper; it was the New York Times, by special delivery.

"Thank you," McFadden said as he took the paper and moved towards the dining room for his breakfast.

"Major?" Mrs. Briers stopped him. He turned to face her.

"Yes, Mrs. Briers?"

"Funny, I've never asked you before, but I just got some in: Are you interested in military antiques?"

"Outside of being one myself, no, Mrs. Briers, I am not."

The Major turned again and moved into the dining room.

"I wish I could warm him up," Mrs. Briers said, sharing the longing.

"How do you mean that?" Tom said, his eyes back on his paperwork, their twinkle hidden but obvious.

Mrs. Briers gave the back of his hand a little slap. "Oh, I don't mean that way! I just mean I like our residents to be a bit more friendly on a day-to-day basis."

"One big happy family?"

"Why not? Why do you think my father-in-law made this a residential hotel? He wanted to offer people more than just temporary shelter."

"From the storm?"

"From a sunny day if they liked. Fletcher had been an orphan; you know, on his own from the age of fourteen, living a pretty hard life, most of it alone. It wasn't until late in life he made any money and got married. He always cared about the lonely; wanted to give them a place to call home."

"I didn't know any of this," Tom said, expressing an unfeigned interest.

"No, few do. Even Duncan doesn't really realize this about his father."

"You worked with him?"

"Yes. Started as a maid at eighteen. Fletcher was quite old then, but he still ran this place himself. He was a great old man. You know what I'm saying? One of those great old guys that are beautiful being old."

"So that's why you named the antique store Fletcher's?"

"Yes. He always called himself an old antique. I thought it was appropriate. Anyway, I'll be in the store, working on the accounts. Call me when the Comstocks arrive."

"Will do."

Mrs. Briers walked through the lobby and into Fletcher's, saying a cheery good morning to Allison Carr as she came down the stairs for breakfast, carrying, as always, a book. When Allison entered the dining room, Frank greeted her.

"Ah, beauty and grace have just entered the room!" Frank announced to all, all being few this quiet morning. A transient, as the non-residents were known, looked up at the sunny outburst and smiled at Allison's reaction: a giggle and a blush. "Frank, you're always so cheery," she stated as he led her to her table by the window with the view of the sea. "Why should I be anything else?" Frank said. "Especially when you walk in the room." "Well, there might be a million reasons, the world being the way it is, but I do appreciate it." "You're more than welcome. Who would want existentialism for

12

breakfast? Trudy!" Trudy bounced over. "Trudy, please bring Mrs. Carr her fresh OJ and tell Julio to prepare her...?" He turned to Allison. "Eggs Benedict, I think this morning," Allison said. "Eggs Benedict, Trudy. And tell him not to skimp on the hollandaise." "Okay!" Trudy sprinted away on her mission as Allison thanked Frank again for his consideration.

All of which was overheard but not observed by Major McFadden, who kept his eyes on the New York Times and its report of troubles in a desert where boys he may have once commanded were feeling the pinch of world politics. They were probably dirty, sore, and tired, he assumed. They probably had existentialism for breakfast. That thought caused a subtle little snort, the kind that replaces the laugh of knowing recognition when you want to keep it to yourself. The snort was not so subtle that the transient, who was sitting at the next table, did not notice, looking at the presumed source and seeing a head of close-cropped grey hair and a strong stony face that revealed none of the irony that the snort had seemed to announce. The transient was, in fact, not sure the snort came from this tall man so deeply concentrating on his newspaper, which, in another fact, was an illusion, for Major McFadden was concentrating only on appearing to concentrate on his newspaper, being quite aware that he had inadvertently gathered the transient's uncomfortable attention and was determined to deflect it, which he did, the transient going back to his pancakes. No existentialism there, only griddle cakes and slow, sweet syrup. And none to be had in his own breakfast on order: eggs, plenty of them, with a bowl, not a cup, a bowl of salsa to complement. And two sausages, good, fatty pork ones, hash browns, and plenty of coffee, hot and black. No! Damn! This is Tuesday; that's Monday's menu. I had that yesterday. Shit! In a panic over this breach of the menu—not the dining room's but Major McFadden's own—he looked around quickly for Frank or Trudy, but both seemed to be off the floor. Damn! He had to change his order! Now! His chair had been pushed back, and he was just about to get up when Julio came out of the kitchen carrying a hot bowl of oatmeal with chopped walnuts and raisins on top. He walked over to the Major and placed it before him. "I figured you didn't really want Monday's breakfast," Julio said. As calm set in and the Major sat back down, he nodded his head in acknowledgment and relief. His "Thank you" was barely audible, but Julio knew it to be sincere. After Julio left, the Major put three pats of butter on top of the steaming oatmeal and watched them melt for a moment before he spooned on four teaspoons of sugar. He never added milk. Then he stirred, gathered a spoonful, and fed himself. He went back to the New York Times, back to the desert, back to his men as Mr. Briers entered the dining room from the kitchen, pushed in a wheelchair by Dmitri, who took him to his special table for breakfast.

"Can I go now, Mr. Briers?" Dmitri whined.

"What, so soon?"

"I've got school."

"What grade you in again?"

"Mr. Briers, you know I'm a senior."

"Oh-ho, cock-o-the-walk time, right?"

"Huh?"

"Never mind. Got your books?"

"They're in my locker, Mr. Briers."

"Didn't you have any homework, Dmitri?"

"Yes, of course. It's in my locker."

"Undone, I take it."

"I was going to do it before my first class if I could get there early enough."

"Why didn't you do it last night?"

"I had things to do."

"What things?"

"I don't know—things."

"You don't know?"

"Mr. Briers!" The whine mixed well with the plea.

"Where's your lunch?"

"I don't eat lunch."

"You've got to eat lunch."

"No, I don't, Mr. Briers."

"What did you have for breakfast?"

"Sugar Pops."

"Sugar Pops?"

"It's fortified with all kinds of vitamins."

"Bullshit!"

"It's not bullshit. It says so right on the box."

"Frank!" Mr. Briers called out to his head waiter, who came over quickly. "Make a turkey salad sandwich for this kid to brown bag, will ya, so he can get some nourishment in his skinny body."

Dmitri tried to protest as Frank left, but Mr. Briers cut him off by telling him to retrieve his newspaper from the front desk. With a slump of his bony shoulders, Dmitri slowly moved out of the dining room on his errand and was not back until his sandwich arrived, carried by Frank in a brown paper bag. Dmitri handed the paper to Mr. Briers, and Frank handed the bag to Dmitri. Dmitri opened it and looked inside. "Did you put mustard on it?" he questioned, fearful of the answer.

"Yes, of course," Frank said.

"I don't like mustard."

"Dmitri, you git, it's a free meal. Now be grateful and get out of here, or you'll be late for school."

Dmitri left quicker than he had moved the whole morning.

Mr. Briers looked up at Frank. "You know, Frank, I can imagine a person slower and more dimwitted than Dmitri, but I don't think I'll ever run across one in my lifetime."

"Why do you employ him?"

"I'm afraid to fire him."

"Why?"

"I'm convinced his father is with the Russian Mafia. If I fire the kid, his father will probably come and break my legs."

"Yeah, but you wouldn't feel a thing."

"Ah, yeah, that's right. My arm then, my remote-control arm!"

"Ouch!"

"Yes, imagine going through life being an invalid like that, suffering the looks and sneers and snickering of heartless humanity. No, I'll play it safe. The kid's assured a lifetime job with me. God knows no one else is going to hire him."

As Mr. Briers started in on his scrambled eggs, which Trudy had brought him, Frank turned to survey the rest of the dining room to see if anybody needed anything. Allison seemed low on her tea, so he quickly retrieved a pot of hot water and went to her table.

"More hot water?"

Allison, nose in her book, said nothing.

"Mrs. Carr?"

Allison gave a little chirp of startle as she anxiously looked up. It was a small and subtle upset, but enough of a one to cause Frank some guilt.

"I'm sorry, beautiful; I was just wondering if you wanted some more hot water for your tea."

Understanding settled her eyes, and she smiled. "Oh, that's okay, Frank. Sorry. I guess I was just so engaged. Sorry."

"No, no, Mrs. Carr, you're the guest, I'm the server, that makes me the sorry one."

Allison chuckled and said, "I can't imagine you being sorry about anything."

Frank poured the water, "You're right. Hot tea means never having to say you're sorry. What'cha reading today?"

"Oh—" Allison closed the book, keeping a finger in her place, and read the spine, as if she wanted to be sure exactly what she was reading, which was Nicholas Nickleby "—just a little Dickens."

"There is no such thing as a little Dickens."

"Oh, I'm sure you were a little dickens when you were a boy."

"Absolutely not! I was a model child."

Allison did not believe him, but she should have. He had indeed been a model child, chasing after the compliment, running away from the punishment, and always eager to please. It was with some pain that Frank had a momentary memory of all this as he returned to the kitchen.

Julio was cooking; Maria was doing dishes; Trudy was gathering an order, ready to take it out. An Oldies station was playing on the radio, and a mophead told Frank he wanted to hold his hand. Which was not as wonderful as being told that you were a lover's favorite work of art, but it was better than being screamed at in some atavistic tongue of ancient anguish or being called to violence in a rhythmic chant. The kitchen was warm with cooking and steam, and Frank felt okay. Then Trudy, who had left with a load, returned empty-handed with a bound.

"Can I take my break now?"

"Why? You've only been on—"

"I know, I know, but Austin is here."

"Oh, Austin is here. That's exciting. I think I'll take my break too."

Trudy gave Frank an open-handed little tap on the chest. It was surprising and—fun. "No, listen, it's Austin, from, you know, the theater. He brought in the application form for me and wants to explain a few things. It will only take ten minutes."

"Oh, okay then. Anything for the theater."

"Thanks." Bounding again, she was just about through the door when she turned back and said, "Oh, and can Austin have a Danish, warmed up, and a pot of decaf," then she was out the door, which continued to swing back and forth on her momentum.

"When did she become the boss of me?" Frank asked the universe. Maria turned from her dishes and smiled her answer.

When he brought the Danish and the pot of decaf, he took a good look at Austin, a relatively new resident, for the first time. Frank guessed him to be a man no younger than he, in his late forties, but with the blue jeans, yellow shirt, and leather jacket of a man who wasn't stopping to think about it. He looked like the dedicated sort and evangelical about his dedication. His eyes peered into one end of a tunnel that ended at Trudy's eyes, and he spoke words that told of exciting things. When he touched Trudy's right hand with his left to make a point, Frank was tempted to bring the hot pot of coffee down on them. That was a curious, quick bit of male emotion, Frank thought, as he avoided the hands just enough not to touch but sufficiently close to break the contact.

"Oh, Frank, the theater will be so great!" Trudy said as she nodded yes to a cup of coffee.

"When you opening?" Frank asked Austin.

"Don't know yet. But the renovation of the building is almost done. So soon, I guess. Ms. Heatherton would like one production before the end of school, although I thought of waiting until summer. Summer seems the best time."

"Why?"

"Well, because it's summer, and this is the beach."

"This is Leech Beach. You can't quite equate it with any other."

"Really? Why's that?"

"Have you taken a good look around? We are probably the only beach in America off the beaten path."

"That's what I like about it."

"That's what I like about it too, but I'm not trying to get people here to see Shakespeare."

"Not going to do Shakespeare. 20th Century American playwrights only."

"Oh."

"And The Briers seem to get people here."

"Yeah, for peace and quiet and old furniture. You going to do Odets?"

"A bit heavy."

"O'Neill?"

"A bit rough. Ah, Wilderness, maybe"

"A lot of Neil Simon, then."

"Yeah, I like Simon."

"And Miller and Williams?"

"The Glass Menagerie and Death of a Salesman, certainly."

"August Wilson?"

"Well—with Wilson, if you commit to one, you must commit to them all. Might do Raisin in the Sun, though, if I can find the cast."

"Yeah, blackface would not be good."

"It would get us noticed," Austin chuckled out.

"There's no such thing as bad publicity?"

"Exactly."

Trudy had no idea what they had been talking about but smiled through it all, just the same.

Happy with her hollandaise at her nearby table, Allison Carr did have an idea what the two men were talking about. She was even sensitive enough, where Austin may not have been, to feel the prodding of Frank's needle-like questions. Just little pricks they were, no thrust, no insertion, but poignant, just the same. She found Frank an interesting if confusing man, not fitting the handy profile his black pants, white shirt, and simple black bow tie indicated. She liked him. And not just because he greeted her like she greeted the dawn each morning, arms open, wide smile, appreciation on his lips, but because such a greeting, not exclusive to her, indicated a happy man, a man more than satisfied with his lot in life. But what was his lot in life? Frank had demonstrated to her many times, not just this morning, that he had a soul more expansive than was necessary for a morning shift headwaiter at an out-of-the-way residential beach hotel. But was this a bit of prejudice? Workers should be workers with a workers' concern of three meals a day, bills to pay, God, what a grind, is the beer cold, look at the jiggle on those jugs! Sure, such a portrait must be less than true for all cases; people are, after all, individuals. But often, they were individuals strolling with the crowd. Frank, though, seemed to stand alone. What was his story? Allison, who loved stories, was curious to know this one.

Frank was there, hot pot of water in hand. "How about I restore some warmth to that cup of yours?" Frank asked, indicating her cup of tea, half drunk and fully cooled again. "Oh, yes, that would be very nice," she said as she watched him pouring the steaming water. Then he said, quietly, "Here, I found this floating in the air," as he dropped a new tea bag out of his palm into her cup to make this second refill as strong as possible. It was a fun little kindness he enjoyed at such a small cost to his employer. It was sweet, and Allison smiled at the fact, thanking Frank, then stopping his exit with, "Uh, say, Frank, I was just curious—what did you do before coming here?"

She saw an instant and very brief shock of cold come to Frank's eyes. It startled her; she knew she had crossed a line she should not have. It passed, though, and Allison wondered if it had indeed been there as Frank, with a smile, said, "Well, Mrs. Carr, you know, my parole officer said I really shouldn't talk about such things." "Oh," she had felt the little nudge pushing her away. "Okay." Off Frank went, retrieving dirty dishes from the Major on his way to the kitchen.

As he had come in at four in the morning, as he did every morning, Frank was off at noon, turning the dining room over to Joe. He took off his clip-on bow tie and went into the employee restroom to change his clothes, slipping off his ill-fitting black pants and putting on his comfortable easy-fit khakis with the front pleats that complimented the pudge he carried. Frank kept the white shirt on but put his brown jacket over it and zipped it up. He said his goodbyes and walked out the door into the cold, seaside air. He took a deep breath and tried to pass a ring of relaxation from head to toes but found himself still angry—unreasonably so—but still angry over Allison's question. How can people be so damn insensitive? I'm a man in his late forties waiting tables at a beach hotel. Did that seem like a rung on an upward ladder to her? What possible story but a sad one did she expect to elicit from such a question? Not that he was depressed about it, it had all been his choice, but anybody not residing within him, not understanding what he understood, would see it as sad and offer silent pity. Shit!

He walked along the boardwalk, heading towards his car, then stopped. He was tired, sore from eight hours on his feet, eight hours on his guard, never allowing the "Frank" now sitting down on the bench with him to be anywhere but in a back corner of his brain doodling, sketching, envisioning. He breathed in some cold air, breathed it out warm, and then snatched some cold again. It felt good and—and honest, Frank supposed. He didn't know why. Frank closed his eyes, concentrated again on the cold going in, and ignored the warmth going out. When he opened his eyes, he was looking at The Briers.

What a strange building. It was built by Thaddeus Tiberius Leech in a not easily defined style, although undoubtedly a building from the 1930s. And yet it featured architectural frou-frous here and there which reached back into pasts little understood, hinting of the Victorian, the Moorish, castles along the Rhine and the glory that was Greece. Built with wood, stone, brick, and stucco, it was an odd, ugly building, oddly appealing nevertheless—Frank loved it. Large and looming, it sat on the lopsided end of the boardwalk Fletcher Briers had installed when he converted the mansion into a hotel. It was not a very long boardwalk with several empty narrow one-story buildings and a few occupied ones. There was a bait and tackle shop, a thriving tattoo parlor as it was the only one in a hundred miles, and a boat rental shop. At the other end, there was a wide two-story building that used to be a dance ballroom that, during its fruitful years, featured big bands that never played on the radio, rock & rollers who never recorded, imitation British bands, and Peace and Love flower power groups that never made it to either San Francisco or Woodstock. Its musical history stopped there, and the building stood empty for years. But now Austin of the blue jeans and leather jacket was converting it into a theater.

The Briers owned it all. Briers Beach, Frank thought they would have renamed it, but they never had. It remained Leech Beach. A joke in so many mouths, a comedy of expectations. And a tragedy in life when its strong undertow and mean rip tides murdered Mrs. Thaddeus Tiberius Leech (known as Lottie) on that day of celebration of completion, the completion of her life leading to no celebration. It was a beach with tufts of long grass of some name no one had the interest to learn, popping out of the tops of the little dunes that seemed to give the beach its very own waves and that started or ended close to shore itself, leaving but a thin strip of smooth, uninterrupted sand before the breaking waves. It was not a good swimming beach. Nor a good sunning beach as fog usually hung around much of the day and most of the year, rare all sunny days, like today, being bright exceptions.

When the fog did lift, the view out to sea—expansive and fulfilling though it was—was pockmarked by little islands of oil rigs drilling-drilling-drilling. At night though, until the fog returned, the oil rigs became a small constellation of surface stars, which was not unappealing.

The ring of relaxation finally took, Frank began to doze, drop into that always dark but comfortable country where sounds of thoughts competed with sounds surrounding. At this moment surrounding sounds of waves surging forward, running back, birds screeching protest, a car horn honking, and a shout to a friend to bring the hooks all merged with thoughts of the giant dog coming forth and the stack of plates that slipped and fell and crashed...

His body dropped the ball of his head but quickly recovered, jerking it up. Then he was aware of light too bright, the day, cool breeze, and the smell of salt in the air.

Home. Time to go home.

Frank got up from the wooden bench and headed to his Celica, an old brown one bought used but not used up. He sat and started the engine, which kicked into life with a satisfying roar. He turned on his radio. NPR was talking about poverty in the Southern hemisphere. He looked but couldn't find a place in his heart that cared. He pushed in the cassette already in place—young Louis Armstrong singing sweetly. Okay, now he could drive.

To reach Leech Beach and The Briers, you had to travel a winding two-lane road of some ten miles that saw moments of elevation into hills of trees and interesting geological formations. And then other moments of penetration into valleys. Farms were in the valleys, primarily small, family farms, some with nice houses and painted barns, some with nondescript habitations and structures that stood by the grace of some power not observable from a moving car. There were fields of strawberries, groves of walnuts, patches of soybeans, and hillside-grazing land with dots of cattle and horses to complete the picture. Frank could see none of this when he drove to work in the fourth hour of the day. Leech Beach Road was then just a thin ribbon of existence minutely illuminated ahead of him and as frightening as Hell. Frank had gotten used to the curves, dips, and elevations; repetition can lead to a reliable guide if the mind does not drift. But if it does, you suddenly seem to be in a black box, not knowing what is immediately outside it, maybe a sharp right, perhaps a drop to the left (slow down!) to suddenly descend the last drop and see the lights of The Briers at the bottom haloed in fog. It was always a relief and not a bad way to start a workday—glad to be alive. But on the way home, once out of the fog, if it had crept far inland, Leech Beach Road was one of those drives that seemed organic, part of the landscape and not a rude slash through it, offering an almost giddy drive. Not a bad way to end a workday—glad to be alive.

On this clear and bright day, Frank noticed things he had never seen before. Including a large mailbox with a bold printing of a name: ANDOVER—Trudy's last name. Ah, yes, she once mentioned that she lived close by. His car suddenly pulled to the right and stopped among a scatter of gravel at the side of the road. Did I do that? Frank thought, surprised by his impulse. Beyond the mailbox was a short road that led down a slope to a house, neat and trim, with flowerbeds surrounding it. It was a two-story abode with an expansive patio, rocking chairs, and a certain sense that it could be a cover for Country Living magazine. However, the photographer would have to angle the camera to avoid getting the huge TV satellite dish in the picture.

Deeper in the property and to the left was a barn. In front of which a man worked on the engine of some farm implement. Two dogs lay on the ground nearby him. The faint squeak of a screen door drew his attention to a woman emerging from the house to shout at the man. Frank could not hear the words, but the intention was clear. Lunch was on the table. The dogs competed in a dash. And the man wiped his hands on a rag and headed towards the house. It was a pleasant scene. It must be good to own your farm, wake up in the morning, stand on your land, and watch life grow out of it. Just about to enter the house, the man noticed Frank's car. Frank put the Celica in drive and left with a feeling of guilt. Why? Frank had no idea. But it was interesting to see where Trudy lived. Why? He had no idea.

Leech Beach Road ended at a four-lane interstate that Frank turned right onto, taking him past larger farms probably owned by corporate families and ranches with cattle thick enough to scent the air. It led him into Rubenton, the small town where he lived. Not a dreary place, not a cheery place, just a place with a small strip of downtown, small houses in old neighborhoods, and apartment buildings as the main feature of what used to be the outskirts. For no apparent reason, Frank's building was called The Mandalay. It was a complex of furnished singles. Frank parked his car in its assigned stall and got out, the work he hoped to get done that afternoon on his mind. First, he would take a shower, though, certainly a shower before work. But when he got to his single—one long room he had divided with a free-standing wicker screen into "bedroom" and "living room," with a kitchenette at one end and a bathroom at the other—Frank thought maybe a touch of the erotic was called for. Yes, he thought, maybe so. Then, after its outcome, he could shower and emerge refreshed and comfortable.

Frank got out of his clothes, took a videotape from a drawer, placed it in the VCR, turned on the 13-inch TV that sat on the VCR that sat on the dresser, and then laid down on the bed. A fun couple fornicating appeared on the screen. He began to manipulate his manhood, which he had been doing regularly since his boyhood, dismayed once again that, while it stiffened, it never got hard anymore, not stone hard, not that hurting hard he had loved so much in times past. He blamed it on the quality of current pornography. It was all just sex! There was never any story anymore. At least not in the ones he could afford, the 3 for $3.99 videos of what used to be loops in machines in booths in adult bookstores. It was like Hollywood product writ small and naked, all just action, spectacle, and special effects, no engagement in real characters, no involvement in their lives, nothing for the mind. Sex was all mental—didn't they understand that? They had to set the scene, tease us with exciting situations, and show the cut and thrust of erotic conquest, not just cut to the conclusion of the chase when the hound set on the fox and the dirty deed was done.

Oh well. The blonde in the last one was cute, and the brunette in this one is—is reminiscent of Helen. Remember Helen? Remember when she had come over that last night, you were house-sitting for Bob? She brought the vodka and the tonic; you had Bob's excellent sound system and fireplace. You had a fire, even though it was August, you danced to Billie Holiday in front of it, warm from the fire, warm from the vodka, she whispered in your ear that she wasn't wearing any panties, you gently pulled up her skirt and, son-of-a-gun, she wasn't! Your hands on her buttocks felt so good. Then you were on the couch; her skirt hiked, the beauty of her furry pubis glowing in the firelight, a sight of wonder. As was her smile as she sipped more vodka, then suggested bed, Bob's bed, where she took you, laid you down, mounted and had her way with you, the monster, she was great, up there above you, ascending, descending, ascending, descending. Then that smile wrapping around your stone hard hurt, such envelopment of warmth, such gentle play with her practiced tongue. You were so afraid to ask, but you asked anyway, and she never left her station; she simply nodded permission. Now you were the monster, a well-oiled piston—the transportation into an alternate universe of pure pleasure being...

The phone rang. Frank looked at the video: another blonde of curly hair had replaced the brunette. The phone rang again. He turned everything video off remotely with his left hand and went to reach for the phone at his right and slightly behind him on the night table. He stopped—his right hand was much too sticky, and like a fool, he had forgotten to grab a paper towel as a bedside companion. The outcome of his memory play with Helen now covered his chest, threatening to run down his side, and was pooled in the crease of his pudge bottomed by his navel. The phone rang again. Frank slid to his right with great care, balancing the liquid of life between his pectorals. He wiped his right hand on his right thigh, unpleasant but necessary, and managed to reach and punch the speaker button, despite the threat of a dislocated shoulder.

"Uh, hello?"

"Frank?"

Oh, great. It was his ex-wife. Or the wife that would be ex if she ever actually filed for divorce.

"Donna, hi."

"I'm sending you the divorce papers."

"You wouldn't kid me, would you?"

"No. I'm going to do it this time. Really."

"Okay, fine."

"Because, you know, I'm going to get married."

"Again?" The outcome was beginning to grow cold and uncomfortable.

"What do you mean again?"

"What engagement is this?"

"Only the second."

"What about that Tom guy?"

"Tom died before he could ask me to marry him, and you know I'm still sensitive about that, so thank you very much for bringing it up."

"Sorry. Uh, listen, could I call you right back? I've got to—"

"No, I've got to give you some information about what to put on the divorce papers so that everything will sail through. David and I want to get married as soon as possible."

"Why, are you pregnant?"

"Don't be rude! And yes."

"You're kidding? You're too old."

"I am not! Plenty of women my age—"

"Yeah, but—"

"Well, you would never give me a baby!"

"Well...."

"You son-of-a-bitch!"

"Look, I—"

"I've heard all your excuses. It was mean, and you're a shit!"

"Well then, obviously not great father material."

"A baby would have changed you, Frank. It would have deflated your ego, brought you down to earth and made you human."

"But what if I didn't want to be human?"

"You're the single most selfish bastard I've ever meant."

The single most selfish bastard Donna had ever met was beginning to crust over, which caused an itch that his sticky right hand had no choice but to scratch.

"Look, Donna, I'm in the middle of something." Or something's in the middle of me, he thought.

"I've got to give you this information."

"I don't have anything to write with right now."

"You? Don't have anything to write with? No pen, no pencil? I've never seen you without one or the other. Where are you, in bed?"

"Well, yeah, actually, I am."

"What?"

"I came home with a terrific headache; I was lying down."

"Well, get up and get one. This is important."

"Look, can I record you?"

"What?"

"My answering machine has this two-way record button. I'm going to hit it; then I don't have to take notes, okay?"

"I guess."

"Okay, so I'm going to hit it now. You'll hear a beep, then give me the information."

"Okay."

Frank, like a contortionist, felt for the right button. Finding it, he pushed it with the tip of his finger. The machine beeped, and Donna started rattling information as Frank slid off the bed and dashed for the bathroom; the outcome not yet crusted flowed, a drip or two hitting the carpet before he could get to a washcloth.

When he came back, Donna was saying, "Frank? Frank?"

"Yeah?"

"Did you get all that?"

"Sure."

"Okay, so I'm mailing the paperwork today. Fill it out exactly like I've said. I've put a self-addressed stamped envelope in there, so you'll have no excuses. Bye."

"Bye. Oh, Donna?"

"Yeah."

"Congratulations."

"Oh, thanks. David's a nice guy."

"Let me know when the baby's born. I'll send you a gift."

"That would be nice. How about a nice drawing of a teddy bear or a ducky?"

"I don't do requests."

"I know. That was always your problem. Bye."

Before in Frank's life, a shower had just been a shower. A necessity if you want any reasonable association with others of your kind. Now, though, a good, hot shower was the demarcation of his day, the border he crossed—a refugee from a land of bare subsistence—to enter the Promised Land. It was not a promise made by a god on high or a shining land looking for wretched refuse, but a promise he made to himself, a land of his creation.

The hot water was good. Especially on Frank's back, between his shoulders where it hit and spread, massaging the little bit of tightness that always developed there. And his lower back, crushed like a tin can, he imagined, by the weight of himself. And his head, his hair, enveloped by a tunnel of hot wet, then luxurious lather, then the hot wet again to wash it away. And a blast on his face—he could take it, throw it all at him, throw all the shit ya got!

The shower off; the cool air clamping onto him; the big, brown bath towel to chase it away—it is not so much that he wanted to come out of the shower a new man; he just wanted to come out a true man.

Refreshed and dressed, Frank left his single number six, walked down a narrow hall with a strange cut to the right, and then straight again to the single apartment nine at the end. He took out his key and opened the door. The sunlight from the two big windows that looked out over the parking area was satisfactory. Frank went to the old white drafting table he had dragged with him through the last twenty-five years of his life and looked down at the unfinished drawing taped to the center of the slanted surface. The wet, rocky landscape extended far into the distance, light breaking through the black cloud cover on the horizon. Whether sunrise or sunset, it illuminated the oversized hound in the background striding forward, panting out deep menace with his visible breath. In the foreground was the head of a man that had just turned to face the viewer. The details of his visage were all down, finely etched, except for his eyes. There was a patch of blank paper where the eyes should have been, but it was not pristine and untouched. The wear of multiple erasures was evident. It was the eyes; he had to get the eyes right. For if he got the eyes right, if they communicated what he intended to be on the man's mind at that instant, then the drawing would be funny, very funny—at least to Frank. Fuck the rest of the world.

Allison Carr finished her book at breakfast. The Life and Adventures of Nicholas Nickleby had concluded, and those who deserved to be happy were. This meant that she had finished the bookcase. Now had to pack up the books it held and drive into Rubenton to the storage company, where she had a 40X40 space lined with very tall bookcases filled with books. In the center of the area was a comfortable chair, a table, and on the table a battery-operated lamp. Here she would bring the books she had finished and choose others to refill the bookcase in her room. She loved putting the read books back in the little gaps they had left by their absence. She adored leaving fresh gaps as she chose the new books by an intuitive process she did not care to understand. The books here were arranged as in a library— alphabetical by the author for fiction, by subject matter for non-fiction. For this is what, of course, this was—her library.

She had spent years building it up, buying books that interested her, classics and new releases, fiction and non-fiction, many subjects, colors, and tones. She bought them at a rate far outstripping her time to read them. But she didn't care. She wanted to own them, shelve them, come across them in a later browse—Ah, yes, I'll read this one now. It's just the mood I want.

Sarah, the housecleaner, would help her pack them, always curious over the titles. "Is this one good?" she would ask, holding out a weighty tome. Allison knew she that what she was actually asking was why anyone would read something so big. "I liked it," was the only commitment Allison would make. "What's it about?" Sarah asked. The cover clearly spelled it out, but Allison graciously answered, "World War One." Sarah looked at the cover seeing the haunted faces in the trenches. It looked awful. "Was that the one with Hitler?" Allison had just blown the dusted off Vile Bodies. "Sarah, you really have to dust my books better." "Sorry." Sarah hung her head, making Allison regret the admonition. "And Hitler was World War Two." "God, there were two of them?" Placing the last book in a solid black plastic Fairfield Dairy milk crate, Allison stood up. "Yes, Sarah, there were two of them, although some might contend that Two was just a continuation of One. But normally, they are considered two separate conflicts. Can you get someone up here to take these down to my car?" "I'll do it." Sarah felt proprietary about Allison and her things. "They're heavy." "I'm strong. I'll get the dolly." "Okay." Allison gave Sarah her car keys. "I'm going down to lunch; bring them back to me there, okay?" "Sure." Then Allison grabbed her purse and her current book, a short, staccato-like hard-boiled mystery, a change from mean human hearts to the mean streets. Sometimes Allison felt the need for the satisfaction of flesh pounding into flesh in a righteous cause.

Mrs. Briers sat at her desk in Fletcher's, very pleased with herself. Mr. and Mrs. Comstock—a lovely couple, was her first impression—

had gone right from check-in into Fletcher's, excited, they said, to see the pieces Mrs. Briers had e-mailed them about. Mrs. Comstock, a tall, dark woman of sharp, elegant features emphasized by her pulled-back hair and the two long curved cuts of her eyebrows, gasped at the four armchairs. "Perfect, they're absolutely perfect," she declared to Mr. Comstock, almost as tall, very light in contrast to his wife with his pale to pink skin and his not very natural blond hair fully covering his scalp, but short and brushed forward. Mr. Comstock agreed in a British accent, posh but with a shade of Cockney, but the 1930s cocktail cabinet delighted him even more, so incredibly Nick & Nora, he said. Their clients, they declared, were going to love the pieces, plus the others Mrs. Briers had set aside, plus items the Comstocks spied on their own.

The Comstocks happily laid out $13,987 of their clients' money, made the shipping arrangements, agreed to have dinner with the Briers that evening, then went up to their suite to rest.

Duncan wasn't going to be happy. He hated these dinners with buyers. "Emily, must I?" he would ask as he always did, contorting his face into a portrait of exhaustion. "Yes," Emily would always answer. "We are the Lord and Lady of this manor, and the Lady does not entertain alone." But Duncan would always be charming, telling some stories from his Hollywood days—so many tales for so few days. And if the guests had seen one of his few films, especially if it had been the one now considered a minor classic, they became just a little giddy in his presence.

Chicken, Emily thought. Roasted chicken, mashed potatoes and—and peas. The dining room offered nothing that could ever be considered gourmet. Even though the clientele she endeavored to cultivate for Fletcher's might be used to the exotic in food, spending more time than was necessarily useful discussing it, Mrs. Briers preferred to offer meals that could be prepared at home but rarely were. Which now made those meals—now that she thought about it— somewhat exotic. That is why she always hired cooks and never chefs.

She looked out the window at the bright, clear day, which she could have taken as a nice compliment to her current mood, but didn't as she had always been ambivalent about the sun. The half-day shroud of fog, which more often surrounded The Briers, and the overcast, which usually hung around for the rest of the day, were the atmospheres she preferred, never feeling constricted but quite comfortable in their embrace. The first time she saw The Briers, it was just emerging out of an evaporating fog, as if it had traveled here from the past, obviously with several stops along the way. It was love at first sight, as the past had become her obsession, as the present had never offered her any rewards. She had been born in Rubenton to parents always in the present, especially as presented on TV. They were two unattractive people or two people uninterested in being attractive. Her father had worked at something that greased his clothes; her mother read only the Reader's Digest, TV Guide, and the Church newsletter. They were not young when Emily was born and was perplexed about what to do with her. They fed and clothed her, sent her to school, and took her temperature when she seemed to be ill. Otherwise, they left her alone in her room with the dolls, stuffed animals, and picture books Emily had occasionally asked for, and they never hesitated to give her. One of the books had the most detailed color illustrations of a Victorian house, both interior, and exterior. She would spend hours staring at them, fascinated by the designs, which were so much more—she didn't have the right words—curly and round, shapely with cones and tubes, toned in red, it seemed, or rose, and dark woods. Textures, there were textures everywhere. When she would take her nose out of the book and look around at her home, her neighborhood, and her town, all she saw were straight lines and ninety-degree angles defining boxes of brown or grey or dull white, flat rectangular doors with blank knobs, windows with nothing much to see through, whether looking in or out. Visual white noise, she was later able to explain to herself when she had the words. It was all just white noise instead of symphonies, quartets, tone poems, and songs with sparkling lyrics. She found more strange but wonderful music in other books on buildings from the past: Cathedrals and castles, palaces and the Parthenon, the farms of ancient Rome, the cottages of Shakespeare's day, the labyrinths of legend.

Oh, how she learned to hate her boxy surroundings. To get out was all she thought about—but to where? To somewhere where the past still existed, or at least the fossils of the past, elaborate, faceted shells now housing the present, looking forward to the future, but still elaborate and faceted fossil shells. She wanted to go to an old college of brick and ivy, but her grades and her parents' finances would not allow it. Or to the Old World reachable by jets, passage on which she could not afford. Or just some old town built before they had settled on the box. But how was she to get there? Money, as it so often is, was the answer. She had heard about The Briers Hotel her whole life and had always wanted to see it. But her parents, of course, had never taken her out there. "What for?" was always their response. She could never come up with a satisfying answer. But when she was eighteen, just graduated from high school, and she saw the ad in the newspaper for CLEANING STAFF HELP WANTED, she had an answer they could understand. Still, her father was reluctant to drive out there. "You can borrow the car," he said, pulling the keys out of his greasy pants pocket.

Fletcher interviewed her.

"Are you a hard worker?"

"I don't know. I've never worked before."

"Cleaning rooms can be hard."

"I keep mine immaculate."

"Immaculate?"

"Yes. Not just clean, but everything placed neatly in the proper order."

"But that's your room. So you have a vested interest."

"I'll treat all your rooms as if they were my room. I can't offer any better assurance than that."

"Nor would I ask for any better. All right, Emily, you can start tomorrow if you want."

"I do, but I have to figure out transportation first."

"Don't you have a car?"

"No. But my father does, and I think I can get him to give it to me."

"That would be very nice of him."

"We live five minutes from where he works. The walk will do him good."

Fletcher liked her immediately. She was no-nonsense and practical. So unlike his wife, now deceased. And his son, on a flight of fancy trying to be an actor, producer, or both in Hollywood. Both had abandoned him to run the hotel by himself.

Emily liked Fletcher immediately. He was a beautiful older man, very elegant and Old World in his dress and manner, with silky white hair still covering most of its natural territory.

They became lovers. Or as much of lovers as they could be, given Fletcher's age. It was not energetic love, but soft and gentle, with a lot of caressing and little whisper kisses. She couldn't keep her fingers out of his hair, and he couldn't keep his lips off her nipples. On occasion, she made sure he climaxed. He did his best for her.

She was not a maid for long. Her advancement, though, had little to do with their intimacy, for Fletcher knew that Emily was not in love with him but with his hotel and that when she made love to him, it was the personification of the hotel she lay with. He was delighted, for he loved the hotel and soon found that he could no longer run it without her help. The day he made her the desk clerk, she returned her father's car to him and took out a loan to purchase her own. The day Fletcher made her the assistant manager—a position that had never existed at The Briers—she stopped thinking of faraway old colleges of brick and ivy. Instead, she took some management courses at the local community college, housed in buildings all stucco and steel. The day he made her the manager, stepping himself into the higher realm of just being the "Proprietor," she canceled a plane reservation that would have taken her to London for her first vacation. Then Emily moved out of her parent's house and into a room next to Fletcher's.

That was when The Briers became truly hers.

Trudy hated the last two hours of her shift. Frank was gone, and Joe was on as the afternoon headwaiter. It was not that Joe was bad or anything; it was just that he was the typical adult boss who felt that whatever he was in charge of was, at that moment, more important than just about anything else in the world. If everything was not just right, Joe grumbled and cursed and let you know just how stupid he thought you were without ever actually saying it. And when he did things superbly well, which, Trudy had to admit, was often, he never failed to make a general announcement of it. Whether he genuinely thought people could learn and improve by his example or whether he was just waving the flag of his personal nationalism was never quite clear. He always did it with a rising, blaring announcement that settled into a serene self-satisfaction evident by his slight smile.

Not that Frank did not make mistakes. "Oh, you didn't want the sour cream?" he would say to a lactose intolerant customer who sat aghast at the cloud of sour cream hugging the top of his baked potato. "I'm sorry, I thought you said you did," Joe would swear, laying the blame on the customer as he had laid the sour cream on the potato in a great big glob. By contrast, Frank would have been sincerely apologetic if he had made such a mistake, which he rarely did. And he would have rectified the situation immediately and added something— gratis—to the order, a pastry, or a little bowl of sliced fresh fruit, to compensate for the inconvenience. Frank was not just morning to Joe's afternoon, but day to Joe's night. He kept things light, fun—and funny. Frank could be hilarious. Even when he was being critical of you, he made you laugh about it. Old as he was—and Trudy didn't know exactly how old he was, but he was old, sort of like her parents— old as he was, she never really thought of him as an adult. She thought of him as just a person, a fun guy she liked to see in the morning, and was sorry to see him leave in the afternoon. So, the last two hours were work as just work, five fifteen an hour, ten dollars and thirty cents she earned to feel oppressed.

All this is one reason she wanted to be rich and famous—except for the first eight years of her life when she had been blissfully free of this ambition. Then in the first quarter of her ninth year, Cissy McMann, America's Favorite Girl, also in the first quarter of her ninth year, came suddenly into her life. Cissy McMann was born in the womb of an eight p.m. TV sitcom where she was cute beyond all reason, witty beyond all belief, and—from the second season of Trial by Erin— compensated beyond all comprehension. America's Favorite Girl wrote her autobiography at the age of fifteen. It was hardly necessary. The press had covered the story of her life, broadcast media had detailed it, and supposedly all had been revealed under the gentlest questioning by talk show hosts—even the late-night ones. The details of her days were seemly known by all and had been committed to memory by Trudy.

Trudy wondered why this life could not have been hers. She had every episode of Trial by Erin on DVD and would run a scene, then run through it herself in front of her bedroom mirror, taking all of Cissy's lines. She was delightful. She could do it all: The little catch in the voice; the meaningful stance that had become a signature; the right emphasis on the right syllables on what had become America's catchphrase, "Don't blame me—it's biological!" Trudy loved, admired, and nearly worshipped Cissy. But why, she wondered, is she America's Favorite Girl and I'm just Jack and Carla's kid living on a farm off Leech Beach Road when I can do it just as good as her? Trudy was too young to know the details of either fate if fate existed or the shattered

33

and scattered mirror that was the randomness of the universe if it didn't. All she knew was that she wanted to be the one that other girls imitated in their bedroom mirrors. This feeling probably would have passed if Cissy McMann had had her day and was, by now, at nineteen, a has-been, lost somewhere in a drug-induced stupor, as other child stars on occasion were. Then Trudy might have left her behind, like the dolls she had left behind. But Cissy McMann had not fallen. Trial by Erin had run its course, but by that time, Cissy had developed a rather astute head for the business. She moved from cute to sensual and trained a voice that she took to Broadway in a groundbreaking new musical, of which the financing she had partly secured. Then Cissy won an Academy Award for her searing portrayal of—of course—a teenager lost somewhere in a drug-induced stupor. She remained America's Favorite Girl. So, there was no escape for Trudy. Instead of oppression at five dollars fifteen cents an hour, the freedom of fame and fortune continued to star in the life Trudy should have had. But also, importantly, continued to preview the life Trudy was sure she would—no doubt about it—eventually have.

And eventually might just start today at two p.m.

"Got to go, Joe," she said as she rushed to change out of her waitress uniform at 1:50 p.m.

"Hey, wait a minute. I heard you were late this morning."

"I know, but Frank said it was okay, and Mrs. Briers said it was okay."

"Said what was okay?"

"That I still leave at two. I'm coming in a half hour early tomorrow to make up."

"Doesn't help me much."

"I'm sorry, but I've got an important audition."

"Audition?"

"For the new theater?"

"What new theater?"

"Down the boardwalk. They're refurbishing it now, haven't you noticed?"

"I thought they were going to make it a movie house."

"No, it's going to be, like, a real theater, you know, with real actors. And I'm going to be one!"

"Damn! I was looking forward to seeing some movies without having to drive to Skidmore."

"Can I go, please?"

Trudy did not wait for an answer, and Joe did not give one, both knowing it to be a waste of time. Instead, she ran into the employee restroom and quickly stripped out of her waitress uniform. Trudy hung it on a hanger in the vinyl closet, standing in one corner. Almost simultaneously, she grabbed her new blouse, which she quickly slipped into, and her low-riding jeans. Trudy jumped into the jeans even before buttoning her blouse, which she tried to do as she was also trying to zip her jeans up. Besides letting her midriff show, the blouse allowed the airing of a "so very feminine" black filigree tattoo on the small of her back. She checked it out in the restroom mirror by twisting her torso farther than biology was comfortable with and jumping to get the image of her lower body in the mirror, set well above the sink. In a flash, she saw it there and reassured herself that it was very, very cool. Then she did her face, enjoying the soft caresses of tiny brushes.

She left in a rush saying goodbye to all, and exited The Briers, entering the world, which was, as Frank had warned, cold and clear with a breeze off the ocean that chilled. She longed for her jacket, but it was such a dumpy thing, and now was not the time to sacrifice impact for comfort it might provide. She walked down the boardwalk quickly, heading to the theater. Her body warmed a little with the activity, but not enough to prevent her nipples from rising and pushing at the blouse, which (tit for tat?) pushed back. Trudy noticed this and admired these two points justifying her decision to leave the jacket behind.

They were points well taken by the construction crew working on the theater. One comically dropped his hammer; another gracefully buckled his knees; all grinned broadly and asked Austin how the hell they could get his job. Austin told them to cool it and led Trudy into his office, a part of the renovation that had been completed. The heating system, though, had not been, and his office was as cold, if not colder than the outside. Of course, there was no breeze in his office, but that was hardly compensation.

"What are you doing without a coat?" Austin asked as he directed her towards a chair in front of his desk and sat.

"I forgot it," Trudy said, realizing that she was shivering and that her teeth would soon begin to chatter.

"You forgot it? Where, back at the hotel? Why don't you run back and get it?"

"No, I left it at home."

It was a simple bit of information but hard to comprehend.

"What time do you get to work?"

"Six."

"Wasn't it even colder at six?"

"My dad has a heater in his truck. And then I'm in the hotel. I thought it would be warm by now. And—"

"You didn't know I would be without heat?"

"Yeah."

"You want to go back to the hotel and talk there."

"No!" Trudy said, handing him the application form she had filled out on her second break and looking around, seeing books of plays on shelves and pictures and posters of past productions. "I want to be in the theater."

"Well, what a wonderful introduction to the cold life it can be."

"What?"

"Would you like a jacket?"

"No, I'm okay."

Austin got up and went to a coat rack in the corner. "Don't be silly," he said and grabbed an oversized puffy insulated sports jacket. "Get up," he commanded, and Trudy got up. "Turn around." Trudy turned around, and Austin wrapped the coat around her, his arms enfolding her for a moment. Warmth came immediately, and she gathered the sides of the jacket together, cocooning her and shutting off from the elements her breasts, the nipples that punctuated them, her midriff, and the feminine filigree. But she was cozy. Austin laughed. "What?" Trudy asked with a coy edge of having been affronted in her voice. "You look like a cute little kitten," he said, "all wrapped up in a blankie."

It was not the impression she had hoped to make, but it did not seem entirely negative.

Austin was wearing the leather jacket he had had on earlier, and it creaked a little as he sat back down in his chair, drew Trudy's application towards him, and studied it for a moment. He had a nice body; she had noticed this at the hotel. Slim, like the boys she knew, yet with just enough flesh to make him a man. He looked great in jeans. He had sandy hair, lots of it, with cute grey temples. And he had a cute face. No, not cute, not anymore. It had been cute when he had been Trudy's age. Now it was, at his age—and she supposed he was maybe as old as forty—boyish, which was pretty cute on an older guy. She analyzed all this as she peeked out from under the jacket, into which she had hunched.

"Well," Austin said, looking up from the application to see Trudy sit up straight and let the sides of the jacket go, "you went to Rubenton High School."

"Yeah. Everybody around here does."

"I'm going to be teaching there this spring."

"Really? What are you going to be teaching?"

"Speech and drama."

"Really? Not fair. We cried for a drama class for years."

"Well, I guess your cries have been heard."

"Yeah, but I'm not there anymore!"

"But you're here," Austin said, indicating their surroundings. "Look, let me explain everything, and that'll give you more details on my plans here, what I expect to accomplish, and what I'm going to expect from company members and students."

"But I thought I was going to audition."

"Oh, we'll get to that. But if what I'm doing here doesn't sound like what you'd be interested in, why waste the time?"

"Yeah, I guess."

"Well, look, a little bit about me and my background, first. I got my B.A. in Theater Arts at Northeastern University in Oklahoma, a really, really good school, had some fine professors there, and got a good, you know, an excellent grounding in my art. But then I decided to go east, so I did my M.F.A. in acting at a small university in upstate New York. After I got that done, I, of course, as we all do, headed for New York, you know, the city and got involved in theater there. I already had a friend from Northeastern who was part of this experimental theater company, so I started with them. But what they were doing was so—out there and—well, I'm sure they thought they were being revolutionary, but I found it hard to defecate on stage on cue, you know what I mean? To be that precious about poop was not my idea of theater. And, of course, they didn't pay anything. Well, hardly any theater at that level does, but the point was, if I'm not going to get paid, I might as well not get paid to do something I liked. And I had made contacts and got into the scene enough that I was able to get involved with other theater groups. So, I got extensive experience doing everything from the fringe and off-off-Broadway, even some off-Broadway..."

Without really understanding any of it, Trudy was fascinated by what Austin had to say or, more accurately, by his saying. But then Austin was fascinated by it and had been well trained to convey and share emotions. It was like listening to a song whose lyrics you can't quite understand, but the tune is catchy. She almost wanted to move with the music. Then, on occasion, something was said that caught her understanding. Austin worked on one off-Broadway play with Sean Bach, who was hot right now and a real cutie. And Austin did six weeks on a soap opera her mother loved. Then, Austin appeared in an independent film that she had heard about if never seen, because Jack Stafford, that old actor from the old days, had a small role in it that he won an Oscar for just before he had this heart attack and almost died. So there was a lot of publicity on it.

Then Austin talked about moving to Los Angeles.

"It just got too hard to live in New York. And I heard that there was a vibrant theater scene in L.A., although no one in New York would believe it. But I heard it was true, so out there I went..."

It was the same tune, a bit sunnier perhaps, of working on theater for very little money and doing the odd guest shot on T.V., but with the variation of Austin beginning to teach acting. He spoke the names of actors he had taught, and even the ones Trudy had never heard of impressed her as Austin mouthed their names like poetry and gave the rhapsody of their credits.

She wanted to reach out and touch him—him who had touched...

"But L.A. can depress the hell out of you. You know what I mean?"

No, Trudy did not know. L.A. was the home of so many so well known. How could that depress?

"There's a lot of theater there, sure, possibly more than in New York, in fact. But it makes absolutely no impact on the community. I mean, film and television overshadow everything there; anything else is meaningless to the common mind. So, your audience is basically just other theater people. Theater people watching other theater people— you can't get more incestuous than that! And theater that makes no impact on the community is useless, vapid, and is simply not fulfilling its function."

Was there fire in his eyes? There may have been. Trudy had no idea what materials were burning, but she liked the glow.

"Fed up with it all, I just started searching on the Internet for ideas of things to do and places to live. I ran across this notice for a drama teacher at Rubenton High. I called them up, your principal, uh, Ms. Heatherton, and told her about myself, and she invited me here to talk about it. When I came here, we really clicked, but it was apparent they had no idea how to put together a drama department. And the facilities at your school leave a lot to be desired. But she brought me to The Briers for dinner, and I saw this building, and I just had, you know, a great inspiration. Suppose the school would help me renovate this building into a theater. In that case, we could do all the high school productions out here, plus I could run a commercial theater company that the students could intern at, get some practical experience, and we could give something back to the community. She loved the idea, loved it! She talked to Mrs. Briers that night and got a good rental deal on the property. I told Mrs. Briers we could do a special Dinner and a Show deal, and I would put up out-of-town actors at The Briers if she could cut me a deal, and—well, it all just worked out. Ms. Heatherton is working on an emergency teaching credential for me, I've got to take a few classes to qualify for a permanent one, but that's no big deal. So, the upshot is, this is going to be the Stafford Theatre—I named it after Jack—home of the Rubenton Theater Company. I am going to try to find local talent to train—both here and at the high school—to become a permanent stock company, plus I hope to bring in name actors—you know, people I've worked with—to help attract a crowd. Terrific actors, I don't care how famous, love getting away from the glamour and glitz and going to some out-of-the-way theater to get back to their craft. It's really, you know, really invigorating for them.

"So, how does that sound, Trudy? Does that sound like something you would be interested in?"

Trudy sat up. She was now almost too warm in Austin's oversized jacket. She let it drop from off her shoulders, which she threw back, just a little bit, with enthusiasm. "Sure, it sounds neat. But, um..."

"You have any questions?"

"Well, you're going to train me to act, right?"

"That's part of what I'm here for."

"And then I have to be part of this permanent company?"

"Yes, our stock company, the Rubenton Theatre Company Players."

"Does, well, does that mean I can only act here?"

"No, of course not. You can act anywhere you want."

"Well, how long do I have to stay here?"

"Trudy, if I accept you, you can stay here as long as you want—as long as you pay the dues."

"So, I could go to Hollywood or Broadway if I want?"

"Do you want to?"

"Of course."

"Why?"

"I want to be a rich and famous actress."

"Oh. Not the purest of motivations."

"What?"

"Do you care about acting at all?"

"Of course. I can do it. I'm going to be good. There's no one I've ever seen in film or television who did something I didn't think I could do."

"Well—self-confidence is an asset."

"I know what I know. You want me to show you? Should I audition now?"

"Well, the stage isn't finished yet. I thought just a first interview today—"

"No, look, I can do it right here, okay?"

"Well—sure, okay?"

Trudy jumped out of the chair, leaving the coat behind, and found a good spot to stand, facing Austin. She took one deep breath and then started:

"Okay, so once again, Dad was right. I—"

"Wait a minute," Austin stopped her.

"What? Did I do something wrong?"

"What are you doing?"

"You said to prepare a monologue."

"Yes, I know. But, I mean, what monologue are you doing? What play is it from? What's the character?"

"Oh, well, it's not really from a play. It's from TV"

"Oh. Okay."

"Trial by Erin. You know how at the end of each show, Erin looks into the camera and does a monologue? Well, I'm doing one of those."

"Oh. Well, I've never seen any of those shows—"

"You haven't!"

"No. I did audition for them once."

"You did! Did you get to meet Cissy McMann?"

"No, you audition for a casting agent."

"Oh, God! I would have insisted. I mean, to get that close and not to be able to meet her."

"It doesn't really work that way."

"Really? How sad."

"Well, it is what it is. Okay, so since I know nothing of this show or the character you're doing, uh, fill me in briefly and then start."

"Well, you know, it's Trial by Erin, and Erin is this girl that lives with her dad, who's like a Law teacher or something at this college. And her mom is dead, so it's just her and her dad, and she gets into a lot of trouble that her dad has to get her out of, and they kind of fight a lot, but they really love each other. And when the show started, she was nine years old, and I was nine years old at the same time. So, I grew up with the show until it stopped when we were seventeen. So, this is, I mean the monologue, this is from when we were sixteen, so you have to imagine me as a sixteen-year-old if you could do that."

"I'll give it a shot."

"Good. Okay, so this show is about Erin being asked to a dance by Brad, who she has this huge, big crush on. But he asked her after this new kid in the school, Loren, asked her. Loren is, like, this skinny loner who answers all the questions right in class and reads a lot and stuff, and Erin said yes when he asked her because she didn't think at that time that anybody else was going to, and because, you know, her dad felt she couldn't say no to him, because it wouldn't be right. So, anyway, she tries to work it to get Loren to un-ask her so she can go with Brad because, her dad said, for her to decide not to go with Loren on her own would be a breach of contract, which, I guess, is something against the law. So, this Brad turns out not to be so great after all. And it all is, you know, okay at the end. So, this is what she says at the end of the show, okay?"

"Okay."

"So, I should do it now?"

"Sure. Go ahead."

Trudy took another deep breath. "Remember, I'm sixteen, okay?"

"Okay."

"Okay, so, uh— 'So once again, Dad was right. I hate that. I really hate that. I mean, my score with Dad on being right and not being right is something like 0 for 20,000. Who made that a law of the universe that kids can't ever be right? I mean, I was convinced, absolutely convinced, that Brad was a superhuman sailor of love on the U.S.S. Dreamboat sailing on the Sea of Forever! But Dad knew that Brad was nothing but, to put it in Dad's words, "A sub-human engineer of lust stoking the boiler of an atavistic steamer on the one-track line of Kiss You Today; Kiss You Off Tomorrow." I mean, Brad couldn't have had more hands on me if he was an ambidextrous octopus! And Loren! Besides having a name that could be a girl's name, it was obvious to me that he was so uncool that even the geeks wouldn't invite him to their lunch table. You know, the one by the big trashcan. How was I to know that he had, again in Dad's words, "Deep resources of intellect and sensitivity and was a fine poet to boot." Although, why anyone would want to boot a poet, I don't know. And his poem? The one he wrote to me. Well, I had imagined that my skin would glow at his touch when Brad first took me in his arms. Instead, when he had his hands all over me—it just crawled. But when I first read Loren's poem, all alone in my bedroom, with his hands nowhere near me, I could have read it by the glow I gave off!

'So, I guess I'm going to the dance with Loren. However, I will have to teach him how to dance first. It's not going to be a pretty picture. Unless, of course, Tommy Bradford asks me. You know Tommy? He's the tall blond one in my Social Studies class. The one on the football team. And he—he really knows how to dance.

'Hey, don't blame me—it's biological!'"

Trudy ended the monologue in the exact Trial by Erin pose that Cissy McMann struck in more than a thousand photos. Despite what Austin had indicated, he knew it well, for it was now a cultural landmark having achieved, through constant repetition, what Marilyn Monroe in her blown-up skirt had achieved by doing just once.

Trudy popped out of the pose with a little jump of joy over her superb performance. "Well, what did you think?"

Austin would have loved more time to fashion an answer, but his number was being called. "Jesus, it's as if you were channeling."

"What?"

"Trudy, that wasn't acting; that was an impersonation."

"Isn't that acting?"

"Well, it can be if that's the goal, but what I really need to see is what you can bring to a role—what individuality, what spark of your spirit you can bring to it."

"But I did it just like Cissy McMann."

"I know—that's the problem."

"I guess I shouldn't have picked something from TV. But see, I don't know any plays because they never would give us a damn drama class."

"No, that's not the problem. You could have done the same text but given it your interpretation, not Cissy McMann's. That would have told me a lot."

"Oh." A confused sadness clouded Trudy's head while an agitated panic screamed from her chest. "But everybody—everybody's always loved it."

"Of course, they did, Trudy. It's a good impersonation. But it's all surface. Do you understand what I'm saying? It's like tracing something instead of doing an original drawing."

"So—so I can't join the acting company?"

"To be honest with you, Trudy, I don't know. We'll see. As a teacher, I can't start with nothing. I need students with the raw talent I can help shape and form. What you did today shows a talent for imitation, but I'm not sure I can work with that kind of talent."

Trudy returned to the chair and sat down hard on it, sitting on Austin's jacket, a large button making a bad impression on her. "Ow!" She jumped up, gathered the jacket, and handed it back to Austin.

"Put it back on."

"No, I guess I should leave."

"Put it back on and sit down."

Trudy did so, finding it a comfort to sulk in the enfolding warmth of the jacket.

"Trudy, acting is not about becoming rich and famous. If anything, money and fame sully the purity of the craft and art. Why do you think I came here? It's because I wanted to do my craft and art for the pure joy of it, not for some—some race to get on magazine covers. You can do that only in places like this, in regional theaters. Not that I don't want appreciation for my craft or even recognition, but the proper kind, the pure kind, not the paparazzi kind. Do you understand what I'm saying?"

Trudy nodded yes because she was afraid not to. Then she got up, removed the jacket, and, this time, instead of handing it back to Austin, tried—and failed—to sling it onto the back of the chair, the jacket falling to the ground. "Sorry," she mumbled sadly as she, with her back to Austin, leaned over the chair to retrieve the coat. It was an awkward move causing her blouse to ride up her back and her low-riding jeans to slide to crack level, making the filigree tattoo on the small of her back an arresting point of focus.

"Neat tattoo," Austin said, needing to say something.

Trudy grabbed the jacket and righted herself with some enthusiasm. "Do you like it? Mom and Dad got really upset after I did it because I got sick for, like, three days after."

"Then why did you do it?"

"It's pretty cool, don't you think?"

"I almost hate to admit it, but yeah, there's something kind of attractive about it. But it may just be the location."

"Yeah, that's what I like about it." She had gotten the jacket securely on the back of the chair. "Well, I guess I'll go now."

"Do you want to borrow the jacket to go home in?"

"No, my dad's picking me up. I'm sure he'll bring me a jacket."

Trudy started to leave. Austin stood up. "You know, I'm not rejecting you."

Trudy stopped and turned to him. "You're not?"

"Of course not. But I need to see more before I can accept you. You don't need to be perfect; I would have nothing to teach you if you were perfect. But I need to evaluate your true, individual talent. Not Cissy McMann's."

"Oh."

"So, look, here—" he reached over to a bookcase and pulled out a small but thick paperback book "—take this. It's a book of monologues for actresses. Read them and find one you want to do. Memorize it, rehearse it, and then you can give me a proper audition."

Trudy took the book and looked at it. Her stomach suddenly felt empty, the haunting of an old feeling—it was like getting a homework assignment. "Oh, okay. When?"

"Whenever you're ready."

"Thanks." She turned to go again.

"Hey, Trudy."

She stopped again and turned to Austin.

"Don't be so sad, okay? If you want to be an actor, in a pure way or even for fame and riches, you will likely face many rejections and disappointments. But if you really want it, you stick with it. Look, that's what's going to be good about what I'm doing here. If you have some talent, and my instincts tell me that maybe, you know, you may just have some, then here we can develop that talent in a nurturing atmosphere. So here in our own little kingdom by the sea, we can get you to be good at acting. Maybe even more than that. Then, if you want to go 'out there,' where all the monsters are, you'll be better equipped and stronger. Do you know what I mean?"

Trudy nodded yes because she was afraid not to.

Every day, after school, Dmitri came back to the hotel. His first duty was to take Mr. Briers for a "walk and roll" along the boardwalk. Duncan liked to stop in at the few businesses there and chat with the owners, trading jokes, mostly dirty ones, and discussing whatever was disgusting them at the moment about the outside world as presented on TV and in the newspapers. Dmitri paid no attention to the talk, despite having more than once been informed that if he would only listen, he might learn something. Instead, he usually moved away to stand and stare out at the ocean or into the fog, depending on how late it lingered. And there he stood until Duncan yelled, "Dmitri— onward!" Dmitri would then sigh and amble back to the man in the wheelchair and push him on to the next stop. Today the view was as sharp as the cold. He could see out to the oil rigs and wondered about getting a job on one after he got out of high school. They made a lot of money, he heard, which would be a good way, he thought, to support the car he wanted. But they live out there too; he had also heard. You don't need a car out there. And the work was probably hard. How could it not be? Oh well.

"Dmitri—onward!"

Dmitri sighed and went to Mr. Briers and pushed him out of the bait and tackle shop and started to take him to the boat rental shop, but Duncan said, "Hey, no, take me to the end; let's see how they're doing on the theater."

"Why? Are you going to act there?"

"Act there? Why would I act there?"

"You're an actor, aren't you?"

"No, Dmitri, I'm the owner of a hotel."

"I saw your movie."

"Really? Which one?"

"I don't know. You were a zombie bank robber."

"Ah. Dead Dillinger. I also produced that one. Did you like it?"

"No."

"No? Why not?"

"It was stupid."

"Of course, it was stupid, you git. That was the point."

"What's the point of making something stupid?"

"So it can grow up and become a cult classic."

"Is it a cult classic?"

"Sadly, no. But it has made several Worst Films lists."

"Is that good?"

"Well, it's not as bad as America's Ten Most Wanted."

"So why don't you act in the theater?"

"Why do you keep on about that?"

"I don't know. It seems, you know, you own the theater, you could do whatever you want."

"Dmitri, have you, by any chance, noticed that I'm in a wheelchair? Just exactly what am I supposed to play? I suppose I could do Sheridan Whiteside in The Man Who Came to Dinner, but I would have to have a stand-in—literally—for when he suddenly jumps out of his wheelchair."

"I don't understand."

"You and so many others, Dmitri, you and so many others. Now push."

On their way to the theater, Trudy walked by, head down, arms hugging herself, one hand clutching a paperback book, her quick steps pounding on the boards of the boardwalk.

"Hello, Trudy," Duncan said.

"Hi," Dmitri said.

But Trudy did not acknowledge them as she headed back towards the hotel. "I really like Trudy," Dmitri said after she passed.

"How do you mean that?"

"What do you mean?"

"I mean, what do you like about her? Do you like her sparkling personality or just her body?"

"Well, I've never really talked to her. She was a senior last year."

"So, it's just her body?"

"I guess. So what?"

"So, nothing, Dmitri. It's just nice to know that you are not completely oblivious to your surroundings."

"What does that mean?"

"Push, Dmitri, just push."

By the time Trudy reached the hotel, she had a plan. It was scary, almost horrifying. But she was proud of how she had worked it all out, how she wasn't going to do anything impulsive but do it step-by-step to do it right. She thought about it as a whole thing, the sequence of events she was planning all squeezed into one second of thought. It gave her a chill, the good kind, more of a tickle really, the kind you get from a lovely caress. Her dad was waiting for her in the lobby. He had with him her jacket. "Thanks," she said and bundled herself up quickly. They left the hotel and got into the pickup.

"How'd it go?" her dad asked. "Really good," she said. "He really liked my acting." "That's good, huh?" her dad said as they started up Leech Beach Road. "It means I'm on my way." "And this is what you want to do, huh?" "Oh, yes—more than anything." "Well, okay. Just remember what you promised, when you get rich and famous, you'll buy me some new farm equipment." "Dad, I'll buy you a whole new farm." "Don't need a whole new farm. Just need some new equipment." "Whatever, Dad. Oh, and look, I think I have a ride home tomorrow, okay? So you don't have to pick me up."

That night the Briers had a successful dinner with the Comstocks. The roasted chicken was delicious; Ana, the evening cook, had done a fine job. Emily and Mrs. Comstock discussed a particular furniture maker of the 1780's that they both had a passion for, the rarity of pieces as much as the pieces themselves. Mr. Comstock talked of home, England, and the annual trips he and Mrs. Comstock made there looking for exciting finds. Then Mr. Comstock had a quick, bright idea and suggested they all plan a trip together. Emily was thrilled by the thought; Duncan, in a very amusing way, declined, giving them all the reasons why, despite modern accommodations for the disabled, he would never travel again. But Emily, Duncan said, should go, must go. It would be her first trip out of the country on an antique hunt. Just time it to when she was comfortable making Tom, the desk clerk, the assistant manager. So that the day-to-day running of the hotel—of which he had divorced himself from years ago upon the occasion of their marriage, "Divorced and married all in one day," he often proudly proclaimed—could continue smoothly. Emily paused to think about that—even if she left her ship in a good state, what state would it be in when she returned? "We're not going again for nine months," Mr. Comstock said. Nine months, Emily thought out loud: Could she create Tom in her image in nine months? "Of course, Emily can," Duncan assured all. "Look at what what's-his-name did in seven days." Emily looked around, stopping momentarily at the eyes of each of her three dinner companions, finding encouragement at each stop. "Okay, fine," she said, "I'll plan on it." "How long are the trips?" Duncan asked. Two weeks was Mr. Comstock's answer. "But this one, with Emily coming, should be special. How about a month, Honey?" Mr. Comstock said, addressing Mrs. Comstock. "Then we could do the continent. We are very weak in Scandinavian contacts. Danish design, even as early as the 1950s, was inspiring. And Italy? We must go to Italy. It would be a whirlwind, exciting, exhausting, but we would love it!" Emily became giddy at the thought. Duncan found that charming. "Of course," he said. "Yes! It must be a month." Mrs. Comstock, though, saw the sadness of it. "Leaving you behind, Duncan, for a whole month?" "Don't worry about me," he said, "I have my amusements." "And what were those?" Mrs. Comstock asked. The question made Emily nervous, for she did not find old movies amusing, and she did not think her husband spending a good deal of his time watching them was amusing. But far less amusing was explaining his amusements to others. Duncan was not insensitive to this. "Taking the profits that Emily somehow squeezes out of this hotel and investing them. It's a lot like old movie serials." "Old movie serials?" "Didn't you ever hear of them? Adventure stories told chapter by chapter every Saturday afternoon at the local theater, each chapter ending with a cliffhanger, the hero, it seemed, in a fix too terrible to escape alive." "Oh! Yes! My dad watched them—on video. He would watch five, six chapters at a time." "Not the way to watch them." "Well, I guess they weren't in theaters anymore." "TV took over." "Yes, TV took over." There was a moment of silence. Nobody really knew why. But they knew it was time to wait. Finally, Duncan smiled and said, "So there I am, many mornings, in front of my computer screen, cutting a rather dashing, if sitting, figure, as I go up against the evil forces of Market Conditions. With my trusty sidekick—Benny the Boy Broker—I buy, being a man of action; or I sell, being a man knowing when to retreat, or I hold steady, being firm like a rock in my loyalty and resolve. And, at the end of each chapter, when the market closes, I am either standing on the cliff, breathing deep, enjoying the view, or hanging from it, the pit of my stomach trying to decide whether to throw up its contents. It's all highly entertaining." And with computers, the Internet, and the international markets, Mr. Comstock pointed out to Duncan that he could do it all day long. "No, thank you, the American markets are enough. It's just a hobby," Duncan said, smiling. "I wouldn't want to get obsessed."

With the dinner done and the evening over, the two couples parted. Emily wheeled Duncan into the kitchen, where they thanked Ana and the staff and said their goodnights. Then, with Ana holding open the back door, Emily wheeled Duncan to their small outside private elevator. They entered, and it took them up to their balcony. They exited and entered their apartment through double glass doors.

"What was that you said about Dmitri?" Emily asked as she headed them towards their bedroom.

"What?"

"When you were telling them some of your Dmitri stories."

"Yes, I'm beginning to collect a lot."

"They're a bit mean."

"The truth often is."

"Anyway, what did you call him?"

"I'm not sure. I call Dmitri so many different things."

"It was a funny name."

"Oh. I called him a 21st Century white Russian Stepin Fetchit. I don't think they got it."

They reached the bedroom, and Emily kicked off her shoes.

"I didn't get it."

"You laughed."

"We all laughed. It was such a funny name."

"Stepin Fetchit was a black actor in movies in the Thirties and Forties. He usually played a lazy, slow-talking, uh, 'nigger,' as they would have said in those days."

"That's awful."

"What? That I called Dmitri one, or that one existed in the movies?"

"Yes, the last. Your old movies are but the record of our bad past."

"Why don't you carry a line of antique slave manacles?"

"Duncan!"

"Don't tread on my movies."

"I was just pointing out—"

"In 'all-Colored Movies' made for a growing 'colored audience,' I think he usually played the romantic lead."

"Have you ever seen one?"

"No."

"Why?"

"I'm not all-colored."

"Duncan!"

"Can I change the subject?"

"I suppose."

"I visited the theater today."

"Oh," Emily sat in a large wingback chair and put her feet on an ottoman. "How's it coming along?"

"Okay, I guess. But why are you letting this happen?"

"Why not? It could bring in business."

"From where?"

"You'll see. People will travel to see good theater."

"You're assuming it's going to be good."

"Why are you being so negative?"

"Do you remember the suggestion I had for that space two, three years ago?"

"No. I don't think you ever had a suggestion about anything to do with the hotel or anything else around here."

"I got the tattoo parlor in."

"Oh, yeah. I was against it."

"The business from the oil rig guys alone pays his rent."

"I'm no longer against it."

"But two or three years ago, I suggested we find someone to convert the old ballroom space into a movie house showing nothing but old movies, a revival house."

"Oh, yes. I remember now."

"Whatever happened to that idea?"

"You never found anybody."

"Because you were so unenthusiastic."

"I was unenthusiastic about the tattoo parlor, but that didn't stop you."

"No, you had qualms about the tattoo parlor; you were deeply unenthusiastic about the revival house."

"Who wants to come and see a bunch of old movies?"

"Who's going to come and see theater?"

"I've read studies—"

"Yeah, I know."

"It could put us on the map."

"We never wanted to be on the map."

"You never wanted to be on the map."

"I've been on the map."

"It was a pretty small map."

"Yeah, but it was still hard to fold."

"Look, Pattie Heatherton really wanted it."

"Oh, Pattie really wanted it."

"She's my best friend."

"I'm your husband and business partner."

"Those—those are just words, Duncan."

"Words defining the truth."

"You are Duncan. I am Emily. We are both tired. So let me lift you and get you in bed." She stood up, crossed the room, and pushed Duncan to bed. Then she locked the wheels on his chair. "I hope you're too tired to watch a tape because I want to go right to bed."

"You've got to get ready, don't you? That'll give me at least a half hour."

"All right. Do you have a tape in the machine?"

"Sure."

"What are you watching tonight?"

"The Man Who Came to Dinner."

"Is that a good one?"

"Sure. Kaufman and Hart. Came from the theater. I play it to honor you."

"Thank you," Emily said as she grunted to stand Duncan up. She steadied him, grabbed his pants, and yanked violently. The pants, a garment of two halves joined by Velcro at the seams, fell apart, and fell to the floor. Duncan himself reached up to his shirt and pulled. It also broke away into sections and fell to the floor. He then stood there in boxer shorts and a T-shirt. Emily unlocked the wheels on the chair and pushed it back. "Timber!" Duncan yelled. "Timber!" Emily repeated, letting Duncan go, directing his fall towards the bed. Duncan fell and giggled, as did Emily as she grabbed his dead legs and swung them around, positioning Duncan correctly on the bed. With his strong arms, Duncan took over then and made himself comfortable for a half hour with Sheridan Whiteside. Emily went into the bathroom to undress, wash her face, and shuddered slightly over certain absurdities in her life.

BY THE SEA (II)

Chapter the Second

Like all girls her age, Trudy loved her bed. Not the basic from-the-factory box spring and mattress, of course, that was just a skeleton, but the enveloping creature of comfort she had created from it by layering on the flesh of smooth sheets of a particular delicate lavender; soft purple blankets that hugged; a patterned down comforter that embraced, and pillows, lots of marshmallow pillows that held so lovingly her head and the dreams it spun. Of course, there were analogies to infer. A cocoon was one; the womb would not be hyperbolic; even a man's loving, protective arms would mix well with the company. But the truth was far more direct, for the bed was not an outside thing at all but part of Trudy herself. And when she snuggled in and down under the covers, she was simply folding into herself, gathering herself to herself, happy to be herself, the loveliest comfort of all.

The curse of the alarm clock was a disruption of this comfort. It meant leaving the pureness of the self to confront objects animate and inanimate—cold floors, missing slippers, cats underfoot, cheery intimates, or miserable ones. Most days, Trudy cursed the curse of the alarm clock, but not today. Today she woke five minutes before the alarm was to scream. She hugged, embraced, and enfolded herself in her blankets as she watched the illuminated digital numbers change in unbelievably slow advancement, wondering why time had to choose this moment to be interminable. Then, finally, an electronic blaring that was louder, it seemed, than when it rudely intruded on her sleep caused her to burst forth.

She needed to be thirty minutes early today, but she was determined to be forty-five at least to put Frank in a good mood and to have a relaxed moment with him, for Frank was the key. Having showered before bed the night before, all she needed to do was quickly washed her face, brush her hair, and throw on some clothes. Much to her father's surprise, she showed up in the kitchen as he watched the coffee drip, waiting to claim a cup.

"Good morning, Dad!"

Jack Andover was happy to see his daughter early. Usually, he had to rush her to get ready, so he could take her to work, and, of course, he could never get any breakfast down her at all. "Well, hello early miss. Making eggs and bacon, how about some?"

"Can't, got to be at work early. Can you take me now?"

"Now?" It was both a question and a plea for mercy. "But I haven't had breakfast yet." Jack Andover was a man who liked his breakfast; indeed, it was his favorite meal of the day. He liked to hear the eggs fry and the bacon sizzle; he liked the taste of the mini cinnamon rolls his wife bought at the Sav-Rite Market. "You know, I don't need the truck today. Why don't you take it."

"I can't!" It was just a prick of panic, but the alarm was there, and her father noted this but didn't know what to make of it. "I told you; I'm being picked up from work today."

"Oh. Who by?"

Trudy had, of course, anticipated this question and had the answer waiting. "By a boy, Dad."

"Oh. A boy. How odd."

"We're going into Rubenton."

"Rubenton, huh? How odd."

"I'm going to help him shop for clothes."

"Well, given the fashions I see you kids wear, that'll be the oddest thing of all."

"Dad, stop kidding. Can we go?"

"Can I finish my coffee?"

"Yeah, sure—in the truck. Pour it in that mug-thingy with the top," Trudy said, referring to a promotional item from the John Deere company, a large wide-bottomed insulated mug with a magnetized bottom and a tight lid with a drinking hole and gloriously emblazoned with the John Deere logo.

Because he loved his daughter and often found her amusing, Jack Andover did as she asked, and soon they were on Leech Beach Road, moving slowly through the return of the thick fog, an animated white surrounding that turned the open road into an enclosed passage. Trudy, bundled in her oversized, ugly coat, marveled over this passage and turned it into a metaphor that she hoped would lead to a new maturity, a certain knowingness, and the application of same in the pursuit of justice

When Trudy entered the kitchen of The Briers Hotel at 5:15, she found Frank and Maria dancing to a hot salsa number flowing from a little boom box placed on a high shelf. Maria danced beautifully, Frank ridiculously, and Julio laughed from his position by the oven. The song ended, and the DJ announced in Spanish that this was the station of mas romantico music, and Frank repeated the term but altered it to mucho romantico because he liked better the way it pursed his lips. He gave Maria a big hug and announced, "Mucho caliente romantico!" Maria laughed, and Julio warned Frank to keep his hands off "my woman," Maria laughed even louder as she returned to the slicing of tomatoes. Then Frank noticed Trudy.

"Trudy!" Frank exclaimed, "Tardy no more!"

"I'm even here fifteen minutes early."

Frank looked up at the round wall clock provided by the coffee wholesaler. "Yes, you are. Congratulations. Are you going to want to leave fifteen minutes early?"

"No, I'll work till two."

"You will!" he said in mock delight.

"Don't kid me."

"Why not? You're a kid, aren't you?"

"Nineteen is not a kid. You have to be, like, twelve to be a kid."

"That's from your short-range perspective, kid. But from my long view, you are such a kid—and I mean that in a nice way."

"You do?"

"Sure. Nice or envious—one or the other. Why don't you get changed and get the tables laid? It would be a big help."

"Okay, but can I ask you something first?"

"Sure," he said as he prepped the coffee makers.

"Would it be possible for you to drive me home today? My dad has to be in Rubenton all day and can't come and pick me up. I'm on your way home."

Frank turned to her, the inconvenience becoming concrete in his mind. "Well, yeah, Trudy, but I get off two hours before you do."

"I know, but I sometimes see you take a walk on the beach after work. So I thought maybe today you'd want to do that."

"What? Just for the privilege and pleasure of taking you home?"

"Well, I don't know about privilege, but I might be able to give you some pleasure."

Rarely did anything stop Frank. But this stopped him. "Oh-oh-oh!" He heard Maria at the meat slicer say in a rising voice that perfectly matched the blush blooming on his face. As well as another rush of blood not in his control.

"Huh, well..."

"Ah, come on, please! I don't want to have to walk home."

"Um ... well ... yeah, okay, I've got some stuff I could do to kill time, I guess."

"Great! Thanks!" Trudy said as she ran off to the restroom to change.

"Caliente romantico," Maria said with her big, wide, tooth-full grin.

Frank was speechless, and Maria heartily laughed as she shook symbolic heat from her hand.

Allison opened the drapes of her tall window that morning and found that the fog had returned, and it stood there before her, a moving, textured entity of some interest. Allison did not consider the fog a fiend for cutting off her view, for she was happy for it to be her view. Indeed, Allison often saw the fog as an old friend keeping her safe behind its shroud, amusing her with its relaxed manner. She looked down to the boardwalk and saw the row of lamps that ran along it struggling to illuminate through the flowing white, barely succeeding in that task. The expected and always welcomed accompaniment to this scene, the foghorn, sounded. Allison smiled, closed her eyes, and, cracking the window that opened inward, breathed deeply of the fingers of flowing white and cold that entered. Goosebumps appeared on her naked body, and she let the chill fully awaken her. Just as she was closing the window, the phone rang, startling her, for rarely did her phone ring, and never this early in the morning.

She walked to her bed and put on her forest-green terry cloth robe, dousing the chill in immediate warmth, then went to the phone and picked it up.

"Hello?"

"Allison?"

The voice was as recognizable as it was unwelcomed.

"Oh, hello, Mavis."

"Allison, I'm sorry, I'm, well, I have some bad news."

"Yes."

"Jerry is dead."

"Gerald?"

"Yes, Gerald."

Allison honestly did not know what to say. Mavis reported to her, but she wasn't sure the fact was relevant. So, she said nothing, just listened to Mavis's breath as Mavis, she assumed, listened to her.

"Allison—do you want to know the details?"

"Sure."

"Are you okay?"

"Yes, of course."

"Do you need some time? Do you want to call me back?"

"No. Tell me what happened," Allison said as she decided to sit and be comfortable, so she took the phone over to the wingback chair and sat down.

"Well, it was—well, a freak accident, sort of, I guess. Well, Jerry was, I don't know, I guess fooling around with some of his friends—"

"Who?"

"Oh, some guys, you wouldn't know them, just some guys he, you know, used to hang with."

"Hang with?"

"They were out at Milliard's Bridge—"

"He was hit by a car?"

"No ... no, it was ... well, I ... I guess they were trying to bungee jump."

Allison had nothing to say to that. It was a concept she understood but, in the context of Gerald, not one she could grasp.

"Did you hear me?" Mavis asked.

"Yes, yes, of course, go on."

"Well, I guess they didn't really have a bungee cord, you know, a real one, so they hooked together a bunch of those—oh, what do you call them?—I don't know, those elastic things with hooks on each end that you tie things down to your car with."

Allison closed her eyes. It was like a joke, with a lousy pun ending that you could guess.

"Jerry went first and—"

"Did anybody go second?"

There was a measure of shock in Mavis' voice. "No, of course not, not after—"

"Yes, they probably wouldn't have been that stupid."

"I'm—I'm sorry, Allison."

"Okay."

"The funeral is Thursday."

"Okay."

"Are you coming?"

"No, I don't think so."

"Allison, he was your son."

"No, I don't think so."

"Just because he was adopted—"

"That was Jim; Jim wanted that, I—"

"Look, it would mean a lot to Jim."

"No, I don't think so."

"It would, Allison. It really would."

"No, I'm just reiterating that I'm not coming. I didn't like Gerald, you know. I pretty much loathed him, you know. I detested every moment I had to take care of him. I could tell from when we got him; even at six, I could tell how he would turn out. So, I'm not surprised he jumped off a bridge inadequately prepared. But Jim loved him. He was truly Jim's son—or Jim's boy at least. So, do tell Jim I'm sorry. I truly am. But I—I won't be there. If he asked you to make the call, it was wrong of him."

"No, I just thought—"

"Then you thought wrong."

"I'm sorry then."

"That's okay. Thanks for letting me know, though. I would not want to have not known."

"Yeah, okay, yeah, I thought you should know, of course."

"Of course."

"Well, goodbye."

"Goodbye, Mavis." She could hear Mavis begin to hang up. "And, oh...!"

"Yes?"

"I'm glad Jim's got you now."

"Oh. Oh, well, thanks. That's sweet of you to say."

"Goodbye, Mavis."

"Yeah, goodbye, Allison."

Allison hung up the phone. A chuckle jumped out of her before she could suppress it, but why should she suppress it? So she laughed, laughed at first as an elaboration on the chuckle. But soon, it was a hearty thing all its own flowing out until it hit a quick image of poor, dumb Jim in grief because, certainly, he would grieve. He would sit and cry, not understanding, not even understanding enough to question. So he would cry with pure, thoughtless grief. The image turned her laughter into a bawling, sudden, swift, tears and mucus-forming bawling so outrageous she had to laugh at herself. She laughed as she crossed to her bedside table to grab tissues to wipe and blow and clear it all out, and force herself to stop, catch her breath, stop the silliness, finish it, finish it with a chuckle.

Then she took her shower mixing far more hot than cold, causing sting and steam, and she scrubbed hard, and when she got out, she wrapped herself in a big, fluffy bath sheet and sat on the closed lid of the toilet, breathing in the leftover steam, a warm fog of her creation. She sat there for forty-five minutes and tried to think of nothing.

Besides having to go to The Briers Hotel so early in the morning, before school even; on Saturdays even, to take care of old fart Briers, Dmitri hated that he had to drive along winding Leech Beach Road always in the dark and often in a fog and that he had to do it in the old, crappie Ford Escort of his dad's that his dad let him use now that his dad had a new car, a really cool Trans Am, which his dad never let him drive. What all this meant—winding, dark, fog; crappie old car constantly breaking down—was that he had to go too damn slow. And although Dmitri, from any objective observation, seemed somewhat slow himself in movement and other attributes, he hated driving slow. Speed was all. If he had been clever enough to declare a life's motto, Speed was all would have been it. Dmitri loved high-speed roller coasters, fast-paced video games, and the quick-cutting Slam! Pow! Of modern action movies, anything that allowed him to move fast while sitting still. To drive at a snail's pace; forced to be careful as he negotiated the dark, fog-enshrouded curves of Leech Beech Road, hoping not to hit something; hoping the Ford Escort's shit engine didn't die. This was, for Dmitri, an essential, soul-numbing irritant.

But at least he could play his music. And play it loud—very loud—for wasn't loud the aural equivalent of speed? Sure, it was. And Rock and Rap and Hip-Hop; one could play it no other way. Have you ever tried to listen to them at a low volume? Stupid. The music makes no sense that way. It certainly doesn't move you; get into your gut; pull out your truly individual beat or rhythm (oddly, in total sync with the music's), not to mention your extraordinary abilities on the air guitar. So, he had his music at least, as he lumbered along on four wheels toward a morning of old fart Briers' potty, bath, breakfast, and lumbering along on four wheels.

But the old fart paid well. Much better than Dmitri's last job at McDonald's, especially after they kept cutting his hours until he was down to only four a week. At minimum wage, that's hardly worth showing up. The old fart paid him two hundred a week to show up before and after school and at those exact times on Saturdays to pick him up, put him down, and push him around. Boring, very dull, especially when the old fart wanted to talk, saying things Dmitri was not interested in hearing, mainly because he was never quite sure what the old fart was talking about. But as boring as his job was, he found interest in his savings account. Dmitri loved to get on the Internet, using the modern, near-futuristic convenience of online banking to check his balance, which grew by one hundred dollars weekly. By graduation, he would have enough for a reasonable down payment on the NSX he wanted, a more than cool car, a totally fast car, because the Japs really knew how to make them. Then, after high school, he could make the payments with the old fart's job alone while he looked for a really good-paying job. Or maybe he'll go to the local community college, like his dad kept telling him to, to study accounting because accountants, his dad always said, always make money because there will always be money to count. And with today's computers, you don't need to be that good in math, which, God knows, Dmitri wasn't, but he wasn't so bad that that should stop him because the computer will figure it all out in the end, and Dmitri is just going to have to note the bottom line, that's all.

As Dmitri thought of himself as a bachelor accountant, relied upon by businessmen and the wealthy, known for tooling around in his genuinely excellent NSX, probably the only one in Rubenton, and for being able to handle with relaxed confidence the curves of Leech Beach Road at speeds most people would shit-in-their-pants if they went—his two front tires blew out.

Followed in no time at all by his two rear ones.

"SHIT!" Dmitri yelled as he struggled to break and regain control of the Ford Escort, which was not that hard. He had not been going that fast.

Dmitri pulled off to the side and stopped. Death was the musical demand on his radio, but the call abruptly cut off when Dmitri turned off the car's engine. He took a deep breath and wondered when his heart would stop beating so hard. Then, after a moment, he got out of the car, looked at the tires, and couldn't believe it. Four blowouts! He looked down the road to where he had come. Through the fog, he could just see—just—something lying on the road. He walked over to it and couldn't believe it. It was a piece of plywood, the kind you use to board windows, studded with maybe a hundred nails all pointing up.

"What the hell! What fucking asshole did this?" Dmitri exclaimed as if anyone could hear him.

"I did," came a voice from the fog, followed by its source, a man of some sixty hard years in overalls. "You did that pretty good. Know how to handle a car, don't 'cha?"

Dmitri wasn't getting it; all he knew was: "I could have fucking been killed!"

"Nah, you were going too slow. Besides, I figured with all four tires going; you wouldn't lose too much control of the car."

"I should fucking kill you!"

"Yeah, well, you should notice that I have a shotgun here, so you probably won't be able to."

"You're crazy. I hate old people. They're all crazy."

"I was just trying to get your attention."

"Why?"

"You play your music too loud."

"What?"

"Your God damn Rock n' Roll and that urban black stuff. It's too loud, too early. Scares my cows and chickens. Scared cows and chickens don't produce milk and eggs."

"What?"

"Did you ever think of that? Did you ever consider that you're coming by our farms at six in the morning blaring that stuff, disturbing the peace?"

Consideration, of course, was not something Dmitri had much of to give. "What?"

"No, I didn't think so. I was going to flag you down and ask you nicely to keep it down, but I thought, Nah, that never works with young people. So, I decided to do this. Pounded all those nails in the plank myself. Bit of a job, I can tell you. But every morning you come along this road blaring that stuff, that plank going to be somewhere to greet you. You get it?"

"You're an idiot!"

"I'm not the one with four blown tires."

"How the fuck am I supposed to get to work? Mr. Briers is really going to be pissed."

"I figured you worked at the hotel. I've got to deliver some eggs and produce; I'll take you in."

Dmitri was disbelieving. "You're going to give me a ride?"

"Sure. I got ya four brand new tires to put on your car. Figured it was worth it to make my point. Of course, they're retreads, all I could afford, but they're still probably better than the four you had. But I'm telling you, son—if I have to blow your tires again, you'll be shit-out-of-luck. Get it?"

"Yeah, I guess."

"Yeah, well, don't guess, know it in your heart of hearts, okay? Now give me your keys. I'll change the tires while you're at work and drive the car to the hotel myself."

"But I only work for an hour or so. I don't want to have to be stuck there all day!"

"Don't worry; I'll get it done in time."

There being no other possible thing to do, Dmitri gave the man his keys and got into an old Ford pickup the farmer led him to. After driving the Ford Escort off the road, the farmer got in himself, settled down, started the engine, and turned on the radio. Stupid, twangy, shit-kickers music came gently and softly out of the speaker, and Dmitri silently groaned. He groaned again, not so silently, when he realized that the old Ford pickup went even slower than the Ford Escort.

Major Philip McFadden had been a good soldier. He had been a good soldier since he was two years old, and his father had taught him how to salute correctly, with his arm at the proper angle, which was challenging in a body forming but not yet formed. He did it, nevertheless, and his father was proud and gave him a snappy salute back, which from that time until the day his father died meant, I love you.

Master Sergeant Mike McFadden grew up uneducated in anything but survival in the streets of urban America during the 1930s when more than just those streets were depressed. He had been a tough kid, violent, when necessary, not respectful of the law, rough and unfair in his dealings with the opposite sex. Then the war came, boiling over from molecules of agitating events in Europe and Asia, events Mikey McFadden had not paid much attention to and so knew little about. But it was a fight. A fight the other guy picked—unfairly—and that was enough for Mikey. So he enlisted in the first wave of reflex patriotism and soon found himself in North Africa, a changed man. At first, hating all authority, like any tough guy from the streets, he soon found that he loved the precise stratification of the Army. For the streets had been chaos, and chaos is a whirl that spins perception. But in the Army, there was no chaos. Discipline, the Army called it.

There was comfort and joy in having a place to occupy. Mikey liked knowing who to answer to and who must answer to you. He was a sergeant by the time they landed in North Africa. He was a sergeant the first time he saw a man's guts explode out of his body. And seeing that man, still conscious, realize he was now a ripped-through bloody hunk of flesh—the incredible shock and surprise on the face of Pfc. Nick Pappas, as he watched himself flowing away into nothingness, never left Mike McFadden. He carried the vision of it until the day he died. It showed him how stupid he had been as a youth and how reckless he had been with his life. He changed again. Still loving the

Army and the place it gave him, he now became a lover of life, of being alive; of breathing, because the air was sweet and supported life; of food, all kinds of food, because it was delicious and extended life; of love, because it was pure pleasure and made life. A sense of place and a sense of purpose and a love of life; this is what the Army gave Master Sergeant Mike McFadden, and he wanted nothing less for his son.

Young Philip McFadden had always loved his father; had never passed through a rebellious stage ruled by conflict. His father was his hero. And his father wanted him to go to West Point. So, Phillip did. As the Army had been his father's life, it had become his. His father was exceedingly proud on graduation day and was happy to salute his son, now an officer who outranked him. And his son was pleased to salute back; trading loves very sentimental but no less genuine for that. Genuine, though, could not define every display of emotion by Lt. Philip McFadden that day. That sense of place so loved and proselytized by his father was nowhere to be felt within the new lieutenant. Only a lifetime of viewing his father's display of that love allowed him to do the same in a mockery so accurate he fooled his father—but did not make a fool of him.

Austin O'Brien knew nothing about any of this, of course, as he considered the ramrod individual sitting in The Briers Hotel dining room having his breakfast of Raisin Bran and yogurt, grapefruit juice, and "very hot" coffee. "Wouldn't bring it to you any other way, Major," Frank, the waiter, had said. "After all, you know how to use a gun." Frank's style and manner—light, with a smile, and an eye that twinkled—belied any snide tone that the ramrod individual might have perceived, and, indeed, Austin saw a slight smile cross the ramrod individual's lips.

"He's a resident, right?" Austin asked Frank when Frank came to his table.

Frank looked. "Oh, yes. Moved in about a month ago. Retired Army major."

"He looks it."

"Yes, doesn't he. He's very—orderly. Not particularly friendly, but not, not friendly, you know what I mean?"

"Striking looking, though, isn't he?"

"Yeah, I guess. It's that military bearing. I think it is, you know, that career officer look. Makes them kind of alien-like. I wonder if he will loosen up now that he's a civilian again."

"What's his name?"

"Ah, gee, I don't know. We all just call him the Major. You ready to order?"

"No, I'm waiting for someone."

He was waiting for Pattie Heatherton, the principal of Rubenton High School. They were having another of many such meetings about the Stafford Theatre. They often met here at The Briers as it was more convenient for Austin to stay close to the theater, and, besides, all the blueprints, plans, and paperwork they might have to consult were here in his office. And before the office was ready, the meetings had been in his room. For Pattie's convenience, they met on Saturday mornings. It was not too upsetting for her family life as her husband, Harry, always went golfing on Saturday mornings with his "cronies" and rarely came home before three in the afternoon after a long and mostly liquid lunch at the Fore! Cafe. And her boys were in their late teens and quite happy not to have mom around on Saturday, as they had had to deal with her dual authority over them (mom and school principal) for the previous five days.

"Guess what!" Pattie's excited voice hit Austin before a view of her did. She came around his back and swung herself into the chair opposite him. As Austin had still been considering Major Ramrod, who was just now leaving the dining room, walking with a perfected grace of bearing Austin found aesthetically pleasing, he was not immediately yanked into Pattie's existence.

"Austin!" Pattie yanked again.

"What?" he managed to say, now considering the woman before him. A dark-haired beauty, there was no doubt about that, despite her being in her middle years and the few sparsely allocated strands of white hair picking up highlights under the institutionally charming hanging lamps of the dining room.

"I saw you on TV last night!"

"Really?"

"On an old rerun of Dori Hart."

"Oh, yeah. Did a couple of those."

"You were the killer!" Pattie said with an odd measure of delight.

"Well, it was a mystery show. Somebody had to be the killer."

"It was so strange to sit there and watch you on the screen and think to myself, I know him! And in the flesh too!"

"Pattie! Not so loud."

"Oh, no one's listening, and fewer care."

"Still..."

"It was just so neat to see you. When did you make it?"

"I don't know. Five—six years ago."

"Your hair was longer."

"I was supposed to be one of her students taking Forensics in order to plot the perfect murder. I think that was the last time I got away with playing someone much younger than myself."

"Why? You could still do it. You don't look anywhere near your age."

"Thanks. I know I should take that as a compliment, but for an actor, youth, being inherently uninteresting, is uninteresting to play. But, at least in this episode, the guy was nuts, and nuts is always fun to play."

"Well, I enjoyed seeing you. It was such a surprise, it was such a—well, I was channel surfing, bored, thinking about this morning, but, you know, not trying to think about this morning as Hairy-butt Bastard was in the room reading the paper, when suddenly, there you are, all blond and cute. I stopped changing channels and started to watch, which drove Hairy-butt Bastard out of the room because he hates Kelly March for some reason. 'What are you watching that bitch for?' he says. 'I don't know,' I said, 'looks interesting.' 'You've never watched this show before,' he says. 'Quiet, Harry,' I tell him, 'I want to watch this—besides, that blond guy has the most gorgeous schlong you've ever seen in your life!'"

"Pattie! You didn't!"

"I did! After he left the room."

"Hi!" Trudy bounced up, menu pad in hand. "Hi, Ms. Heatherton!"

"Hello, Trudy. How are you?" Pattie said, suddenly with the demeanor of a woman whose lexicon did not include Schlong (slang) —N. A Yiddish word, simply meaning a penis, but often used by Gentiles to indicate a penis of admirable length and mass.

"I'm great!"

"Trudy is auditioning for the theater," Austin said

"Really? That's great, Trudy. You were always the highlight of our talent shows."

"Yeah, I know. Thanks. Can I take your order?"

Trudy took their order, noting it meticulously on the menu pad. Later, when she brought the hot and steaming materialization of her notes to their table, Austin asked if she had picked out a scene yet, and she said no; she's still looking them over, and he said, if she wanted, he'd recommend one, and Trudy said she would get back to him on that. Pattie suddenly intruded in the exchange to inquire if his office was heated yet? When Austin answered no, she expressed extreme disappointment. Still, Austin said it was okay because he had all the paperwork and the lighting equipment catalogs up in his room, and they could go over them there. Frank passed by just at that time and overheard the conversation, reporting it with a not very admirable glee to Julio once he got to the kitchen, the end of the report being heard by Trudy just as she came in.

"Excuse me? Are you saying that—that Austin and Ms. Heatherton are—are...?" Her mouth continued to hang open, but nothing else came out.

There was acknowledgment in Frank and Julio's eyes and smiles.

"Eww...!"

"I thought you weren't a kid anymore," Frank said.

"I'm not. Not now, not after that!"

"Yep, that's when you grow up. When you realize life is full of uncomfortable surprises," Frank said as he started to walk away.

"Hey. Hey...!" Trudy stopped him. "You're taking me home, right?"

"Right, sure, I said I would."

"Don't forget."

"I won't forget, kid. I'm a grown adult used to responsibility. Now, why don't you get back out to the dining room."

Major Philip McFadden (U.S Army, Ret) crossed the lobby, acknowledging Tom, the desk clerk, with a nod as he started up the stairs to his room. When he entered, he went straight to the bathroom to floss and brush his teeth. The Major then urinated and washed his hands thoroughly with soap and hot water, drying them on the hotel's somewhat embarrassingly fluffy towels. He then went into the main room and sat down at the antique, but not valuable, desk to face the yellow legal pad waiting for him. The pages of the pad were blank. There were two other pads full of his tight, neat, and orderly handwriting stacked at the upper right-hand corner of the desktop. He was writing his memoirs. It was the only thing he knew to do. When he had left the Army, not as the four-star general Master Sergeant Mike McFadden had hoped for, he had no idea where to go or what to do. Having been an Army brat, he had no hometown, no ancestral seat to return to. Having been a combat soldier, the Major had no skills that translated comfortably into any legal civilian profession. But also, not having married and raised a family, he had savings and investments, not to mention his pension. They would see him secure for many years, indeed up to and probably past his eventual demise, no matter how long that may be delayed by the exciting world of geriatric medicine.

So, having nowhere to go, he looked around and found a place that was, essentially, nowhere. And having no future except existence, he decided to spend his days in his past.

He titled his memoir Soldier. His goal had been to try to capture not only his life as a soldier, not only the life of a soldier in general but the life force of the Soldier, the historical and human concept. Thus, he wanted to deal with the essential and crucial ideas of Duty, Honor, Loyalty, and Love of Country. But to his surprise, his distress, his disgust on some days, his fascination on others, he found himself not just dealing with cold concepts that one laid emotion on, but also with emotions of which he could not find the concepts.

The beauty of a soldier's body, which he had written just the day before, has inspired artists of all ages. I mean specifically, the combat soldier. Ready and willing to fight, one that knows his body is part of his weaponry. It must be as well tended to as any weapon, from his M16 which should always be clean and well oiled, to his combat knife, which should always be so polished that the sun's reflection on its blade could daze an enemy. Its edge should always be so sharp and honed that it could slit through his enemy's flesh, muscles, and sinews with just the slightest pressure. However, in modern warfare, who can appreciate the soldier's body, so covered with head-to-toe combat fatigues and body armor and backpacks full of high-tech instruments and helmets meant to extend this human soldier's perceptions towards the realm of the superhuman? You would have to go back to the days of the ancient Greeks and images on pottery or carved from marble to see a true celebration of the soldier's body as an instrument of war. Or, in modern times, you must go into the communal shower of the barracks where soldiers, naked and glistening, cleanse their tools of war.

He had struck out the last sentence before going on to a consideration of a soldier's mental preparation. But notwithstanding the bold intersecting pencil line, it was still on the yellow legal pad.

◆ ◆ ◆

At noon, Frank left work and went straight to his car, intending to jump in and leave for home. But his self-vaunted sense of responsibility lived up to his earlier declaration. It caught him by the scruff of the neck and pulled him out of the car.

"Oh, shit!" he said. Oh, well, he thought.

He slammed the car door shut and then went to the trunk and opened it up. He pulled a blanket, a sand chair, and his sketchpad from it. He was just about to slam the trunk shut when he remembered to grab his pencil pack. Then he closed the trunk unemotionally and walked out onto the beach.

The fog had lifted, but the gray had not. There was no wind, but a good cold stood its ground. Frank zipped his jacket up and walked down the beach away. He went around a curve in the shore and out of sight of The Briers. He went to his usual spot and set up the little sand chair, all seat and back, and no legs, then laid the blanket before it. He threw his sketchpad and pencil pack on the blanket, then sat down on the chair. He sat between two small dunes, each topped with tuffs of scrubby grass providing cover. Now he began to thank Trudy silently. Two hours of this cold, grey isolation was not such an awful way to spend his afternoon.

"He...hello."

Frank turned his head to the left to see Mrs. Carr, bundled in a great coat over pants and practical walking shoes over thick, gray socks. A pink stocking covered her head; gray streaked blonde hair fell from either side.

"Oh, hello, Mrs. Carr. You going for a walk?"

"Beh...." Allison said and then quickly needed to catch a breath.

"Sorry?"

"Beh...been for a walk ... went too far ... just coming back." She took one more deep and deeply appreciated breath. "And I'm exhausted."

Frank could see that, and he jumped up from the sand chair and offered it to Allison, who accepted it gratefully. Frank helped her by awkwardly grabbing her at the elbow and guiding her down. She plopped but laughed and seemed quite happy to sit.

"Ah—that's better. Unfortunately, my ambulatory ambitions sometimes outstretch my native abilities."

"You ought to be more careful."

"Oh, I'm okay. Just a bit winded."

"Well, just rest here."

Frank was still standing over her.

"I'm sorry, "Allison said when she noticed, "I've taken your chair." Then, she started to get up.

"No, that's okay, look," Frank descended gallantly, "I'll sit here on the blanket—by your feet, my lady."

"But—"

"Don't argue," Frank had gathered up his sketchpad and pencil pack and now held them on his lap. "What better place to worship you from."

Allison laughed—surprisingly—a young girl's laugh. "You're the nicest man, Frank."

Frank tossed the compliment off. "Well—what the hell? I'm just after your money."

The young girl laughed again. "Oh, so that's what you really are: A gigolo."

Frank's sudden stare, unintended and not caught in time, embarrassed them both.

"I'm sorry," Allison said. "I seem to have intruded again."

Frank just looked at her and smiled.

"I mean, I wouldn't want you to get into trouble with your parole officer."

"No—no, that would not be good."

Both were quiet. It was a moment when only the ocean spoke in an unbroken monologue; the whispered one of a calm sea. Frank turned his eyes to that ocean. Allison kept hers on Frank.

"Did you learn to draw in prison?"

"What? Frank turned back to her.

"Sketchpad," she said, indicating it.

"No."

"Because there was no prison."

"Well, not one of metal bars, at least."

"Did you major in art?"

"No. completely self-taught."

"Why?"

"Because no one could teach me. Never was a good student."

"What do you draw?"

"Whatever the hell I want."

"Ah. So, probably never to be exhibited in a group show."

"Ha-ha!" It was a laugh jerked out. "That's true. Not likely to have a one-man either."

"Why?"

"Well, I don't know. Maybe I'm just not an exhibitionist."

"So, you're a waiter...."

"An honorable way to pay the bills."

"Wouldn't you rather do it through drawing?"

"I already did—for many years. Paid pretty good, too."

"And you walked away from it."

"Or it walked away from me. In any case, it was all that is called in contractual terms, Work-for-Hire. To you and me, it's called being a hack."

"You don't mean you were no good?"

"Oh, no, of course not. I'm a superb artist. No, by a hack, I mean, you know, like a taxi driver. Someone hired to take someone where they want to go. Now, of course, there are bad hacks, average hacks, and great hacks. A bad hack is a driver who hardly knows where he's going, much less how to get you to where you're going. An average hack, now there's nothing wrong with him, he always knows how to get you where you want to go, but he always takes the most typical route. But a superb hack, an excellent taxi driver, will say to you, 'Hey Mac, how adventurous are ya? 'cause I can take you where you want to go by the normal streets, or I can take you a way that will be full of surprises and beauty and things you've never seen before. You game?' That's the kind of hack I tried to be. But, unfortunately, most passengers just want to get where they're going as quickly, cheaply, and mundanely as possible."

"So now you sit on the beach drawing seascapes?"

"No, no, God, not seascapes. I never draw what's in front of me."

"Seemed to have worked for Michelangelo."

"Ah, yes, but he was just a hack driving around the Popemobile."

Allison laughed. She liked the tap of the dance of Frank's quick wit.

"So, what do you draw?"

"What's inside my head."

"Why?"

"Because I like what's inside my head."

"I see. And it has the advantage that no one can challenge your interpretation."

Frank looked at Allison, noticing what he had admired before, now seeing something else as well. "There's a bit of wisdom behind those stunning blue eyes."

"One of the perks of getting older, I guess."

"No, don't sell yourself short, Mrs. Carr. Young fools usually grow up to be old fools. And the gray and wise were usually sharp youths. Got to build on something solid, you know."

Allison smiled, and Frank smiled back, then they allowed the ocean's whisper dominance again as they both breathed in the cold air and felt the comfort of the gray. After a moment, Frank, in a natural move, opened his sketchpad and pencil pack and began to draw. Allison did not notice this as her eyes were out to sea.

"You know, often when I sit on the beach like this, starring out at the surface of the ocean wondering what's down there below, I'll see, or imagine, of course, but it's like I can see it, I'll see a great sea monster—"

Frank stopped his drawing and looked at Allison.

"—rising, breaking the surface, so huge it's not relatable to the surroundings. I mean, it almost dwarfs the sky, the beach, and me, of course. I mean, I'm so tiny before it. But I'm not scared, it's not a 50's movie monster, where I suppose I got the image, I'm not scared, I'm— I'm in awe of its—its grand size, its grandeur almost, its beauty. Its beauty, yes, beauty and strength and grace as it—"

Frank quietly turned the page of his sketchpad and quickly began to draw. "—moves its huge head on the end of its long neck and turns to look at me. Me. And I feel it acknowledges me, tiny though I am. And then, again with such grace of movement, it turns and dives, almost folds itself back into the sea, sending up great sprays of water, some of which, seconds later, blows cool onto my face."

Frank shut the sketchpad just as Allison looked at him.

"Pretty weird, huh?"

Frank laughed. "Well—unexpected. I'll never be able to look at the ocean the same way again. But, you know, I like it. Better sea monsters below than just drilling equipment."

"Ah, yes. Well, I guess I should be getting back home."

Frank stood quickly, offering his hand to help Allison up. With grace, Allison accepted and allowed him to pull her up. She found it an enjoyable cheat of gravity, and Frank noted with surprise how soft, smooth, and gentle her hand was. He was ashamed to realize that he had been expecting a dry leaf.

"Don't walk so far next time," he told her.

"I know. I just lost track of where I was. Things on my mind, you know."

"Mysterious things?" Frank asked, immediately wondering if he had just flirted with her.

"Well, no ... it's just that ... you see, I heard this morning that my son was killed."

"Oh my god! Mrs. Carr, I'm so sorry."

"No, that's all right. He was adopted. I never liked him. Still—passages, you know, passages."

"Of course." Frank did not know what more to say except, "How old was he?"

"Oh—not yet thirty. A young fool," Allison said acknowledging their shared wisdom. "At least now he'll never be an old one."

The sex had been so wild and passionate and thrilling that Pattie felt like a young girl again, like one of the teenage girls that surrounded her five days a week during the school term. They were her sacred charges, and yet they pissed her off because they flaunted their youth, their supple bodies, and specific knowledge that they had no business having yet and which was no part of the curriculum Pattie had set. She sat in bed stretching her torso, hands reaching for the sky, a sly, satisfied smile on her face, aware of her naked breasts now pulled up to an approximation of where they had stood twenty years ago. It was a pretty picture she was trying to paint for Austin, who was just slipping back into his briefs.

"I feel like I'm glowing," she said, "Am I glowing?"

Austin rose to full height and considered Pattie and her question with admiration on his face. More likely, it was admiration for his performance than her glow, but he had studied the role well.

"Like a hundred-and-fifty-watt bulb," he said with a patented smile.

"Mmm," she said, pleased and complimented. "You fuck so good."

"Sometimes it's not the artist; it's the subject."

"Ahhh." Hearing him was like taking a sip of a drink that was both refreshing and stimulating. "You are the sweetest thing." He was undoubtedly sweeter than her husband, Harry, or "Hairy-butt Bastard," as she often referred to him in private.

"You better get dressed."

"You're only the fifth man I've ever fucked, you know." She liked saying "fuck" and the word meaning something wildly illicit and, quite frankly, fun.

"Oh? How do I stack up?"

"Please! One of them is Hairy-butt Bastard, two were in college, and the first was hardly a man. We were sixteen and stupid. However, he was more stupid than I was. Sixteen-year-old boys don't have a lot of finesse, you know."

"Yes, I remember being sixteen."

"Oh, but I can imagine you were the exception to the rule."

Austin smiled. "Well..."

"Ah-ha!"

"I, uh, I had had an older lover."

"Oh, you liked older women even then, huh?"

Austin felt a rush of embarrassment, but he talked himself out of it. "What are you talking about? You're not older than me."

"No, but I'm still an older woman. Older, I'll bet you, than most of your show biz lovers."

"Well—that's show biz!"

"Okay, I've had five. How many lovers have you had?"

"Pattie!"

"I'm not jealous, just curious."

"You need to get dressed. We haven't even gone over my update on the theater."

"Oh, we don't need to. I trust you." She jumped out of bed, happy in her nudity, and stood in challenge before Austin, now in jeans and an unbuttoned shirt. "Come on, how many?"

"Do you really think I've counted them?"

"Don't all men?"

"No."

"Really?"

"I don't think so."

"Notches on your belt? The number of 'kills' painted on the side of your fighter jets? You guys love to count your conquests."

"Not all of us guys. Some of us have a little more—"

"Class?"

"Yeah, I guess."

"Class and a nice ass!" Pattie locked her arms around his hips and squeezed his buttocks as she took his left nipple into her mouth.

"Pattie!"

But he made no impression on her as her arms returned to the front, undid his pants, slipped them and his briefs down as she went down herself, and quite joyously slipped her mouth over his penis. Feeling the thrill of its bulk, she proclaimed silently to herself, "I have a lover, a big stud lover—damn, it's wonderful!"

Austin, realizing this would be a two-a-day, screwed up his courage by giving consideration again to the perfected grace of bearing displayed earlier by Major Ramrod.

Duncan Briers had laughed loud and long when Dmitri, not intending to solicit laughter, told what the farmer had done to him that morning, expressing a great deal of umbrage—a word Dmitri did not know but an emotion that could sting him.

"It's not funny!" Dmitri claimed with even more umbrage.

"The hell—the hell—it ain't," Duncan said between laughs. "Serves you right. I've had to repeatedly tell you to turn your damn radio off before pulling into the parking lot. You know, some people are still asleep this time of the morning."

"I've been turning it off!"

"Not always."

"When?"

"Last Wednesday"

"Oh, yeah."

"Oh yeah, indeed."

"Well, sometimes I forget."

"Well, if you didn't have your damn radio blasting that shit you listen to in the first place, you wouldn't have to remember."

"It's my radio; it's my car!"

"But it's not your—world. Don't you understand that?"

"I've got a right."

"Yeah, you've got a right to sing the blues."

"What does that mean?"

"Never mind."

"No, what does it mean."

"I said, never mind! Now get me into the bathroom."

In the bathroom, in his bath, Mr. Briers couldn't help but laugh again. It was a little unfair, he knew, maybe a bit mean, he understood, but he couldn't help it.

"It's not funny!" Dmitri shouted from the bedroom.

"I'm sorry," Mr. Briers said, then laughed again, well aware that he forced it. And he immediately regretted it.

"I said it's not funny, damn it! That goddamn, fucking old bastard, I'm going to get him," Mr. Briers heard, then heard a crash.

"Hey, what are you doing out there?"

"Nothing, I just knocked over some of your video tapes."

"Holy Christ! Did you break any?"

"No, they're fine. I'm picking them up."

"Well, calm down, for Christ's sake, and be careful!"

"Well, I am! I'm going to get that old fuck! He could have killed me!"

"Yeah, sure, you're going to get him. How are you going to get him?"

"I don't know. Poison his cows or something!"

"Hey!" Duncan was cold in his bath water, suddenly as chilling as Dmitri's intent. "Stop talking like that and get me out of here!"

When Dmitri entered, Duncan had already unplugged the tub and was pulling down a large bath sheet to wrap around himself. He picked Mr. Briers up, positioning the bath sheet over his back and shoulders. He then stood him up on a rug by a wall with handles for Mr. Briers to grab and hold himself up with while Dmitri rubbed him dry, leaving the genitals for Mr. Briers to dry with one hand as he held onto a handle with the other.

"Okay, get my robe."

"You don't want your clothes?"

"No, damn it, my robe! Now!"

Dmitri got him into his robe, his bedroom, and his wheelchair. Duncan told Dmitri to sit on the edge of his bed and then gave him a deep, intense look, which Dmitri found very hard to meet, as it was so weird coming from Mr. Briers.

"Listen to me, Dmitri." Dmitri kept his eyes averted. "Are you listening to me?"

"Yeah."

"Then look at me!"

"I can hear you."

"But I want you to look at me."

"I don't want to."

"Why?"

"It hurts my eyes."

"That's the stupidest thing I've ever heard."

"It is not! You're looking weird."

"All right, okay, listen—are you listening?"

"Yeah."

"You are not—do you understand me—you are not to do anything in retribution towards Hendrickson."

"What's 'retro-bution'?"

"Oh, for Christ's sake!"

"Well...?" It was practically a pleading for his life.

"You are not to do anything to get back at Hendrickson."

"You're not my father!"

"I'm your employer, I pay you far more than you're fucking worth, and I'm the ticket to that speedy little car you want. Right?" Dmitri seemed to be contemplating his knees. "Right?"

"Yeah."

"Look, Hendrickson made a point. Somewhat dramatically, I'll admit, but he had a point to make. And he's willing to compensate for the damage he caused. So why aren't you listening to that, taking all that in, rather than plotting bovine murder?"

"What's bovine?"

"Cows, you git!"

"Because I hate him. I mean, he's, like, an old bastard that thinks he's so smart. He's just a fucking farmer. I mean, what's that? He's just like everybody else who think they're so fucking smart but don't really know shit! I mean, what does he know?"

"He knows your damn loud music disturbs his livestock."

"Oh, big deal."

"It may be to him."

"I betcha it doesn't really scare his cows and chickens."

"I don't know; what do I know? But it disturbs him during a time of the day that should, by all rights, be quiet and peaceful. Don't you think that's enough of a discourteous thing to do?"

"I like my music."

"Goddamn it, Dmitri! You just refuse to understand, don't you?"

"I don't know."

"Yeah, that's the thing—you don't know. Well, listen, if I hear of anything happening to Hendrickson, or his cows, or his chickens, or even his goddamn vegetable garden, I'll know you did it, right? So even if you didn't do it, I'd assume you did it, then I'll take action. And it won't be a good thing for you. Do you understand?"

"The old fuck," was all Dmitri would say.

"Jesus Christ! If I could only stand up, walk over there, and beat some sense into you."

"Yeah, well, you know, I would hit back."

"Metaphorically?"

"What?"

"I meant it metaphorically. Would you hit me back metaphorically?"

"What's meta-for-cally?"

"Oh, for Christ's sake!"

Duncan sent Dmitri downstairs, instructing him to tell the kitchen to send his breakfast up. But not before he had him go through the videotapes he had knocked over, which were now in a jumbled order, to find his copy of Way Out West with Laurel and Hardy. Duncan did not intend to watch the whole movie; he needed to do some work on their investments this morning. But he also desired— right that very moment—a little oasis, a bit of beaming from the TV screen some display of thought or feeling so much purer than he had ever been able to find outside of the box or off the screen. He needed, essentially, to irradicate the taste of Dmitri out of his head. He hit PLAY, put the machine on FAST FORWARD, and watched Stan and Babe quickly enter the Western town. He stopped as the boys reached the front of the saloon to listen to a relaxed cowboy band sitting casually on the wooden sidewalk, playing and singing a song that instructed the listener to commence to dancin', which is precisely what the boys do.

It's the sweetest moment in cinematic history, Duncan thought. For the dance of the boys was a dance of pure joy, of simple delight. Here, in a bit of charming choreography, these classic "Two minds without a single thought between them" revel without harshness, their smiles—worthy of saints—projecting pleasantness and good-heartedness. Duncan wanted to hug them, take them into his arms, to feel a connection with something that would not bite back, burn the skin, or bruise the flesh. This is a good thing that movies once did in Happy Hollywoodland. It's what had made Duncan gravitate towards there, only to find that Hollywood was not always—in fact, rarely was—happy. Indeed, he found Hollywood to be nothing but hills and valleys of Dmitris trying to entertain Dmitris while biting, burning, and bruising each other. Drunk was the only way Duncan could take it. A weakness on his part, he was sure, just couldn't cut it, couldn't play with the Players, couldn't—

But why, goddamn it, why think of all this now? He picked up the remote and ordered the boys backward, then requested, that they, once again, commence to dancin', please.

After Frank saw Mrs. Carr to The Briers, he returned to his spot on the beach, sat and grabbed his sketch pad, and furiously worked, surprising himself that he was drawing an image from his brain that had not originated there. He kept his eyes on the surface of the sheet he was reshaping, obstinately not looking up at the actual ocean. Maybe Frank worked fast to get it out because it was alien, but he was not unhappy to do so; he was, he had to admit, having fun. My god, he thought, could Mrs. Carr be my muse? He had never had a muse before. Donna certainly had not been one, although she had tried to motivate in other ways. Helen had inspired, but not to art. The few other women he had been intimate with really did not care about his art, concerned, as they were, only with being cared for, so, no muse for this boy. Nor had he ever had a mentor, for that matter, not really. There were those he had admired, whom he would have loved getting close to so they could have admired him in return, but none ever seemed willing. There were the odd, occasional encouragers, but they had always understood only a bare fraction of his true talents. So, muse-less, mentor-less, he always had lived in a single, even when he was married and lived with Donna.

"Frank!"

The voice came from far off, down the beach, delivered by chilled air, fresh and bubbly. It was Trudy in the distance, a small waving figure. He looked at his watch—it was 2:05. It was time to go.

◆◆◆

"You weren't really serious, were you," Trudy said as they pulled out of The Briers parking lot and onto Leech Beach Road, "about Austin making it with Ms. Heatherton?"

"Well, I've never actually seen them do it, but they seem to spend a lot of time together in his room."

"Yeah, but—"

"And she has that certain look when they're together."

"What look?"

"That look that women get when they are in the act of possessing."

"That's silly!"

"You don't think—"

"Men can look dopey too, you know."

"I didn't say it was a dopey look. The dopey look comes when women are in love, often before the possession is secured. What I'm talking about is a much more haughty, triumphant look. And it doesn't necessarily have to be preceded by love."

"You think you're smart, don't you?" Trudy asked, but, surrealistically, not in accusation.

"Not smart. Knowledgeable through experience; aged, some might call it."

"And cynical?"

"I wouldn't say I was cynical—factual, but not cynical. A cynic is nothing but a disappointed romantic, and I have never been a romantic."

"And you're unemotional about, you know, about love and sex and relationship stuff like that?'

"It seems so. Much to my soon-to-be ex-wife's dismay."

"Good!" Trudy said quite emphatically.

Frank briefly took his eyes off the road and looked at Trudy with some surprise. Then he turned his eyes to the road and said, "Well,

I've never really been dismayed by it, but I'm surprised you aren't chastising me."

"Why?'

"Because girls usually like the warm, fuzzy, and emotional."

"I don't have time for that."

"Oh, you don't."

"I need you to be cold."

It was so categorical, so much a prelude to a demand, that Frank felt her gathering his strings and did not care to feel the tug.

"Well, I don't know if I'm completely cold—"

"And calculating."

"Christ, what do you want me to do, kill somebody for you?"

"No. Just teach me to fuck really good."

Unfortunately, they had hit a curve in the road, and Frank, his head quickly twisting to face Trudy's smiling face, did not steer the car to follow suit. Fortunately, peripheral vision and great reflexes brought the Celica to a gravel-churning stop just before it was scheduled to fly off into a small ravine.

Frank's heart was racing. From what cause—a male-fantasy-fascinating proposal or near death—he had no idea. Trudy sat there with a bright-eyed, smiling face that was guileless, pleasant, and more than sincere. She did seem to be breathing a little rapidly as the eye-catching rise and fall of her breasts attested to, but, again, from what cause, he had no idea.

"Ah, well—" Frank managed to get out.

"I want facts, techniques, with an emphasis on what a guy really likes. I made it with a few guys in high school, but they hardly knew anything themselves, so I thought I would go to someone who is, well, you know, like you said, knowledgeable through experience. Aged!" Trudy seemed to like the word a little more than Frank did.

"Uh—" Frank suddenly realized that the car was still in DRIVE and not going forward into the ravine only by the extreme pressure his right foot was applying to the brake. He quickly put the car into PARK and jerked the parking brake tight. "Is there any reason you want this, uh, these, uh, information, instructions, and um..."

"Yeah, I want to seduce Austin."

"Austin?"

"So he'll let me be in the theater company."

"Trudy—"

"No, really, it will work. You see, I'm not sure Austin 'gets' me yet, because he's so, you know, kind of in love with the theater and all that stuff. Which is good, of course, but I'm all about being, you know, really, really good at being, you know, myself. Which the camera, you know, I think, will just love. But I need experience—obviously—I need experience. But, you know, at doing the kind of things that will show me off doing, you know, what I can do. And I'm not sure Austin gets that. I think he, maybe, thinks I need to do, you know, really acting sort of stuff. So, I got to change his head a little bit on that. Now I've read a lot about Hollywood, you know, I've read a lot of books, so I know what goes on there, and it's obvious for, you know, for females there, the best way to change a man's head is to, you know, turn it first. So that's what I want to do, to turn his head so I can get him on my side so I can become a part of his company, and then he'll pick plays that will completely show me off, and then when his friends, you know, come out from Hollywood, I'll be discovered. Now I know that all sounds so, sooo calculating, really, you know, a bitch thing to do. But I knew somehow that you would understand because I knew you are such a nice guy, but not, you know, a wimp kind of guy that might think—well, you know. And now! And now that you tell me that Austin's making it with Ms. Heatherton, which is a completely yucky thought, I mean, I didn't think I was going to have any competition, not that I truly think she's competition because she's, you know, kind of really an old type. So, I can handle that. But not if I'm not any good because, again, you see, she's probably knowledgeable through experience too, and aged and all that."

Trudy's long explanation had given Frank time to think, but he was not sure he had used the time efficiently. His mind had been diverted by the confusing combination of pleasure and pain that was the bold signature of a fully engorged penis. And by his silent, repetitive recitation of Mary had a little lamb/little lamb/little lamb, which was a technique he had first employed during school hours at the onset of puberty when he suddenly found his penis engorged at the most inopportune moments. It was usually at school just when the bell rang, and he had to vacate his desk-attached, lap-covering seat to stand up and leave. He had found that the nursery rhyme had a good deflating effect, if not always a rapid one. But he always managed to weather the delay through a skillful twisting of his body, strategic placement of his hand-held textbooks, and because his mother always clothed his pudgy self in roomy, husky-style jeans. So he never suffered the embarrassment he had been so deathly afraid of.

On this reminiscent occasion, though, Mary and her little lamb were not having the desired effect at all. Probably because years ago, some witty and clever guy in a bar had recited to Frank, Mary had a little lamb/Some salad and dessert/Then she gave me the wrong address/The dirty little flirt. And ever since, the original and unadulterated version had lost some of its potency.

"You're excited about the idea, I see," Trudy said, having had her attention drawn to Frank's crotch by his involuntary shifting of hips for comfort's sake.

"Uh, Trudy," Frank said, forming a very concrete image of himself as an older, responsible adult with a reasonably solid moral base, "there are so many things to consider here that—"

"You do want to fuck me, don't you? I mean, you always have, right? I mean, who wouldn't?"

"Uh, well, I can't lie, can I? You are, well, you are an attractive girl, and—"

"Look, I'm nineteen, you know; I'm not jailbait anymore or any of that stuff, so that's not a problem, right?"

"Well, yeah, sure, I mean, legally, but you are a lot younger than me, and—"

"Ah, come on, old guys fuck young women all the time. I'm not stupid, you know. Plus, it's not like I'm asking you to date me or anything embarrassing like that. I just want some instruction and practice, that's all. I mean, you have coaches for sports, right? And drama coaches? And they're always older people, right? I mean, they must be, mustn't they? So all I'm saying is, be my sex coach. Because I think I have only one shot at Austin, and I don't want to blow it."

"Or maybe you do," Frank said, making the joke before he could censor it. Trudy got it immediately and laughed heartily. Not a girlish laugh; it had a honk to it. But it was the laugh of an individual fully aware of and happy with her senses. To show her delight, Trudy leaned over to Frank, grabbed the back of his head in her left hand, guided it to her lips, and gave him a vigorous, probing kiss as her right hand settled on his crotch, making the most of manipulation.

Frank, being a man, especially being a man with an engorged penis now stimulated by an outside and attractive force, found the image of himself as an older, responsible adult with a solid moral base becoming quite abstract and hard to pin down. A great rush of joy filled his head, his heart beat out a happy tune, and his breath rapidly brought in the intoxication of Trudy's intimate behavior. Then, in age-old and automatic response, his left hand went to Trudy's right breast, and the recapturing of a certain adolescent giddiness once he had felt the firm but giving substance of it surprised and delighted him.

Nothing, not a damn thing, could be wrong with this; the universe seemed to shout at him. And who was he to argue with the universe?

◆ ◆ ◆

When they got to Frank's single apartment, Trudy proclaimed it "cute" as she dropped her bag on the floor and moved around the wicker screen to see the bed.

"Oh good, you've got your TV where you can see it from the bed."

"You want to watch TV?" Frank asked, slightly confused, wondering if there were a soap opera, game show, or low-brow talk show full of people you would never want to know telling you all their emotional trauma that Trudy never missed at this time.

"No, I want you to put on some of your porno. You know, something to study. I've never seen any porno, but I figure it's got to be really instructive about what guys like because, you know, mainly guys watch it."

"How do you know I even have any porno?"

"You're a guy. You're single. And you live alone."

Frank was stunned by the wisdom of the assertion. "Are you sure you're only nineteen?"

"Nineteen's not as dumb as you might think. Plus, I overheard Julio and you talking about porno and where you get the best buys."

"When was this?"

"Months ago." Trudy was now sitting on the bed, taking off her running shoes.

"Julio and I talked about pornos in front of you?"

Trudy stood up and undid the metal button of her jeans. "No, you didn't know I was near. I can be real stealthy when I need to be" She linked her thumbs in the top of her low-riding jeans and quickly pulled them down, leaving her lower half covered only by cherry red thong underwear. Frank drew in a breath, which seemed to puff out his eyes.

"Julio wants to fuck me, you know, but I wouldn't ever let him. Not because he's Mexican or anything, but—"

"Salvadorian," Frank found the voice to say.

"What?"

"Julio is from El Salvador."

"What's the difference?" Trudy linked her thumbs again and pulled the thong underwear off.

"Ah..." was all Frank could say, responding to either Trudy's sad lack of geographic knowledge or the stunningly perfect beauty of her pubis and the silken strands of the hair covering it. As Platonic Justice seemed to be demanding his non-platonic fingers in that hair, it was probably the latter.

"You're not getting undressed," Trudy was kind enough to point out to him.

"Ah, I thought I would wait for you."

"Oh. Should I have done a sexy striptease or something?"

"No, this has been fine."

Trudy smiled. "Good." She then pulled her red sweater off, leaving behind a cherry red bra, which did not remain the lone survivor for long.

It was her skin Frank most appreciated. Not that he wasn't completely sold on the form that skin encased. Trudy's beautifully shaped legs, pillars of pleasure; her waist, begging to be held; her breasts, alive with her breathing, were all creatures to be embraced, kissed, and loved. But her skin was brilliant in its acceptance and reflection of light, putting out a light olive glow of smooth youth; non-aged, unused material of the most luxuriant look, feel, and, he assumed, even taste.

It was, he thought, a matter of aesthetics—he would have loved to have drawn or painted in this material. But some matters mattered quite a bit more at this moment, and he found he was light-headed and breathless as hormones and fluids in pleasing active states took control of the situation. He was so grateful. Exactly to whom he had no idea, but that did not diminish the gratitude.

"Your turn," Trudy said, unmistakably meaning that Frank should now strip as simply and quickly as possible.

A sudden shyness Frank had not felt for years, possibly through all his adult years, hit him with a rush of anti-nostalgia that was nauseous. He had not considered this aspect of the afternoon Trudy had planned for them. Somehow his head filled with the image of a classroom with charts, illustrations, and graphic designs on the chalkboard and him lecturing, not only fully clothed but in the robes of an Oxford don, on the ins and outs of how to "fuck really good." "Ah..." Frank inarticulately began.

Standing there completely nude with her hands on her hips, Trudy said, "You don't want me to turn around or anything, do you?"

"No, of course not, but, um, look, I gotta tell you before I, uh, strip, that I'm not anywhere near an Adonis here, and I—"

"What's an Adonis?"

"Uh, Adonis was, in Greek mythology, a young man beloved of both Aphrodite and Persephone because he was so, uh, gorgeous and, and—well, he was the ultimate in male beauty."

"So, you're telling me you're no beauty under your clothes?"

"I am nowhere near that, I'm afraid."

"Do you think I expected you to be? Frank, you're no great beauty with your clothes on either. But don't worry, I'll take care of the beauty stuff. You just take care of the instruction and put me through my paces."

If it were at all possible for Frank's penis to fill with any more blood, it would have burst out of his pants.

Frank quickly took his shirt off, losing a button in the process, and undid his belt and pants and slipped them off awkwardly due in part to the impediment protruding from his groin. But also because he had not bothered to take his shoes off first. Eventually, though, he stood nude before Trudy, whose eyes followed the slow drip of a long, thin, crystal clear drop of viscous moisture.

"Wow. Does that always happen?"

"When you're as excited as I am at the moment, yes."

"What is it?"

"Uh," Frank looked down at it, "I suppose it's a lubricant."

"For you or me?"

"I think it's for our mutual benefit."

"Well, wipe it off; it's weird looking."

Frank did so with his hand, wiping it over his thigh.

"Hey, I like your love handles," Trudy said, perfectly sincere. "They're cute."

Frank looked down at the pudge he had grown so used to. "Thank you. I grew them myself."

Trudy giggled. "You're funny." Frank was about to thank her again when she said, "Okay, where's the porno? Let's get started," Trudy looked around as if the porno would be prominently displayed.

"They're in the drawer over there." Frank pointed to his dresser, where the TV and the VCR sat, "The bottom drawer.

Trudy went to the drawer and pulled out several tapes from under four folded sweaters.

"Why are you hiding them, Frank?" she said with some amusement. "You live alone, right?"

"I don't know. It's just what you do with porno. Gives it, I suppose, a certain forbidden romantic charm."

But Trudy ignored his explanation as she was reading the titles.

"Cum Fly With Me; Facial Fetish; Rock 'Em, Suck'Em; Cum Blow My Horn. So, which one is the best?"

"I don't know. Pornos are all about the same. Cum Fly With Me is the most unique. They shot all the bits on airplanes."

"Really? Is it like a story?"

"No. These are just one fuck scene after another."

"Cool. Nothing to get in the way then."

Trudy took Cum Fly With Me and put it into the VCR. The remote was on top of the TV, and she grabbed it and turned the set on, putting it on channel 3. Immediately on the screen, there was a shot of a shot of cum heading towards and landing on the cute face of a blonde with a button nose.

"Eww! Do men like to do that?"

"Uh, well..." Frank's penis was in utter confusion. The basic situation—the live nude girl before him, the video flying cum—had it boiling over to blow, but Trudy's nonchalant attitude and her—relative to the situation—intellectual questioning was a bit deflating. "Yeah, I guess, some guys. But most, I think, like to see it more than do it. Climax is much more intense when you come in one of several orifices, not outside of them."

"Several?"

"Uh, the vagina, of course. Or cunt, to be nasty about it." The magic of words commenced re-inflation. "The rectum—"

"Or asshole, to be nasty about it," Trudy said, intensifying the re-inflation.

"Or bunghole, if you prefer."

"Bunghole?"

"Yeah."

"I think butt would be better than any of them. Not so technical, yet not so crude."

"Good point."

"And the third?"

"Well, the mouth, of course."

"Oh, that's an orifice too?"

"Last I looked."

"I need to be able to give good head; I know that."

The ache of full intensity now called for immediate contact.

"Well, the next one coming up—uh, so to speak—is going, uh, well, as you can see...."

On the screen was the head of a woman giving head to the head of a multinational corporation in the head of his private jet.

Trudy watched with fascination as she moved to the bed and lay down. Frank assumed he should follow, so he did, lying beside her. Never taking her eyes off the screen, Trudy positioned herself somewhat like the woman in the video, grabbed Frank's penis—none too gently—and headed down towards it. Unfortunately, given the amount of time Frank had remained in a heightened state of alert, Trudy's mere touch—ham-fisted though it was—was enough to cause an eruption. She was greeted in mid-descent with a hot and salty surprise as Frank bucked like a man receiving shocks from a defibrillator.

As Frank and Trudy drove Leech Beach Road heading towards her home, neither spoke. The anti-climactic scene had been one of Trudy reacting partly with disgust, partly with desperation for something to wipe off her face. Frank had jumped off the bed and ran in a pressured frenzy—as Trudy vocalized, "Eww! Eww! Eww!"—to find that something, naturally going for some paper towels in the kitchenette. Finding his roll of them depleted, he pulled a new one out of a small cabinet and struggled with the plastic wrapper with the picture of the macho guy on it. Failing in the struggle while Trudy shouted, "Hurry!" in the background, he finally grabbed a knife. He slashed at the macho guy—and much of the roll beneath—then yanked off the wrapper, pulled a handful of mutilated sheets off the roll, and ran back to the bed, bumping his shin along the way, only to find Trudy wiping her face with the case she had just slipped off his pillow. On the TV screen, the head of the multinational corporation was unloading his burden onto the willing face of the mile-high, button-nosed woman. Frank grabbed the remote and turned the TV off.

"Well," Trudy said, finding a dry spot on the pillowcase to wipe the last vestiges, "I suppose you're pretty much empty now, right?"

"Uh—yeah—for the time being."

"So maybe you should take me home."

"Okay."

They dressed in silence. They walked to Frank's car in silence. And drove in silence until Frank stopped at the top of the long driveway that led to Trudy's home.

"Do you want me to drive to the house," Frank offered, although it was the last thing he wanted to do.

"No, this is fine," Trudy said as she got out of the car. After closing the door, she motioned to have Frank lower the passenger window. "Can we do it again tomorrow?" She asked.

"You serious?"

"Sure. The first day of class is always a bummer."

"Well—"

"Pleeease."

"Trudy, I—"

"I think I can borrow dad's truck, so I'll meet you at your apartment, so you won't have to wait around for me. Okay?"

"Well—"

"Okay." Trudy turned to go, then turned back and thrust her head into the car. "You know, it doesn't really taste all that bad!" she declared with a girlish delight and smile, then pulled her head out of the car and ran down the long driveway toward her house.

BY THE BEAUTIFUL

Chapter the Third

For several weeks Dmitri followed a new pattern. He no longer drove Leech Beach Road early in the morning with his radio blasting some well-remunerated screech. Instead, he traveled it silently with single-minded intent, allowing his anger to fester, but not well up. He imagined himself an avenger of meta-human control, knowing this fog-shrouded road so well that he knew exactly when to break to slow down to an ominous roll, then a complete stop in the middle of the road, right in front of Hendrickson's farm. He would then hit one long blast on his horn to make sure that the old bastard, who was always up and somewhere outside tending to some farm thing, knew he was there. On the first day he did this, the day after Hendrickson had blown his tires, Hendrickson thought he was just greeting him, saying, "Good morning to you." So he gave Dmitri a big wave. But Dmitri did not acknowledge the gesture; he just simply, and very slowly, rolled down his window and stared at the old farmer, then very slowly rolled the window back up and, at about five miles an hour, moved on beyond the farmer's sight. Dmitri convinced himself that this was a totally terrifying thing to do. Especially in the fog. And so he repeated it daily, sometimes throwing in a variation by getting out of the car and standing against it with arms crossed, staring out through superfluous sunglasses. Then, one day, sitting in the driver's seat, he displayed a gun, checking it over as if to see that it had been properly cleaned, oiled, and loaded. It was, of course, a fake, a realistic toy he had had since his tenth birthday, but one that had done imaginary service in the slaughter of Dmitri's many enemies.

Hendrickson, while never taking it seriously—certainly never feeling threatened by Dmitri's daily routine—was also not amused by it. That is until one morning of a dense fog when he could see Dmitri's car only because of the lit headlamps. As he slowly stepped out of the car and took his, to his mind, intimidating stance, Dmitri himself was only a mere outline of a trace of a phantom, and therefore, Dmitri was sure, scarier than ever. Dmitri stood there for a self-allotted and counted-off three minutes (three minutes, he had decided, was far more effective than one, much scarier than two, yet not as boring as four). Then he slowly got back into his car in the middle of the road.

Dmitri had just started his engine and put the transmission into drive when a hell of a horn blast broke through the air. A large white truck, one hour late, was making its second weekly delivery of linens to The Briers. It loomed in Dmitri's rear-view mirror like a ghost ship. Dmitri screamed and hit the gas sending the Ford Escort off the road and into a ditch as the ghostly truck passed by, its driver assuming the asshole in the other vehicle was all right, but if he weren't, that would be all right too.

Hendrickson ran to the car and, once he saw that Dmitri was uninjured, laughed loudly with an annoying delight. Not pleased with this, Dmitri cursed the farmer with various vulgarities, each one more, it seemed, amusing to the farmer than the previous one. Finally, Hendrickson stopped laughing and said, "Listen, you little rat's turd, you better start being nice because only me and my truck's going to get you the hell out of that ditch." It was a point Dmitri could not argue. So, for the second time within a month, because they found that the Ford Escort now had a broken axle, Dmitri was taken into work in the farmer's truck listening to stupid, twangy, shit-kickers music the whole way.

In Allison Carr's storage unit library, besides fiction of various sorts and non-fiction of different subjects, there had been two photo albums filled with pictures of her adopted son, Gerald. They had been a "divorce gift" from Jim. The day after she had gotten the news of Gerald's death by dumb behavior, she made an unscheduled trip to her storage unit, pulled out the albums, sat in her chair there, and went slowly through them. It was a ceremonial act in lieu of going to his funeral. A gesture not in celebration of Gerald's life—Allison had always prided herself on not being a hypocrite—but in simple acknowledgment of his life. She owed him at least that, she felt.

Of course, Jim had always loved the little bastard. It was a determined, almost ideological love: "He's my son, damn it! My son!" He would emphasize and dwell on the word, issuing it as a sacred sound. The irony, always lost on Jim, was that "son" was accurate only in a legal sense. Gerald was not from his loins, of his blood; no C, no T, no G, no A had split off from his own to pair to meld with that of a female. Jim had not collaborated in what has often been called the wondrous, mysterious miracle of new life. But to be realistic about it, it was nothing to wonder at—although wonderful on a case-by-case basis—for the process was no longer a mystery and far from miraculous. It was, in fact, completely mundane. Mundane or not, birth through sexual coupling was the only honest, truthful, non-spiritual way to put in a bid for immortality. And that had an emotional component of rightness about it that Allison, from her first pubescent stirrings of hormones to the day the doctor told her she could not have children, had embraced as one of the more rational parts of existence.

But all that was genuinely meaningless to Jim, for he was like a converted believer in an unforgiving god, adopting adoption as a new capital T Truth that outshone all others and competed with the sun. Gerald was his son, and that was that. The boy was the light of his life; he did not need the light of the sun.

His non-son son was not the only irony lost on Jim. All irony was. One of the first comments Allison ever made about Jim when they were in college was, "For one so tall, a lot goes over his head." Despite this, she developed a massive crush on this big, tall football player she tutored. Jim was in jeopardy of losing his scholarship, which meant that the small liberal arts college they went to was in danger of losing their most valuable quarterback. No one wanted that to happen because they were having a winning season for the first time in twelve years. So little Allison Carr, an academic star, was made a commando of knowledge and sent in, often under the cover of darkness, to rescue Jim.

The second thing Allison learned about Jim, after discovering his immunity to irony, was that he was the sweetest creature on the face of the planet—a killer only on the football field, a Ferdinand the Bull off it. And it was perfectly genuine. Jim liked people. He always thought the best of them, always saw the best in them, and always wanted the best for them. Whether just a good habit or a genetic mutation, it made him, later in life, a dynamite salesman of sports equipment, and then, mixing in a little of the killer from the field, a crew motivating district manager, which soon made him a natural for regional manager. Then, skipping regional general manager, by applying a little more of the killer, he became an excellent regional VP. His success got him great notice from world headquarters, not to mention a roomy office with a big window, as he became a Senior VP, then a Senior Executive VP. Under his corporate nickname of "The Velvet Killer," he soon occupied the luxuriously large, redecorated at a stunning expense, corner office of that strange duality of modern corporate life—President and CEO.

But in college, Jim was just a big, irony-deficient lug who loved to hug people. Including Allison, who he nearly crushed on several occasions until he realized that he liked her more than anyone else because she had done such a fantastic job helping him get his grades up to well-deserved Cs.

Allison was a petite, blonde, bookish, not unattractive young woman when she paid attention to her looks. Which she did after Jim started saying, "Why don't you get contacts?" and "Why don't you wear your hair down a little bit?" and "Hey, you got a nice little figure, you know, you shouldn't be hiding it in those bulky sweaters." And makeup, Jim loved makeup on women; he felt it was natural to them, so Allison became an expert in applying it to her face. They became a couple almost without noticing and engaged without a big announcement. Soon after they graduated, and Jim got his sales job with the sports equipment company, they got married and wound up living in a state bordered by no large body of water, which began to depress Allison. The saving grace was that they lived in a community with a college with an excellent graduate studies program. She finished her Master's degree, got her Ph.D., and found employment at an exclusive private school, all of which amused Jim. Then Jim kept getting promoted, and they kept moving, always becoming the oddest couple in the two divergent communities they inhabited in each new location they occupied. He well over six foot and she well under. But their physical attributes were the least of it.

Jim being Jim, he was always selling—himself if not an actual product—and therefore lived for the society of his fellow man. Literally, for he was usually quite uncomfortable in mixed company. But put the "boys" together with some Scotch and cigars, Jim was happily comfortable. And he was happy to be the center of these tiny universes, and the other men were glad to orbit around him. The talk, between sips and sucks, was mainly about sports, although politics did rear up now and then, especially when they considered it a competitive sport. They talked little else except for the state of the economy and what a lousy job the current administration was doing to aid struggling businessmen. Regulations—if they were not railing against this quarterback or that pitcher who just could not throw if his mother's life depended on it, they were railing against the impact that goddamned government regulations made on the smooth, profitable conduct of their various businesses.

Jim enjoyed the railing because the men railed with good humor. He liked the man who could make a particularly cutting remark that brought forth from the guys a loud burst of laughter, that communal high sign of pals, buddies, bros, and compadres. Despite his relocations, Jim was always able to gather around him such buddies. The personnel changed, but the general experience was always the same. That is until a new subject was suddenly on the table when several of the sippers and suckers had children.

It was sudden because Jim had little noted the gestation required for these events, outside of the odd chuckle over the jokes about morning sickness and how big the wifely boobs were getting. But when gestation was over and generation accomplished, the talk of sleepless nights, and strange colored shit, and silk shirts ruined by spit-up put Jim off. Not to mention the time, effort, and help their wives required of the men.

"Why isn't Joe here?"

"He's babysitting."

"What?"

"His wife had to go somewhere."

"What?"

"So, he's babysitting."

Joe had once brought the baby with him. And because even these men knew they couldn't blow smoke in its face, the afternoon was ruined.

When these strange shitters and spitters started to walk and talk and hug their fathers, squeezing them around their necks and calling them "Daddy," Jim took a new interest in the childish talk that had invaded their camaraderie. The men doing the talking had lights in their eyes and strange, affecting smiles on their faces and enthusiasm for life and the future that may well have been contagious. Invariably, at this time, as the buddies and pals would break up a session and prepare to head on to their various homes, someone would usually say, "So, Jim, when are you and Allison going to have a kid?"

This was a question that Allison occasionally wondered about, almost from a sense of obligation, but usually dismissed as there was just no time to think about it. After each new move following Jim's rising star, she was always able to secure a new teaching job because her credentials were that good. Sometimes at a local public school full of the rambunctious spawn of the suburbs, but more often in a private school, always quieter and more refined. She was happy as a teacher, which invariably meant that she soon found herself an administrator following an upward path somewhat parallel to Jim's.

Allison tried to put off the inevitable by declaring that she had no time and was far too busy. But Jim kept insisting that there was no time like the present, and soon their attempts at procreation became, as Jim called them, a constant celebration of their love.

When conception was neither immediate, nor even soon, it was considered the luck of the draw. But when the lack of conception became unreasonable, Jim and Allison knew they had a problem. They were both checked for fertility. Allison had none and never would. Jim rejected a child by test tube as just too weird. Both refused to consider a surrogate, as they were uncomfortable with a third wheel in their relationship. Adoption seemed the only option. Jim embraced it enthusiastically, not only for their sake but also for the humanitarian aspect that they would be giving love and a home to an abandoned child. Allison considered the idea horrifying. But then, she was the kind of person who would never accept hand-me-down clothes or buy from a thrift store. She even had an aversion to perfectly good used books, always preferring to buy new ones, fresh ones, ones that, once the virginal purchase was consummated, were hers and hers alone.

But Jim—now referred to by business colleagues and friends alike as Big Jim—would not be denied. So, as Big Jim designated it, a full-court press effort began to find him a son. No discussion of a daughter took place, although Allison might have liked to have had one. But by this time, Allison was Dean of the English Department at a private girl's school, and she was getting old enough to start to see her charges as surrogate daughters. So, it was neither important nor necessary to disconcert Jim as he picked out a seven-year-old boy named Gerald.

Gerald was a pain in the ass from day one. Besides several fine art objects destroyed by him, and a neighbor's dog damaged, he was diagnosed as having any one of several learning disabilities generally known only by their initials, which flowed off the tongues of professionals and readers of weekly newsmagazines with stunning grace. He seemed always to be running where he should not, jumping on things he should not, and yelling when quiet would have been much more appreciated. Jim excused all this by non-creatively declaring that "Boys will be boys." "Too bad he's not gay," Allison said in one of her more unguarded moments. Jim went wide-eyed in shock. Allison handed over the discipline of their "son" to Big Jim, and Jim handed it over to the sweet creature within him, never ceding any authority to the killer that also resided there. Gerald never knew any effective discipline until the day he entered a military school from which, six months later, his parents, under orders, retrieved him. Only Big Jim's standing in the community and his honed salesmanship kept Gerald, in his teen years, from having a juvenile police record, not to mention suffering incarceration with others of like lack of mind. But he was Jim's son, and Big Jim loved the little bastard.

Oddly, one of the things Allison contemplated as she sat in her storage room library looking at the photo albums was whether she should take one of the photos of Gerald. It was a slick 8x10 glossy taken in a photo studio under strict conditions. Should she take it back to The Briers to be framed and put up on her wall to occupy a space she had been trying to figure out how to fill? After she had taken early retirement and divorced Jim to the shock of many, she had hoped never to see Gerald again. Now that she knew conclusively that she never would, she felt the need to have some remembrance of him. Not all the days with Gerald were terrible. There were some moments to remember, especially around the age of nine, when Gerald suddenly grew very affectionate towards her, clinging on and demanding hugs and kisses, and wanting to spend all his time with her. This, at first, made her nervous, but less so as his little hand in hers grew increasingly more comfortable. Just as she was beginning to enjoy the situation, Jim demanded it curtailed, possibly thinking of Allison's old, offhand "gay" comment.

Allison took the 8x10 of nine-year-old Gerald out of the photo album and decided to take it back to The Briers, putting off the decision of whether to frame and hang it until later.

It never was framed and hung. Several days later, while Allison was downstairs for breakfast, Frank handed her a sizeable stiff manila envelope and told her there was a present inside for her.

"Don't open it now," Frank said as she started to. "Wait until you get back upstairs."

She did, and with—this fact amused her—trembling hands, she opened the envelope and pulled out a piece of sketchpad paper mounted on stiff cardboard that had on it a rendering of her sea serpent image that was so perfect she gasped, quickly laughed into her hand, and shed a tear. Framed that day, her "Day at the Beach with Sea Serpent" filled the space on her wall to her continuing delight, and once again she could comfortably forget Gerald.

The theater was coming together. It was much less a site under construction now than a real theater receiving finishing touches, the last bit of polish. Every emotion stirred in Austin over this fact stirred into a heady brew.

Austin sat alone dead center in the mass of 433 seats laid out in rows in an ascending sweep from the front row of seats to the last row. The seats were staggered, not one directly lined up behind another. The sight lines would be excellent! The seats, just installed, the workmen left; Austin was the first person ever to sit in the house of the Stafford Theatre in these brand-new seats. Well, at least the upholstery was brand new. The seats came from a movie house seventy-five miles away, gutted to become a vast clothing store.

Pattie Heatherton had heard about this and traveled the seventy-five miles to negotiate personally for the seats as a donation to the theater, she hoped. She got the seats, but not as a donation. The owner of the clothing store, a man of grand retail dreams, scoffed at the idea of a charitable write-off; he wanted cold, hard cash. However, Pattie did get them at such a meager amount of cold, hard cash Austin had to wonder if Pattie's re-energized sexuality had not come into play here. A bit of strategic flirting—or more—to seal the deal to the gratification of all?

Then Pattie got a local upholster, who had had six children go through her school, to agree to recover all 433 seats for free, but someone else would have to provide the material. She got the material by going to a fabrics wholesaler and saying, quite bluntly, "What have you got in large quantities that you can't sell? What huge mistake can we take off your hands?" Austin was amazed by Pattie's grasp of commercial psychology, but he should not have been. Hairy-Butt Bastard had made many such mistakes in his commercial life, and his experiences had ensnared themselves tightly into several neural nets within Pattie's brain. The wholesale fabric supplier did not hesitate to show her bolts of material that were undoubtedly too weird for any regular, mundane, or rational purpose. But for the theater, for their theater, Pattie and Austin decided that the material was perfectly funky. The supplier quoted them a cost that they had no idea was absurdly high, but he was happy to donate the material to their non-profit theater. It was a matter Pattie and Austin did not have to be concerned with, just one that might someday come under consideration by the Internal Revenue Service.

Austin sat in the center of these funky seats of his theater and reveled. He looked at the classic proscenium stage he had ordered to be built. Austin had wanted nothing funky, odd, or experimental here; there was even a curtain. He breathed deep and almost teared up. He thought how fabulous it would be, how pure and essential and extraordinary. Theater, for the sake of theater, live with the direct, psychic communication between actors and audience achieved nowhere else.

In designing the first season, Austin was intrigued by the idea of reviving that old 1920s chestnut of men-at-war, What Price Glory. He had no idea why. Austin had never seen the play in production, he had never read it, nor had he even seen the 1952 John Ford film version with James Cagney, and he had certainly never seen the original silent film version. But he knew about it; he had heard and read about it in histories of the Drama; probably saw production stills from the original Broadway run. Austin liked the title. It had men in uniform at war, and he liked the title. Somehow that made it appealing. But how could he direct it? What did he know about men in uniform at war? He had no answer for himself. But he would first read the text; that was the first thing to do, then he would worry about his competence to interpret.

To his delight, Austin found that he had a copy of the play. In an anthology, Best American Plays of the 1920s, he had in his small library of mainly used theater books he had collected over the years. He grabbed it eagerly and devoured the play as if it was something he had been searching for his whole life. What was this instinct he had about this play? He couldn't quite figure it out. He just knew that What Price Glory would make an excellent premier production for the Stafford Theatre. Maybe it was because he and his theater were not sitting in the middle of the urban-liberal environments he had been used to, Manhattan and Los Angeles. They looked to the edgy, the experimental, the out-there, non-TV type of plays; the anti-establishment, anti-traditional, and anti-plot on occasion. He and his theater were sitting in the middle of that other reality that was most of America. A place of basically good, decent people, too whacked in the head by TV, certainly, but didn't that make them open to the experience of live theater? But don't be an asshole, he thought, don't challenge their cherished assumptions, not at first anyway. This theater had to get established; the classics are established; do the classics. It was simple. Plus, for an actor, there was nothing like a well-crafted traditional play to allow you to shine. What Price Glory, for example. Austin knew he could perform well as either Captain Flagg, the hard-drinking, superior soldier brighter than those who commanded him, or Sergeant Quirt, the battle-hardened, bitter man of war—professional warriors both. He could bring out one of any number of moderately well-known actors he knew in LA or New York to trade the parts with him. Yes! One night he would be Flagg; the other, he would be Quirt. The next night they would change roles, he Quirt, the other Flagg. It would be a great hook! It would help fuel the publicity. Maybe it would get people to return, to see the two actors in both roles and compare; perhaps he could offer a two-for-one-discount-price to encourage such exploration. As for the other parts? Well, it was a more extensive cast than he should have for his first production, with 24 different male roles. But with make-up and costume changes, he could double-up on several of them, and many of them were small parts of young, green soldiers—Pattie's high school kids could play them. After all, that's partly why the Stafford Theatre was coming into being. As to the one lone female role of Charmaine De La Cognac, the local innkeeper's daughter, a bit of a French tart, it would be perfect for Trudy if he could get her to do a French accent. To make it easy, he would just get a copy of the old Cagney film and have her mock whoever played it in it, as she had learned to mock Cissy McMann. That should work.

And we'll be giving the good, decent people of this mainstream America a view of two-fisted he-men-at-war, albeit in a play somewhat cynical about war, somewhat questioning the purpose of it all, but only lightly; entertainingly so. And as long as it wasn't a play being cynical about the current war...

But there was one thing that was missing. Austin knew he could give a fine performance as either Flagg or Quirt. But he wanted to give a brilliant performance. He needed to dig deep. How could he do that? And how could he, as the director, bring verisimilitude to the performances of the other actors? Him, whose least favorite members of society had always been the fascist cop and the vicious soldier? He, who had never even spoken to either? What was he to do? Besides renting and watching Patton about ten times?

Ah! He had almost forgotten. Major Ramrod! Maybe Major Ramrod could help him.

Having checked at the desk as to his actual name, Austin went into the dining room at breakfast and walked right over to the Major, who was intensely reading his New York Times and eating a breakfast of eggs, plenty of them, with a bowl, not a cup, a bowl of salsa to complement. And two sausages, good, fatty pork ones, hash browns, and plenty of coffee, hot and black.

"Major McFadden?" Austin found the words strange coming out of his mouth. It was as if he was in the moment in the middle of a scene written by someone else.

The Major looked up in a snap from his Times and breakfast and then suddenly stood almost at attention. Austin jumped back a little bit, surprised by the action.

"I'm sorry, I—I didn't mean to disturb your breakfast. I was just wondering if we could, um, well, talk for a moment."

"Talk?" Major McFadden asked as if in mid-grasp of the concept.

"Well, yeah, I mean, we're both residents here. I see you every morning; I just thought it was about time I introduced myself. Um— I'm Austin O'Brien. I'm going to be running the theater you may have noticed they've been building at the end of the boardwalk."

"Yes, I had noticed something going on over there," the Major said as he continued to stand and face Austin.

"May, uh, may I sit?" Austin asked.

"Certainly. Would you like to join me for breakfast?"

"That would be wonderful. Thank you." Austin pulled out a chair and sat.

Trudy was immediately over to take his order. "Morning, Austin."

"Good morning, Trudy. Fruit and yogurt, please, and mint tea."

"All righty," Trudy made a note and started to leave, but Austin stopped her.

"Hey, Trudy, you been working on that scene? I've been waiting for you."

Trudy smiled a not-so-simple smile. "Oh, I'm working on it."

"Good. Are you getting confident with it?"

"Yeah, I think. I think it's coming along. I'll let you know when it's ready."

"Well, soon, I hope. I'm interested to see what you do."

"Okay, I'll try to amaze you."

"Good."

"I'll let you know," Trudy said as she headed towards the kitchen.

"Is she going to be an actress?" the Major asked.

"Well—she wants to be, unfortunately, for all the wrong reasons. But I'm not working here with a huge pool of talent. So I'll bring actors in from the outside for the major roles. But part of what we're doing, you know, is we are aligned with the high school to make it sort of a theater lab for their students to develop their talent."

"Sounds—civic-minded."

Austin laughed a short, knowing laugh. "Oh, yeah. Also, I couldn't have done it without some finances from the school district and, you know, a great deal of help from Mrs. Briers. But I think it's going to be very exciting. I don't think people around here have ever seen much live theater."

"I wouldn't know. I'm new here. But I've been to a lot of places, and I've found that places tend to surprise you."

"Well, yeah, that could be. What about you? Have you seen much live theater in all these places?"

The major looked at him now, pretty much eye-to-eye. "Only that which the USO brought in. I was a combat soldier, Mr. O'Brien. I was more likely to be in a theater of war than a theater of—theater."

"Well, actually, that's why I wanted to talk to you."

"Okay."

"You see, I think the first production I want to do is a wonderful play from the 1920s called What Price Glory."

"Interesting title."

"Well, yeah, it's an interesting play. It's about men at war during World War One. But it's not really about warfare, although—and I'll be honest about this—" and somewhat embarrassed, Austin found "—it is a tinge anti-war."

"Every good soldier I have ever met was at least a tinge anti-war."

"Oh, well, then you might really relate to this. Because it's really about the soldiers; it's a portrait of them. And, to be honest with you, I was never in the military, so I don't know how true this play is."

"You don't know how accurate it is in its portrayal?"

"No, not really, I don't. And I'm not sure how much modern-day accuracy is required. But enough, certainly. And—and, because I like the play and I want to do it, but I want to be able to direct it with some sense of knowing what I'm talking about, so I was—well, I was wondering if you would come on board as a sort of consultant to the production."

"Really?"

"Well, as you said, you've been a combat soldier. There are experiences you've had and things you could share with me, although it's not the same as going through the experiences myself, I know that, but it would at least help me get a handle on it."

"What would I have to do?"

"Well, first, read the play and give me your notes on it. Tell me what you think about it. And then as we put up the production, just be that little angel on my shoulder telling me if I'm going in the right direction or not."

The Major became quiet. And Austin had nothing more to say. The only sound coming from their table for a moment was that of the Major's knife being dragged across his plate as he very precisely carved a sausage link into bite-size pieces, holding his fork in his left hand, his knife in his right. He then took a slice of sausage and placed it into his mouth. He chewed methodically.

Trudy placed a bowl of fruit and yogurt before Austin, which startled him, and he jumped a little. The major did not acknowledge the incident.

"Don't be scared, Austin," Trudy said, "I won't eat you." But he did not hear her as Major McFadden had just said, "Okay."

"Yes? You're saying you'll do it?"

"Sure."

"Well, that's great, thank you, I'm—I'm sorry, I can't—I can't pay you anything."

"Money is the least of my concerns right now. It sounds like it might be interesting."

Austin was thrilled. "Okay, great! Well, look, here's the play, What Price Glory. It's in this anthology. So just, you know, read it at your leisure and let me know. You can, you know, um, I mean, I'm in number six. Or most of the day I'm at the theater, so if you want to just to drop by, or, you know, whatever. Knock loud and shout out because I'm the only one in there right now."

"Okay. I'll read it today," the Major said as he took possession of the book.

"Well, you know, no hurry. I don't want to put any pressure on you."

"I never procrastinate."

"No—no, I bet you don't. But, well, listen, Major..."

"Call me Philip."

"Philip?"

"Philip."

"Why not—why not Phil?"

"I hate Phil."

"Oh—well, okay, Philip. I'll see you later, then."

"That will be fine," the Major said. Then Austin, who had never touched a bite of his fruit and yogurt, left, and Major McFadden returned to his New York Times.

Frank and Trudy had been scrupulous in allowing no one to learn that they shared an outside activity. Frank was still the boss, and Trudy was still just a waitress, and they still verbally bantered because if they didn't, people would have thought they were mad at each other, and why should they be mad at each other? But they shared no intimacy that others could view, neither verbal and certainly not physical. Several times, in fact, Frank almost lost his balance making quick moves to avoid even accidentally coming into physical contact with Trudy. Especially if it was to be skin-on-skin contact because if Frank was to touch that soft, smooth, warm, and vital flesh, he was not sure he could contain himself despite the location and situation of work. But then he knew he would soon be touching it, which comforted him as Mary and her little lamb manly tried to keep him flaccid. The latter being especially important in the first week of their—What? You couldn't call it an affair. A student/tutor association, then? In any case, Frank remaining flaccid was necessary, for he was suffering from what Trudy called his little "nick on the prick."

When he left work the day after the "first day of class that had been a bummer," Frank drove a little too fast down Leech Beach Road and eventually into Rubenton. It may have been anxiety, but he preferred to think that he was just pressed for time. He went to a small electronics store and bought a nice-looking portable radio/CD player on his credit card, then walked down the street to the record store and found—a good omen here, he thought—just the right CD of Billie Holiday. He then drove to a liquor store and found what he hoped would be a good bottle of white wine and other necessities. Then he went home and quickly, yet thoroughly, dusted and vacuumed his apartment and took a quick shower. Finally, dressed in clothes Trudy had never seen him in and wearing nine-year-old cologne, Frank was ready to receive his student—who did not arrive until three-thirty.

She should have been there at three at the latest. Instead, Frank spent a lousy half-hour disappointed and angry and worried and regretful and feeling foolish. But the knock at the door came at three-thirty, and the quick rush of adrenaline nearly floored him.

Trudy spoke the moment the door opened. "Well, I hope you'll show some better control today." Then she walked in and started unbuttoning her blouse.

"Stop!" Frank ordered.

Trudy turned around and suddenly realized the atmosphere in the room. The curtains were closed, so the light was subtle; the place was tidy. Some woman was singing some old song on a radio or something. And the table in front of the couch was bare (the day before, it supported a pile of newspapers, books, and a crusted-over bowl that had once held Grape Nuts) except for an ice bucket with a bottle of wine and two long-stemmed glasses. And Frank; she looked at the change in Frank.

"You look nice," she declared.

"Thank you. This is how I look like when I'm not a waiter."

"I like it."

"Thanks."

"So, we going to fuck, or what?"

"Well, eventually. But, you know, Trudy, there's more to a good fuck than just fucking."

"Not according to the boys I've been out with."

"Austin is a man, not a boy."

"I thought all men were really just boys."

"Well—in every man-boy, there's a boy-man struggling to get out."

"What does that mean?"

"I haven't the foggiest notion."

Trudy laughed. Somehow it made her skin look even more luscious.

"Let's sit down and have a glass of wine."

Trudy sat down with alacrity. "Are you going to get me drunk?"

Frank sat down beside her on the couch and poured the wine. "No. In fact—in deference to your age—I will ration you to just one glass, although I may have more. I want you to relax with a civilized glass of wine and some music."

"Oh yeah. Who's that singing?"

"Lady Day—Billie Holiday."

"She's got a weird voice."

Frank took some offense to that, but he didn't show it, hiding behind his first sip of wine. "Weird but wonderful."

"Yeah, I guess." Trudy stopped and truly listened for a while. "Yeah, actually, yeah. It's okay." Trudy took her first sip of wine.

"Do you like the wine?"

"Yeah, it's okay. Better than beer. I hate the smell of beer. Especially after it's been thrown up."

Was she consciously trying to pollute the atmosphere he had worked so hard to create?

"Uh, would you like to dance?"

"To that?"

"Sure?"

"Well, okay."

They got up, and Frank took Trudy in his arms and led her into a gentle slow dance. Frank was not much of a dancer, but this kind of dancing was not about the steps but the contact. He held her little right hand that was so smooth it was like holding warm velvet. He couldn't believe his good fortune in being able to put his arm around her waist, touching her skin directly as she wore again a blouse that did not fully cover her midriff, just as her low-riding, hip-hugging pants did not come up to it. The vibrant give of her flesh lightened his head and elevated his pulse.

"Hey!" she suddenly said, pulling back a little.

"What?"

"I remember dancing like this with my dad when I was tiny. Only I stood on his feet."

"Well, please don't stand on mine."

"Okay. Plus, you don't remind me of Dad."

Frank was happy to hear that. And happier still when Trudy moved in close and put her head on his shoulder. Billie was singing "I Must Have That Man," and Frank thought it could not have been more appropriate.

The next song was a little too upbeat, far beyond Frank's competence to lead, so they stopped and picked up their wine glasses and sipped, still holding onto each other, looking into each other's eyes. There were questions in Trudy's. Questions she had not known she would be asking. Frank leaned in and kissed Trudy, to her surprise, but no protest. It was a simple kiss, but a brush of the lips, a brief trading of breath. Then Billie started singing "Foolin' Myself," and Frank put down his wine glass, took Trudy's and put it on the table as well, then started a slow matching of the rhythm, bringing Trudy very close, putting his mouth close to her ear so she could hear him breathing as he could listen to hers. Soon their lips were together again, their mouths were open, and they shared the same heady wine-tinged oxygen. Time passed this way as Billie moved effortlessly into "Easy Living" as Frank effortlessly unbuttoned Trudy's pants and slipped them down along with her thong underwear. Trudy stepped out of them as Frank went to his knees to see, to smell, and to be excited by her gorgeous pubis. The slight moisture there confirmed his good effect.

Trudy took in a deep, surprised breath when Frank first touched her with his tongue. Then, as he applied it, she grabbed his head and pulled it to her, saying, "Oh, you devil! You devil!" This amused them both.

The CD ended. Billie was over. Frank stood up, unbuttoned Trudy's blouse, and extricated her from her bra. The glory of her breasts was undiminished from yesterday. He bent down to them and kissed each one delicately on the nipple, leaving a little lick behind. Then he led her around the wicker screen to his bed. She sat on the bed and then laid back on it. Frank methodically took off his clothes and stood there fully erect, once again with a clear stream in a slow drip from the end of his penis. Trudy reached out for it with her finger, gathered it up, then brought it to her mouth and tasted it. Frank leaned over and kissed her, then traveled down her body, joining her on the bed, settling between her legs as he worked—or possibly played—to bring her to a full climax. She shuddered and squealed and grabbed his head again and almost smothered him. But then she relaxed. He raised his head and smiled. A sense of wonder graced her face. Frank moved up to lie beside her, kissing her breasts again along the way.

"Now, Trudy," Frank said. "As you can see, I'm exercising complete control. So, it's time for you to..."

He did not have to complete the sentence; Trudy scooted down and grabbed his penis too enthusiastically.

"Ah—gently, Trudy. My penis is one of my best friends, treat it gently and with care, and it will do right by you."

"Sorry."

"Hold it with enough pressure only to move the loose skin back and forth. Ah—yes, that's right. No! No, don't speed up; keep it slow for the moment. Now see more of the stuff coming out of the tip. Take your thumb and gently rub it around the head. Ah - ah, yeah, good. Okay, now, I think you better put it into your mouth. Slowly is good, yeah, that's good. Gently bob your head - ah, no, keep your mouth open wider, don't bite; I'm not that kind of guy. Ah, yeah, that's good, that's—that's—oh, yeah, well, uh, I'm going to start moving now, okay, don't be scared, I'll tell you when I'm coming if you want to pull it out...."

Suddenly Frank was a madman, pumping away almost uncontrollably, while Trudy was like a bronco rider holding on for the best time. Then Frank's penis slipped out, and he groaned in disappointment, which moved Trudy to grab it and slip it back in, forgetting exactly how wide her mouth should be.

"Aaaaahhhhhhh!

"Ooowwwww!

107

"Ow! Ow! Ow! Ow!Ow!"

Afterward, all Trudy could say was, "maybe it was my chipped tooth."

"You have a chipped tooth?" Frank said as he held a wet and warm washcloth to his penis.

"Yeah. Haven't you ever noticed?"

"No!"

"Well, it is back a little way."

"Have you ever thought about getting a crown?"

"Yeah, I'm supposed to do that."

"Well, class is temporarily suspended until you do!"

Three days later, Trudy was in her dentist's office getting the crown. Frank gave her the time off from work.

Pattie Heatherton sat on the end of her Super King Size bed in her quite impressive master suite with the sizeable connecting bathroom that had two sinks sunk in Italian marble; the most comfortable toilet she had ever sat on in her life; a bidet; a towel warmer; a whirlpool bathing unit, and a multi-stream shower stall that could have accommodated ten people if it had ever been deemed necessary. She sat there and stared at Hairy-butt Bastard's hairy butt. It was much broader than when she had first seen it, long ago, when she was a high school freshman with fresh hormones, and Harry Ogg mooned her Girl Scout troop, which was camping on Leech Beach. Harry was a junior at the time and known as one of the coolest guys at Rubenton High, mainly because he had a great head of long hair and a good bod. Although he wasn't an athlete, athletes he considered to be ass-kissers always appearing at Lion's Club lunches mainly to say "Yes, sir" to all the crap-ass civic leaders to get scholarships. Harry had a renowned sense of fun and good times, often at someone else's expense. But that only led to the great laughs everyone enjoyed while in his company.

And, of course, there was that great 1964 Ford Mustang that he and his brother Richard (always Richard, never Dick) rebuilt, painted, made noisier than most cars, and drove all over town as if they were always in the middle of a race.

Harry no longer had a great head of long hair. He did not even have an adequate head of short hair. Harry had gone bald early, leaving only a fringe wrapping around the back of his head from ear to ear that he thought looked too "dufus" to tolerate. So, he shaved it off and kept it shaved. Harry's butt, though, had lost none of its youthful hair and had only expanded in the number of follicles in its fleshy roundness. Harry's back and shoulders were also pretty much mat-like, and a plush carpet resided on his chest. The hair on his arms could have been braided. All this personal somatic landscape—the desert above, the various lush forests below—would have been enough to engender the nickname Harry sported in the outside world, Ogg the Ogre, but sadly—Pattie had always thought—the nickname came directly from his personality. Harry's look was just an incredibly suitable coincidence.

"Where the fuck is my new dress shirt, Pattie?" Hairy-butt Bastard said to his wife as he stood stark naked at the entrance of their large walk-in closet, looking in but seemingly unwilling to commit to the action of entering. "You know, the stretchy one."

"Isn't it in the closet?"

"I don't see it."

"Maybe if you actually went into the closet."

"I shouldn't have to go into the damn closet, Pattie. I should be able to see it from here. It should the fuck be popping out at me right now."

"Why?"

"Why?"

"Yes, Harry. Why?"

"Because I fucking say so, that's why."

"What is that? The divine right of Harry Ogg?"

"Oh, shut the fuck up, Pattie! I want that shirt. Richard's making me go to this big deal meeting today and told me to look sharp and wear a suit. All my other shirts are uncomfortable; that stretchy one isn't, so that's the goddamn one I want!"

"Lose some weight, and the other shirts won't be so uncomfortable."

"Oh, shut the fuck up, Pattie! Now, where's that shirt?"

Pattie sighed, got up off the bed, came up behind Hairy-Butt Bastard, and pinched his hairy butt.

"Hey!" he said as he jumped.

"Well, get out of my way," Pattie said as she walked into the closet, went right to the stretchy shirt hanging among five other white shirts, and picked it out. She took it off the hanger and threw it at Harry.

He grabbed it and pulled at the material to confirm its ability to stretch. "Yeah, good," he said as he threw it on the bed and went to the dresser to retrieve some underwear.

"You could say thanks."

"Yeah, sure," he said as he slipped on some boxers and went into the bathroom to powder his testicles. Otherwise, they would be testy all day.

"What's the meeting about?" Pattie asked, although she was not at all interested in the answer.

"What?" Harry answered, not having heard her question, only that she was asking one. Nevertheless, it irritated Pattie.

"What's the meeting about?" She shouted back the re-run with some anger.

"Hey, you don't have to fucking shout," Harry said as he returned and started to put on his stretchy white dress shirt.

"Well, I already asked."

"Well, I didn't fucking hear what the fuck you said, okay? Jesus, sometimes you can be such a bitch, Pattie. You know that? And you used to be such a sweet girl. You know that?"

"Well, one, I'm no longer a girl. And two, the general sourness around here has overpowered any sweetness I may have had."

"So, it's my fault, of course."

"Well, the boys aren't sour."

"No, they're good boys," Harry said as he slipped on his suit pants and sucked in his gut to button them.

"How the hell that ever happened, I'll never know," Pattie wondered.

"Hey, every man fills out a little bit when he gets older."

"I don't mean your gut; I mean our boys and how they turned out to be good kids."

"It's got to be your influence. Because I'm just mean."

"Harry, you're the most self-aware son-of-a-bitch I've ever known."

"Hey! I'm Ogg the Ogre! And you should be damn happy I am, or you wouldn't be living in this big house with all the neat amenities. Business is doggy-dog, baby, and I'm the meanest damn dog around."

"It's dog-eat-dog."

"What?"

"Not doggy-dog, which makes no damn sense, Harry. It's dog-eat-dog, meaning eat the other dog before he eats you."

"Really?"

"Yeah."

"I always thought it was doggy-dog."

"Well, you were wrong."

"Well—what the fuck? Tie the damn tie for me, will ya?"

Pattie stood up and tied Harry's tie, an ability he had never been able to master.

"But when you're mean, Pattie, you see, when you are mean, you don't have to be right. You just have to scare the shit out of the guy who is. See this meeting you asked about; it's with one of our distributors. He's not doing a very good job. His sales figures are way down. Now Richard—Richard sent him memos and called him on the phone and always took his excuses as gospel truth, which, hell, for all we know, they may well be. But even Richard knows we can't let the truth stand in the way of upping our profit. So, he sets up a meeting so I can ream the bastard's ass. But the bastard don't know I'm going to do that. We fly him in, put him up at The Briers, get him a whore if he wants, make him feel really secure. Then, in the middle of his meeting with Richard, when Richard's being so nice to him, I come in, looking very serious in this here suit, and separate his asshole for him and plunge my fist in it. Symbolically, of course, I mean. I guarantee he'll go back home determined to up his sales figures."

"Richard having nothing to do with it, of course."

"Hey, my little brother's a damn genius, you know that. And he's damn good with the figures and all that, but he couldn't put fear into a pussycat. No one does business with you because you're a nice guy. They only do business with you if they're afraid not to." Harry put his suit coat on and tried to button it. The fear the coat felt was intense. "What the fuck. Looks better unbuttoned anyway," Harry said as he left their master suite and headed downstairs for a breakfast of eggs, sausage, and hash browns prepared by the diminutive Juanita. She never failed to make his breakfast precisely as he liked it—she was afraid not to.

Upstairs, as Pattie began her routine of showering and getting dressed, she asked herself, as she had so many times before, what the hell she had ever seen in the hairy-butt bastard?

The unfortunate thing was—she always had the answer. Spending her educator's career not only among teenage kids but also at the same high school where she had been a teenage kid herself gave her no license to take on the adult conceit of finding teenagers unfathomable. So she knew what she had seen in Harry—a teenage girl's shallow, hormone-soaked brain's opinion of an Alpha Male of potent sperm and protective strength. But, oh, what a joke our pre-historic, barely sentient animal antecedents have played on their vastly more sophisticated, socially more complex, technology-commanding-near-masters of their environment descendants. Maybe the future will be better, Pattie thought. But she had got stuck with a present stuck with the past, and so she got stuck with Hairy-butt Bastard after he had stuck her sometime in her senior year when he was really, really cool because he was no longer in school.

Their parents rushed them into marriage before the pregnancy could show. Which was going to happen—thank goodness—after Pattie's graduation. It would have been a bit of an embarrassment to have the Class Valedictorian give her thoughtful address in front of all the school and community, expectant not just of a bright, shining future but of a child.

Harry's brother Richard, who graduated with Pattie, the unofficial Class Geek, was the Best Man. The brothers were as close as brothers could get, despite their differences. But they also had things in common, especially a love of automobiles and the engines that ran them. And both were very protective of the other. Harry of Richard because he knew damn well that he was the stronger and that Richard, being kind of weird and spending too much time reading books, especially geeky, weird, sci-fi shit, couldn't defend himself from a mild insult, much less physical abuse. Richard of Harry because he was smart enough to know—among many arcane things—that Harry was a simple innocent completely unprepared in any mental development sense to deal with the rapidly approaching, sure to be complex, 21st Century. It was true brotherly love, pure and simple.

The only A that Harry had ever received was for Auto Shop, so the plan became that the fathers of the bride and the groom would finance his certification as an auto mechanic and stake him to a little garage and gas station. Pattie's father used the money he had saved for her college education, which shocked her. But he told her bluntly, with a certain level of disgust, raw and red anger, and a much more subtle, deeply hurting disappointment, that she had made her bed—somewhat literally—and now she must lay in it as wife and mother only.

The blackness of her mood after she had realized what had happened to her bright, shining future may have led (although how could one really know?) to her late-term miscarriage.

At first, she had the feeling—one she never shared but reveled in privately—of shackles breaking and falling away. It was a good feeling but short-lived, for the bonds may be gone, but the prison walls were still up. Although she thought about organizing a jailbreak, several facts intruded. One was that she did, she guessed, sort of, in a way, love Harry, who had been devastated over the loss of the child and was now newly vulnerable, which she found endearing. Her college money was gone, and to go to college, she would have had to take on a full-time job that paid, rather than the one she found herself doing for Harry. Ogg's Garage was now up and running. And Harry had her handling the books, paying the bills, and dealing with the customer complaints that he was a rude son-of-a-bitch. Harry said he "really, really" needed her to do this so he could just concentrate on fixing engines. And if she had left him and the garage, where could she have gone? Back home, to live again with mom and dad? Neither, but especially dad, would have welcomed the idea.

Pattie settled down to an acceptance of the situation and thought— what the hell—she would try to get pregnant again!

It was Richard who came to the rescue. He had gone to college as a chemistry major but worked at the Ogg's Garage during his vacations. The combined inputs into his still-forming brain led him to create a new formula for a friction-proofing additive for engines that was 73.02% more effective than the leading brand. As he was a smart enough boy also to be taking some business classes, he had the resources to draw upon to get the formula patented and to set up a company to manufacture what Richard named Ogg Brothers Friction Proofing. He made Harry his partner because Harry was his brother, and he loved his brother.

The success of Ogg Brothers Friction Proofing and the other engine products from Richard's fertile mind led to positive write-ups. Not only in the local paper and national car magazines but in Time, Newsweek, Business Week, and, of course, Entrepreneurial Magazine. A picture of the brothers Ogg standing with arms around each other dressed in racing attire (they both became competent amateurs) giving the thumbs-up signal that all was right in their world accompanied most of the pieces.

Pattie immediately started taking the Pill again as she found herself the still very young wife of a rich man who could now afford to send her to college. Not that Harry wanted to, but Pattie became determined, and Harry, outside of domestic violence, could not figure out a way to stop her. He did make one condition, though. He—and Richard, he said—had no intention of ever leaving Rubenton. They intended to someday be the town's largest employer and run the city. Harry, because he thought it would be fun, and Richard as a geek's revenge. So, Harry said to Pattie, whatever fancy education you get, you better be prepared to use it right here in Rubenton.

And so, Pattie spent her serious adult professional years as the principal of Rubenton High School after serving her time as a teacher, a counselor, and the assistant principal within the halls of her adolescent frivolities.

But, more importantly, she became the Queen of Rubenton, as Harry was the King. He, as the largest employer, and she, the custodian of everyone's young, basically ran the place. And could do just about anything they wanted to.

Frank discovered that there was particular difficulty in putting a bandage on your penis, as the penis is the only organ that changes its mood. It could be argued, of course, Frank thought, that the heart is also an organ that changes mood, but only "metaphorically," and, besides, the heart is more muscle than organ. The brain is, of course, an organ, but as it is the mother of moods, Frank considered it above consideration in his current contemplation. Plus, he could not think of any possible reason the heart—or the brain—would ever need a bit of protective gauze held down by an adhesive plastic strip.

However, Frank's poor penis did need such protection, for Trudy had taken quite a bite out of it. Or rather a bit of a slash. Some loose skin had gotten caught on a jagged bit of chipped tooth during a heightened moment of piston-like sexual aggression, and now the consequence was sharp alerts sped to his brain upon even the subtlest of moves.

When he thought to bandage his member, his first consideration was whether to apply the sticking savior to it while erect or flaccid. If while erect, Frank assumed that when his penis headed in the other direction, the bandage would bunch up, and it seemed to him that that would cause new problems. On the other hand, if the dressing were applied while his penis was at rest, the Band-Aid would have to match its growth when it suddenly awoke, as it was bound to do despite Frank's intimate acquaintance with Mary and her little lamb. Despite the pain of the memory, Trudy was rarely far away in his fertile imagination, not to mention in a physical location. All bandages have a certain amount of elasticity, of course. Still, no sticking plaster, as the English would say, could match the elasticity of the male member, which has a rather extraordinary amount of elasticity if one thought about it. Although, "elasticity" is probably not the right word or attribute. But is "extendibility" a word? In any case, the thought of wrapping his penis in just plain gauze was not appealing, as the mental image of the raw, ripped skin rubbing against the gauze as his penis responded to moods was not pleasant and was soon banished from his mind.

He concocted—if that word can be used—the idea of filling a condom with petroleum jelly. But besides being messy, he did not know how to secure it in place for the mood changes. Then he remembered that he had a small bottle of a liquid bandage product. Frank symbolically slapped his forehead, moved like a cowboy celebrating fifty years on the range to his bathroom, and found it in the medicine chest. He quickly opened the bottle and brushed the magic stuff onto the wounded area.

It stung like hot holy fucking hell! Inspiring him to create a new dance.

Once the dance was over, he thought maybe he had taken care of his problem. But unfortunately, liquid though the bandage was, once dried, it was not very fluid. And now Frank had a dry crust on his penis, which cracked with movement and, adding a strange insult to injury, itched.

Finally, Frank gave up and put on a pair of boxers shorts and thanked the chaotically random universe surrounding him that he was of the age to wear easy-fit pants.

It was tough the week after the second day of class with Trudy. People kept asking him what was wrong as he moved gingerly, deliberately, with a slight hint of that old cowpoke. "Wrenched my back," was his answer, which, whenever she heard it, solicited a giggle from Trudy, leaving people with the impression that she had a previously unknown mean streak. Despite his precautions, those sharp alerts went off in his brain every once in a while, causing him to jerk one leg up and out and exclaim, usually under his breath, unless he was in the kitchen, "Fuck!" This left people with the impression that he was in the early stages of Tourette's Syndrome.

One morning when Pattie Heatherton was once again having breakfast with Austin O'Brien, she noticed several little jerks of Frank's. When he came over to refill their coffee cups while Austin was in the restroom, she said to him in a whisper, "Baby powder."

"What?" Frank asked, wondering if she wanted some and why.

"My husband uses baby powder."

Frank was not sure what he was supposed to do with the information except acknowledge it. "Okay."

"Down there."

"Where?"

"The balls."

"What balls?"

"His balls."

"You mean—" Frank was groping, but what else could he do? "—his golf balls?"

"No, his testicles, silly."

"Oh." Now he understood.

"I can see you've been having a problem. All that loose skin can get sweaty; stick together. Baby powder takes care of it. My husband swears by it."

"Sounds like a good idea. I'll give it a try."

"Be careful with those black pants, though."

"Why?"

"Because they're black. The white powder creeps through. Just brush your pants off before you come to work. You wouldn't want to be embarrassed."

"Oh, I don't know. I'm getting quite used to it.

"Oh, I didn't mean to...."

"Don't worry about it. You're a teacher. Comes naturally. Anyway, I'll pick up some baby powder after work."

"Good. You'll thank me."

"Hey, I'm thanking you now!"

Red alerts in the nether regions were not all Frank had to concern himself with in the days after Woman Bites Dog. He was still an artist, and the call of creativity was strong. Even on that day, after the driving hormones appreciating Trudy's smooth, clear, luminous flesh had diminished, Frank found himself, after the torture of the short walk to the single that served as his studio, sitting pant-less at his old drafting board. He covered a blank piece of paper with a more finished and refined version of Allison Carr's sea behemoth vision. Why? He should have just laid himself on his bed with his penis sheaved in a nice wet, warm washcloth, hoping for a miracle healing, which is what he did after Trudy had left, giving him first a big, wet, tongue-intensive kiss as a consolation—although it was not much help. But he had grabbed his sketchpad to avoid getting bored and found the quick sketch he had made as Allison had talked on the beach.

Frank had forgotten about it and looked at it with virgin eyes, and a certain power in the drawing struck him. And he thought about Allison and knew then that he had to take her vision to the next step. He wanted to do it, do it now, do it for her. How odd. He didn't particularly like doing art for other people; that's what this, this life he now led, was all about. But maybe it was the power of the image. Could Allison become his muse? No, he dismissed this bit of romantic crap. Perhaps it was the death of her child, although such sentiment did not move him much. Or maybe it was how surprisingly soft, smooth, and gentle her hand had been when he had helped her to her feet. Yes, perhaps it was something as simple as that touch.

Late at night, near the noiseless transition from one day to the next, Emily Briers sat at her desk in Fletcher's, going over the accounts, somewhat joyous, amazed, and disbelieving that she could track three separate significant inflows of income. One inflow was from The Briers and nearby properties, which she had always been able to manage in the black. One was from Fletcher's, a true delight, for Emily had started this business for her inner satisfaction, expecting to take a loss. But found that her love of the fine designs of the past was easy for her to communicate, especially over the Internet, one modern thing she adored, for Fletcher's would never be the beneficiary of foot traffic. The last was Duncan's doing, trading stocks and such on the computer. It had been an idea that had scared her deep enough to scar her, but there had been no way to stop Duncan, a man most comfortable with his eyes focused on a screen. At least this screen dealt with reality as opposed to that tube in the bedroom full of primarily dead actors from a bygone era arrogantly acting as if they were still alive. But Duncan seemed savvy at the task, and money flowed in.

They were rich! What a tickle and giggle that was! By both their efforts, by both their talents, they had become wealthy. She often had to think about this very concretely, very precisely, very black-figures-on-ledger-paper, to find an emotional and authentic response that would allow her not just to be rich—but to feel rich. It was vital for her to feel rich because then, maybe, she would be more comfortable with the knowledge that everything she wanted to surround herself with she now could. And she wanted to surround herself with the Old World, mainly, or at least the last vestiges of the Old World, which was probably enough of the Old World for her. But for some reason, she could not do it just because she could. She could not do it just because it was there and she had the wherewithal to get there. She could not do it just because she had the desire. What kind of reason was that? She did not want to be a tourist to the surroundings she wanted to be surrounded with, which, she felt, would be like wearing borrowed or rented clothes. The fit may be fine, but it was false. She wanted to be there with purpose, be a part of the commerce of her surroundings and meld in. She did not wish just to stand aside or before and gawk at the past that had made it into the present—examining it like a guided tourist on an obligated walk through a great museum trying, with sophistication, to so very much admire how real that apple in that bowl in that painting looked. She had always wanted to be a natural part of all she admired and not just be a visitor, alien to the thing itself.

It was Fletcher who told her how.

"Hell, if you want to dwell in the past, make the past your business."

"It's not the past, Fletcher; it's things from the past. You know, from something as small as a stereopticon to something as large as houses, streets, areas, districts unchanged but still functional."

"Antiques, then. You should be a dealer in antiques."

"Should I?"

"Of course."

"But I love The Briers and working for you."

"Do it here. Hell, we got some antiques here I wouldn't mind getting rid of."

"But I love them. I love being around them. I wouldn't want—"

"They're ball and chains, kiddo, ball, and chains, keeping you here. Hell, I feel like an ogre who's locked you up."

"Fletcher, no, but...."

"Sell them, find buyers, empty the place of them, create a hole in your soul you gotta fill. Then go out, travel the country, and find more. Go to old things in old places with purpose. Just always come back and run the place. I need you, can't do without you. But you got to have some you too. Think about it."

"Okay."

"You promise?"

"Sure."

"Sure what?"

"Sure, I promise."

And she kept her promise. She had thought about it. In the wrap of the fog of Leech Beach, she had thought about it.

Then Fletcher acted. He died.

He left The Briers to his only child, Duncan, a son, a sometimes actor in sometimes okay movies, which he sometimes produced himself. But Fletcher put into his will the proviso that Duncan had to retain Emily Stump as the manager with a lifetime contract. If Emily Stump were not retained, the hotel and the land would be given to the state and turned into a Museum of Seashells. As Duncan had a desire for the income generated from the hotel, but absolutely no desire to return to the rather strange scene of his unusual childhood to run the place, he was happy to acquiesce to his father's wishes. He was not particularly happy with another provision of the will, though, that gave all the furniture in the hotel to Emily Slump. Including the beds in the rooms and the tables and chairs in the dining room. But only if she agreed to stay on as the manager for life. And take all the furniture that could be certified as antiques and use them as the beginning stock of an antique store to be established in The Briers. If she would not agree to this stipulation, then the hotel and land would be given to the state to become a public Park of the Modern, although Fletcher did not precisely delineate what that was. Emily agreed without hesitation and with a smile.

"I guess my father has arranged a marriage of convenience for us," Duncan said over the phone to Emily, a woman he had not yet met.

"Well," Emily had replied, "a strange sort of partnership at least."

"As good a definition of marriage as I can think of."

"Sounds like Hollywood cynicism to me."

"There's no cynicism like show cynicism," Duncan sang the adapted lyrics to the proper tune. "And, talking about cynicism, I will send my accountant out there once a month to audit the books."

"You don't trust me?"

"How can I trust you? I don't even know you."

"Your father trusted me."

"I probably would too if I was his age, and you were sucking my dick."

Emily gasped louder than she thought possible.

"Dad wrote to me once a week. He was a man. He liked to boast."

"Was that all Fletcher said about me?"

"No, but I don't want to embarrass you with the sentimental crap."

Duncan had felt wonderfully tough after he had hung up, almost mean, which was good. For he was trying to cultivate a mean demeanor to go along with a certain toughness and lack of emotion that would begin to guard him against the tough, emotionless, meanness that had so often battered him into a sack of hurt in Hollywood. Duncan wanted to stop being a victim and, if he had to, learn to victimize in preemptive strikes. It wasn't so hard, he thought, right after he had talked to Emily at ten-fifteen that morning and right before he took his second drink of the day.

The first time Emily heard from Duncan's accountant; it was not about when he would be there to audit the books but to inform her that Duncan Briers had slammed his new Mercedes—which the accountant had advised him not to buy—into a tree while driving the curves of Coldwater Canyon. It was after his more than disturbing meeting with a little snot-on-two-legs Warner Bros baby-faced executive. Duncan had tried to play hard-ball with the little humanoid shit but lost embarrassingly and with tears when the little navel-fuzz-for-brains Warner Bros baby-faced executive exercised the only real power he had and simply said: "No."

After six months in the hospital, where his flesh and internal organs healed but his legs never regained their usefulness, he asked to be sent home to The Briers. Installed in his father's old suite, which Emily had left untouched, Duncan was cared for by a big male nurse for a while until he decided he was not ill enough for a nurse; he just needed mechanical aids. So he had an elevator built on the outside of the building connecting with his balcony. And then he got a state-of-the-art self-propelled wheelchair, which he did not like, so he replaced it with a simple, plain wheelchair and, eventually, Dmitri, who was not state-of-the-art but was pretty much mechanical if you thought about it.

And then he considered an occupation. He would never go back to Hollywood. If he could barely stand up for himself when he had legs that worked—how could he do so now? Six months in the hospital, six months inside his head allowed him the luxury to admit that he did not have the right stuff to be a Player in Hollywood, for the right stuff seemed to him to be the wrong stuff. But was that just the whining of a wimp? And was it just Hollywood? No, it was probably anywhere that money, power, and fame were at stake in the center of some engaging activity. Better to hug onto some fog-enshrouded edge of land no one else wanted.

What had sent him to Hollywood in the first place? Not money, power, or fame—silly him—but the product: movies. Spinning tales in flashes of light, stories of triumph and glory and love of family and fellows and mates, of sweet people finding happiness, and good besting bad, of justice being real, fairness being tangible, and happiness with tears of joy being not only possible but sustainable, happy endings that were not the endings of happiness. In other words—lies. But they were lies he liked. He had made the mistake that he could be true to such a product while making such a product. He could not. He was not a survivor. But the product survived. The product was there, was everything, and was—its greatest asset—repeatable.

Better than booze, he was happy to admit now that booze was no longer a part of his life.

Could this then be his occupation? Not employment, not productive activity traded for money, but an occupation that occupied his time. Could he become a full-time movie watcher? A full-time soaker in of life that actually made sense told in stories of internal logic about people whom he liked, except for the people in the stories you were not supposed to like, and who never won and often died of humiliation or in a spectacular cessation of life making real the concept of Justice. Why not? There is not one person in the world who really likes reality; reality is just what they are stuck with. They run from it down many paths: booze, drugs, religion, self-delusion, conspiracy theories, marriage, divorce, passion for causes, and causes for passion. Like birds eating fermented berries to get high (as if they could not go high enough as it is), people do whatever it takes to keep their brains soaked in something happy to counteract the deluge of reality pouring in. Unfortunately, most can only do it part-time. Thanks to the awful truth of legs lacking purpose, Duncan now had the luxury to soak his brain with improved reality full-time. What a life he began to lead! He fell in love with hundreds of women and had many stalwart best friends. His wide-ranging adventures kept him active in his inertness and gave him, over and over, a lovely sense of extraordinary accomplishment. Pratfalls and clever wit allowed him to laugh at the abyss. Well-mannered, glorious deaths made him grieve and feel ever so profoundly human.

It was a grand occupation.

Until he realized he had a bed sore on his ass.

He had done this movie-watching in bed. And why the hell not? He couldn't walk!

It was late at night, and the damn thing hurt like hell and had woken him. It had been mildly sore there and uncomfortable for a few days, but he hadn't thought much about it; he had just shifted his position as best he could while keeping his eyes on the screen. But now, hell, now this hurt! It was not sore no more but sharply painful. Duncan grabbed the phone by the bed and called downstairs to the night clerk, a nineteen-year-old kid who he scared the hell out of, screaming that he was in mortal pain. The desk clerk did not want to, but it was his instructions in the case of an emergency, so he called Emily, who was not happy, but she padded to Duncan's room in slippers and a loosely tied robe and asked him what the hell was the matter?

She had not liked Duncan for several reasons. First, he had come home and occupied his father's suite, which she had been planning to move into, and that she had essentially been living in any way. Duncan was aware of this, as he was of the intimacy that had taken place there. That was the second thing she didn't like about him. He was her boss, and he was a stranger, and Emily felt herself to be the boss, and she didn't like strangers. Except those that eventually checked out in the morning. But Duncan owned The Briers, toward which she felt proprietary. An uncomfortable paradox. Then there was the fact that she considered him a slug. An awful, slimy thing that sat in bed all day and watched old movies. How could she respect a man who could not stand on his own two feet? She understood, of course, that it was not Duncan's fault that he could not stand on his own two feet. But she meant it metaphorically, meaning a man who would not stand on his own two feet, even if he could not stand on his own two feet, which should not be any excuse.

But there he was lying in bed on his stomach, pouring out uncontrollable tears and a well-considered stream of profanities, with his bare ass displaying its rather large bit of putrid flesh. Although Emily would never admit that her heart went out to him at that moment, as Duncan later wanted to believe, she would confess that a nurturing/nursing instinct did kick in. After declaring, "Jesus, what a mess," she tended to the infected area with the most tender care. Emily bathed it in warm water. She cleaned out the infection. She applied an antiseptic and dressed it in a bandage.

In the calm coming after such a dramatic late-night painful emergency, Duncan thanked her, an expression somewhat muffled by being stated into his pillow. He raised his head and declared it again, then said, "God, I hate sleeping on my stomach."

"Stomach or side, that's going to be it for a while. And once you can, you better get out of that bed more often, or you're going to wind up just one big pustulant bedsore."

"Thanks for leaving me with that image."

"Yeah, well, sweet dreams."

It became Emily's responsibility to see that Duncan got out of bed more often, which meant spending time with him. A lot, at first, as he would have no one else nurse him.

This Nightingale turn gave Emily a compelling perspective on the generational passing of physical traits.

"Well, I see you are your father's son."

"Yeah, nice schlong, huh? And it works too."

"Yes, I can see that as well."

"I'm sorry, but I think you turn me on."

"The wounded often fall for their nurse."

"You doubt my sincerity?"

"Not yours. It's your schlong's sincerity I worry about."

Duncan laughed and declared his love for Emily, which was not meant to be nor taken to be a serious declaration.

But several months later, Duncan made an earnest proposal.

"I think you should marry me."

"What?"

They were on the boardwalk where Emily had wheeled Duncan out for some fresh early evening air. It had been a remarkably clear day, and as the light began to dim, they could see the lights of the many oil platforms on the horizon.

"It makes a great deal of sense, you know," Duncan said.

"I'm still not sure I heard what I heard."

"I proposed to you."

"Oh, I did. Damn, I thought I had misheard you."

"We're a near-perfect match, I would say."

"How near?"

"Pretty damn near. Certainly, as near as your relationship with my father."

"I didn't marry your father."

"You should have. Then you would probably own The Briers, and I would be living here only upon your sufferance."

Emily was stunned. She honestly had never thought of the possibility of marrying Fletcher, and he had certainly never proposed. What a stupid, young, naive woman she had been! For it would have been easy to have gotten him to propose. Hell, she could have proposed. She would have slapped her forehead if it did not look so stupid. But even without that, the whirl her mind was going through was quite evident to Duncan.

"So now you can make up for your mistake: community property, Emily. Half ownership is only fifty percent of full ownership, but at the same time, it's a hundred percent better than no ownership. Whereas unmarried, I will have my Last Will and Testament stipulate that the property become a Cultural Center for the oil riggers. You know, displays of famous pin-ups throughout the ages and a ground-breaking show on beer can designs." Duncan smiled. "I am my father's son."

Emily stared down at Duncan, this not bad-looking man who could never walk by her side down the beach before them, who would not be able to lift her and carry her over the threshold, who...

"Would we have to have sex?" She asked the pertinent question.

"Certainly. That comes with the institution, normally. But don't worry. Given my limitations, you will always be on top. I'll just lay there and be your love toy."

"You're a bit sick; you know that?"

"Hey, you're the one who was into senior sex."

"Your father was the sweetest man in the world. It was an honor to give him a little pleasure."

"Well, I promise I'll try to become sweet by the time I'm an old man."

Emily was thinking, Duncan could see that. She was thinking about the proposal, and seriously too. Duncan's heart raced to his throat.

"You'll—" Emily finally said, "—you'll have to become something."

"What do you mean: become something?"

"Well, you'll have to be more than just a damn cripple who watches old movies. And I don't mean taking an active part in the running of The Briers. Hell, that's the last thing I mean. But you have got to do something. I can't be married to a man I can't respect."

"Would you like me to get a job on the oil rigs?"

"You know I don't mean that."

"Yes, I know. Well, don't worry; I've already thought this all out. Before the accident, I was starting to do some trading on the stock markets. I've got a pool of cash from my Hollywood days, residuals still coming in, and insurance money. All I need is a computer hooked to the Internet and—"

"You'll become a professional gambler."

"It's a bit more respectable than that."

"I don't know."

"Listen, until I prove myself, I will not use a penny of income from The Briers."

"But if I'm married to you, your debts...."

"I'll incorporate; it'll be fine."

It was now dark, but the moon had come out, and moonglow romantically spread its influence. How wonderful it all was, Emily thought as she looked out over the beach and the ocean and breathed in the air of stunning stimulation. She thought how awful it would be if I let this perfect atmosphere affect me.

She should have worried more about Duncan, for it was affecting him, especially as he looked up at her face reflecting moonglow and so beaming as if lighted by Old Hollywood's best black & white cinematographer.

"Look, Emily, I love feeling emotions, but I guess I'm not very good at expressing them. I'm offering you this deal because it's the deal that I think will attract you. But don't think I am not, at the same time, offering my love."

Emily turned to Duncan and looked at him closely, deeply. She could find nothing false in his eyes. And so Emily kissed him. She meant it to be a sweet, quick one, but long and deep it soon became as Duncan put his right hand on the back of her head. When they finally broke, Emily did not come out of her awkward bending position, for their eyes were locked, as lover's eyes should be. Then Duncan, with his two strong arms, managed to tip Emily over and spin her around to fall into his lap. She screamed a laugh of delight, threw her arms around his neck, and kissed him again.

"Hang on," he said as he turned his wheelchair around and began to roll them back up the boardwalk, back to The Briers, back to their Briers.

They were married at The Briers in a civil ceremony with the residents and staff in attendance. Both bride and groom seemed so happy it softened the cynics, and a hell of a party ensued with the many toasts to the happy couple leading pretty much to a bacchanal with Duncan reigning as the joyful god though not imbibing himself. But Emily imbibed and improvised a rather radical wedding dance with complicated steps as she wheeled Duncan's chair in a manner no less extreme, especially regarding the intent and purpose of a wheelchair. Duncan found himself spun, tipped, jerked, and abruptly halted. As the chair did not come equipped with a safety belt, Duncan just hung on tight and found great joy in the ride, as evidenced by the loud, uncontrollable laughter forced from his lungs.

Emily finally collapsed onto Duncan's lap and into his arms, happily drunk and completely exhausted. Maria wheeled them outside to the elevator and sent them up to their suite. Upon opening the elevator door, Duncan wheeled his bride over the threshold, and she threw up on his chest.

Emily and Duncan's quasi-marriage of convenience became a real one of conviviality as they played Host and Hostess at the hotel to their residents and to the friends from Rubenton they started to cultivate. Duncan was a little less happy about this than Emily, but only because he thought it suited his personality. He protested every new dinner engagement Emily arranged, grumbled about it with bits of wit, and then thoroughly enjoyed himself. And afterward, after the "Timber!" of getting him into bed and Emily's undressing and cleansing of her face, she joined him there, took the remote, turned off whatever old movie he was watching, and snuggled into his arms.

But that was the occasional evening. During the day, and often late into the night, she was married only to The Briers, with Fletcher's being her licit lover. Emily thought it had been a satisfying life as she sat in Fletcher's now in the first hour of a new day. More than she probably ever should have expected, being Rubenton based. But now, with the offer from the Comstocks, she realized that despite the satisfactions she felt, she also felt a specific ache. It was a precise desire to place herself among the surviving edifices of the Old World and not just gather some odd chips from the block that happened to fall her way. Of course, she truly wanted time travel, which was impossible. But those things that had traveled through time to reach now, there was no reason why she should not greet them. What had stopped her in the past? A kind of fear, she supposed. And the unambitious goal of being happy with leftovers. But from Fletcher's Will to the Comstock's offer to the support of Duncan, courage was gathering, and an insistence on all seven courses of the meal was easier now. She was excited. A tingle to add to the giggle and tickle of knowing she had the wherewithal. It was now one-fifteen in the morning, and she felt like she should be running down the boardwalk, taking the occasional leap and shouting at the top of her lungs. Instead, she closed her books, went up to her suite, did not bother washing her face, slipped into bed with Duncan, and surprised him awake in the manner she had often surprised his father.

The body's capacity to heal was wondrous, Frank thought as he informed Trudy that classes could resume. Ever the eager student, she was at his apartment that afternoon, and not a damn thing went wrong.

During his convalescence, he had had time to think out a syllabus, and he stuck to it, taking Trudy on a trip through the various ways a heterosexual couple could stimulate and enjoy each other's intimate company. Only a religion that could offer such a heaven would get Frank's attention. But then, here it was on Earth, although, Frank assumed, it would not be eternal. That fact and Trudy occasionally declaring, "Wow, I can't wait to try this out on Austin," were the only negatives Frank could find in his mentoring of young Trudy. That is if he didn't include her never quite getting above a C+ in the fine art of fellatio. But at least she never again pulled the automatic F of ripping flesh.

They kept their relationship a secret as life at The Briers went about its course. The Briers' life seemed so much grayer and duller than theirs. But then Frank and Trudy did not know of Emily's excitement over an upcoming trip abroad; of the Major's reading of What Price Glory, which he found both fascinating and fault with; of Austin's growing love of the theater, not in the abstract, but of the physical Stafford Theatre itself; of Pattie's delight in her sexual secret, which was not much of one, but which made her feel thrillingly alive and youthful; of Dmitri's festering anger, and Duncan's concern about it. And they certainly knew nothing of how Allison Carr sat up in her room reading a good book contentedly and occasionally looking up at the framed picture of her sea serpent. A simple act—the looking up—possibly not worthy of note. What would Frank have thought had he known that Allison derived from the picture a pleasure as satisfying as she was getting from the book in her hands? Possibly a finer, deeper one, for the image was so close to the core of Allison Carr that she felt it an extension of her presence in this world and not just something attendant to it.

SEA

Chapter the Fourth

The President of the United States of America was nude. Completely. Stark naked, it might be said, using a term that used to be titillating but now seemed clinical. He sat upon an ornate, vaguely 19th Century toilet seat such as one might imagine would be in the private residence of the White House. He stared out at you, sporting that smile of his that had fallen into a strange, popular imagination no man's land, somewhere between famous and infamous. It was a smile of pleased self-confidence to those who liked the man. To those who did not—approximately the same amount of people as those who liked him—the smile was nothing less than the goofy smirk of the least admirable kid in the class. How an objective eye viewing this scene should feel about the man was dictated by the relatively large roll of toilet tissue on the wall by the President's side that was—despite the text being upside-down—obviously fashioned out of the Constitution of the United States of America.

Allison Carr found the drawing funny and laughed hard, and Frank was very pleased. Encouraged, he showed another of his Presidential Suite of drawings. Here she saw a wet, rocky landscape extending far into the distance, light breaking through the black cloud cover on the horizon, illuminating an oversize hound in the background that was striding forward with toxic menace panting out with his visible breath. In the foreground, a man's head just turned and faced the viewer. It was the President of the United States of America. Words worked into the drawing, finely etched and in an elaborate graphic style, stated:

ONE OF THE DOGS OF WAR COMES BACK TO BITE HE
WHO LET THEM SLIP.

Allison exploded out one boom of a laugh, then said, "Oh my God,
this is brilliant! God, I love his eyes; they're so damn knowing. I mean,
you can hear them saying, 'Oh-oh!' How the hell do you do that?"

"I don't know. You just keep at it until it's right. And I'm really
please you saw that because I worked on those eyes for a long time.
But they're still not quite what I had imagined."

"Can they ever be?"

"No, probably not."

"Then don't touch them again. The communication is there; trust
it."

"You don't find them offensive?"

"Of course, I do; that's what's wonderful about them. Although
maybe subversive would be a better word."

"How about this one?"

He showed her a drawing of the aged Pope in full regalia in an
ornate public restroom designed as a miniature St. Peter's Basilica,
urinating into what looked to be a jewel-encrusted solid gold urinal.
The letters here, looking to have been cut out of an illuminated text,
spelled out: JESUS MAY HAVE BEEN ABLE TO TURN WATER
INTO WINE, BUT THE POPE CAN ONLY TURN WATER
INTO URINE.

"Oh, well...." Allison said after viewing it for a while, with no
chuckle, laughter, or guffaw. Frank, in an instant, felt sick. Maybe she
was Catholic? Carr, was that an Irish name? Was subversive politics
okay, but the Holy was the Holy, and you don't mess with the Holy,
see?

"This ex-communicates rather well, doesn't it?" Allison finally said
as she turned to Frank and smiled a smile that was somewhat more
wonderful than wicked, although it was certainly that.

Allison was the first person to see these drawings, and Frank still
disbelieved that he had allowed her to. But he had found this short,
vital woman very persuasive, even after being somewhat rude to her.

Allison had come to him the day after he had given her the sea
serpent drawing with such effusive gratitude that he found himself
embarrassed and was short with her in his thanks as he gingerly made
his way to the kitchen to escape. He was still suffering from his
wounded penis, but he also did not want to prolong the conversation,

as no one at The Briers knew anything about his life after work. Not even Trudy, who had not been invited to his single number nine and did not even know that it existed. Allison was only momentarily taken aback by Frank's reaction, for she had had the experience of Frank being reticent to discuss anything that was not just a simple pleasantry or something to do with the meal he served you. And yet, they had had that time on the beach, and he had taken the time to realize a simple yet meaningful mental image of hers. She had hoped...

Allison returned to the beach daily, hoping to catch him sketching again. Instead, for weeks each trip was a failure. Frank seemed to be otherwise engaged.

Then the day came when Trudy whispered to Frank in the kitchen, "Okay, I think I'm ready."

"For what?"

"Austin, of course. I think I'll seduce him this afternoon."

"Oh."

"I've rehearsed one of his stupid little scenes, but I don't think I will have to do it."

"Well, you know...."

"I can't wait any longer. The theater's finished. Austin will be auditioning others soon, so I've got to get in there now."

"I did want to show you...."

"Believe me; you've shown me enough. I feel completely prepped."

Frank could not believe the strength of the jealously he felt. He was happy to admit that it was atavistic and not worthy of a modern, rational man but would not let such self-knowledge stop him. He entered the walk-in freezer and punched a big hole in a large cardboard tub of strawberry ice cream. Only the fact that it had just sat in the warm kitchen for a half hour after its delivery before Maria had thought to put it in the freezer saved him from breaking his hand. After he had extracted his ice cream-covered fist, he struggled to think up an explanation, finally settling on, "Hey, does anyone know what happened to the ice cream? There's a hell of a fucking big hole in it!" Everyone was baffled—and destined to remain so.

After work, Frank did not feel like going home. Instead, he grabbed his sketchpad, chair, and blanket and headed toward the beach. As he walked, he realized that it would be the first time he had put pencil to paper since he had done the sea serpent drawing for Allison Carr that now he wished to hell he had not done. Was that right? He had not drawn since...? Frank stopped to think about it. All his recent memories were of pain or copulation; there was none of drawing. Was it that he had done what he had sworn he would never do again, draw the dreams of others? It certainly could be, for it seemed fitting that it would derail his whole creative drive. But then, long afternoons of exciting, adventurous sex with a nineteen-year-old girl did tend to eat up time and be creatively fulfilling in its own too pleasant way. Not that he wanted to "create" with Trudy. Good God, no! But let's face it, the basic urge to create can manifest itself in various forms, some mundane and obvious, some more unique. Had he traded the extraordinary for the ordinary? Well, it was only supposed to be for a short time anyway, and now it seemed to be over.

Goddamn it to hell.

He went to his favorite spot far out of sight of The Briers and settled into the sand. It was overcast, which was fine, for so was he. He opened his sketchpad and picked up a pencil but did not draw. Instead, he looked at the ocean, traveled it from horizon to shore, and then back again.

Allison Carr's magnificent sea serpent rose out of the sea, gallons of water falling off its back. Then, with a slow but deliberate gait, it came ashore and, with great, huge legs, stomped over to the boardwalk and stepped not so lightly on the renovated old ballroom, now known as the Stafford Theatre, crushing it into the ground.

Of course, there was no sea serpent—just a dumb figment of imagination, not even his own. There was just the sea, a deep pool of murderous thoughts churning, despite its calm surface. And a seagull, which had suddenly landed and hopped a few times in front of Frank as if it was happy to see him.

"What the fuck do you want?" Frank asked the dumb bird. "Unless you're an art lover, I've got nothing for you. And even then, you're pretty much out of luck," he said as he showed the bird a blank page.

The bird seemed to agree, for he hopped a couple more times, the last hop taking him back into the air. Frank was jealous. Hop, hop, fly! Wow, what a great life that would be! Frank turned his head to follow the ascent of the bird and found himself looking up at Allison Carr.

"I thought maybe you had given up drawing on the beach," Allison said.

"Been busy," Frank said.

"Doing what?"

"Uh...."

"I'm sorry," she said, although she wasn't. "That's none of my business, is it?"

"Well...."

"I guess I just hoped it was still drawing. Just somewhere else, I guess."

"Would you like to sit in the chair, Mrs. Carr?"

"Call me Allison, or I'll kick sand in your face."

"Mrs. Briers frowns on such familiarities."

"We are not at The Briers at the moment."

"I think they own the beach."

"No, the beach is public. And no, thank you for the offer of the chair, but I think I'll sit on the blanket."

She sat and arranged herself for comfort. Then she picked up the sketchpad and saw that it was blank. "Of course, maybe I should leave. I could be disturbing you, getting between you and your muse."

"My muse?" It was funny that she brought that up.

"The ocean."

"Oh. No, that's just a big body of water I happen to be sitting by. Besides, it seems to be your muse."

"Well," Allison looked out to the sea, "I love it."

"Damn thing's gray most of the time."

"That's what I love about it. You can't think on a sunny beach in front of a blue ocean—only feel."

"You would rather think than feel?"

"Oh, sure. My thoughts," Allison held up a book she had brought, "or the thoughts of others."

"Yeah, I notice you always have a book."

"I'll bet you that outside of The Briers, you always have a sketch pad."

Frank smiled. There was no need to confirm her suspicion.

"I want to know why," Allison said after some moments of silence, "an artist of your abilities is working as a head waiter at The Briers?"

"Aren't we back into the territory of None of Your Business?"

"Sure. So what? Tell me what I want to know, or I'll ask Mrs. Briers if I can display my new art acquisition that I'm so proud of in the lobby. I'll ask her quite loudly as I tell her who the artist is."

"Jesus, you're tougher than you look."

"I was a teacher, then an administrator at several exclusive girls' schools. I found that sometimes the best way to motivate an uncooperative little bitch was to throw her greatest fear in her face."

"So, I have no choice," Frank said while realizing he was thrilled by the fact.

"Come on, Frank—talk to me. You said you once earned a lot of money doing art."

"I did?"

"That day here on the beach."

"Oh, yeah. Well, I did, once. But I wasn't happy doing it."

"Why not?"

"Too big of an ego. I got paid well to do art that supported other people's egos—which were also too big."

"What kind of art?"

"Illustrations. For kid's stuff."

"Kid's stuff?"

"Well, look, let me start from the beginning, okay?

Allison nodded.

"You see, I was a kid who always drew. I mean, from a very early age. Of course, all kids do from an early age, but I kept it up daily. People could see that. I mean my parents and teachers and such. So, I was encouraged and put into special art classes. But whenever people tried to tell me how to draw, I got real upset that they were bugging me. I was not a popular student. My genius—I mean, you know, in an ancient world kind of way as that thing inside you that makes you do the art—my genius was a jealous guy and didn't want anyone else mucking with me."

"You must have been an unpleasant child."

"Yeah, I pretty much was.

"With a big ego."

"Hey, you can't accuse me of something I've already admitted. Now, my problem out of high school—I didn't go to college, didn't feel the need—was that the only people being able to give full vent to their egos in the art world at that time were abstract expressionists and other purveyors of art that looked like shit. Whereas my art only looked like shit when I drew an actual piece of shit. The art world thought it was being kind when it called me an illustrator and pointed me in that direction. But I didn't want to be an illustrator; I wanted to be a painter doing huge canvases of some importance. Plus, I didn't know how to become an illustrator. It was a whole—profession-thing I didn't want to take the time to figure out. I just wanted to do my work."

"And you wanted the world to come to your door and be thrilled by it."

"Exactly."

"But you discovered...."

"The world don't go looking for nobody. It just sits there, and you must jump through embarrassing hoops to get its attention."

"So?"

"So, I worked odd jobs, busboy, phone sales, pizza delivery guy. Finally, I got a job in this theater's ticket booth. Not in a movie house, but live theater. It didn't pay much, but I liked the job and the people. They were passionate about what they were doing, and I could relate to that. It was a small theater that struggled all the time, but everybody seemed to have fun there.

"Anyway, I was in the theater one day when they delivered the sets for a children's play that they were doing. They were awful, just, just, real crap. As if the designer thought, 'Oh, it's only for a stupid kid's play, so I can slap any old thing together, the kids won't mind. Well, the head of the theater company was livid but no more so than me. So I started railing against the shit. I really lost it. I got so mad I said, 'Here, here's what you should have,' and I grabbed a pencil, and on the back of the sheet of paper that I had listed the last night's receipts, I—in a snap—designed, quite frankly, a brilliant set. First, they dropped their jaws because they had no idea that I could do that. Then they hired me."

"You must have been happy."

"No! I was miserable. Designing their damn set was going to take away time from doing my work because I still had to run the box office; that's how it is in regional theater."

"But you did it anyway."

"Yeah, sure."

"Why?"

"I was an exceptionally nice person then."

"You're an exceptionally nice person now."

"Not really. I just know how to play the part."

Allison smiled, understanding that there was more to it than that.

"So, you designed the set."

"Designed it, built it, painted it."

"And it was good."

"It was brilliant—magical. Every time I saw it, I fell in love all over again, as if I was seeing it for the first time."

"So, you should have been happy. Admit it; you must have been, even a little bit."

Ah, come on, Allison—Frank silently pleaded—get off this happy track. "Remember me talking about hack work?"

"Ah. Yes, I do."

"I admit to being a happy hack. But not a happy artist."

"So why didn't you just go back to your ticket booth?"

Frank laughed. "Images of genies, open bottles, and barn doors no longer closed come to mind."

"Ah. The failure of success."

"Exactly. Someone coming to the damn play was a publisher of children's books. She loved the set and gave me the commission to illustrate a book she had coming out. Something about Easter gift rabbits in the city being let loose in the country when they got too big. It was supposed to be an allegory about culture shock or something so 20th Century like that. But the damn thing sold well."

"Because of your illustrations?"

"I would like to think they helped, but it also was a very funny book. But I was associated with it, so commissions started coming in. I was stuck."

"You became a children's book illustrator."

"Please, saying it makes it sound even worse."

"You don't like children's books?"

"No."

"Why?"

"I don't like children. I know women hate hearing that from a guy."

"Not all women."

"Really?"

"You'd be surprised."

"Well, maybe there's hope for humanity in this grossly overpopulated world after all."

"Not likely. But go on."

"What more can I tell you? I started earning a very decent living, met a gorgeous girl who was impressed by my very decent living, and married me. I say she married me instead of 'I married her' or 'we got married' because the whole thing happened, I think when I was out of town."

"Dare I ask if you had children?"

"I managed to avoid it."

"How?"

"Vasectomy."

"Your wife knew about this?"

"To this day, she's never known. I mean, she knew I didn't want children, but...

"So, you're no longer married."

"No, I'm still married. But not for long. My wife kicked me out when, besides not giving her children, I suddenly started turning down commissions and just sat in my studio drawing images that she considered quite awful. If I had had any guts, I would have up and left her like a modern-day Gauguin, shucking off all domestic responsibility for my art. But I didn't have the guts to jump. I had to be pushed. So here I am. Welcome to my Tahiti."

Allison looked around. "Not quite the same inspiration Gauguin went for."

"Yeah, I know. And around here, you can't just live easily on breadfruit and nubile young natives." Not that nubile young natives were unavailable; Frank had to admit to himself. "But I work the shift I want, which leaves me with good afternoon light."

"Here on the beach?"

"No—at home. I have a bit of a studio. Not perfect. Totally inadequate for where I want to go. But for now..."

"Take me there," Allison said as she suddenly sprung up and stood above him with her fists on her hips, like Wonder Woman. Frank did not quite know how she did this so quickly, but it seemed a move far too gymnastic for a woman her age.

"What?"

"Now." Allison swept her right arm down to scoop up her overcoat and then swung it behind her to hang, hooked on her finger.

"Well...."

"Don't argue, Frank. I want to see your work."

"Why?"

"I like your story."

"My story?"

"I'm going to treat you like a book."

"Why?"

"I like books."

"Do I have a happy ending?"

"That's what I want to know. Come on, let's go."

◆◆◆

They traveled in two cars, as Allison would not hear of Frank having to drive her back to The Briers. She said she had to pay a visit to her storage unit in Rubenton anyway. When they arrived at the Mandalay Apartments, Frank took Allison to number nine. He stopped for a moment as he put the key in the lock.

"Forget something?" Allison asked.

Frank turned to Allison. "Uh, I've got a little bar refrigerator in here, and I was just trying to remember if it's stocked with anything I can offer you to drink."

"Water will be just fine."

"Well, maybe we ought to go to the apartment where I actually live and...."

"Frank."

"No one has ever been in here before but me." It was a plea for understanding.

"Afraid of losing your virginity?"

"Well...."

"Frank, stop being so damn selfish."

"Selfish?"

"Keeping your work to yourself and not sharing it. Why? Most artists too eagerly want to share their work—usually just looking for praise."

"And devastated as hell when they don't get it."

"You know the feeling."

"No, I don't. My work is what it is. Praise or criticism isn't going to change things."

"Are you really that pure?"

"Yeah, pure as the driven over snow. Look, I'm just saying...."

"Open the damn door, Frank."

Frank looked at Allison and noticed her stunning blue eyes again, as blue as ever but now also quite commanding. "Mrs. Carr, you're surprising me with the force of your personality." He moved the key in the lock and opened the door. Allison, without hesitation, passed through.

"Surprise is good for the complacent."

"Complacent?" Frank followed, closing the door behind him.

Allison looked around. In the middle of the room was a white drafting table angled to catch the light coming in from two large windows. Next to it was an old TV cart covered with art supplies. On one wall was a large metal cabinet with long, narrow horizontal drawers that Allison recognized from the various art departments in the multiple schools where she had worked. On another wall was a couch that Allison thought must have been a cast-off once dumped on the side of the road where Frank may have found it, grabbing it like some college kid trying to furnish his first apartment. She was not too far wrong, except the couch had been cast-off by Frank's wife and had never seen time by the curb. But it was broken looking, and she assumed uncomfortable and was covered with an old blanket to help cover the worn spots. Under the high end of the angled drafting table was a bookcase stuffed with books. Allison, being Allison, gave the books a quick scan. They were on various subjects, and all were lushly illustrated. Art reproductions decorated the walls. None were by Frank, as they were all recognizable, some to the point of fame.

"Small room."

"Yeah."

"Little world."

"Yeah."

"But you're the king of it."

"Yeah."

"Brooking no insurgency from within or without."

"Yeah."

Allison took her eyes off the room and gently laid them on Frank. She smiled. It was an incredibly girlish smile that somehow made the blonde in her hair come out stronger, pushing back the gray. It also shared an unarticulated secret with Frank, nor could he have articulated it, but it comforted him. Allison moved over to the drafting table and around it to view the slanted surface. Frank suddenly remembered what had been sitting there for weeks, waiting for him to put on the last touches. Fear made his stomach cringe as he tried to project a calm nonchalance into the small room.

Allison took only a few seconds to scan the drawing and burst into laughter.

◆◆◆

Positive reinforcement is a wonderfully powerful motivator. An hour later, all the drawers were open, and their contents scrutinized. The last drawing examined was of an alternative Washington D.C. where the White House closely faced the Capitol building, both sculpted out of ivory, or maybe it was Ivory soap. The Supreme Court hung from a tree in the background, waiting for the wind to blow. On the surreal rolling ground between the buildings were groups of individuals facing each other off, pointing accusing fingers at each other. The individuals were all anthropomorphic black pots and black kettles in black suits with Old Glory lapel pins and ties of either blue or red. Here the legend read: A WHOLE BUNCH OF POTS CALLING A WHOLE BUNCH OF KETTLES A WHOLE BUNCH OF BLACK.

"What's to be done with them?" Allison asked.

"What do you mean?"

"All this work—vibrant, angry, opinionated, rude, funny—what do you want to do with it? You can't keep it to yourself, it's good, and it demands an audience. Can you try to get them published in a book? Or can you submit them to magazines? Maybe make, I don't know, limited edition prints out of them."

"You don't understand."

"What?"

"These are not the final works. These are not illustrations." The word, springing from his tongue, snapped at the air like the curse of an old cuss.

"They're not?"

"These are just studies, sketches, ideas for bigger works."

"Bigger?"

"Allison, I want to take these and paint them in oils onto huge canvases. Some will be very painterly, almost High Renaissance in look, old-fashioned, but with a very contemporary subject." Frank became giddy in the telling. "Some will look like huge woodcuts; some I'll paint in oil, in shades of gray to look like quick pencil sketch drawings. I've even planned to make some look like watercolors, although they'll be in oil. But all will be huge, I mean massive, floor to ceiling, not just in your face, but smashing against your whole being."

Allison took one of the drawings and held it arm's length in front of her, "hanging" it on the wall before her. "Wow," was her simple exclamation. "Why haven't you done it?"

"Hell, I can barely afford these art supplies on my salary. And this 'studio' is not quite large enough."

"I'll get you the studio."

"What?"

"And the supplies."

"What are you talking about?"

"I want to see these, Frank. I want to see them huge on huge walls. How will I get to do that if I don't make it possible for you to do it?"

"But...." Frank was having a hard time understanding; he was having difficulty discriminating his feelings, which crowded and pushed and shoved each other. "But it's going to cost—"

"Frank, I've got plenty of money. But this isn't completely charity if you're worried about that. I'm going to make a deal with you. I'll fund your work, but you also must let me be the sole and exclusive agent for it."

"But what do you know—"

"Frank, listen, I spent years in exclusive girls' schools. Many of my former pupils, most of whom I believe liked me, went on to important, high-paying careers, married well, or inherited lots of money. Two of them, inseparable friends in high school, now run what I understand to be a fashionable gallery in New York. And all these contacts are just waiting for me in an address book I keep in my storage unit, which is why I planned to go there after seeing your work."

"But how did you know you would like—"

"Frank, I told you, I see you as a book. If a book doesn't grab you at the beginning and let you know it's going to be good, then you don't bother to finish it. Your story first intrigued me, then grabbed me. I'm going to see it to the end. And more than that, I want to be a part of it. My own story has disappointed me, Frank; I wouldn't finish it if I had a choice in the matter. I want to be a part of your story. I want to be a part of a story that I really really like."

"Are you going to be my muse then? It's funny; I've never had a muse; no one ever cared for the job. But after I did your sea serpent, I wondered if maybe you might become my muse."

"No, Frank, I'm not going to be your muse." She indicated the drawings that everywhere surrounded them. "You don't need a muse. But what I can be, what I want to be, is your champion."

The statement stunned Frank, and the air in the room suddenly seemed hard to breathe. He grabbed Allison, intending only to hug her, which he did, but when pulling away, their lips found each other, and in a deep kiss, Frank found the air he was seeking.

The couch being convenient, love was made boldly, in a space not admitting the vulgarities of time.

Allison left with parting kisses and tender talk on both their parts. She did not want Frank to walk her to the parking lot. From his window, though, he watched her walk to her car and drive away just as a truck pulled onto the lot and occupied the space Allison had just vacated. It was Trudy. "Oh, shit!" Frank said as he left his studio and ran to his apartment, where he caught his breath and waited for Trudy's knock. He opened the door, and there stood Trudy with a drawn, tear-stained face. "Oh, Frank," she said with tortured sadness as she pushed forward into his arms, pushing them both into the room. She hugged him tight as tears burst and a cry wailed, and then she stripped Frank quickly and had her way with him.

◆◆◆

Dmitri had asked his grandmother if it was easy to snap a chicken's neck. In response, his grandmother had thrust out her lower lip and dipped her head and upper torso in a grand nod to say, yes, easy. She knew this because she had snapped many chicken necks while growing up on a not-so-productive collective farm in the old USSR. Then she mimed with her hands the holding of a chicken and the twisting of its head to achieve the snap. It looked much like taking a twist cap off a bottle to Dmitri. The grandmother, ninety-three years old, no longer twisted chicken's heads, for chickens now came to her from Super Manny's Market headless and featherless; naked little bodies, or pieces thereof, ready for the pot, pan, or microwave. She had no complaints about this; she was not a nostalgic woman. Life in Russia had been burdensome, and she would not have minded dying at her half-century mark. Unfortunately, she had come from a region and a family of the long-lived, only one of which was abundantly fertile—and it was not the region. She had often wondered why God had cursed her little part of the globe. To give life—Ah, to breath, love, and laugh—then to make it so miserable—shit, shit, shit, everywhere and everyone, shit—then to extend it among them far beyond the national average. What kind of joke was this?

When she went to bed that night, late as always for sleep held little appeal for her, Dmitri was playing a video game, strange demonic magic to his grandmother. She looked at it briefly before saying goodnight. The images on it moved fast, so very fast, and very credible human bodies kept bursting, splattering blood everywhere. She only vaguely understood that the bodies burst in the air because of the vicarious thumb actions of her grandson. She kissed him goodnight on the top of his head. He did not acknowledge her presence, which amused her.

Later, in the twilight before sleep, she heard the roar of an engine.

Between the kiss on the head and the engine roar, Dmitri had finished his game, went to his bedroom, and donned a set of camouflage fatigues he had purchased at the Army Surplus store. He then blackened his face with shoe polish. Soon Dmitri was speeding down Leach Beech road in the Ford Escort with the brand-new retread tires, slowing down before Mr. Hendrickson's farm and stopping to the side of the road under a tree with low-lying branches. He opened his car door very slowly and got out of his car with completely silent stealth. Unfortunately, in the middle of self-congratulations, Dmitri momentarily forgot his mission and slammed the car door shut with the self-important push he always gave it. It was like a gunshot, and he crouched instantly to hide among the branches and the dark. A dog was barking. But it was far off. Hendrickson did not have a dog; he knew that. "Too many damn animals to care for as it is," he had once heard Hendrickson say. When all was quiet again, Dmitri, maintaining his crouch, crossed the road and entered Hendrickson's property. It was slow progress to the chicken house, but he finally made it and quietly entered the unlocked building. The chickens were asleep and made no note of him. This was good; he was doing good. His original plan at this point was to throw acid on two or three of the chickens. He thought that would have been neat. But he had had absolutely no idea where to get acid. It wasn't like it was on the shelf at Super

Manny's Market. At least he had never seen it there. And he certainly wasn't going to ask for it. He had seen enough TV to know that asking for it would have put a memory in some clerk's head that would have wound up as a clue against him. No, a weaponless, truly natural kill would be best. And soon, he thought, for he did not like the smell in the chicken house.

But it was pitch black in the chicken house. There were windows, but there was no moon. He had picked a moonless night—after struggling to figure out when the next moonless night would be, a teacher finally pointing out these little round and such symbols on his calendar—because it is hard to be stealthy with a lot of moonlight. But he did not think to bring a flashlight. He stood still for a few more minutes, hoping his eyes would adjust to the dark, but in the pitch black, there was not much adjustment to be had. Finally, he moved forward with tentacle-like arms leading the way. His shin caught something hard, and the hurt was immediate. "Shit!" he said, managing to keep it under his breath. Forward once more, his feet now "sniffing" along the floor.

Then a sharp, pressured, piercing pain flared up on his right hand in the soft curved spot between his thumb and index finger. "Fuck! Shit! Hell! Damn!" These exclamations came very much over his breath, and the feathered residents answered in kind in their native language, and chaotic din reined much to Dmitri's consternation. His plan to subtly snap a couple of chicken necks and stealthily leave ruined, Dmitri grabbed out and grabbed out and gabbed out until he finally connected with a chicken neck. He held it in a good grip and swung the damn uncooperative kinetic chicken around until it hit something hard. Standing his ground there, he slammed the chicken over and over and over against whatever the hard thing was until it was a weight very much dead. Then Dmitri burst out of the chicken house—no time for stealth now—and ran across Mr. Hendrickson's farm. He fell only seven times before reaching the Ford Escort, sure that a blast from Mr. Hendrickson's shotgun would soon pepper into his back, sending him reeling forward, to fall, tumble, and possibly expire on this dark, moonless night.

But no blast came. Dmitri started the Ford Escort, gunned the engine, manned the wheel to execute a high-speed, not very elegant U-turn, and sped back to Rubenton.

The chickens soon calmed themselves, and a quiet returned to Mr. Hendrickson's farm. Mr. Hendrickson had remained in undisturbed sleep, one of the advantages of the hard of hearing who take their hearing aids out before going to bed.

When she married Hairy-butt Bastard the year of her high school graduation, Pattie Heatherton was suddenly Pattie Ogg. When she first saw this name in print, she threw up. It may well have been morning sickness, but it also might not have been. The high school annual had already gone to the printers, so there, at least, she would be immortalized as her father's daughter. But the graduation program documenting an event she was such an essential part of listed her as Pattie (Heatherton) Ogg giving testament to the fact that she was in this strange transitional state between being the child of her parents and the wife of her husband. Wife? Husband? But really, he was just Harry. She really was just his girlfriend, Pattie. And why wasn't theirs still just a cute campus romance? As indicated by the heart-shaped photo of them kissing on her doorstep on the night of the Senior Prom that dominated the two-page spread in the Rubenton Raccoons annual documenting all the most popular cute campus couples (Harry still qualified, being an alumnus)? After graduation, the Heatherton she was faded into something ghost-like as she started to be known as Pat Ogg, Ogg the Ogre's wife in the office at the Ogg Garage. This picture, which was not in the form of a heart, did not make her throw up but did unsettle her stomach into ever-present nausea, making her still very young life sour, manifested by a sour face announcing a sour attitude.

Thank goodness for Harry's brother Richard and his genius and friction-proofing. When she went to register as a freshman in college, she registered as "Pattie Heatherton," which Harry thought was too feminist of her. But by that time, Pattie did not give a damn what he thought.

Indeed, Pattie did not give much of a damn what anybody thought, which was her strength. And what made her an effective administrator. But Austin O'Brien wondered if it made her a less practical illicit lover.

"I don't give a damn," Pattie said when Austin said that he thought maybe her discretion was weakening, pointing to the gift she had bought him—a futon couch for his office.

"I mean, honey, I really appreciate it, but everyone knows you can quickly turn it into a bed."

"Yes, I know. That's the idea. You're always so nervous about doing it at The Briers; I thought an option would be a good idea."

"Good and obvious is the problem. You should have seen the way the delivery guys looked at me."

"Who gives a damn?"

"Well...."

"They were nothing but delivery men, for Christ's sake."

"And yet they understood perfectly the concept of the casting couch."

The idea threw a sharp and disturbing image into Pattie's head. "Oh. I hadn't thought about that."

"See, people might think—"

"You could use it as a casting couch, couldn't you?"

"Pattie—"

"You wouldn't, would you?" It was a question reminiscent of an order.

"I have no intention of doing any such thing."

"But how am I ever going to know? Outside of taking DNA samples from the mattress."

"Pattie!"

"You know, Austin, how upset I would be."

"Pattie, I—"

"Upset enough to sic my husband on you. But then, I would have to tell him about us."

"Pattie—"

"Of course, I do have a couple of varsity football players desperate for passing grades."

"Pattie—"

"Oh, Austin, I'm just kidding. No one's going to find out in this stupid little town. And what if they did? So what? Hairy-butt Bastard and I run this town."

"So, you don't mind that someone like Trudy knows about us?"

"How did Trudy...?"

"It seems to be an open secret at The Briers. A lot of talk in the kitchen about us."

"Oh, so what? They don't brand people for adultery anymore, you know."

"But, Pattie, don't you think that if our relationship became general knowledge, somebody might think it not so appropriate since you got the school board to commit a lot of money for this theater? It's not the revelation of sex I worry about; it's a money scandal that could kill this theater. Look, we are at the beginning of something wonderful here, I don't want to blow it, and I don't want to lose it. This theater is becoming my life, my—my purpose. I don't want to sacrifice it just for a little nookie."

Forced to give that some thought, Pattie remained silent for a moment. A finite moment but interminable for Austin. Finally, with a smile as an introduction, she spoke: "One, it hasn't been a little nookie; it's been a whole hell of a lot of nookie. And damn fine nookie, I think you will agree. Two, I was just about to be insulted that you would refer to me or think of me as nookie, a little or a lot. But upon quick reflection, I realized that that's basically how I think of you—as nookie. Damn fine nookie, that I'm not going to give up. Now, as to the theater and my efforts to fund it, that is a completely separate matter that I'm perfectly capable of handling and protecting. I am as committed to this theater as you are. It's good for the school; it's good for the community. I can defend it like a warrior queen and smite any opposition that might arise, I assure you. Now let me show you how this futon is effortlessly transformed from a couch to a bed, and let's inaugurate it with some delicious hot sex. Okay?"

"That's what Trudy wanted to do."

Pattie had effortlessly transformed the futon from a couch to a bed before she turned to Austin and asked, "What?"

"That's what Trudy wanted to do yesterday when she came in for her audition. She walked in, and I swear to God her nipples popped out and pointed to the damn thing."

"Trudy Andover?"

"She tried to seduce me yesterday."

"Why?"

"Because she'll never be a good actress, and she knows it, and she wanted an easy way to get ahead. 'Get ahead by giving head,' the crappy actress's motto."

"But you didn't...?"

"Of course not."

"How can I be sure?"

"Take a DNA sample."

Pattie could not help herself; she felt and looked for a possibly still wet stain. But the futon, which had never been in the bed mode before, was factory fresh. Pattie stood up and smiled. "Thank you,"

"For what?"

"For the nicest compliment that I have ever received."

"Oh, well, sorry, it really wasn't a compliment to you." It was something Austin might normally not have said, but he realized that he was hurting just a bit from the revelation that he was not much more to Pattie than a Homo dildo, ironic as that term might have been. But then, she was not much more to him than a Femme facilitator, making his theater dream come true. "I resent people who want all the perks of hard work without doing the hard work. Trudy doesn't want to be an actress; she wants to be a star. She doesn't want to be an artist; she wants to be famous. Somehow, she thinks that will make her admired, and that will make her happy. People like that piss me off. You don't get anything out of life without putting in the time, sweat, and the pain of hard, sometimes unpleasant effort."

"Oh, is that what I am? An unpleasant effort?"

"I'm talking about something else, and you've got to bring it back to you, don't you?"

"Me is who I'm concerned about."

"Don't be, Pattie. You're a fine fuck, you're a lovely lay, you're a spectacular screw, and you're a beautiful boff. And you damn well know it, and you don't need me to tell you."

"No, I just need you to prove it to me," Pattie said pointedly.

Austin got the point—and dropped his pants. "The irony is I had already decided to cast Trudy in What Price Glory." He walked over to the futon, upon which Pattie was now nude and kneeling.

"Really? Why?" Pattie said as she pulled Austin's briefs down and kissed the head of his penis.

"All the role calls for is young sexuality on two legs with a French accent. Trudy will be perfect."

"Yes, but," Pattie ran her tongue along Austin's now stiff shaft, "can she do a French accent?"

"Somehow, I don't think there is anything French she can't do."

Pattie chuckled at the joke, then engulfed Austin's penis giving a happy moan of satisfaction.

Austin thought Pattie's attitude was rather cavalier—if that term could apply to a female. But why not, he thought, she fucks like a man, very aggressive in her technique. Not that he minded that, for it took a particular burden off him, letting him float off on his own with companions of his imagination, as she got what she wanted, and he got what he wanted. But was the cavalier in her going to jeopardize that? Because what he wanted was not just a good fuck—at least not from her—what he wanted was this theater, the financial wherewithal to operate it well, and the support—the active support—of this community. Pattie Heatherton essentially was the community. But could she lose it? Could she alienate it? Could she be divorced from it? And where would that leave Austin and the Stafford Theatre?

Austin wondered if he deserved such insecurity. Maybe that was one of the "perks" of having—prostituted was the word that naturally seemed to come next, but—oh, face it, by all old-fashioned criteria, prostitution was what he was doing precisely. And that is what he had refused to do while in Hollywood. But to prostitute yourself to get a role on, say, Trial by Erin was one thing. To prostitute yourself for your life's dream was quite another. But would there be Hell to pay? He had to think about that. He had to hope not. If the gates of Hell did open, it would be not by his actions but by Pattie's cavalier attitude. He would just be an innocent bystander, standing by, getting his dick sucked. The moral ground here was shakier than he liked. What would a moral quake here register on the Richter scale? Pretty high, he guessed. Hell, he might as well be living back in Los Angeles.

At least he had not allowed Trudy to negotiate the shaky path. Not that she would not eventually, and probably in Hollywood, but at least he did not start her off.

Trudy had come into his office bright and bouncy, carrying a beach blanket. She was excited to see the futon.

"Wow, that's cool! Can I sit on it?"

"Sure." Austin had answered.

And she did so. "Ooh! It's really comfortable. It turns into a bed, right? Have you slept on it yet?"

"I just got it this morning."

"Oh well, then, it needs to be, uh, it needs to be—what do you do with a boat?"

"A boat?"

"You know, like one of those big cruise liners, they smack it with a bottle of champagne."

"Launch it?"

"Yeah, yeah, but there's another name."

"You christen a ship."

"Yeah, that's it! Let's christen the futon."

"You want to give it a name?"

"Is that what that means?"

"Yeah."

"Well, maybe I do mean launch."

"I don't think you launch futons."

"Well, what do you do when you do something for the first time to get started?"

"Maybe you mean to inaugurate it?"

"Yeah, that's it! Let's inaugurate it!"

Trudy had such a hopeful look in her eyes that he would get her meaning without her having to put out any more effort. Austin hated to disappoint her. But, of course, he had to.

"Trudy, did you pick out a monologue?"

"Yeah, sure."

"Then maybe you better get up and go to the stage."

"Actually, I need to be lying down in a bed."

"Why?"

"It's a scene from, uh ... uh ..." She quickly riffled through the book of monologues Austin had given her. "Whose Life is it Anyway?"

"Whose Life Is It Anyway? That's a bit mature for you, don't you think?"

"Well, uh, I thought it was really—interesting, and, uh, and dramatic, being about dying and all that, and—and I thought it would be interesting to, you know, act while laying down in a bed."

"You did?"

"I thought it would be a challenge. So that's why I brought this beach blanket. You see, I thought I would do it on the stage floor, but now that you've got a bed here, I can do it on the bed."

"I don't think that will be necessary. I would just like to see how you, you know, read the lines."

"You don't want me to lay down on the bed?"

"I would prefer it if you didn't."

"Oh." Trudy sat with palms down on the futon, and she looked at it to her left, then to her right, as if to leave from it was to be a final parting, and she would never see it again, so she needed to burn it into her memory and heart. This took a moment or two, enough time to consult with herself and agree with herself to shift her strategy from the artfully subtle to the boldly blunt. Suddenly she looked up at Austin and declared, "God, you're hot!"

"Trudy...."

"I mean, you are a super sexy guy."

"Thank you. Would you like to read the scene now?"

"Don't you think I'm sexy?"

"You don't really need me to answer that question, do you?"

"So, you do find me sexy?"

"Most men would."

"Yeah?"

"Especially since you're wearing a halter top, no bra, and your nipples are desperate to poke through."

"Oh, you noticed, huh?"

"Trudy, you would have to be Ray Charles not to notice."

"Who?"

"He's a blind singer?"

"Oh. I—I really want to fuck you, you know."

"Yeah, I got that idea."

"Don't you want to fuck me?"

"That's not what we are here for, Trudy."

"But, but, I'm good, I'm really good. A lot better than Ms. Heatherton, I'll bet you."

"Ah...."

"You don't think we all don't know, do you? Everybody at the hotel knows."

"Well...."

"I mean, if you want to fuck an old woman, I guess that's okay."

"My relationship with Pattie is not a part of this discussion."

"But—"

"Trudy, do you want to do the scene or not?"

"Well—yeah."

"Okay. Then, well, just stand up and begin."

Trudy did not stand up. "I'm terrific at sex, you know."

"Fine," Austin's reply expressed his impatience.

"I've been rehearsing."

"Good. That's what you're supposed to do with a scene."

"Not the scene. Sex."

"You've been rehearsing sex?"

"Maybe practice would be a better word."

"How?"

"Well, by fucking!"

"Who? No, wait, that is not a part of this discussion either. So maybe the better question is, why?"

"Well, so I could make you happy, of course."

"Why?"

"Well, because I feel there's a connection between us, a, um, you know, a relationship."

"Are you saying you think you're in love with me?"

"Yeah, sure, if you want me to be."

"Trudy, I don't think it's about what I want, but... Why do you think you want to do this?"

"Because...."

"Because you have it in your head that if we have a special relationship, you'll get all the best roles; that I'll cast you without you having to audition?"

Trudy started to cry.

"Yeah," Austin said, "I thought so."

Trudy started to cry profusely.

Austin walked over to a box of tissues, grabbed it, and then tossed it to Trudy. He should have gently handed it to her, but somehow, he needed to make a gesture of disgust.

"Trudy, do you know how hard actors must work? First, to learn their craft, to perfect it. Then struggle to get roles so that they can prove themselves. DO YOU KNOW HOW HARD THAT IS?"

It was way over the top and like a stinging slap. Austin knew it immediately and was regretful. Trudy responded as one would expect, with even louder crying and many more tears.

"Trudy, I'm sorry, but you can't—you shouldn't do it this way."

Trudy took some deep breaths to stop her crying, wiped her tears, and blew her nose copiously and repeatedly. Then, finally, laying the seven tissues she had used aside, she sat up and arched her back, throwing out her breasts with now deflated nipples, grasping for a potent strain of teenage pride. She said in a challenge, "Are you telling me actresses don't do this, that this never happens?"

She knew, of course, that they did, and it did. And so did Austin.

"No, I'm not telling you it never happens. I'm telling you, it never happens with me. Now, do you want to read the scene?"

Tipsy on the verge of new tears, Trudy said, "I'm—I'm upset now!"

"Good! Use it! Don't you think a dying woman would be upset?"

"Well...."

"Did you memorize it, or do you need to read it?"

"I memorized it."

"Okay. Do it."

"What?"

"Do it! NOW!"

Trudy ran through the monologue. After she had finished and blew her nose once more, Austin, looking down at her, said, "Well—that was a good job."

Trudy's eyes widened and brightened, and she said, "It was?"

"Yeah—if you were in the Fast-Talking Olympics! No, it was awful. This is not Trial by Erin, Trudy. You have no understanding of this character. You didn't even try to understand who she is. You just read lines and read them as fast as possible to get it over with!"

"I'm upset!"

"I don't care."

"You're mean!"

"I care even less about that. What I care about is good acting."

"You're a bastard!"

"When it comes to this—when it comes to this, which matters, yeah, I am a bastard. I am also a son-of-a-bitch and the fucking devil incarnate!" Austin stopped, knowing how loud he was getting, seeing how scared Trudy now looked. It was an interesting effect his performance was having on this audience of one. Sometimes over-the-top is how you had to go. Though when left with a whimpering pup, you needed to beware of strikes to the heart. "Look, Trudy, if you truly want to be an actress, I can help you; I can do something for you."

"What?"

Austin grabbed a copy of What Price Glory from a stack of newly arrived Samuel French play scripts. "Take this home, read it. It's the first play we're going to do. There is one female character named Charmaine. Find the first scene she's in with Captain Flagg. Study it.

Don't memorize it. Come back in three days, and we will read the scene together."

He held out the script to her. She looked at it but did not take it.

"Come on. Do you want to be an actress?"

"Yes!" She declared.

"Well," Austin said, amused by her adamancy. "What I think you really want to be is a star. But be that as it may unless you want to be a star in porno films, you are going to have to try to be an actress first. You can leave now and leave behind the script, and at least you'll have your dream of stardom. Or you can take it with you and show me that you are willing to try to achieve that dream."

Trudy stood up, angry. She grabbed the Samuel French from Austin's hand, rolled it up tight into a tube, and then struck him on the arm with it.

"Does that mean you're going to try?"

Trudy walked out of the room, play script in hand.

It was a hall of rational design and was, in fact, labeled THE HALL OF REASON. Rational in the sense that the size and proportions, while large and expansive, were pleasing to the eye and were not too daunting nor pressed on you too dearly your insignificance. The decorations were plentiful and colorful but not so ornate that their total load on your visual cortex constituted a riot. At one end of the hall, a young, longhaired, bearded man in a sparkling white robe and sandals was exiting through a large door labeled: EXIT TO IRRATIONALITY. He was leaving the hall, leaving the door open. At the other end of the hall was a group of people, male and female, clothed in typical costumes of various historical periods from Antiquity to the Renaissance to the stiff collars of the Nineteenth Century to white lab coats over blue jeans; just about everything except the more habitual clothing of the Dark and Middle Ages. The group seemed in the middle of a discussion, conferring with each other, comparing notes, and imparting information and knowledge. One member of the group, a female in a white lab coat, was turned away from the others and towards the robed man who was leaving, gesturing towards him as an accompaniment to her high-volume verbalization of, "JESUS CHRIST, SHUT THE DOOR! WERE YOU BORN IN A BARN?"

Frank was pleased with the drawing. He chuckled, then laughed, and then wished to hell he could share it with someone right now. But Frank was alone in his single number nine. He had never much minded being alone. Even when he was with people—his wife when he had lived with her; co-workers; people on a busy street—Frank was always so much more in his head that he was essentially alone. But now, he was feeling an ache—an actual ache, right there in the center of his chest close to, biologically, where his heart was. It was not a painful ache, but it was a palpable one. He quite objectively figured it was either loneliness or longing if there was a difference between them. But, of course, he knew there was.

Loneliness was mundane. Longing was romantic. Any dog can be lonely. It took a deep feeling human to long for the sublime. And the sublime he was now longing for was to see his work as it should be seen—finished and in its final form. He had prevented himself from longing for this before. Frank had forced himself to be content with the concept sketch, to enjoy it by himself alone. And to be the only lonely one to know the final form intended. Frank could visualize it so precisely that, as far as his brain knew, it physically existed. But now, with hope dangling on the bejeweled string of promise held by Allison Carr, he could long for it with abandon.

All this had nothing to do with the fact that the day before, Frank had, within the space of an hour and a half, made nearly passionate love with a nineteen-year-old after having made deeply passionate love with a fifty-four-year-old. Possibly that was the point—art as pure escapism. He needed his mind engaged in some reality other than the one he had lived through the day before. Which, as realities go, was truly surreal.

Now that he had finished the piece, though—no—wait—there was more to be considered here. Now that he knew—at least hoped he knew—that he would be able to take this concept sketch into its final form—what form should that form be? As he had been sketching it this morning in the glory of a day off, he had assumed he would finalize it on a large canvas in the form of a High Renaissance painting. Sort of Da Vinci of The Last Supper mixed with a bit of the Tintoretto of Christ Before Pilate, or maybe El Greco; he liked the faces in El Greco, especially in The Burial of Count Orgaz. But he had drawn indications of the whole history of the rational battling the irrational, so how could he stop there? No, no, a large canvas, yes, but divided into, say, yes, it would be six panels, a triptych times two. Hinged? Yes, maybe hinged—do triptychs have to be hinged to be triptychs? Does it matter? But it won't be a triptych, of course, it will be a—what? A sextych?

Here we are back with sex!

Look, start with a panel with the look of Antiquity. Say, black figures on red like those on a 6th Century BC amphora. No! Better red figures on black from a 5th Century drinking cup. The 5th Century would be better, obviously. But did he have to be so date-specific? He liked the style of the fresco paintings from Pompeii. They were fuller, more dimensional, more... Ah, but wait a minute! It was suddenly clear to him what style the sixth panel should be. If he goes with that, the more cartoony pottery art will offer an exciting balance. Okay, so, first panel, 5th Century red figures on black. The second panel, the Middle Ages, of course. Frank jumped off his chair and went around his drafting table to his bookcase. He grabbed a particular book and quickly thumbed through it. Yes, this is it. He was looking at a color panel of The Annunciation by the Master of Flemalle. He loved the lack of perspective, the tabletop that seemed to be tipping forward, and the milky white, rosy cheek faces of Mary and the Angel Gabe. Perfect. Panel three? Now we can do the High Renaissance. For the fourth panel, he decided to do the 18th Century. Gainsborough would be fun. And very pretty in its colors. But when he thought of Gainsborough, he thought of portraits, not big scenes. Not Gainsborough, then, but Hogarth is where he should go. Yes, indeed, he would love to do Hogarth. But Frank didn't want it to be black and white; the last panel would be black and white. But he could give it a sepia tone or, better yet, a faded colored print look. Yes, that would work. The fifth panel would be pure 19th Century: Manet, Renoir, Degas, or a painting by the bastard child issued forth from a creative ménage à trois between them. And finally, the sixth panel—pure 20th Century, of course. But it couldn't be abstract. His idea was so concrete it couldn't be abstract. Hopper was too static, Wyeth too painterly, Picasso too much of a challenge. Besides, the concept was a joke; it was funny. That, in contrast with the historical styles, he hoped would be an addition to the humor making the point. But for the 20th

Century, he might as well be upfront and open about it. He would do the sixth panel in a New Yorker cartoon style.

So, there it was. The same concept, the exact same scene in the Hall of Reason with the Exit to Irrationality being left open but done in six different styles from six distinct periods of history. Damn! He couldn't wait to get started! He couldn't wait to get started on his sextych.

Speaking of sex tick—a thirty-eight-year age spread between two women a forty-five-year-old man makes love to within two hours might qualify.

He was going to have to think about this, wasn't he?

He had had a hell of a time kicking Trudy out of his bed the night before and getting her on the road home before her parents worried. Plus, the next day was not going to be her day off; she had to report to work at six in the morning. If anyone knew what a problem it was when the staff was late, it was Frank. But she was being very clingy. She was a completely different girl. She explained what had happened at her audition in details that Frank knew were very much shaded by her point of view. But, after his initial surprise that Austin had the willpower to turn Trudy down, he did not doubt the essence of those details. Trudy was an aggressive and determined person who just wanted what she wanted and could not see why she should not have it. Frank had always detested the hypocritical game playing a man usually had to go through just to get laid—not that women had often asked him to play the game. So this want of a sexy nineteen-year-old girl offering herself to him with no conditions on a velvet padded silver platter with gold handles was a fulfilled wish not to be abhorred, ignored, or stored away for a rainy day. However, for a man like Austin, romantically handsome in a leather jacket and tight jeans, getting laid was probably neither a mental nor a physical sweat-inducing process. And as he already had a convenient, not bad-looking, bed partner who was also the genie who was fulfilling his, let's face it, much more essential and deeply needed wish, he probably was not in the mood to gamble. Austin was, Frank was sure, more than happy to stay with the current hand dealt to him. Whereas Frank, whose current hand had only been his right one, this new hand, which had announced itself to be a full house before he had even looked at it, seemed no gamble.

But now, this full house seemed more like full arms squeezing tightly.

"You know," Trudy had said to him after she had brought him to, by her reckoning, his second climax of the day, but by Frank's, his third, "maybe it's a good thing. Maybe it was fate."

"Fate?" Frank asked with a slight quiver of fear in his voice because men hate hearing that word from a woman's lips.

"Yeah, because, well—you know...."

"Yeah?"

"Well—you know...."

"What?"

"Well, kind of like—you know...."

"Kind of like, you know what?"

"You're going to make me say it, aren't you?"

"Say what, Trudy?"

"Well, you know, Frank, I ... I think I'm crazy about you."

The crazy part he could accept without argument. The rest...

"Ah—Trudy—"

"Now listen to me, and—and don't talk. I know I came to you for just—well, you know, instructions. But did you ever wonder why, you know—I mean, we really hit it off, didn't we? I mean, except, maybe for that first time. But we did hit it off. I mean, it seems so natural to me."

"Sex is natural, Trudy."

"No, I mean, between you and me, there's a communication; our bodies communicate, don't you think?"

"Ah, well, our bodies fuck, I know that much."

"No, Frank, no, it's much more than that; it's deeper, don't you think? Frank, I'm in love with you; I know that now. This night has been... I love you, Frank."

As they were lying down, and Frank was holding her in his arms, he found it hard to walk away.

"Uh, Trudy, I think you have gone through a—a very emotional situation; you were upset, and you needed to be consoled, and, uh, as I was privy to your plans, I was the only one you could come to, and—"

"Frank, don't try to be—don't try to be smart about it. Don't—don't think about it, just feel. And if you feel, I think you'll agree that you love me too. I mean, how could you not?"

"Well—uh—Trudy, you know, I'm much older than you, and I don't want to take advantage of you."

"Age has nothing to do with love. Don't you know that? I'm only nineteen, and I know that."

"Uh, yeah, well, look, um—I gotta pee."

Frank jumped out of bed, ran into his small bathroom, and urinated satisfactorily and copiously and noisily. Frank was happy about this. Because he thought it was important that Trudy hear him pee so she would not doubt that he had been telling the truth and that he really had to pee and was not just trying to avoid, for the moment at least, continuing a conversation of some consequence.

And then there was Allison. After that most relative stretch of time which seemed both a moment of glory and the onset of a desirable eternity, Frank had fallen from Allison, off the couch, thumping onto the floor. But he felt no pain, no shock, only awe. They were both breathing hard and were wet in patches and sheen. Frank was looking at the ceiling, noticing the cottage cheese roughness of it, an alien landscape supporting no life as he knew it.

"Um—" Frank started to say, but Allison cut him off quickly.

"Don't! Don't say anything. I'm in this wonderful afterglow right now, and I'd prefer not to dim it down with a discussion of the details."

"I was just wondering who seduced whom?"

"I rather think the moment seduced us both."

"Are there many moments like this in life?"

"If there were, then religions would fall like leaves, for what would be the attraction of an afterlife?"

"So," Frank said, "the rest of life is just crappy little mundane moments of uncomfortable reality?"

"Probably so."

"Like when the hot liquids of passion become air-cooled, and suddenly, you're uncomfortably cold."

"That's one of them."

Frank stood up and looked down at Allison lying still on the couch. He noticed for the first time her breasts. They were small but pretty. He had enjoyed having them in his mouth. She stared at him and said, "What are you asking yourself? 'How the hell could I have banged such an old broad?'"

Frank gave a short laugh. "No, actually, I was marveling over the versatility of beauty."

She smiled. "How romantic." She sat up. "Do you have a romantic bathroom in this place?"

"No, I have a lousy small one I never use. But I store my linens there, so I have plenty of towels."

They went to the bathroom, which featured a small shower stall with a glass door. Frank opened it and turned on the water. A copperish stream whooshed out and gathered on the shower floor before being pushed down the drain by the clear, hot water that followed.

"Would you like to go first, madam?" Frank asked with mock formality.

"Oh, no," Allison said, "we're in this together." She pushed Frank through the door, followed, then closed it. Steam was filling the confined space, and Frank grabbed an old, dried, cracked soap bar. He rubbed it between his hands under the stream of hot water and brought it back to lathering life. Then he soaped Allison. Up and down. Front and back. "That feels good," she said. He held her under the water and rinsed her off. Then he started gently poking around her back, mumbling one-syllable sounds. "What are you doing?" she asked. "Counting your moles," he said. She turned around to face him and slapped his chest. "Don't!" She was just a little angry, but he didn't notice that as he looked into her eyes. "God, your eyes are beautiful!" He said it like the boy that never leaves the man, and she smiled and forgot her anger like the girl that never leaves the woman. "Thank you," she said. "Now you." She took the soap from him and lathered him all over, having fun when she came to his genitals. Then she positioned him under the shower's stream and rinsed him off. Then they were facing each other, two wet, clean humans.

There were probably things to say here, but neither spoke up on any subject of pertinence. They just looked at each other rather intensely. Frank looked down at her wet head, the gray and blonde having melded into just slick lightness, beads of water adorning her face like crystals, youth seeming to radiate out of skin whose age was not hidden and certainly was not ashamed. She looked up at a face whose roughness of beard she now remembered having felt; whose slight roundness gave Frank a funny, innocent look. Funny because Allison now knew him to be the most knowing person of her acquaintance. It was not a bad-looking face, she thought. The innate niceness that he had nurtured and manipulated, but was no less genuine for that, despite what he may have thought, gave him a handsome aspect that caused her to smile, which caused him to smile.

A certain sweetness was starting to flow with the water, which was beginning to cool. "You know," she said, "I've always had this fear of slipping in the shower, so I like to hold on to some handles." And, retaining her smile, she grabbed the handles Trudy had called love in each hand. Frank continued smiling and said, "I wish I had a water-resistant pen." "Why?" She knew she had to ask. Frank gave her an up-and-down scan. "So I could connect the dots." She slapped his chest again and then fell into it, bringing her arms around him into a vibrating hug as she laughed. He covered her with his arms and felt the fun of that vibration.

They came out of the bathroom dry but cool and found their clothes all over the room. They gathered them up, assigning them to their proper places, and soon they were dressed. Allison took a brush from her purse and brushed her hair into a logical form. Then she took the brush and conquered Frank's hair, still roughed up from the towel. As she did so, she said, "I am going to go now, but we must talk soon. Not about this—" she indicated their bodies and their recent mutual endeavor—"but that." She gestured with her head towards his drafting table and its many drawings. "That is urgent. This," she stroked his face, "this is not related and can be discussed at any time." She kissed him, assuming he wanted to be kissed. He did, and he kissed back tenderly. She moved to go; he moved to accompany her. "No, stay. Draw." She smiled with her lower lip sucked in. The sight was oddly precious to him. Then Allison turned, opened the door, and left. He closed the door behind her and then went to the window to see her walk to her car and drive away. As he was waiting for his first glimpse of her walking out of the building; onto the parking lot, the need to draw suddenly consumed him, to wave his pencil across a sheet of paper and to make—silly way to put it, but it was the way he was feeling—to make magic.

Ah! There she was.

Ah! What to draw hit him with full force. He could see it without being able to see it, but he would see it once he drew it. He became giddy with the thought, moved to his drafting table, then stopped—no, stay at the window, what if she turned to wave? But Allison did not. And that was okay. It was the right thing to do, to stay at the window until she was out of sight, but visions can be ephemeral, and he was now anxious for her to leave, but not wanting to admit the fact.

Now, though, now her car was backing out of the parking space, and so—

"Oh, shit!"

The vision, the vision, throughout the rest of this very surreal day, he struggled to hold onto the vision. Throughout the pounding of flesh, the sucking of organs, tickles and laughter, and one-sided talk of love, he kept drawing the vision over and over in his mind. Closing his eyes, he struggled to recall the image as various calls of nature grabbed his attention, including the last one for sleep that would cloud his vision with pure darkness.

When he awoke, the vision was still there. He jumped out of bed and ran, nude except for a T-shirt, from his apartment to his studio, passing no one in the hall on the way. Frank grabbed a large blank sheet of sketch paper from his file cabinet. It was almost as large as the drafting table's top. Then he drew, furious at first, but then more deliberately, for the vision was there; he had cemented it hard in his mind; it wasn't, he finally convinced himself, going to go away. And then, there it was—alive on paper, and he could fully relax.

"Jesus Christ," he thought, possibly addressing the image in his drawing, "the ejaculations of man!"

He had an itch and reached to scratch, suddenly realizing that the surreal had not ended as he contemplated the complications of a safe return to his apartment.

Farmer Hendrickson woke up at nearly the same time every morning. This was not due to an alarm clock. Nor, as one might have expected, the crow of a cock. Neither of which could make an impression on the deaf old man. It was due to a life of regular habits and hours and the internal clock set by those admirable qualities. Upon waking, the farmer would get out of his bed and move on slightly unsteady legs out of his bedroom, down the hall, through the living room, and, finally, into the kitchen, where he would push a button on an elaborate automatic drip coffee maker his son, George, had sent him for his last birthday. As he could not hear if the coffee maker had gone into operation or not, and as he never trusted the little red light that came on to offer such an assurance, he stood and waited until he saw the first brown drips coming out of the basket with the ground coffee that he had put in the night before to save time in the morning. As soon as there was dripping and possibly inspired by it, he moved, now on more steady legs, into his bathroom and took a pee. After washing his hands thoroughly with hot water, it was only then that he put in his hearing aids, letting in the sounds of an early morning farm to serenade him as he dressed for the day.

After Farmer Hendrickson had his coffee, which he had always considered to be a tonic for his heart, and his breakfast consisting of two fried eggs, little sausage links, and prefab hash brown potato patties, which he heated in a shiny four-slice toaster that his other son, Joe, sent him last Christmas, and which he smothered in catsup, Hendrickson would make his way outside to attend to the things that needed doing that day. First, though, he would take a moment to stand on his porch to survey the extent of his land, which was less extensive than it used to be. After his sons had grown up and declared that no farmers they would be, Farmer Hendrickson had sold off much of his land to help pay for their college educations and other frivolities. The land he kept, he worked by himself except for the seasonal help of migrant laborers. He liked it that way. Long a widower, he had become an advocate for solitude—just him, the land, things that grew, the relative quiet of the country, and the complete quiet of his deafness.

Hendrickson's attending to the things needed doing that day led him to the chicken house wherein, on the morning after Dmitri's commando raid, he found many loose feathers and a pulverized chicken. As there were no teeth marks on the dead chicken, and, indeed, as the dead chicken was still there, he knew that no four-legged varmint had invaded the chicken house, and he had little doubt about the identity of the two-legged one who most likely had. It did not take much investigating to find two sets of bipedal tracks upon his land. One set laid down in a zigzag pattern heading towards the chicken house, and one, beeline-like, led away from the chicken house, with seven curious impressions along the way as if something big had consistently dropped to the ground. At the beginning and end of these tracks, on the far side of the road, he found tire tracks in the moist earth and muddy ones on the old asphalt of the road itself. The latter formed a near-perfect U shape. On both surfaces, they were clear impressions of tires with only minor wear on their treads.

"Damn that Dmitri!"

The farmer Hendrickson thought of putting out the plywood sheet with nails again but then thought better of it. He decided that the problem would have to be solved by a higher authority.

◆ ◆ ◆

Hendrickson found Mr. Briers in the dining room of The Briers, just finishing his breakfast. Without introduction, he said, "Where's that young shit who works for you?"

Duncan Briers looked up at the farmer and answered, "That's what I want to know. He hasn't shown up yet."

"Maybe because he was up late last night beating the crap out of one of my chickens."

Duncan had dreaded such a scene, but he would not let Hendrickson see his dread. Instead, he said, with a steady composure, "Really?"

"Yes."

"Well, I didn't know that Dmitri had any hobbies. But it's probably not beyond the sad, low level of his intelligence. Have you had breakfast?"

"Of course."

"Would you like some coffee?"

"Yes."

"Sit down."

Not long after Hendrickson had taken his first sip of coffee, delivered by a smiling and beaming Trudy, Dmitri sauntered into the dining room, taking his second U-turn of the morning, when he saw farmer Hendrickson. A sharp, piercing intonation of his name stopped his exit. As commanded by Mr. Briers, Dmitri then turned and walked over to the table. He said nothing, and nothing was said to him as both Duncan and Hendrickson looked with curiosity at Dmitri's face. Not the aspect they were both familiar with and which featured a permanently quizzical look, but at its surface, which was spotted with little splotches of black here and there this morning.

"Dmitri, what the hell do you have on your face?" Duncan asked.

"Nothing," Dmitri answered, possibly believing himself.

"Nothing?"

"Yeah. Nothing."

"Well, I suppose if nothing had a color, it would be black."

"What?"

"You have black splotches in various spots on your face. Did you know that?"

"Uh...."

"I can imagine that you would rarely want to look in a mirror, Dmitri, but certainly, you must have seen your face sometime this morning if only to check for zits."

"I, uh, I got my face dirty."

"You did?"

"Yeah."

"With what?"

"Shoe polish."

"Shoe polish?"

"Yeah."

Duncan leaned to look down at Dmitri's feet. He saw a pair of worn white running shoes splattered with dried mud.

"Dmitri, do you even own any shoes that need to be polished?"

"No."

"Then what were you polishing?"

"My face."

"Why? So you could become a black Russian?"

"Uh?"

"Explain yourself, Dmitri."

"Uh, well, me and some guys went out to play, uh, paint-ball commandos, and, uh, we put on the shoe polish so we would be, you know, camouflaged."

"When?"

"Last night."

"Last night?"

"Yeah."

"In the dark, I take it?"

"Well, yeah, sure."

"Was the paint fluorescent?"

An awesome thought, Dmitri thought, and so he said, "Uh, yeah, sure, it was."

"I don't see any splotches of florescent paint on you."

"Uh, well, you know, that's because I won."

"Oh. You won. Congratulations."

"But I was up really late, and I forgot to set my alarm, so that's why I'm late."

"I see."

"Is there anything I can get you, or do you want me to take you back up to your room?"

"No. Sit down and join us."

"Uh...."

"Sit, Dmitri."

Dmitri sat and folded his hands into his lap and bowed his head as if in prayer, which might not have been a bad idea.

"Dmitri, you'll notice Mr. Hendrickson is here."

"Uh, yeah."

"You didn't say hello."

"Hello."

Mr. Hendrickson said nothing in response, and Duncan expelled a long breath and then said, "Dmitri, why did you beat the crap out of one of Mr. Hendrickson's chickens?"

"Uh, I didn't—"

"Don't try to deny it. I warned you about something like this."

"Well...." was the only word Dmitri seemed able to get out.

"You're not even going to defend yourself?"

"Well...."

"I thought not. Dmitri, here's the thing. The chicken you grabbed and pulverized happened to have been Mr. Hendrickson's prize chicken."

Hendrickson, who had been keeping an evil eye on Dmitri, now looked over to Duncan, unsure if he had heard what he had heard. Duncan's subtle yet telling glance clued him to the need for no queries.

"Now, he had raised that chicken from an egg. From even before the egg because he has been breeding chickens for forty years along the principles of domestic chicken genetics as laid out by the late, great Roscoe Arbuckle of Road Island Red fame. After all this time, he felt he had achieved the near-perfect chicken, and he was going to show that chicken at next month's county fair. If his chicken had won the Blue Ribbon, which it was likely to have done given a weak competitive field, it would have meant $10,000 in prize money for Mr. Hendrickson. Even a second-place win would have meant $5,000. But as it is now, with Arbuckle—oh, he had named the chicken Arbuckle in honor of the great Roscoe—with Arbuckle now a mass of beaten dead flesh, Mr. Hendrickson will be lucky to sell him to McDonald's for McNuggets."

"Oh."

"I see you're starting to understand the severity of your crime."

"Well...."

"You have essentially cost Mr. Hendrickson at the most $10,000 and the least $5000, not to mention the attendant fame which would have put Mr. Hendrickson on the map right there next to the great Roscoe Arbuckle himself."

"Oh."

"Now, Mr. Hendrickson wanted to go to the police about this, but I told him I thought we could take care of this among ourselves. For once you understood the seriousness of what you have done, I told him, even though it really wasn't your intention to hurt Mr. Hendrickson as bad as you have, that you would be more than willing to recompense him."

"What's recompense?"

"To pay him back."

Panic slapped Dmitri. "I haven't got $10,000!"

"But you've been saving for a new car."

"Yes, but—but, I don't have anywhere near that much yet."

"Do you have $5,000?"

"Well...."

"Close to it, I'll bet."

"But—but, it's for my car."

"I understand. That new car is important to you."

"Yeah, well, yeah!"

"You do have something else to offer, though."

"What? I don't have anything else."

"Your labor, Dmitri, the sweat of your brow."

"But I work for you."

"And you will continue to work for me. But now, you will also work for Mr. Hendrickson, giving him whatever help he needs around his farm until you have paid off the $10,000."

"Hey, I don't want him hanging around my farm that long."

"Should he pay off only $5,000 then?"

"Okay. That'll be fine."

"But—but—"

"Dmitri, if you don't accept this solution to a problem you created, then I will fire you. Then you will be unable to make more money to add to your savings to buy your new car. Instead, you may wind up working at McDonald's again for minimum wage, waiting for the dreaded day when you serve poor Arbuckle, in the form of McNuggets, to some snot dripping, whining little brat. And Mr. Hendrickson will call the police."

"But I'll be working two jobs, not even getting paid for one. When am I going to have time to do my schoolwork?"

"Do you actually do your schoolwork?"

"Well...."

"This might even be a blessing in disguise. You'll learn how to work in the soil, like your Russian ancestors. You might find yourself."

"Find myself?"

"Sorry. You can't find yourself if you are blissfully unaware that you are lost, can you?"

Dmitri did not answer beyond the quizzical look that rarely left his face.

After Dmitri had taken Duncan back up to his suite and got him into his bathroom...

And after Duncan had turned the computer on to do a bit of morning trading...

And after Duncan had received from Dmitri, once again, assurances that yes, he would show up at Hendrickson's farm early Saturday morning to work (And Sunday morning," Duncan reminded, Dmitri grudgingly agreeing, "And Sunday morning")...

And after he had dismissed Dmitri, who left the room just as Trudy entered with a tray bearing Duncan's large thermos carafe of coffee and a bowl of one fresh apple, one fresh banana, and one fresh orange...

And after Duncan had noticed and commented on Trudy's even brighter-than-normal smile of satisfaction with life, saying, "You must be in love," getting a drawn-out "Maaaaaybe" from Trudy in answer, causing Duncan to inquire, "Oh? Anyone we know," causing Trudy to draw out even further a second "Maaaaaybe" as she left the room...

And after Duncan looked at the computer screen and the symbols and figures thereon, suddenly being able to make no sense of them at all…

After all of this was when Duncan began to question himself.

What the hell was that performance he had given downstairs? Performance? Shit! Improv comedy! Hendrickson's dramatic report on the murder of the chicken had hit him in the pit of his stomach. It was as if the farmer had been reporting on the murder of Emily. Or a guest of the hotel. Or the President of the United States. Or Slappy Montgomery, the last surviving member of that famous film comedy team, the Goofs. Duncan had refused to react in kind; how could he? It was just the murder of a chicken. Besides, it wasn't the murder he was reacting to; it was the malevolent nature of humanity as represented by Dmitri.

"Oh, good God," Duncan thought. "Must such mean-spiritedness exist in the world? Must such stupid eye-for-an-eye, tooth-for-a-tooth, innocent chicken-for-a-balding set of tires core of vengeance lump itself in the center of humanity?" When he had heard Hendrickson's report, he had wanted to wail, mash his teeth, and pull out his hair. But, of course, he could not have done that, for no one would have understood. When Dmitri came in, he wanted to slap him silly; slap some sense into him. He could not have done that either for the same reason. Besides, it would not have done any good; Dmitri was not a dumb dog, at least not literally. No, Duncan had to maintain control and set up a scene and exercise power over Dmitri, an exercise that had felt too damn good and now, at this moment, sickened Duncan.

Who the hell did he think he was? Humphrey Bogart? The Godfather? James Bond? He realized with some slight horror that he loved Dmitri's stupidity; it was such an easy target. Whereas the malicious stupidity of the powers-that-be (usually the minor powers-that-be) that Duncan had had to deal with in Hollywood he had hated because he had feared because he had never had the wherewithal to stand up to them. He was never clever enough, smart enough, and quick enough to improvise a scene with them that allowed him the upper hand. But Dmitri was a human sponge to be picked up, moved, and squeezed at will. Such an easy target was a mark you could hit blindfolded, the side of the barn, and the fish in the barrow. The sense that power gave Duncan afforded him grace while moving through the world and effortless control over the slings and arrows of not only outrageous but malicious fortune. It may have been an illusion, but, damn, it was terrific!

"Damn!"

The computer screen screamed at him. He had just lost a trade that would have been a triumph. He shut down the computer.

"Hell, I'm rich enough," he shouted to the world.

Well, maybe his stupid little improv, his easy power game, would lead to something good. Perhaps it was not just sentimental slop to think that Dmitri, forced to plant his fingers into the good rich soil of the earth, could grow and reshape himself into something more conducive to a world kind of kind, sort of sweet, possibly pleasant, instead of the maggot covered sphere of shit it is today.

Duncan picked the fresh red apple out of the bowl and sunk his teeth into it.

After she had left Frank the day before, Allison Carr drove down the streets of Rubenton towards her storage facility, wondering why those few people she saw on the road were not stopping to stare at her, maybe smile, maybe greet her with applause, or at least give a friendly wave in acknowledgment that, just a very short time ago, she had been in the throes of a most beautiful sexual passion. One they certainly should have admired, if not envied. She felt like Debbie Sims must have felt and had tried so hard to communicate to Allison when she had admitted during a counseling session that she, at 16, was having sex.

"I feel so real now," the attractive A student had said.

"Real?"

"A real human being. Fully, you know, fully human. Fulfilled, I suppose." She giggled. "I mean, literally."

"Debbie, we don't need to be crude about this."

"I'm sorry, I know, but how can I explain it?"

"Do you feel special now?"

"Well, no—yes, I mean—not special, just not what I was before."

"What? A virgin?"

"Mrs. Carr, please, it's not that black and white—or stupid. I mean, it's like I've risen to another plane of existence."

"Oh, come on, Debbie, 'Please' yourself. You've just done what millions—billions of people do every day."

"I know—that's just it! I feel like I've finally entered the stream of humanity, that I'm no longer this—this neophyte, this human trainee, this—this ungainly half human."

"Debbie, you are very much intellectualizing the simple fact that you got yourself laid."

"No, Mrs. Carr, you don't understand. There's nothing intellectual about it. It's pure feeling."

"Then you're romanticizing it."

"Well, shouldn't I?"

Allison had had no answer for that, for if you could not romanticize sex, then maybe it was just slapping wet flesh and somewhat embarrassing to think about after all. But, still, there were practical matters to attend to.

"Donna, why have you come to me with this—revelation?"

"Well, I need to know how to get on the pill."

"Why don't you ask your mother?"

"Are you kidding? She would fucking kill me!"

Sex was so common. And yet it made one feel so unique. And false though it may have been, Allison was determined to retain the feeling for as long as possible.

But look, Allison pointed out to herself, that woman in front of the drug store with the hips wider than her bust, no chin, a rather prominent overbite, and a head of hair that would drive any self-respecting mop into a salon, sucking on a cigarette and swigging a Coke—surely sex is not a common experience in her life. Allison had a moment of elevation pleasant to experience. Then, three doors past the drug store, she saw a young woman with a beautiful body, much of it exposed, walking to her car. The concept and implications of the slang word "slut" came immediately into Allison's mind. "Not nice, Allison," she said to herself. "Not a nice thing to think at all." Still, she wanted to doubt, and so she did, that either woman had ever experienced the quality of love-making she had, just a short time ago, been privileged to have experienced. Not bad for an old broad.

When she got to her storage facility, she had planned just to retrieve her old address book and leave. But instead, she sat in her chair, the battery-operated reading lamp beside her, surrounded by her books, and thought: This was the intended landscape of my future.

After an adult life of uncontrolled input into her brain of the needs, looks, thoughts, quirks, and desires of her giant husband, her adopted dumb child, her many "daughters," and numerous other entities essentially as foreign to her as she was to them—despite this vaunted interconnectedness of all life—she had opted for full retirement. Not just from her profession, the employment that paid her wages, but from her life, her life story, which she had found to be somewhat less than a page-turner as she hit her mid-fifties. It shocked everyone. Jim never understood her decision and never would. She knew he continued to hope that it was just a phase—that's what he insisted on calling it—as if she was a rebellious teenager. Even when the divorce became final, he would not fully accept it, even after the fifty-percent diminution of his assets. In her retirement, Allison had planned to gain control over the input into her brain. She would allow in other stories, many and various stories, stories of tragic tone, if compelling, and stories of comedic lightness if the light had a bite of either style or substance. And in all cases, stories wherein pages demanded to be turned so that Allison could ignore the fact that the pages of her story did not. She understood some might call this ultimate escapism, a divorce not just from Jim but also from the world, from reality. But she did not care. Reality was what the brain made of all the input it received. Each brain will only last some seventy-six point-something years on average in the United States of America in a universe that is maybe midway in its story of some thirty billion years. Does it truly matter what reality an individual brain of such short duration experiences? But if it's a page-turner, that's the key; if one page demands that you progress to the next, then it matters. What could make a brain happier? As Allison sat surrounded by the books that had the pages she loved to turn; as she wrapped herself with the input she had wanted to be the reality she thought would make her brain the happiest, was it not ironic that she was now contemplating the touch and feel of the hide-bound volume of the story of an artist that she was planning—magically—to jump into and share and influence? As if she was some kid in a kid's book about a kid jumping into a kid's book to have adventures, the whole thing being a Library Association-approved metaphor for the adventure of reading.

What was the first adventure? A sexual escapade. She had not expected this story to have—as they used to say—blue sections. But maybe that was what makes a page-turner a page-turner—jaw-dropping surprises along the way. Allison enjoyed the smile that the happy face muscles made. Where would it lead, though? Given certain circumstances of biological reality, what outcome could there be but one of a final sad disappointment? Ah, but if lessons are learned? Bullshit! Sad is sad. A disappointment is a disappointment. The key will be not feeling like a victim and not getting bitter. You did not jump into this story for the blue parts; you did not know there would be blue parts, so concentrate on the main thread of the plot you thought would be the exciting part: Frank, the undiscovered artist, and you, the far-seeing discoverer. Everything else is just filler, right? Literally! Hey, no need to get crude about it.

As Allison drove away from her storage facility and through Rubenton towards the interstate that would take her to Leech Beach Road, she found a bit of that thread lying abandoned by the roadside. It was a small warehouse vacated long ago by some small manufacturer, now looking for someone to fill its emptiness. Or so the FOR LEASE OR SALE sign indicated. There was a phone number on the poster, and she pulled up to a nearby phone booth to call it.

"I'm interested in your warehouse on Green Street," she told the man who had answered the phone.

"Fine. Why don't we set a time to meet tomorrow, and I'll be happy to show it to you?"

"I want to see it now."

"Well, I'm just sitting down to supper. Can't this wait?"

"By the look of the property, it's been waiting a long time to be occupied."

"Well, times have been tough," the man apologized.

"So why would you pass up any opportunity? Tomorrow, I may not want it."

"Well—okay. I'll be there in fifteen minutes."

And he was. The man, Stan Clinton, opened the building and started to give its history, but Allison was not at all interested. She just wanted to see how much space there was inside.

"If I lease it, will you make alterations?"

"Well, it depends. What do you want?"

"A skylight."

"A skylight?"

"A big one."

"Well, I don't know; that might cost a lot."

"And can someone live here? Could you, say, build a living space into a corner?"

"Well, the zoning laws would have to be dealt with, and the cost—"

"Maybe I should just buy the building. Would that be easier for you?"

"Well, certainly it might—"

"Give me a good price then."

"Well. We've been asking—"

"How long has this place been a burden on your mind, Mr. Clinton?" Allison said, having no patience for dickering. "How long has it been a millstone around your neck? Longer than you would have liked, I'm guessing. So, take whatever price you're thinking, Mr. Clinton, and subtract the peace of mind I'm offering you and don't you dare insult my intelligence."

Stan Clinton stopped and thought and did a bit of figuring in his head and did not insult Allison Carr's intelligence.

YOU AND I (I)

Chapter the Fifth

Major Philip McFadden took seriously his duty to read and consider *What Price Glory*. It was a duty not because Austin had commanded him to read it; Austin had no command authority over him. But because he had given his word that he would. As old-fashioned as it might seem, especially in the civilian world he now inhabited, Major Philip McFadden considered his word his bond, and the fulfillment of a bond was a duty.

The Major sat down in his room and opened The Best American Plays of the 1920s, where What Price Glory began under the heading of ACT I and the sub-heading of SCENE ONE. Immediately the sense of oppression that can occur when one is doing one's duty came over him in an unpleasant and persistent series of waves. He was not used to reading much except for, professionally, battlefield reports, company readiness reports, discipline reports, manpower reports, recommendations for commendations, armament manuals, the Stars and Stripes, and, of course, orders from his commanding officers. For pleasure, he read a few battlefield memoirs, some soldier biographies, histories of wars recent and ancient, the New York Times, and, now and then, just for a bit of relaxation, mysteries, usually of the Hard-boiled Detective or Police Procedural variety. He had never read a play before and found it difficult to distinguish between the description of the action and the words spoken by the characters.

Assessing the problem, the Major decided to look at the text as if he was looking at the markings on a battlefield map. That allowed him to understand the script as a mechanical entity of various parts—some in italics, some capitalized, some in brackets. Once he had accomplished this, the Major began to read the play with more fluidity, except for the abrupt stops he would come to when he had lost the sense of which character was doing the talking. Applying discipline, he trained his eye and mind not to skip the capitalized character names by saying them aloud, then reading their dialog silently. If anybody had been able to observe him at this time, they would have seen a middle-aged man unconsciously emphasizing his healthy body by sitting straight back in a wingback chair, holding in one hand a small paperback book in front of his face and seemingly chanting, although with no perceivable rhythm:

FLAGG   QUIRT FLAGG   QUIRT FLAGG   QUIRT FLAGG   QUIRT   FLAGG QUIRT FLAGG KIPER FLAGG   QUIRT SOCKEL QUIRT.

Only the sudden intoning of CHARMAINE brought some musical sense to the recitation.

After whipping the text into shape, it still took the Major three or four more readings before he understood the play.

He found What Price Glory a bit strange. The main characters, Captain Flagg and First Sergeant Quirt were both familiar and foreign to him, although foreign was not a sufficient word. Antique? Ancient, maybe? No, those were overstatements. Antique suggested equipment, uniforms, and armaments in display cases in musty military museums. Ancient had the scent of texts translated from Greek or Latin, but not this text of wartime bravado among homogenous white male soldiers doing not their duty but just their job, which they seemed to both hate and love. No, not antique, not ancient, not even antiquated, but certainly not of today's modern fighting men from diverse—if mainly poor—backgrounds, doing not just their job but their duty and considering it an honor. Black and white, he suddenly thought, it is like a black and white film! That's what it is like. Close to today, but without the freshness of color. Once he got that image into his head, he sat back, relaxed, and reread the play with a proper fluidity, reeling it out in his head, the words on the page almost disappearing, obscured by the black and white images in his mind. After this last read of the play, he set it down, realizing that he had enjoyed the experience.

The next morning, when the Major entered the dining room carrying The Best American Plays of the 1920s along with his New York Times, he saw Austin O'Brien engaged in conversation with an attractive woman he had previously noticed. Trudy, the young waitress, came up to him with her usual bright smile, greeted him, and took him to a table. Although she did not need to, she inquired whether he would like a cup of coffee; he replied crisply, "Very hot, please." Trudy positioned him, or, possibly, he set himself, in a chair that faced the window, allowing him to look out at the ocean, not allowing him a view of the rest of the dining room, including Austin. There was no way for them to catch each other's eye, which, for the moment, made the Major comfortable, for he would not have wanted to intrude on the conversation between Austin and his guest, a conversation that he could hear was continuing. Hear, but not listen to, as the words of Austin and Pattie Heatherton (who was, of course, the woman) came over to him in waves of senseless sound except for occasional words clear in meaning. Words such as No! Really? Wonderful! And, oddly, Hairy-butt.

This conversation mingled with other sounds to create an aural environment very familiar to the Major, who had spent many years having breakfast in communal dining rooms always infused with the same mix of muted and sharp sounds: human voices hushing words, few of which were distinguished; serving staff moving, dashing, whooshing by as the fabrics they wore rubbed together in murmurs of urgency; sharp, clean protrusions of sound puncturing the air as ceramics clunked ceramics and metal clinked metal, all in a bubble of warmth and inviting scents.

"Here's your coffee," Trudy said as she put the cup and saucer on the table. "Julio already has your breakfast going. It'll be out in a moment."

"Thank you," the Major said, again with a crisp fold to his voice.

"You're welcome!" Trudy said, bouncing her own.

The Major took a sip of the coffee. It was as hot as he wanted it to be, and the Major appreciated that. He picked up his copy of the New York Times and noted the articles he would read first, but he did not feel like reading right now. So instead, he looked out at the ocean, which was the same as usual in its stretch towards the horizon, in its insistent, wet clawing at the shore. Why did an old Army man in retirement gravitate to the ocean? Because he was an old Army man in retirement—he had fought no battles on the sea.

After his breakfast had come and he had consumed it, as well as several front-page articles in the New York Times and three pieces on the op-ed pages, the Major was taking the first hot sips of his just refreshed coffee when he heard, "Philip." His mind noted the sound, but he did not respond until "Philip?" came at him from a slightly different angle as Austin thrust himself into the Major's field of vision.

"Oh! I'm sorry." The Major stood, not quite at attention, but in formal greeting.

"Lost in thought?" Austin asked, amused again to receive such respect.

"No, uh, actually, I didn't recognize my name."

"You did ask me to call you Philip."

"Yes, of course, it's just, I've been so used to being addressed according to my rank."

"Oh. May I sit?"

"Yes, of course, please."

They sat, settled in, and adjusted for gravity.

"So," Austin began, "in the Army, are you always referred to by your rank? When you're off-duty, can't people call you by your name? You know, I mean, fellow officers, peers, not the, you know, what would you call them, the grunts? Friends, I guess I mean."

"Yes, certainly, but—I didn't have that many friends."

The Major revealed this interesting fact with a little smile; the first Austin had seen coming from him. Was there a twinkle in the Major's eye as well? It passed so quickly; Austin could not tell. Nodding toward The Best American Plays of the 1920s, Austin said, "I notice you have the book; I was wondering...."

"Yes, I finished it. I read it. Here," the Major reached into his coat pocket, "I wrote you some notes," and pulled out several sheets of yellow legal-pad paper folded neatly in half and handed them to Austin.

Austin took the papers, unfolded them, and saw on them a dense text of printed words written in a neat hand, headed by the title: NOTES ON WHAT PRICE GLORY BY MAJOR PHILIP A. MCFADDEN (RET.).

"I'm sorry; I hope it's legible. I haven't gotten myself a computer yet. I keep meaning to."

"Legible? It's beautiful. I can't wait to read it."

"Well, I—I hope it'll help."

"Did you like the play?"

"Well ... uh ... yes, but with certain provisos, I go into there, mainly concerning—"

"Look, I've been sitting here all morning having breakfast; you too. Why don't we get up, stretch our legs, walk over to the theater, and we can talk?"

"Uh, okay. Fine."

They left The Briers, walked out into the morning chill, and started down the boardwalk towards the Stafford Theatre. Neither said anything at first, so the moment could not help but be awkward. Then, finally, Austin said, "This is the kind of morning people use to call bracing."

"Yes, I suppose so," the Major said.

"Personally, I just call it cold," Austin continued, hoping for another smile.

"Well, it's cool, certainly," the Major said, not smiling. "Certainly not warm. A lot of moisture, of course, being by the ocean, giving you that wet cold that can be, I suppose, a more negative type of cold."

"Oh yeah—certainly."

The Major suddenly stopped walking. They were in front of the tattoo parlor, but that was not what was taking the Major's attention. Instead, everything was; the whole of their surroundings, which the Major took in by little twists of head and body. "Funny," he said.

"What?"

"I've been here over a month, and this is the first time I've walked down the boardwalk."

"Really? What have you been doing all this time?"

"Well, settling in, I suppose, certainly. I've made some trips to town, set up bank accounts, bought a few things."

"What did you buy?"

"Paper, pens, magazines, vitamins, and stuff. I take vitamins."

"But no computer."

"No—no, I haven't gotten around to that. Nor clothes, for that matter. I have a rather limited civilian wardrobe. I need to buy some clothes."

"Ah, yes. Since I got here, I've been buying a lot of things online. Rubenton is not really a shopper's paradise."

"No, I imagine not."

"So, shopping online might be a good idea for you."

"Yes, certainly."

"But you'll need to get that computer first."

"Yes, of course. I'll go tomorrow."

Austin wasn't sure whether he should start walking again, for the Major continued just to stand, happy to be receiving, it seemed, all the impressions his senses could soak up. Finally, Austin took a chance and moved forward and was rewarded with the Major falling in step.

They entered the theater through its lobby; Austin started to lead the Major to his office when he suddenly stopped and turned to him. "Hey, look, before we sit down to talk, would you like to see the stage? We're just putting in the finishing touches. I'm very proud of it."

"Certainly."

Austin, leading the Major into the theater, led him into a deep black.

"Oh, shit! I forgot. The lights, uh, I've got to turn them on from the lobby. Be right back, don't move." Austin left, leaving the Major in the dark.

The Major stood there, noting the smells of new construction, the lingering smell of cleaning fluids, and the deadness of sound. Then, suddenly, as if at the point of creation or the birth of a bright idea, there was light, and he saw before him rows of uniform seats lined up in an orderly, if not military, fashion, leading down to an area where there arose a stage, an elevated flat plane of possibilities. It was an unusual space with an atmosphere breathable but not typical to him. It gave him an odd feeling of comfort. Not a cold comfort, despite being alone and in an empty space, nor a warm, welcoming comfort; it was somewhere in-between, a comfort that was just comfortable.

Austin bounded back into the theater. "Isn't it just great! Isn't it just—just marvelous? I hate using a word like that; it's just so—so—well, you know, but—" Austin stopped and took a breath. "There's nothing like an empty theater. I sometimes prefer an empty theater to one with a packed house and wonderful actors doing a great play on stage. It's the difference, I guess, between aspirations and realizations, hope and fulfillment. Am I getting too philosophical for you, Philip?"

The Major looked at Austin; the term "eager young chap" whispered from far away. Where did that come from, he wondered. A book? No, it was a bunch of them, a whole series that he had read as a boy about the adventures of time-traveling Boy Scouts. He had not given those books one thought in thirty years. One of the scouts was Jack. The others used to say: "Jack, you're an eager young chap." It was light camaraderie kidding from his fellows. Still, it had perfectly described Jack, the eager one, the gung-ho one, the one always ready for adventure, pushing ahead despite facing the hordes of Genghis Kahn; the conundrum of the Black Death; or the viciousness of the Dalton Gang. He had liked those books. He particularly liked Jack.

"It's always certainly good to express a passion," the Major said, "I—I suppose."

Austin smiled at that. Then he said, "Well, come on, I'll take you to the office."

When they got to the office, Austin gestured towards the futon couch as a place for the Major to sit, then crossed over to his desk. The Major looked down at this strange hybrid piece of furniture sitting low to the ground. It was not the Government Issue he was used to. Nevertheless, he did his best to sit down on it with as much military bearing as he could muster. By the time Austin settled behind his desk, he was greeted with a view of the Major sitting on the futon, his back ramrod straight, his feet flat on the floor, and his knees practically parallel with his cheekbones. Austin couldn't help but chuckle, and he quickly made an apology and an offer, "I'm sorry, Phillip. Would you be more comfortable in my chair?"

"Yes, I think so, if that would be alright."

"Yes, certainly, certainly."

Austin sprang to his feet and tried to ignore the Major struggling to his.

"I'm afraid those futons weren't made for—well, for people of your height. They're more kind of a, you know, college kids-first apartments-lounge around kind of furniture."

"Why do you have one, then?" the Major asked.

"Oh, uh, well—it was a gift. You don't turn down any gifts when you're in my position, trying to run something new in the arts."

"Oh."

"The arts are always struggling. It's a never-ending battle."

"I see. Too bad the arts couldn't have the budget of the Defense Department."

"Oh, yeah, wouldn't that be nice!"

The Major sat down on Austin's chair with great dignity; Austin plopped himself down onto the futon couch.

"It's actually very comfortable once you get used to it," Austin said.

"I'll have to try it again sometime," the Major replied with that little smile.

"Well, you know, you don't have to. Futons are definitely a matter of personal choice."

Silence came upon them again, not quite awkward, but certainly not comfortable, as the Major took a moment to look around the office. Austin had hung pictures of himself in various roles, and the Major's eyes moved to them.

"You're an actor as well," the Major said.

"Oh, sure. That's how I started. I mean, in the theater, you wind up doing everything. I've been an actor and director; I've built sets, help run the lights."

Some of the pictures were from television roles.

"You were on Sgt. McKennen?"

"Oh, that was just a guest shot. I did three of them."

"The service appreciated that show."

"Well, you know, it had a lot of cooperation from the Army; they were, well, you know, it was practically a weekly recruitment poster."

"It did some good, yes, I believe so."

"But it was, you know, it was a good show too. It was pretty good drama."

"It—missed certain things."

"Really?"

"But it was meant to be just entertainment, I suppose."

"Well, yes, sure, but, you know, it strived for accuracy. I know that because one of the producers was a good friend, not to mention Ben Alyn, who was the second lead. I've done several plays with him also. They used to talk about how hard they worked at accuracy."

"Yes, well, accuracy—can be—a fluid concept—battlefield casualty reports, for example. Usually precise when reporting on the death of your men, each number in the count counting for a man you, at the least, respected. But a count of the—dead heads of the enemy, often left much open to interpretation."

"Why was that? You couldn't get to all the bodies to count them?"

"There were those logistical problems, certainly. But when reporting on the enemy's dead, you tried to paint a pretty picture of carnage."

Austin could feel his mouth open. It was not really what the Major said but how he had said it. "God, that's, uh, that's a wonderful way of putting it: 'To paint a pretty picture of carnage.' I'm sorry to be getting off the subject, but I just appreciated that as, well, hell, as a literary turn of phrase, I guess."

The Major did not know how to respond, so he shrugged his shoulders slightly.

"But as long as we're talking literature here, let's get back to the play. I mean, what did you think of its accuracy in portraying the, you know, the fighting man of World War One?"

"The accuracy was—adequate. And I enjoyed the play. I found it interesting that it portrayed the generation of soldiers that came just before my father's."

"Your father was a soldier?"

"Oh yes. Career."

"Was he an officer?"

"Non-commissioned officer. His highest rank was Master Sergeant."

"So, this being close to your father's time, did you think maybe it was something like your father's time?"

"I wondered about that. The soldiers in this play—Flagg and Quirt—you didn't get much information on their background, but you got the feeling, I suppose you would say, of them. And I don't know how, which I found interesting because nothing was, as I said, detailed about their backgrounds, and yet I somehow got the feeling that they had both been men from—from the streets, I guess. You know, normal Joes, maybe street toughs, bad boys at one time, who found a place in the Army, a—a home. Well, that was very much my father. But maybe I'm just reading that into it."

"Partly, but probably partly not. That is the beauty of drama. It can tell you so much by implication."

"Implication?"

"Yes."

"I'm used to cut-and-dried facts stated in a clear and precise manner."

"And what did those facts ever tell you?"

"What do you mean?"

"Did they ever tell you the Truth?"

Yes, the Major was going to answer, or possibly, Of course, or an unequivocal, Yes, of course. Something, though, stopped him.

Austin filled the pause.

"You know, the power of art is that it can give you truths, even if the facts presented are not so cut and dried. And they're never going to be clear and precise. That's why I need your help on What Price Glory. The authors have done their job; you read it and, through their implications, got the truth about Flagg and Quirt. But that's on the page. That's just a starting point for me as an actor and director, for I have to interpret what's on the page. I could destroy the truth by not understanding the facts that are underneath. Do you understand?"

The Major said he wasn't sure but would like to try. That pleased Austin.

Austin and the Major continued their conversation throughout the morning. The Major was never less than his ramrod self, sitting at the desk. Austin was as comfortable as a cat on the futon couch, sometimes with his long legs flung out, resting on the floor; sometimes folded and tied as he sat like an old movie Indian or an old Indian yogi; sometimes tucked under him. The Major couldn't help but notice that it was a somewhat feminine manner. Austin would never have guessed, but the Major viewed and noted all these changes in Austin's position and took much pleasure in doing so. Austin wore jeans, and a faded blue denim shirt open several buttons down; his hair had no discipline except that which it naturally fell into. As he spoke with passion, often with a smile, crinkles shot out from his eyes like beams of light and energy. "Eager young chap is ol' Jack." The Major had always liked Jack.

After agreeing to be a part of the production, to take an active role in advising Austin, the Major got up to leave. Before he did, though, he quickly scanned the books on Austin's shelves.

"Are these all plays?"

"Many of them. There's also books on stagecraft, stage direction, how to act for fun and profit, you know, that sort of stuff."

"Can I borrow some plays?"

"Of course. As many as you like."

Without asking for recommendations, the Major grabbed two or three books, then five or six, and finally 10. With some of the books being anthologies, the Major had thirty plays in hand. He caught Austin's amusement. "You really don't mind."

"No, of course not. I'm thrilled."

"I promise to return them."

"Don't worry about it. I know where you live."

"Yes—certainly," the Major said, that smile blinking. Then he said goodbye and left.

Over the next several weeks, the Major divided his time between his room and reading; and the theater and observing.

The reading was revelatory of things good and bad. The stories that played out on the stage he had constructed in his mind moved him often, made him laugh, or, just as often, perplexed him and daunted him. One play might attract him; the next might repel him, sometimes for the subject matter, sometimes for a particular quality or lack of, that did not meet a standard he found himself developing. One of the plays was by Shakespeare, not one of the more famous titles. It was a comedy, or so the introduction stated. Not two pages could he get through, and he put down the play, disturbed. Wasn't this man the greatest playwright of all time? And if so, and if he couldn't understand him, well, then, what did that say about him? At one point, in the theater, during a break when Austin was auditioning Rubenton High acting students for the smaller parts, the Major was bold enough to mention this. Austin smiled and told the Major not to worry about it. Shakespeare could not be read cold, he was practically a foreign language, but one easy to master with a little study. After this production, Austin would happily take him in hand and guide him into Shakespeare if the Major wanted.

Walking back to The Briers, the Major was excited over the prospect, with an almost kid-like enthusiasm. As he walked into the hotel, Mrs. Briers noticed this. "Hello, Major, you're looking bright and chirpy." "Really?" the Major said. "I have never in my life been so described, Mrs. Briers." "Must be the sea air," Mrs. Briers suggested. The Major only nodded at this thought and headed towards the stairs but stopped and turned back. "You know," he said, catching Mrs. Briers' attention. "It may be the sea air, but it just as well might be the wonderful, home-like atmosphere you've managed to create here, Mrs.

Briers." Mrs. Briers, taken aback with delight, said, "Why thank you, Major, that's probably the nicest compliment I have ever received." "Oh, I doubt that. But it is a sincere one. Have a nice day, Mrs. Briers." "How can it now be anything but, Major?"

Waiting in the room for the Major was Waiting for Godot. At breakfast that morning, he had finished The Odd Couple. He hoped this Waiting for Godot would be as funny. He found that it was not. After a page or two challenging to move through, he set the play aside, right next to Shakespeare, as if he would also ask Austin about this Beckett. After a moment, though, staring at the book as if it was staring at him, something made him pick it up again. He read that the play was only from the 1950s, not so long ago, not so foreign. He started to read again. As complicated as it was, tiring as it was, once finished, he immediately began rereading it. Implications, he was looking for the implications. For his third reading, he read out loud.

Not just the names of the characters, not just ESTRAGON and VLADIMIR and POZZO and LUCKY, but their dialog, their words, what they had to say; so easy to understand, so hard to get—but it was fun. He was amused. He began to like these characters, slovenly and dirty though they were. He also saw his mother straddle a grave (hers? his?) as she gave birth to him. Hell, how do you repair such despair? Like Estragon and Vladimir, he found himself standing in the middle of his room, still and not moving—and yet going on.

The next day, as the Major sat in the theater and watched Austin coach Trudy, the young waitress from The Briers, in the French accent she would have to use while playing Charmaine, an idea struck the Major. It was wild and stupid and impossible, but he could feel his heart beating faster over the thought. He wanted to share it with Austin, but not here in a theater filled with the young people from the high school. Pattie Heatherton was there as well. She was a woman the Major did not like. He did not quite know why, but when Trudy had made, quietly, a disparaging remark about the woman, he found himself, to Trudy's delight, nodding in agreement.

The day was wrapping up when Austin called everybody to gather around him on the stage for an announcement. The Major continued to sit in the back of the theater, where he usually sat. Austin called him up and said he would find this interesting. The Major stood on the stage for the first time since coming to the theater. The view from there, down onto the empty seats, intensified his feeling over the wild, stupid, and impossible idea.

"As you all know, I have not yet cast the role of Quirt," Austin began his announcement. "That's because I've been waiting for a confirmation from my first choice. Well, that confirmation came in this morning, and I'm thrilled about it, and I want to thank Philip—"

"What!" The Major was scared that Austin was talking about him, all could see that, and there was some laughter.

"No, no, Philip, I'm not casting you. You just gave me the idea of who to cast."

"I did," the Major said, perplexed.

"Remember that first day in my office when you looked at some of my performance photos."

"Yes, certainly."

"Remember picking out the one from Sgt. McKennen"

"Yes, you said—"

"I said that Ben Alyn, who played Captain Goodman in that series, was a friend of mine, which he is. Well, after you left, I suddenly thought he'd make a perfect Quirt. Not only that but with his association with Sgt. McKennen, it's a marketing dream."

"Are you saying," one of the high school boys said, "that Ben Alyn is going to play Quirt here?"

"That's what I'm saying," Austin said with a grin.

There were wows, cheers, excitement, and not a little wonder among the cast and crew. Sgt. McKennen had been a long-running hit show; Ben Alyn was famous because of it. Famous—and he would soon be standing on the very same stage they were now standing on themselves.

"Oh, Austin," Pattie Heatherton said, coming to his side, sliding her arm in his, "this is wonderful, fantastic. I don't know what to say. Except, what's it going to cost?" Pattie, taking on the role of producer, was beginning to worry about such things.

"Equity minimum. But don't worry, Ben has agreed to turn around and donate his salary to the theater. We'll just have to name the lobby after him or something."

There was applause and agreement that Austin had reached a near-God status, an elevation he was comfortable with.

The day was over, and everyone started to drift out of the theater, leaving Austin, Pattie, and the Major, who was about to say goodbye and leave when Pattie started poking fun at Austin by poking his belly, which had begun to expand lately.

"I know; it's the damn good food at The Briers," Austin said. "Not to mention all the snacking I do around here."

"Well, what are you going to do about it? Is Flagg described as having a potbelly? Not to mention its effect on, um, other roles you might want to play."

"We could jog on the beach," the Major said.

Austin and Pattie looked at him.

"I've been thinking of starting. I've been thinking that I've been far too sedentary since my retirement. I've noticed a problem with my clothes, so I was going to start. If you want to join me, we could run and do several exercises that are very good for toning up. I could have you looking like a soldier in no time."

"Oh, that's a great idea!" Pattie said with the easy enthusiasm of the non-participant.

On the conceptual level, Austin agreed that it was an excellent idea. He just was not sure he wanted to be involved in its execution. He suddenly saw early gray mornings of exertions and much sweat produced despite the cold.

It was a prescient vision made completely flesh the following morning and many mornings after that until Austin, as they finished up a run on their fifteenth straight day, begged for a day off. The Major acquiesced and said that from now on, they would only run five days out of seven and do the complete program of exercises he had instituted on only four days. Austin was grateful and expressed it between deep breaths.

"But admit it," the Major said. "Don't you feel much better now? Don't you have much more energy?"

Austin admitted it, for it was true.

"Listen, uh," the Major said, "I want to ask you for a favor in return."

"Ah," Austin said, "but I did not ask for this favor. It was imposed upon me."

"Certainly. But I'm going to ask a favor anyway."

"Of course."

The favor had to do with the wild and stupid and impossible idea that had struck him that day, two weeks before, when he sat in the theater watching Austin work with Trudy. The Major had held it in abeyance while he and Austin got back into shape, running across the beach's wet sand, jumping and squatting, and sitting up to a rhythm shouted out by the Major in the voice that the Army had so well developed. The idea, though, had never left his mind and never failed to engender those same feelings he had felt in the theater when it was newly wild and stupid and of something he knew he could not do, and yet...

"I want to write a play."

Austin, who was still being melodramatic in his efforts to catch his breath, stopped the performance and stood up straight to stare the Major in the eyes, now breathing in effortless.

"Really?"

"I've actually—since I got here—I've been working on a book. It is about the soldier in history. Although, there are parts that have become more like a memoir, and other parts that are pure think pieces. It's all over the map, out of control, and messy. Disorderly, I'm afraid, it's become disorderly."

"You don't feel in command of the facts anymore."

"Yes, certainly, that's it. And then, after reading all your plays and watching the process of you directing the play and seeing it up there for real, well, I guess, I just got to wondering—"

"If you could work in a form that didn't need you to command the facts but offered some truths that would lead—if you were willing to follow."

"I would never have thought to put it that way."

Austin smiled. "I think it's a great idea. What do you need from me?"

"I don't know how to answer that. I just know I need some help."

"You need a sounding board."

"Okay."

"Possibly a mentor."

"Certainly."

"You need someone who will offer his judgment but not be judgmental."

"That sounds about right."

"Well, I'd be more than happy to fulfill that function, Philip, more than happy."

"How do I get started?"

"How did you get started writing the book?"

"I sat down at the desk like a good soldier and started writing."

"It's the same thing. Except, you know what, here's what I would suggest: Before you do that, besides these lovely jogs, use this beach for some lonely walks and try to imagine scenes for your characters to play out. I'm assuming you have some characters in mind."

"Some."

"Good, that's a start. Next, take your characters for a walk on the beach—that is my first suggestion. Then when those scenes come to you, get them down on paper. Did you ever buy that computer?"

"No."

"Let's go to town today. There's a computer store there. Let's buy you a computer."

"Uh, well, you're very busy."

"I am swamped, but you know what? I want to do this. Come on, let's go back, get dressed, and—"

"It's early; the store probably won't be open."

"Well, we have to eat first, Phillip," Austin pointed out.

"Yes, that's right, certainly."

"This is exciting, Philip."

"Certainly, yes, I think it may be."

"Maybe nothing; it's exciting, Philip. Hey!"

"What?"

"Give me a smile."

"A smile."

"Yeah!"

"Give me a big smile."

"Any particular reason?"

"Just because I want you to, Philip."

The Major smiled. It was a big smile.

Austin laughed.

"What's wrong?"

"Nothing. It's a great smile, Philip. Come on; I'll race you back to the hotel."

"We've just had a long run."

"I'll race you back to the hotel, Philip, and I'll beat you too!"

"That's unlikely."

"I'll bet you breakfast."

Without another word, without even a beat, Philip took off running.

"Hey!" Austin ran after him.

Philip paid for their breakfast that morning.

When Trudy Andover got home the night she had declared her love to Frank, she did not stay up too late watching TV as she usually did despite having to be at work at six the following day. Instead, she came in, said a quick hello to her parents, and then went into the bathroom to take a short, hot shower for obvious reasons. Then, once she was squeaky clean and dry, she slipped into her polyester-that-felt-like-silk pajamas, climbed into bed, and snuggled down into the purple and lavender of her bedclothes.

She had some thinking to do, and she liked to think in bed. She pulled the blanket and comforter up over her shoulders, tucked the sides under her body, and reviewed a day that she thought was one of the most monumental ones in her whole life.

With some bitterness, she re-ran her failed attempt to seduce Austin in near cinematic detail. Where had she gone wrong? As a strategy, she still felt it was a good one. It's not what you know; it's who you know, she gathered from the many books she had read about Hollywood (if four can be considered many, and if novels by over-made-up, designer-labeled women of manufactured glamour counted). And what better way to know a person than intimately? Get a person to care about you, and then they will care about what you care about—that was logical, wasn't it? That's why Austin was doing it with Ms. Heatherton, wasn't it? He really cares about this theater; Ms. Heatherton is really making it happen for him, so he does it with Ms. Heatherton.

Why else would anyone do it with Ms. Heatherton? Except maybe her husband. But then he has to, doesn't he? Still, Trudy magnanimously thought that I wouldn't have stopped him from doing it with Ms. Heatherton if he had given me a chance. As long as he would care about what I care about while he was getting Ms. Heatherton to care about what he cared about. Trudy was a bit angry that Austin had not given her a chance. How could he have not even given her that chance? That was the real question. Maybe the minute she got into his office, she should have stripped. Perhaps that's what she should have done. But, instead, she had to go and talk about it. Maybe that was the mistake. Guys are so damn visual; look at Frank and his pron. She sometimes thought guys would rather watch it than do it. If she had just walked in, not said a word, stripped—slowly, maybe, nonchalantly, as if she was getting into the role of someone dying in a bed—well, no, the whole death thing might have been a turn-off. No, if she had just stripped, grabbed him, kissed him, not let him talk first, especially about all that shit about how hard actors must work, she could have broken through his—his pose as this great, pure, theater guy thing, and found the man beneath, the one with the cock, that lovely snake that was so easy to charm. After he had been inside her, then she could have gotten him inside her to understand how important it was to her that the world gets a chance to see her because of what a lovely view she was. How could he not have seen it then?

Instead, she got a lecture. She hated lectures, especially one-on-one lectures with the one doing the lecturing using a raised voice. What did that mean? That the person hated her? She hated the thought that anyone could hate her. She even hated the word hate. "Don't use that word," she would tell people when they used it at work. "Hate is such a strong word. Don't use it, don't give hate the strength."

This is why she was always determined to be upbeat at work, to give people smiles, to be cheery, and to make them smile. She loved to make people smile; people should be happy. She hated being sad, mad, angry, and distressed. Come on, people, cheer up! Trudy hated to cry like she cried when she left the theater after she had smacked Austin with his stupid play and ran to her dad's truck and drove, crying, sucking back the snot into her nostrils instead of grabbing one of her dad's old oily handkerchiefs on the seat, wiping tears from her eyes with the back of her hands so she could see the curves of Leech Beach Road. People should not ever have to feel this way. It's terrible, it's wrong, it's dumb, and it hurts.

Cheer up! Cheer up! She could cheer people up; that is what she thought. Just like Cissy McMann had always cheered her up. What a wonderful thing to do for people! And I can do it, I know it, I feel it, inside, as if it was an actual organ, as if it sat there, right next to my heart, beating even more robust with a happy, snappy rhythm; I know that I can cheer up more than just the dining room at The Briers! I just need the entrance, the opening, the opportunity. I just need to be me in front of millions, and the millions will get it. Why couldn't Austin? Why did I fail in this first step? What in the hell got in the way? Now, if it had been Frank...

As Trudy thought his name, she realized several things as she traveled Leech Beach Road—that she had passed up her house a while back, that she was heading towards Rubenton, that she was in love with Frank. Yes, of course, that must be it! I'm in love with Frank, and somehow, I knew it! My mind knew it, my heart knew it, and my heart and mind made me do a lousy seduction on Austin, caused me to fail because—because—of course—I'm in love with Frank!

When Trudy woke up the following day and looked at herself in the bathroom mirror, she contemplated what it meant to be in love with an older man. How interesting did that make her? Did it make her more mature? As if rubbing up against Frank made some of his age rub off onto her? Possibly mature was not the word. Sophisticated maybe; yes, perhaps that was it. She would have liked to be sophisticated and, in tastes a bit more—what was that word, oh, God, she couldn't remember, it was something simple though, something like, like, refried. No! Refined! That was it. Stupid, how could she forget a word as simple as that? Anyway—tastes a bit more refined than her peers, especially those of the male gender, all of whom she had found silly, stupid, and crude. Possibly that was why she had fallen in love with Frank. Frank seemed to know things. Frank seemed to understand things. Frank made her laugh. It was true that he was no Adonis, as he had admitted. It was also true, though, that she did like his love handles; she did not mind that in a man, especially a man who could help her become sophisticated and refined. Already he had an influence. She had looked up Adonis at Rubenton's small but adequate library. The librarian was thrilled. She had not seen Trudy there since Trudy had left high school. Trudy used to come to the public library ostensibly to do her homework but spent most of her time reading movie magazines and checking out Cissy McMann's autobiography, Don't Blame Me, It's Biological! Thirty-two times Trudy checked it out. It was a library record.

"Where can I look up Adonis?" Trudy had asked the librarian.

"Adonis?"

"I think that's the name."

"You mean the character from Greek mythology."

"Yeah."

"Well, you might find it fruitful to look under Greek Mythology."

"Okay. Which is where?"

"Would you like me to get you a basic book on the subject?"

"That would be good."

She read of Venus, accidentally pricked by her son Cupid's arrows, then seeing Adonis and falling in love with him because he was beautiful, it seems, but also because of the prick. Trudy was not quite sure about which was which. In any case, Venus was crazy about Adonis and stopped doing all her usual goddess stuff just to hunt with Adonis, who really liked to hunt. Which was a lot like, Trudy guessed, going to action movies with a guy you liked even if you don't like action movies. But he got hurt by a boar in a hunt, even though Venus had told him to be careful and not hunt the really dangerous animals. He should have listened to her. Because she was smarter, wasn't she? Because she was a goddess. But he didn't. So he got hurt and died. Venus loved him so much that she mixed some nectar with his blood and made some pretty red flowers.

Wow, Trudy thought, I get this—this isn't so hard. Why fall in love with a beautiful but dumb guy who is going to get himself killed doing something stupid? When he's dead, what's left? Nothing but flowers—which will just wilt—better to give yourself to a guy who can give you something more than flowers.

At the time, that "something more" was supposed to come from Austin and would open the door to her life's dream. Now, though—now it was sophistication and refinement from Frank. That can't hurt, can it? That could help her eventually, couldn't it? In reaching her life's dream, right? They're all sophisticated and refined in Hollywood. Frank could run a hot, trendy restaurant while I'm a star!

Her dad would not let her have the truck that day, so she could not rush out after work to see Frank, but she called him on her break.

"Oh, hi," Frank had said. "I'm in the middle of something. Call me later, okay? I'll be home all day."

"Sure."

When she got off work at two, she called again, but there was no answer. She left a message on Frank's voice mail.

"Hi, it's me! Are you busy? You said you would be home all day. Anyway, I was just calling to say hi, to talk. But, um, um, don't call me back, at home, because, well, you know. I wish I had a cell phone, damn it. Dad won't let me get one. I don't know why; I could use my own money. Well, actually, I do know why, because they don't work so well around here, so Dad said to wait until they get better, which, you know, should be soon, but I don't have one now. Anyway, don't call me at home because, you know, I don't want Mom or Dad to answer the phone, and, anyway, I'll call you tomorrow, okay? Bye! Love you!"

The next day when she went on her break, she got Frank's voice mail again. As she also did at two when she called after getting off work.

"You must be busy, uh, running a lot of errands and stuff on your day off. Umm, so I guess I'll see you tomorrow. No, wait a minute—I don't work tomorrow. Um, okay, you know, well, maybe I can get the truck in the afternoon. I'll meet you at your apartment after you get off work, would you like that? I'll call you at work tomorrow, and we'll see. Okay? Okay. Bye!"

When tomorrow came, so did a plan. Trudy remembered that Austin had asked her to "study" this scene from—what's this play called? What Price Gory, or something, to come back in three days to read it with him. And that was today. Of course, she was not going to; she had written off Austin, she had written off the play. But why should she? She quickly read the scene.

Oh my God, this girl is French! What are these guys doing? What war is this? Like wanting to know about Adonis, she suddenly had to know, so she read the whole play. It was kind of okay, she guessed. Austin was right. Charmaine was the only girl in it, so that would be neat. If she could get the role, she would be on stage with all these guys. But did she want to? Yeah, sure, why not? Anyway, it gave her an excuse to go to Leech Beach that day; she could drop by the hotel and say hi to Frank.

Trudy dressed totally cool. She had a low-cut sweater that she liked, so she put that on, and a nice tight skirt. She told her dad that she had to have the truck because she was auditioning again for Austin; she even called it a callback because that sounded professional and important. Her dad had no objections. So she took the truck, drove to Leech Beach, went to The Briers, and went into the kitchen to say hi to Frank.

"Oh, hi," Frank said while checking on an order. "You look great! Wow!"

Julio was there; Julio was amused. Frank moved off to a corner to check on some stock, and Trudy followed.

"Where have you been the last two days?" she asked.

"Yeah, I'm sorry, I got your messages, but you said not to call back."

"Yeah, well...."

"I mean, you were right; I had a lot of errands."

"Well, when can I see you again?"

"Um, sure, drop by after work. I mean, give me some time to get some things done. How about, you know, four o'clock?"

"Okay!"

"Would you like to go out to an early dinner?"

"Really?"

"Yeah, sure."

"That would be great."

"Okay, um, I'll see you—"

"Frank! Your order," they heard Julio call.

Frank took off quickly, "—at four."

"Okay. Bye!"

When she walked out of The Briers and started walking down the boardwalk, she suddenly realized that she had just made a dinner date with a waiter. Was that even lawful? She wondered humorously. Was it strange, weird, odd, peculiar? No, it was fine, it was okay, it was not a waiter, it was Frank, and she was, after all, in love with Frank.

Austin seemed happy to see her.

"I thought maybe you weren't going to come back, and I would have to come after you for that copy of the play."

"Well, I was kind of mad."

"I noticed you haven't waited on me lately."

"No, that's just where you sat."

"Really?"

"Of course; what do you think?"

"So you're not mad now."

"No, of course not."

"But do you understand what I was saying to you?"

"Yeah. So you want me to read?"

"Have you studied the role? Do you understand this character?"

"Uh, sort of. She's a French girl, and she likes these American soldiers, and she wants the captain to take her to Paris."

"Yeah, that's sort of it. Okay, I'll read the part of Captain Flagg."

"Well, I didn't think you were going to read Charmaine."

"I thought you weren't mad anymore."

"I'm not. It was a joke."

"Oh, okay. So, you know where we are starting."

"Yeah, here, where Charmaine '...slips in.'"

"That's it. Okay, let's go."

"Do I have to do it in a French accent because...?"

"No, that's something we can work on later."

After they had read the scene, Austin said, "Okay, fine, okay."

"What does that mean? That—that I was good?"

"Um, no, it means, okay, you've got the role."

"I do?"

"Yeah?"

"So I was good?"

"No."

"Austin, you're mean!"

"You were not good, but you were okay. And if you stop thinking I'm mean, I can make you good, or, at least, good enough."

"I don't want to be just good enough."

"Stop thinking I'm mean and start listening to me."

"Will you promise not to yell at me?"

"No."

"Austin!"

"Look, I am who I am. But if you will listen to me when I speak softly, really listen and try to do what I ask you to do, then there is a good chance we'll never get to the point where I will have to yell at you."

"I've really got the role?"

"Yes, you have the role; you will be Charmaine."

"On the stage?"

"Yes."

"In front of people?"

"Yes."

"Wow!"

"Are you excited?"

"Yes!"

"Take that excitement and make it work for you."

"Okay."

"We're going to have to work hard, you understand."

"Okay!"

Trudy was excited. She did want to work hard, despite not truly knowing what hard work was. For the moment, though, now that she knew she would be Charmaine, she was convinced the hard work would be fun. She wanted to rush back to The Briers and tell Frank this exciting news. But, no, better she should tell him at dinner, at their first romantic dinner.

"How neat," she thought as she drove home along Leech Beach Road. "I'm an actress. I have an older man for a lover. I'm sophisticated!"

When Dmitri's father heard Dmitri would be spending his weekends at Hendrickson's farm and why he just shook his head and left for one of his two jobs. When Dmitri's grandmother heard, she laughed, finding it very amusing. As pissed off as he was over the reactions of his family, Dmitri decided not to avoid this responsibility he had taken on, for even he had enough native wisdom to understand that doing so would only lead to trouble exceeding that which he was in currently.

Dmitri showed up at Hendrickson's farm at the early hour Hendrickson had demanded, surprising Hendrickson, for he had been sure that Dmitri would fail in this first task.

"Do you drink coffee?" Hendrickson asked, offering him a cup.

"No."

"Do you drink tea?"

"Yes."

"Do you want a cup?"

"No."

"Hot cocoa?"

Obstinately, Dmitri was about to refuse this offer as well. But the cold of the morning and the warmth imagined upon hearing the adjective "hot" applied to a taste easily craved swayed him. "Okay."

"Fine. I'll make you the best hot cocoa you have ever had in your whole life," Hendrickson said, receiving only a slight shrug of his shoulders from Dmitri. Nevertheless, Hendrickson fulfilled his claim with no sense of wasted effort in his heart. First, he poured some milk from one of his cows into a saucepan and placed the pan over a low flame on the stove. Then he grabbed a tin of cocoa from a cabinet and set it down on the stove counter. While the milk was heating, neither of them spoke a word. Soon there was steam coming from the milk, which Hendrickson watched with a practiced eye, taking it off the stove at just the right moment. He then took a clean, large earthenware mug and put it on the counter next to the cocoa tin, which he opened and drew from it the required amount of cocoa, stirring it into the steamy milk until it completely dissolved. Next, he opened the refrigerator and pulled out a bowl of cream he had whipped himself. "The secret," Hendrickson said, "to making the world's best hot cocoa is to take a dollop of whip cream and put it into the mug before you pour in the hot cocoa." He followed his own instructions exactly, pouring the hot cocoa into the mug very slowly, moving it in tight circles over a dollop of whip cream, thereby infusing the two yummy elements into each other. Finally, he poured, leaving a little space at the top of the mug. "Then, of course, you put a dollop, maybe two, of whip cream on top of the hot cocoa." He then took, with pride, the mug of hot cocoa and placed it before Dmitri, who was sitting at the kitchen table.

"This is how I always made it for my sons."

Dmitri looked up and said, "I don't like whip cream in my cocoa."

"Shut up and drink," Hendrickson said with a not kidding tone of threat in his voice.

Dmitri did so, his eyes widening at the first taste. When he brought the mug down, he had a whip cream mustache.

Hendrickson chuckled. "Good?"

Dmitri wiped the whip cream mustache off his upper lip with the back of his hand and had to admit, "Yeah, good."

"Chicken shit," Hendrickson said.

"What?"

"You're going to be cleaning out chicken shit."

Hendrickson thought it was only fitting that Dmitri's first chore be the cleaning out of the hen house. Dmitri was unhappy about this but decided to do it without grumbling, fearing more dire consequences.

He entered the hen house with apprehension, convinced that the hens would recognize him, and it is true that when he entered, they did not seem happy to see him. They did not attack en masse, though. Once he had convinced himself that they were not going to, he looked around. He discovered that it was not so much chicken shit that he would have to deal with—although there was much more of it than most people would want to deal with—but all the loose feathers caused by his rash actions scattered throughout the structure. He saw a dirty, filthy, awful stretch of time before him. Nevertheless, he began cleaning the hen house as Hendrickson had instructed and worked without complaint until finished, doing a reasonably good job.

Later that day, he shoveled cow manure. The next day he hacked at weeds.

By the end of Sunday, every muscle Dmitri had was sore, and that evening his grandmother covered him with an old Russian remedy balm and put him to bed early. He slept like the innocent baby he may well have once been.

The following Saturday, he showed up again on time, looking forward to a hot cup of cocoa. In the next weeks, Dmitri did tasks he never thought he would have to and got far dirtier than he thought possible. He talked more to Hendrickson. Hendrickson talked more to him. And it seemed as if a relationship not painful to either was developing.

But unknown to Hendrickson and intimately known to Dmitri, time was just being bided as he waited for an opportunity.

The day after Trudy had declared her love to Frank right after she had made love to Frank, Frank entered his apartment with a towel wrapped around his waist that was still damp from the drying of his and Allison's bodies. As he closed the door behind him, dropping the towel, the phone rang. "Oh, hi," he said to Trudy, who was on the line. "I'm in the middle of something. Call me later, okay? I'll be home all day." He had not wanted to talk to Trudy for various reasons, not the least because he wanted to keep his mind traveling the six panels of the Jesus sextych. It was a trip he was enjoying, and he wanted no detours.

When Trudy called later—a later she had been looking forward to, had watched the clock in anticipation of, and had had many warm

200

feelings about—and got Frank's voice mail, it was not because he was either occupied on the toilet or the victim of a massive heart attack, both of which had made their case in Trudy's mind, but because he was not there. For Allison had showed up at his studio door at one-thirty. Luckily, when she knocked, Frank answered, for she had no idea what apartment he lived in, nor did she have his phone number. But she could not have imagined him being anywhere else.

"Hi!" Frank said, a certain headiness accompanying the greeting.

"Have you had lunch?" she asked with a smile.

He pointed to the remains of a pizza recently delivered.

"Good, then we don't have to waste any time. Come on."

"Where are we going?"

"You'll see."

There was something both exciting and disconcerting about Allison's take-charge attitude. He pleaded the need for a jacket and his wallet and walked her to his apartment to retrieve them. She looked around his single, not quite judgmental, but not quite approving.

"You, uh, managed this space well."

"Well...."

Frank's bed had not been made and was more than a little rumpled.

"Did you have a hard time getting to sleep last night?" Allison asked.

"Ah...."

"Looks like you tossed and turned quite a bit."

"Well...."

"Bachelors are not good housekeepers."

"Normally, I am. But I woke up this morning inspired."

"Really."

"Yeah, I didn't show you my new—"

"When we come back."

"Okay."

She took him in her car to the warehouse she was buying from Stan Clinton, explaining nothing along the way, preferring to remain mysterious, so Frank remained perplexed. His perplexity intensified as Allison confidently withdrew a set of keys from her purse, one of which she used to open the building.

"Come on in," she said, hitting a switch and illuminating the interior with a few bare light bulbs. "Welcome to your new studio."

"What?"

"I'm buying this building. I've already had a contractor and an official from city hall here today. I can get all the permits I want. So welcome to your new studio—and home."

Frank looked around the empty interior of the building that had once stored tiny but vital components of lawn mower engines. A sign on the wall, aged and darkened, said: PETERSON PRECISION PARTS—WE PUT THE PUTT-PUTT INTO ENGINES. It was cold in the building, and there were puddles of water in various spots on the bare, concrete floor. Frank took it all in, unsure what he was feeling if he was feeling, and if he was feeling, he was not sure what he was feeling was proper. All he could manage to say was, "Allison...."

"See that corner over there," Allison pointed to the far-right hand corner of the building, "we can build you an apartment there; we can put in a full bathroom, a kitchen, small but functional, and a living space. Then inside the main part here, which will be your studio, I figured skylights—you'll have to tell us where to get the best light you want. Now, look at those walls; look how big they are. That is where we will hang your work for display. You see, this won't just be your studio; this will be your showroom where we will bring people to show them your art—"

"Allison—"

"It will take a while, of course, to build all this; you won't be able to move in for, I don't know, maybe six weeks, maybe two months, maybe more. But, if you want, you can quit your job now and concentrate on your art. I'll pay your expenses."

What the hell was he supposed to say? What the hell could he say? Suddenly he felt like a kept man, like—could you believe this?—a boy toy. Like George Peppard in Breakfast at Tiffany's. Would he have felt this way if he had not recently had sex with this older woman? A scene of righteous indignation played out in his head: I am not a plaything you can buy! Curse you and your damn money!

Before the sex, though, what had she said? Champion. Allison wanted to be his champion. His knight in a shiny armored truck. Did that make him the damsel in distress? Or did it merely make him an artist with a patron, a once honorable tradition? Indeed Allison was as fine a person as any old pope. But sex had happened, and—and it had been—sublime—and—and hot—hot mamma with a shiny armored truck. So what the hell was he going to say? What the hell could he say? Nothing.

Frank broke out into song instead.

Have you ever seen a dream walking?

Frank accompanied himself with a bit of soft shoe as he gestured towards Allison.

Well, I have.

Then he grabbed Allison in a dancer's embrace and began to twirl her around.

Have you ever seen a dream talking?

Taken by surprise, Allison began to laugh as her legs moved furiously to keep up.

Well, I have.

"Frank!" Allison was both pleading and acclaiming.

I don't know the rest of the lyrics.

Frank spun Allison around, letting her go like a top, striking a pose with his arms out wide.

But what the hell!

Allison stopped and tried to catch her breath under the difficulty of still laughing.

"Or how about this one?" Frank started a combination of ballet and tap, neither of which were competent. Both of which were joyful.

I'm singing in the rain, just singing in the rain!

He jumped and came down with both feet dead center in one of the puddles of water that spotted the floor.

What a glorious feeling.

He skipped and leaped to the next puddle, timing a splash for the end of his song,

I'm happy again!

Again, he ended in a pose, arms wide out, a big smile on his face matching the one on Allison's as she came to him, entered his arms, and wrapped hers around him. And then, in this most unlikely place, among the cold and damp and the ghosts of parts that had put the putt-putt into engines, they kissed.

Later as Frank and Allison sat in a roadside diner drinking coffee and tea, it was time to talk business.

"I don't think I'll quit The Briers right now," Frank said.

"Why not?"

"Well...."

"Don't you want to get started on your work right away? And I'll need your help to plan the conversion of the warehouse."

"Allison, I'm off two weekdays and noon on the three that I do work."

"But your art—"

"I've got a huge filing cabinet of pieces. I won't have any problem starting on the final versions."

"I would have thought you would have wanted your freedom as soon as possible."

"Mrs. Briers has been very good to me. I owe her a lot."

"Yes, but—"

"And two weeks' notice."

"Oh, well, two weeks' notice, of course."

"Well, I want to stay a little longer than that, but when I leave, I want to give two weeks' notice. And health insurance, I mean, they've given me a good health insurance plan."

"Frank, I'll buy your health insurance."

"Well, you see, how is all this going to work? I mean, I know you want to be my exclusive agent, but what does that mean? How do you get your money back?"

"Let me worry about that."

"I'm uncomfortable with that."

"Okay. Well, I haven't really thought it out. I suppose, as your agent, I would take a commission. I don't know how much; I'll check with my friends in the business to see what's standard. I can either assume I will see profit from that, less my expenses or I that can take my commission after deducting my expenses."

"But your expenses are going to be huge."

"I know."

"So when, I mean—I hate these kinds of discussions—when do I see money from my art, you know, as opposed to just from you?"

"Depends how successful you are, I suppose."

"And if I'm a failure."

"Frank, don't worry, you won't be. But if you are, it will be my loss. I'm the one taking the risk."

"I hate words like risk."

"Don't let it scare you."

"I would hate to think you would lose money."

"This is where you need to stop being a nice guy. This is where you must be blatantly selfish and concentrate only on your art. I'll take care of everything thing else."

When Frank got home, Allison was with him. The softness of her hand that had long been in his had given him a great desire to make love to her. She had said that it wasn't necessary, that she knew he would probably be getting up very early the next morning, that he was probably tired. He answered her by taking her by the hand and leading her to his studio. He showed her his latest work. She roared with laughter. He told her his plans for the piece. She opened her mouth in awe over the concept.

"Now, wouldn't you like to make love to the man who's going to do that?"

She nodded demurely, like a young woman just blossoming.

"Plus, I have tomorrow off."

Allison smiled. There was nothing demure about it.

Upon returning to Frank's single to make love, Allison noticed the blinking light on Frank's phone.

"You have a message," she said.

"Oh," Frank said as he looked at the blinking red light that seemed to be saying: TRUDY-TRUDY-TRUDY. "It's probably just my soon-to-be ex-wife. I'll deal with it later."

"Well, you never know when there's an emergency."

Frank said nothing more. He simply began to undress Allison.

The Major walked along the beach with battles in his head. Some were battles fought with comrades-in-arms in well-trained group efforts to destroy before being destroyed. Some of those battles featured bullets that rapidly tore at structures—buildings built by the mind and hand of man—precisely pecking away at concrete utilitarian wholes, reducing them to useless abstract parts. Missing was a consideration of these structures as anything other than objectives or obstacles. All thought that these structures had once been homes, or places of commerce, providing a warm continuity of day-to-day living, were suppressed while explosions of varying degrees piled rubble upon rubble in a cold continuity that eventually converted rubble into dust.

Other battles had no bullets, were classic in their divisions of offense and defense, and some featured mind-to-mind if not hand-to-hand combat.

Some battles were internal. Which side was offending? Which side was defending? Do you plan a big push, a major offensive to conquer the enemy? Or do you sit and abide while you wage a war of attrition?

These were the battles in the sand of Major Philip McFadden. Chaos created; order strived for—the duality of every good soldier.

Emily Briers had received a letter on beautifully embossed heavy-weight paper from the Comstocks saying how pleased their clients had been with all the antiques, all $13,987 worth of them that they had purchased from Fletcher's. Of course, Emily took pleasure in that, and pride, and every other good feeling due her. But the part of the letter that pleased her the most was the Comstocks' detailing of their forthcoming European trip, which Emily would be joining. The trip was still months away, but it had become every Christmas every child had ever waited for while daily declaring that they couldn't wait for it. So it was never out of Emily's mind. The forthcoming trip shared space with details and decisions regarding the hotel's running. With the continuing management training of the desk clerk, Tom. With needed decisions about purchases of new antique stock. And with some modicum of concern for Duncan, who seemed not to be completely himself lately.

"Of course, I'm not myself," Duncan replied when Emily had a moment to ask him about it. "My legs don't work."

"Duncan, your legs have not worked for quite a while now. Like it or not, you're a man whose legs don't work."

"Are you saying I'm a natural-born gimp?"

"I'm saying you reconciled yourself to your situation long ago. Something else is bothering you."

"Don't be fooled by my jaunty surface. I'm half a man, damn it, Emily, I'm only half a man!"

"You weren't last night in bed."

"Oh, yeah. It was good, wasn't it?"

"Except for the fact that I was too tired for it."

"You seemed to perk up all right."

"It was you who perked up. What choice did I have?"

"Tell me you didn't enjoy it."

"I enjoyed it fine, Duncan. Now tell me what the matter is."

"The world is a pool of piss with nothing but turds floating in it."

"Duncan!"

"Well, isn't it?"

"No. The world is, or at least can be, a wonderful place full of grace and beauty."

"Sure, if you spend your time living in the past."

"Are you accusing me...?"

"The past was pretty crappy too, you know."

"Don't depress me, Duncan. There is no reason why there should be two of us in this mood."

"People are little bags of rotting flesh fed by contaminated blood and held up by brittle bones supported by muscles of pure meanness."

"Did you lose money on the stock market today?"

"No, I made thirty-four thousand nine hundred and seventy-four dollars and forty-three cents."

"Surely that's something to be happy about."

"Despite centuries of misinformation on the subject, money will not make you happy. Granted, the lack of money can make you seriously unhappy, and therein lies the confusion. But money, in and of itself, cannot make you happy."

"But surely it can lighten your mood a little."

"Only if you are a little bag of rotting flesh fed by contaminated blood and held up by brittle bones supported by muscles of pure meanness."

"Okay, I'm leaving; I've got things to do."

"That's right, desert me in my hour of need."

"You only need to vent."

"So let me vent."

"I don't have time—"

"Well, who else?"

"Well, if you had some friends—"

"Can't have friends."

"Why?"

"Because people are little bags of rotting—"

"Goodbye, Duncan; I'll see you tonight."

Emily left their suite and escaped to the kitchen to test the new recipe for a cobbler she had found. Then she went over some figures with Tom and then settled down in the subtle light and coolness of Fletcher's, sitting at her desk that Henry T. Malone had handcrafted in upstate New York in 1883. Henry was a God-fearing family man and community leader who took his own life at the age of 57 after the discovery that he was a God-fearing family man in duplicate, also having a family (wife, children, and in-laws) in Lower Manhattan. But his desks were exquisite.

YOU AND I (II)

Chapter the Sixth

Frank had avoided talking to Trudy because he did not quite know what to say to her. Of course, he knew what he should say to her, but in this case, that "should" represented such a cessation of certain sensations that Frank was concerned about his heart breaking over the loss. Nevertheless, he knew he should tell Trudy that it was ridiculous to think that she loved him and that they should end their intimacy. Although, of course, they could remain friends.

Another matter was whether Frank would have had the good sense to adopt this position if his life had not just turned a corner from a narrow dirt path to a potentially wide boulevard possibly paved with gold, which he had no mental room left to consider. As it was, millions of synapses in his lovely spongy self were firing with considerations of Allison. Allison as a muse; Allison as a patron; Allison as his moneybag. And Allison as a sexual entity, used, to be sure, but not used up—just like his car.

Millions of other synapses were sparking to the delight of his art, to projections of inspirations into conceptions on paper then vitally enlarging to spread across surfaces of vibrant canvases. A whole class of neurons enumerated the pairs of eyes other than his that would fall upon these canvases while simultaneously registering predictions of positive reactions while negating any negative ones.

All this mental activity was like a profoundly dark cloud, edging towards black, churning with the action that would bring a storm. Yet, it was not a storm to fear but a storm to anticipate, waiting for the cleansing rain of self-satisfaction, happiness, and joy.

With all this to embrace and look forward to, initiating the proper behavior dictated by that "should" should have been easy.

And yet...

Trudy had walked into the kitchen at The Briers bouncing a bounce different from her waitress bounce. This bounce had a stimulating effect on her mostly exposed breasts and affected in no negative way her smile, her eyes, and a certain glow her skin seemed to have picked up. Frank had not expected to see her that day; he had hoped to receive a phone call, during which Frank would arrange a time when they could speak so that he could do what he knew he should do. He would be subtle in the phone conversation; serious, he would forego any humor and not hesitate to hint that Trudy should prepare herself for doing the right thing. But now, here she was, so corporeal before him, so alive, so breathing steadily in and out, as if it came naturally to her.

So he invited her to dinner.

It was not that he later regretted having done so, as he lamented his forthcoming efforts to control the situation. Changing where they were going to meet, for example. He should not meet Trudy at his apartment, then go to dinner, for she was likely to want to feed upon the nourishment of love first, which could turn into a one-course meal for the evening. Or she might promise a special dessert for when they got back, and with that to look forward to, how could he do what he knew he should do at dinner? And if he did manage to do what he should do at dinner, think of the awkward drive back. No, they needed to meet at the restaurant and be able to leave in separate vehicles. It should be simple and clean—especially the getaway.

Frank decided to leave her a note on his door instructing her to meet him at the restaurant. But why would he do that? It seemed odd unless Frank turned it into something that a lover would do, which would turn it into a cruel trick. But the evening would probably end with Trudy hating him anyway, escaping in tears from the restaurant, running to her dad's truck, and speeding away; he guessed the hate would just have to be a little more intense. So he wrote the note: TRUDY—I DECIDED OUR FIRST DINNER TOGETHER HAD TO BE PERFECT, SO I HAVE GONE AHEAD TO THE RESTAURANT TO ORDER A VERY SPECIAL MEAL AND OVERSEE ITS PREPARATION MYSELF. MEET ME THERE

AT 5. IT'S THE LAMPLIGHTER ON THE ROAD TO BURL CITY. YOU CAN'T MISS IT. UNTIL THEN, FRANK.

He avoided writing "Love, Frank" as that would have been too cruel.

He taped the note onto his door and headed off to the Lamplighter where he did, indeed, intend to order a special meal, which was easy enough, for he had good relations with the staff. The Lamplighter was where he went when he wanted to be the one waited on.

At five o'clock, Frank sat at the best table in the restaurant, satisfied that the fine meal was in preparation and that he would have that, at least, to offer Trudy. He was also nervous and not looking forward to the planned unpleasantness. Nevertheless, it should be done, and he was determined it would be done.

Then Trudy entered—another dream walking. How surreal his life was becoming!

Trudy's hair was different—up, he assumed, piled in some exciting configuration. Her body had achieved an impressive elevation through high-heeled shoes, which she walked damn well in, for she seemed to flow towards him wrapped in a light-loving dress plunging at the neckline, soaring at the hemline, and lovingly clinging to everything in-between. And her face—the face he thought he knew so well—had been restructured through painterly tricks, retaining its slight exotic quality while now becoming mysterious. It was a lovely combination, indicative of a maturation achieved while building the mystery.

Trudy, flushed and excited, breathlessly said, "Hi! I've got to pee. Where's the restroom?"

Frank said nothing, not wanting even to attempt achieving a steady voice, so he just pointed the way.

"Thanks," Trudy said with some of her regular bounce and headed in the direction he had indicated.

Frank closed his eyes. He would have welcomed unconsciousness—yet there were so many beautiful things for his conscious mind to contemplate. Trudy's smooth skin carried a sensual scent, and her hair ran soft and cool to his touch. Her hands, with their long, tapered fingers, so talented with their delicate opposable thumbs, were definitely worth dwelling upon. Her breasts, pliant yet pushy, topped by responsive nipples, were wonders to behold and hold. He loved the lie of her flat tummy. And to lie on it, kissing, licking, and squeezing it. He thought of traveling her legs, never tiring of the trip.

And her mouth, he formed a mental vision of her mouth, always ready to fly into a smile that lit up her eyes. And her full lips bordered a safe harbor offering warmth, comfort, and the classic verities of an oral tradition. One could not discount her lips.

"I'm so excited; I cannot tell you—" Trudy was pulling out her chair and sitting down when Frank stopped her.

"Wait!"

Stopped, she waited, her eyes wondering what for.

"You look great," Frank said.

"Oh, thanks." She completed sitting.

"That's a stunning dress."

"Thanks, it was my prom dress."

"That was a prom dress!"

"Yes."

"I thought they were supposed to be, you know, kind of frilly and— and long, and—and with a corsage."

"Maybe when you went to high school, but this is the Twenty-first century."

"Yes, well, indeed it is."

"Our theme was, 'Sophisticated Ladies and Dashing Gents.' It was my idea."

"In Rubenton?"

"Hey, if not here, then where?"

"Well...."

"But that was high school, you know. I'm out of high school; I don't want to talk about high school—hey, Frank, I got the part!"

"The part?"

"In the play, in Austin's play, he cast me!"

"He did? Well, that—that's great, good for you! And you didn't even have to—"

"—Fuck him. Yeah, I know. But then I couldn't; I told you that. My body knew I was in love with you."

"Well...."

"But I think he must have been, you know, complimented that I wanted to."

"No, Trudy, I don't think—"

"No, I'm not saying that's why I got the part. I'm just saying that Austin didn't wind up hating me or anything."

"Well, of course, he couldn't hate you. Who could hate you?"

"He says I'm not a good actress."

"Oh."

"But he says he can make me one."

"Well, that's good, isn't it?"

"But he's just so mean about it."

"Sometimes the best teachers are," Frank said, quite aware that he had no personal knowledge of this fact.

"But it doesn't matter because I'm determined to become good because, you know, I actually am. I just haven't been able to show Austin yet, I guess, or, maybe, you know, well, it's, you know, I can feel how good I am. I've always been able to feel that. It's just inside me; it's there, as real as, as, you know, anything, this table, you, your shirt, my tits." Trudy grabbed the last-named item and pushed them up.

"Oh, they're real, are they?"

Trudy smiled a smile that combined innocence with sin, a thrilling accomplishment, and said, "Frank, you know they are." Then she leaned in close to him and whispered, "Not to mention aching for your tongue and lips."

Frank drew in a needed bit of breath and said, "I think I'll have the lamb."

"What? Oh, should we order?"

"No, no, we don't have to, not just yet."

"But can we have drinks? I'm celebrating. I need Champagne."

"Champagne?"

"Don't you think? My first role?"

"Yeah, but we're not at my apartment; we're in a public restaurant."

"Frank, look at me. Do you really think they're going to card me?"

It was not an argument Frank could win, nor did he want to, so he ordered Champagne.

After a bottle and a half of the Champagne and a meal that had fascinated Trudy in its sophistication and her first ever after-dinner brandy, Trudy said, "I always hated being a girl."

Frank—who was feeling his head hovering over and just a little bit to the right of his body—was shocked by the revelation. "You? Hate being a girl."

"No, Frank, you know, not a female, you know, a woman. I mean a girl. You know, young."

"Oh."

"I always just wanted to grow up."

"Sort of a reverse Peter Pan."

"Yeah. Maybe that's why I'm attracted to you."

"Because I'm old."

"No! But because you're older, yes, and I'm still, sort of, you know, a girl, and I don't want to be one. So, I want you to make me a woman. I want you to grow me up."

"Grow you up?"

"Yes."

"You seem pretty grown up to me."

"On the inside, Frank, I mean, on the inside. Because you see, this play is just the beginning. I am going to go to Hollywood, and I will be a star. And that's a serious thing; I know that. I need to be a woman, not a little girl, to make that happen. So I don't want to play games; I want to take it seriously. I need a man to keep me serious."

"How do you know I'm serious?"

"Frank, you're funny, and you don't always seem old, and you play around a lot. I mean you—you know—you even make work fun. But I know that's all covering a brilliant man who's pretty darn smart."

"Well, one would seem to follow the other."

"What?"

"Never mind."

"I love you, Frank. Because you're going to be smart for me."

"Well, Trudy, actually—"

"I've got it all worked out. We'll take some time here for me to get good with Austin and for you to grow me up. Then we'll go to Hollywood. I'm sure you can get a job at one of those famous restaurants where all the stars go. And I'll soon be acting. It'll just take that one special part where I can really delight people with me, and then I'll be a star. And then, with that kind of money, I'll buy you a great restaurant, which you'll make the best, and it'll be the hottest one in town, and we'll both be famous. Me like Cissy McMann, and you like that Wolfgang guy, and it will be, you know, a real, adult life of—" Trudy suddenly, with no warning to Frank, and little to herself, yawned a wide yawn. "Gosh—gee—I'm sorry, I must be getting tired."

"I should get you home."

Trudy smiled and leaned close to Frank. "You should get me to bed."

"Trudy—"

214

"Dad thinks I'm having a sleepover with Nancy Pacheco. He still calls them sleepovers. Isn't that cute?"

"But you're so tired."

"Driving the truck back to your place will wake me up."

"Oh, Christ, I forgot. I can't let you drive."

"Can you drive?"

"Of course, I'm a man."

"Then take me to your place and fuck me sober. Then we'll come back here to get the truck."

What other option was there? He took her back to his place. Slowly stripping her out of her prom dress was one of the most exciting things he had ever done. Their sex boarded on lovemaking, and she was wide-awake when it was over, although Frank could have used a nap. They drove back to the restaurant, retrieved the truck, then returned for what sleep they could manage. As Frank was leaving early in the morning to arrive at work at four, he set the alarm so that Trudy could get up in time to get to work at six. He promised he would not be hard on her if she were late.

Driving to work on the pitch-black Leech Beach Road, Frank felt myriad emotions and had a thousand thoughts, not the least being a painful admission that the previous evening he had not done one thing that he should have done.

Harry Ogg was pissed. It didn't change his demeanor much, for so many things in life irritated him that he always seemed pissed. But seeming pissed and being pissed were two different things, and if you didn't understand that as Harry understood it, then you could never get life by the nuts and squeeze them to your satisfaction.

Harry had always been a satisfied man. To have irritations was to have standards, and if you had standards, you were superior. If you didn't have standards, then you weren't irritated about all the things in life you could be irritated about, and if you weren't irritated about them, that meant you were nothing but a wuss, a wimp, and a non-entity. Harry liked that last word—his wife had taught it to him.

His wife is what he was pissed about currently. For years his wife had irritated him without pissing him off; that was just part and parcel of the married state, especially his marital state, having married a strong woman—what a mistake! Although, if he was going to be honest (not a condition he preferred), it took a strong woman to put up with an ogre; anything less, he probably would have flattened into a non-entity by now. And the idea of having a non-entity for a wife frightened him—it might be contagious. Still, being married to Pattie had been a trial. Like having an extra steering wheel on the passenger side of a Formula One. But she had never really pissed him off before, and he wasn't quite sure why she was pissing him off now.

It was some change in her. Here was how it had been: They woke up in the mornings in the most prominent house in town, situated at the highest elevation above sea level for miles. Neither offered a "good morning" as neither had yet gathered enough information to make that assertion. And both were far too old ("life-experienced," Pattie might have said) to be naive enough to make such a wish for fear that they would only curse the following six hours or so. They took their showers first thing—occasionally together for a quick bit of what they called "good, clean fun"—then grabbed some time together at breakfast prepared by the diminutive Juanita. During this time, each morning, they renewed their vows by enumerating a series of mutual irritations. For nothing knitted two hearts into one like shared needles of disgusts.

They had many of these sharp implements. Such as un-mowed lawns in untidy yards; other drivers on the road; disrespectful sales clerks in mediocre shops; tiny dogs which they called little turds on legs; restaurant food not delivered hot; other parents at their children's sporting events; fat women in shorts; fat men in tee-shirts; fat people period (despite Harry's growing tendency); fat people who were ugly, which was most of them; men trying to dance at weddings; weddings; fat people dancing at weddings; people who thought they were so smart just because they had an advanced degree from a university; politicians with an advance degree from a university; poor people who didn't quite understand just how low they were; Rap music, of course; the fortunes made from Rap music; the terrible taste in clothes the fortunes from Rap music allowed Rap musicians to indulge in; Europeans, Africans, Arabs, and Asians; and—most of all—the lack of civility in everyday life.

Any one of these mutual irritants, discussed, bemoaned, and laughed over at breakfast, could give them the strength to face the day knowing that a like mind, if not an actual soul mate, would always be there at the end of the day to bring sanity back into their world.

That was the way it had been.

But lately, when they woke, Pattie would stretch her still lovely body, stretch her mouth into a smile, and say "Good morning!" as if she had some secret knowledge that it indeed would be. Not knowing how to respond, Harry would grumble, "Yeah, sure," or possibly, "One can only hope," then head into the bathroom to take his morning pee. Then he would jump into the shower, often hoping his wife would join him for some good, clean fun. Although the hope was occurring about as frequently as it used to, the joining was not. Recently, when he was getting dressed and Pattie was taking her shower, he heard singing. At first, he thought the damn clock radio was still on. But that was not it. He soon discovered that the singing was coming from their bathroom, their shower, ultimately, from Pattie, and that was as strange a phenomenon as Harry had ever witnessed. What she chose to sing was nothing he liked—they were Broadway tunes, Pattie told him— and as she didn't really know them, she just sang the first few lines of each—over and over and over. Harry found this to be irritating.

That is the way things had changed on mornings when they still breakfasted together. Of course, there had always been some mornings when they did not have breakfast together, but that was when Harry had an early morning business meeting dictated by his brother. But, other than those days, he could always rely on having breakfast with his wife because Pattie had a schedule set by the school's schedule, which she, of course, had set. As she had always been a woman who had liked a set schedule, which to her was the temporal equivalent of A place for everything and everything in its place, her not very original but damn utilitarian motto), Harry was disconcerted when mornings would break with him not waking up to the clock radio but to the sound of Pattie in the shower getting ready for an early morning breakfast, not with him, but at The Briers!

It all had to do with this damn theater and the new drama department, which was a far more complex undertaking than Harry could imagine, according to Pattie.

"Busy, busy, busy," she would now often say when he asked her how she was. "It's such a complex undertaking, Harry, far more than you can imagine. But important, very, very important."

"Important? What, a bunch of damn kids dressing up and playing make-believe?"

Suddenly she was showing him studies about how vital a drama department could be to the academic standing of a high school. Did he care? Why did he need to be convinced? It was her damn high school. "Do what you want. But why must it take up so much of your damn time?"

"Well, it's not just the drama department, Harry; it's the theater, the theater!"

"Yeah, the theater!"

And this guy who talked her into it, this Austin guy. She was all a twitter because he had once been on TV. Big deal!

"This is a major thing for a town like Rubenton, Harry, a major thing. I mean, this isn't some 24-year-old MFA from Rutgers we have here—"

"A what? What's an MFA?"

"A Master of Fine Arts, Harry."

"Oh, a master. You wouldn't want a master, of course."

"No, Harry, we wouldn't. Austin is no theory-bound avant-garde artiste that we're bringing in to teach the kids, but a real, working actor. I mean with experience in New York and Hollywood. I mean, he knows his stuff. He says there is nothing like a real, working theater to give the real and proper training an actor needs."

"Well, why do you suddenly have to be training actors?"

"Because drama is life, Harry, and training in drama is training in life and isn't that what it's all about? Preparing kids for life."

"Oh, so this is why I wound up putting money into this theater? Because I'm preparing kids for life?"

"No, Harry, because you, as a civic leader, joining with Emily Briers and others, have put money and other considerations into this theater as a joint school-community effort because this theater will attract people to Rubenton. And that will attract business. And that will raise taxes. And that will increase the revenues for our schools. And you will be a hero having done your civic duty."

"Oh, so that's what I'm going to get out of this. Well, I'm glad I'm going to get something, 'cause I know damn well, looking at the paperwork, I ain't going to get any profits."

"No, Harry, it's a non-profit organization. Your money was a donation. You'll get your tax deduction."

"Don't you worry about giving me tax deductions; I can take care of tax problems."

"Harry, this is a major undertaking of importance, I'm sorry if it takes up my time, but it does. This is my job."

"Oh, yeah, well, okay, well, enjoy yourself."

"I do, Harry. Thank you."

But it wasn't so much the breakfasts they missed that upset Harry as the breakfasts they still had. They had changed also. Now when Harry went off on some rant about some irritation, Pattie rarely joined in for a duet. Now she would say things like, "Oh, Harry, it's not so bad." Or, "Oh, Harry, you need to have some understanding." Or, "Jesus, Harry, cut 'em some slack, will you?"

He was now singing solo, and she was not even humming along. Harry had never felt so alone in his life. And it pissed him off.

Frank made his knee-jerk dinner invitation to Trudy (although it was not his knee that jerked) because he knew he would not be seeing Allison that evening, for Allison would be on a plane for New York.

Frank and Allison had spent a lot of time together during the previous two days on matters of much importance, and it would have been as natural for them to have spent time together on the third day as it was for there to be gentle rain in the spring. But Allison wanted to go to New York without delay to see two former students of hers who now owned an art gallery in SoHo so that she might get a quick education in the art market.

It was like an assignment, a mission, a duty, and a passion. And Allison was in a most excited state as she drove to the local airport; as she took the twin-engine commuter plane to the major hub; as she boarded the 727; as she flew first class—not only the only ticket she could get at such short notice but her declaration of self-confidence in the future—to New York City.

The 727 landed at Kennedy Airport at nine-thirty at night. Her former students had instructed Allison to take a taxi to their apartment on West 74th street, just off Columbus Avenue.

As the taxi came over the Queensboro Bridge, Allison sat in calm anticipation of the first glimpse of the city. She had never come into Manhattan at night before. And when she caught that glimpse, the joy that beat out of her heart caught her by surprise. Damn! It's all light and noise—wonderful light and noise; light, brilliant light standing still and shaped into towers, rushing to and fro along the ground and speeding overhead with whoop-whoops of joy. And noise, purposeful noise, surrounding but not smothering, possessing a beat, if no melody, a tone, if no harmony.

She suddenly realized that it was the attention-grabbing opening chapter of a new story, a new book—Frank's book? That is what she had thought; that is what she had sought. But maybe it wasn't just Frank's book.

Maybe...?

All the feelings Allison felt on the bridge magnified once the taxi was traveling on the island. She caught herself gawking out the window, and she didn't care. It qualified as a thrill ride, a natural, organic, no artificial ingredients added thrill ride. And like the experience of thrill rides manufactured in America's amusement parks, she was sorely disappointed when it was over. Had she been with companions she could jump up and down and giggle with, she would have shouted to those companions, "Let's do it again, let's do it again!"

But her companions of the moment were somewhere upstairs in the building she now stood before.

The taxi that had been hers alone sped off, leaving Allison's story to find another in which to be a minor character.

It was a nondescript building tucked among other nondescript buildings along this narrow West 74th Street, one block off Columbus Avenue. Its entrance was a glass door, not very wide, which opened into a small lobby, not very elegant. She pushed the security system panel button that would alert her former pupils that she had arrived, and in response, the voice of Bebe Hutchinson poured out.

"Mrs. Carr?"

"Yes, Bebe, yes, it's me."

"Oh, we're so thrilled! Come on up. Third floor."

The door buzzed with the same thrill that Bebe had expressed. Allison opened it, lifting her large suitcase (she had consistently overpacked in her life) over the threshold, then put it down on the patterned linoleum floor to wheel it over to the elevator.

What a piece of work was the elevator door! It featured an Art Deco pattern of diamonds and bolts of lightning in red and silver that was interesting, odd, and delightful. While studying it, Allison almost forgot to push the button to call the car to pick her up. When she did, the hard, harsh sound of the elevator arousing itself to come to her to fulfill its limited duty made her jump back in anticipation. What, my god, what would be behind the door when it slid open? The elevator's empty, not large interior was the simple answer, clean but not competitive with the door.

A little disappointed, Allison rolled her suitcase into the elevator, positioned herself to exit at the end, and pushed the button marked 3. The door closed, and the elevator ascended. When the door opened again, she had a view of the third-floor hallway, and the right side of her vision caught the image of two heads poking out of a door. They were the heads of Bebe Hutchinson and Tilly Fordham, co-valedictorians of their high school graduating class and co-habitants of apartment 3B.

"Mrs. Carr!/It's so good to see you!/Welcome to New York!" they said, who was saying what Allison was not quite sure as it was all confusion as Tilly and Bebe rushed towards her, both of them giving her a big hug. Then Tilly grabbed the handle of her suitcase and took over the burden of its pulling, and Bebe launched her arm into Allison's and launched them off toward their apartment.

The apartment disappointed Allison. Why had she expected something from a sumptuous layout in the New York Times Magazine? How could she have been so ingenuous? Not that the apartment was awful or dirty or destitute. Indeed, it was impeccable and lovely, the eye and mind of the artistically inclined evident in every detail. It was just small or seemed small given Allison's expectations. As you entered, there was a tiny kitchen immediately to the right and a dining room/living room directly ahead. The floor was hardwood and gleaming. The furniture for sitting was well designed yet, at the same time, inviting. On the walls were pieces of art she longed to linger over when there was time. Two broad and tall bookcases stood on either side of a unit featuring a television and stereo equipment. One held in neat order oversize books, both tall and fat, on arts and artists. The other, at a glance, had novels, mostly hardback, and those that weren't were trade paperbacks of the same size. All this satisfied Allison and took the sting of smallness away.

"Oh, my God, Mrs. Carr, I can't believe you're really here," Bebe said as Tilly pulled Allison's suitcase down a dark hallway, quickly returning. "We were so surprised to get your call; it was so wonderful to hear from you."

"We heard you retired," Tilly said.

"And—" Bebe said.

"And—" Tilly said.

"Divorced your husband," Bebe said.

"Yes, I did both those things."

"And then people said—" Tilly started.

"You just up and disappeared—" Bebe continued.

"And no one knew where you were," Tilly finished.

"Actually, I found myself a lovely little beach hotel to live in."

"Really?" said Tilly.

"Where?" Bebe inquired.

Allison told them.

"You're kidding!" They both said.

"No. It's exactly where I wanted to be. Where I guess I needed to be."

"Like a shell," Bebe said.

"Yes."

"A seashell," Tilly offered.

"Yes!" Allison found she was thrilled over the analogy. "Yes, I suppose, exactly. Seashells can be quite lovely, don't you think?"

"And here you are now, here in New York to see us!" Tilly said.

"Yes. I've missed some of the girls. You two the most, I think."

"Mrs. Carr, that's wonderful of you to say so," Bebe said.

Allison smiled. "You know, we're all out of school now, and you are adults now. So I think it's about time you dropped Mrs. Carr and started calling me Allison."

"On, no!" Tilly responded with some agitation.

"We could never do that," Bebe emphasized. "You will always be Mrs. Carr. In fact, we like the formality you instituted at the school, all of us calling each other Miss Hutchinson; Miss Fordham, you know, never using our first names. And we've carried on with that in our gallery. I call Tilly Miss Fordham at work, and she calls me Miss Hutchinson."

"And we call all our employees by Mr. Miss, Ms. or Mrs."

"You're kidding," Allison said, truly surprised.

"No, of course not," Bebe said. "There's a measure of respect in it; that's what you always taught us. So why should we drop that respect? And we are here in New York City, and somehow it works in New York City."

"Very New York Times," Allison said.

"Yes, and why not?" Bebe put the question.

"Besides, it's fun; it truly is," Tilly said.

"So, Mrs. Carr, would you like a cup of tea? Herb tea, of course. It's too late for black tea. Or a glass of wine?"

"I would love a glass of wine," Allison was happy to reveal.

Tilly dashed into the kitchen as Bebe indicated to Allison that they should sit, which they did. Tilly soon returned with three glasses of wine and a selection of cheeses and fruit. It was all beautifully laid out on a tray, and Allison said so. Bebe raised her glass, Tilly following suit, and offered a toast to Allison, welcoming her to New York, declaring again how happy they were to see her. Allison, pleased, offered one back, stating how pleasant it was to know that students did not fade away on the day after graduation, but went on to live lives interest, hopefully with great joy.

As they talked of the school and their time together, Allison noted the change and maturation evident in each girl. In aspects, of course, but also in style. Bebe had dyed her hair jet black and wore it short with bangs. She wore large round black eyeglasses that complimented the cut. Her nails were polished a deep, eggplant purple, and her lipstick, while not as dark, was also a shade of purple. Tilly, who had always had mousy-brown hair, was now a platinum blonde, her hair flowing long and down in thick waves. Her nail polish was shock red, as were her lips, and she wore a dress that emphasized her figure, which had made her famous among the male students at the local public school who became rabid fans of the school soccer team she had captained.

After the talk about their shared past had been exhausted, Tilly asked why Allison decided to make this trip to New York. Allison explained that it was, in essence, a business trip and that she specifically came to talk to them for business reasons. Upon hearing this, the two young girls she had helped shape into budding women suddenly became women—businesswomen, both interested and cautious. But mainly cautious.

"Oh, yes," Bebe said.

"I've discovered an artist," Allison explained. "A rather incredible one, I think. I want to take him in hand. I'm going to sponsor him, be his patron, I suppose. But also his representative, on, you know, on a commission. But I know next to nothing about the art market. I need to learn. I would like us to reverse our old positions. I need to be the student; I need you to be the teachers."

"Oh," Tilly said and then had no more to say or no more she wanted to say out loud.

Bebe had more courage. "Mrs. Carr, the fine art business is not easy, you understand. It has complexities and myriad rules of the game that are hard but essential to adhere to, so—"

"Let me show you some of his work," Allison said. "I've brought some. Where's my suitcase? I'll go get—"

"No, not tonight, Mrs. Carr," Bebe cut Allison off. "Tomorrow, tomorrow evening. We take an early morning train to Buck's County to see one of our artists, but we'll be back in, oh, well, probably in the late afternoon. So we'll meet you back here, have dinner, then talk about it."

"Oh," Allison said, disappointed. "Okay, sure."

Tilly stood up. "You must be tired, Mrs. Carr. Would you like to go to bed?"

"Yes, I am. It was an exhausting trip."

"Well, we've got a bedroom all prepared for you."

"Surely, we can put something together here on the couch; it looks comfortable. I don't want to put one of you out."

"Mrs. Carr," Bebe said, knowing this was the moment she and Tilly had both been excited about, even as they had dreaded it. "We've prepared the guest bedroom for you. We sleep in the same bedroom."

"Oh." Allison did not know whether to express being shocked, which she was not, or to laugh, which would be rude even though she knew it would not have been derogatory. "Girls, you call each other Miss Hutchinson and Miss Fordham at work; what do you call each other at home?"

Without hesitation or a blink, Tilly answered, "Sweetie-pie and Honey Bunny."

"Mrs. Carr, didn't you know we were lovers?" Bebe asked.

"I didn't have a clue."

"We became lovers at the school. In the third-floor students' restroom," Tilly offered the revelation.

"I always knew we weren't doing as vigilant a job as possible patrolling those restrooms."

"Surely, Mrs. Carr, you don't have any objections, do you?" Bebe asked.

"Absolutely not. Guess I just skipped that chapter."

"What?"

"Never mind."

"You sure this isn't going to make you uneasy?"

"Girls, love in this world, I think, is something rarer than we like to admit to. If you guys have it, count it precious, hold it dear, and defend it from all objections. None of which you will get from me."

"That's why we loved you in school, Mrs. Carr," Tilly said.

"You loved me?"

"Mrs. Carr, you were our hero."

"You're kidding."

"I don't think you ever realized how much you meant to the students."

"You know, I don't think I ever did. But now, what sweet thoughts I can go to sleep with."

Before going to bed, Allison and the girls (as she continued to think of them) had decided that they would wake up early enough in the morning to go out to breakfast before Bebe and Tilly needed to leave for the train station. As there was only one bathroom in the small apartment, there was a bit of chaotic juggling for everyone to get showered and dressed, and made up, but at only five minutes beyond the time they had wanted to leave the apartment, they did.

As Bebe, Tilly, and Allison exited the building onto the narrow 74th street—made seemingly narrower by the massive monolith of a block-long and block-like building directly across the street—the delightful perception of it being a gorgeous day entered each one of them, and made itself very welcomed.

"Oh my gosh, Miss Fordham," Bebe said, "I think it's definitely going to be a GMD."

"Oh yes, Miss Hutchinson, I think you're right, a GMD indeed. Too bad we're going to have to miss it."

Allison was amused, as Tilly and Bebe certainly intended her to be, but not patient. "All right, girls, what's a GMD?"

"A Great Manhattan Day," Tilly said. "It's what Bebe and I call days like this, days you can feel from the moment you wake up in the morning or walk out the door that the city is going to be magical, as only Manhattan can be."

"Is it seasonal?" Allison asked.

"Nope," Bebe said, "a GMD can happen during any season, in any weather. It can be a beautiful, sunny day or a day when inclement weather keeps you confined to your apartment. But there's got to be magic. That's what makes it a GMD. When a walk through the city on a sunny day seems like a trip through a golden world—that's a GMD. And a day of confinement in your apartment has got to give you the comfortable satisfaction of being safe in a fortified castle you happen to be the mistress of. That kind of magic."

They made it to Columbus Avenue, and Bebe and Tilly stopped.

"The Cuban?" Bebe asked Tilly.

"Yes, certainly, the Cuban," Tilly answered.

"This way," Bebe directed Allison, and they turned left and walked up the avenue, joining a flow of pedestrians weaving among each other as they all went to some place of some importance to their moments.

"Say, listen, I've got a great idea," Tilly said as she led them, walking a pace faster than Allison thought possible and still holding a conversation. "And don't be offended by this, Mrs. Carr, it's going to sound like such a stupid, touristy thing to do, but I guarantee you'll never regret it if you do it."

Allison was intrigued and excited, the talk of magic making her think of a jewel-encrusted box and Bebe offering the contents of it to her. What was inside, what, what? "I'm open to anything. You can't insult me."

"Really? Well, okay. Bebe, what do you think? Don't you think that after breakfast, we should send Mrs. Carr off to take the Circle Line Tour?"

"Oh, yes, of course, you must, Mrs. Carr!"

"It's the perfect day for it," Tilly said.

"Well, what is it?" Allison asked, anxious to know.

"A boat, like, you know, a ferry boat that takes you completely around the island, you travel on the East River and the Hudson, and you get to see all of Manhattan."

Allison told the girls that far from being insulted, she was thrilled to have a plan for the day.

"Great," Bebe said as she stopped. "Here's the restaurant."

They entered Havana Joe's and were immediately seated by a short, dark man who seemed to be enjoying himself. The girls argued a little over Allison's meal, which they insisted on ordering. Allison, who had never eaten Cuban food in her life, was apprehensive but kept it to herself. When the meal came, she found it not entirely to her liking. She kept this to herself as well while eating every bite of it.

Over their last cups of coffee and Allison's tea, Tilly asked, "So, where did you meet this artist?"

"He's a head waiter at the hotel I live at."

The moment Allison had answered, she knew it had sounded stupid or naive or horrible or unlikely or absurd or some word in some obscure language of somewhere between six or seven syllables that was completely unpronounceable by a non-native speaker without damaging the vocal cords, but that simply meant: Embarrassed by one's stupidity deriving from one's total lack of rational perception. The looks on Tilly and Bebe's faces beautifully mimed the same sentiment.

"Really?" Bebe asked, not truly wanting an answer.

"I know that sounds, um...."

"Well...."

"You see, he's not really a waiter."

"Well, Mrs. Carr," Bebe said, "who really is really a waiter?"

"I am really a waiter!" said their happy Cuban waiter as he brought them their check.

"Yes, Manuel, but is that really how you define yourself?" asked Bebe, who was happy for the diversion. "As a waiter?"

"I am a waiter!" Manuel declared again with no less enthusiasm.

"But wouldn't you really want to be something else, I mean, if you had a choice?" Tilly asked with unfeigned curiosity.

"What else could I possibly want to be? People walk in here, and I smile at them when possibly no one else in this city will. I show them to a table that I have made sure is clean and proper for them to sit at. I then make it possible for them to have some sustenance, which if they do not have, they will die. I bring it to them hot and perfectly prepared and ready to burst into flavor in their mouths. And then, for that moment, all is right in the world. Miss Bebe, Miss Tilly, am I not like a god then?"

Bebe laughed and said, "Manuel, if I was ever to have an image of a god, I couldn't think of a better one than you."

"Of course! The logic is irrefutable."

"But is there anything you like to do when you are not being a waiter that you're passionate about?"

"I listen to the music of my country; I smoke cigars; I make love to my woman."

"And this completely satisfies you?"

"No, this is just life. What satisfies me is my son. My son is going to be a great baseball player. He will join a major league team, break many records, and earn millions of dollars, especially in product endorsements. And then my son, because he loves his father, my son will pay for my early retirement, so I don't have to do this fucking job no more." Manuel smiled a smile of great wisdom.

The three at the table laughed, and Bebe asked, "And what will you do in retirement?"

"Listen to the music of my country, smoke cigars, and make love to my woman. What else is there?" Manuel gathered up the money Tilly had laid out to pay the check. "I'll be back in a moment with your change."

"Keep it, Manuel," Tilly said.

"Thank you, oh beauteous one," Manuel said as he left.

"Oh, jeez, look at the time." Bebe stood up and gathered her things. "Tilly, we must run."

They had given Allison the instructions on how to get to the Circle Line over breakfast. And they gave her a key to their apartment. So they felt fine now leaving her. Then they kissed her goodbye and ran out of the restaurant.

Following the girls' instructions, Allison made her way to pier 83 on the Hudson River, from which the Circle Line tour boat left. She got there just in time to purchase a ticket and board before the crew threw off the moorings, and the ship, crowded with tourists feeling both excitement and obligation, backed off from the pier to find the river's flow. As the island receded, affording Allison a better view, she knew that Bebe and Tilly had been more than correct in sending her here. It was a wonderfully clear day; the city was shining now with its innate light, not just the illuminated product of Mr. Edison's perspiration. The sight was unbelievable, she thought, thinking it to be an embarrassingly mundane description. But a mass of buildings, many taller than they possibly had any right to be, crowded and compacted onto this long, narrow island; who in their right mind would ever have done this?

A crewman who stood by the pilot at the wheel announced into the microphone he held that this was not a guided tour, so don't expect any color commentary. Then he preceded to comment colorfully during the entire circumnavigation of the island. He elucidated not just the history, architecture, horticultural, and engineering of the isle but reported up-to-the-minute rumors and gossip. Allison thought it was the most exemplary lecture she had ever attended.

When they got to the north end of the island, looking up the Hudson River, Allison was surprised by how wild and verdant it still looked, how un-concrete-and-steel it was. She did not feel it stood there in opposition to the concrete and steel but as a beautiful counterpoint. Trees may be works of nature, and buildings may be works of humans, but what were humans if not works of nature?

At the end of the trip, as the boat was preparing for its approach back to the pier, Allison leaned against the railing and looked out over the Hudson. And found her creature, her hyperbolic sea serpent, rising out of the water to block her view of the New Jersey shore. How strange, she thought, for it to have it follow her here. The serpent turned its large reptilian head towards her, winked, and then slowly submerged back into the river.

When the tour was over, much of the GMD was left, and Allison realized she had no idea how she would spend it. Despite the heavy Cuban breakfast, she now felt famished, so she decided to find someplace to satisfy her hunger. Rather than taking a taxi to nowhere in mind, Allison started walking, and when she got to the first busy avenue, she turned right and headed south. She soon found a coffee house, one of a chain that had wrapped its linked coils around all of America and most of the world. It was not unique; it was not a New York institution. It may not even have taken on some smattering of local color, but she had always enjoyed this establishment no matter where she had traveled, which made it a welcome refuge.

Allison entered, ordered a peppermint tea and a sizeable low-fat muffin, and sat down with them at a window seat so that she could watch the passing, though not organized, parade. In the stillness brought on by the hot tea, Allison realized that among the exhilaration still rapidly stirring in her mind, there was a slower-moving worry that disturbed her. It was the fact that the open arms of Bebe and Tilly had closed just a little—if not more—when she had brought up her artist—her Frank. Allison sat there, worried she was on a fool's errand. She had never once in her life considered herself a fool, and to do so now was disconcerting. Take the kid to the big city, and she falls flat on her face! This disturbing image compelled her decision about what to do next. She finished her muffin and tea and went outside just as a taxi passed; she hailed it, entered, and asked to go to the Hutchinson/Fordham Gallery in SoHo.

Allison realized that she had no idea what kind of art Bebe and Tilly liked and represented, assuming they were the same thing. She had followed a simple logic that as art was art, and as they owned an art gallery, and as she had an artist, putting the two together was natural. However, she now understood that she should have done some research and not just assumed that the two girls she had strived mightily to shape to her liking would necessarily find her passions to their liking.

The gallery was on the ground floor of a five-story brick building built in 1923 and had originally housed a company that imported "Novelties from the Orient." There were large modern windows so that you could see the art from the street, with HUTCHINSON/FORDHAM GALLERY stenciled proudly on one of the windows in an impressive script. Knowing that Bebe and Tilly would not be there, Allison knew that she could enter anonymously and was determined to remain so. A handsome young man in a dark suit with short hair pasted to his head, looking fashionably old-fashioned except for the silver nose piercing that protruded from the side of his right nostril, greeted her as she entered.

"Good morni—ah, hold on—" The young man, with an extravagant swing of his arm, positioned the watch on his wrist to where he could see it. "—There's no use wishing you a good morning when there are only thirty seconds of it left, so if you'll give me but a minute, well, just a little less...." He then fell silent as he watched the sweep of the second hand on his watch move deterministically towards the numeral twelve, the passing of which would mark this day's change-over from morning to afternoon. Einstein being correct in this, as he had been in so many things, Allison found this short wait relativistically long. Finally, though, when the second hand had swept past the twelve, the young man beamed and said, "Ah, there, so—good afternoon!"

"Good afternoon," Allison said, "assuming your watch is accurate."

"It's a Rolex, ma'am; some things must be taken on faith. May I help you, guide you, elucidate, and edify?"

"My goodness, what service!"

"Yes, wonderful, aren't I? Probably because I am not a native New Yorker of dubious social standing."

"Oh, but you are a snob."

"Yes, ma'am, but a snob dedicated to service and the propagation of artistic vision."

"Are you an artist yourself?"

"Unfortunately, I am not a creator, simply an appreciator. But an appreciator of such finely honed tastes, you can trust me in all your artistic choices."

"Is this your gallery?"

"No, I am neither Miss Hutchinson nor Miss Fordham, neither of whom are here today, but I have their explicit trust."

"Well, I feel I am in good hands, then, Mr...?"

"George Tobias Lemon"

"Well, Mr. Lemon, I am not a native New Yorker either, although I love this city."

"Whom of us do not?"

"Indeed. I'm just a tourist, curious as to the, uh, current; I guess you should say, fashions in the Art world."

"Ah, fashions. I take issue with that adjective. Not in general, but in particular, here at the Hutchinson/Fordham Gallery. Miss Hutchinson and Miss Fordham have lain out quite specifically that at this gallery, we will only represent artists with enduring value. One cannot invest in fashion."

"You can't argue with that philosophy."

"Exactly."

"So, how would you like to elucidate and edify? I am curious about what current artists of enduring value are doing."

"Well, let's see, where shall we start? Currently, we are featuring Hildegard Penrose. I will show you some of her work if you walk with me."

Hildegard Penrose painted exclusively in shades of white and yellow, which she said were the colors of peace. Her paintings, mounted on revolving disks, could be turned slowly and even spun. Move any side down, any side up, and any side to the right or left, and the painting is changed by an optical trick. The first Penrose Allison saw was an uneven landscape of small yellow flowers of various shades that featured in the background what seemed to be a slightly out-of-focus rocket with a warhead. Rotate the piece ninety degrees, and suddenly you see the fuzzy yellow image of a man in profile with an erect sexual organ in gleaming white. Turn it another ninety degrees, and it became the painting of a white and yellow mushroom cloud obliterating a landscape. One last ninety-degree turn and you had what was essentially an abstract work except for the now perceivable letters on the pointed white bar at the top that spelled out in off-white: SPIN ME.

"Go ahead," said George Tobias Lemon, "give it a good spin."

Allison took up the challenge and gave the painting a good spin.

"Now look at the painting, stare at the center, and within seconds you should feel a rush of calm, peace, and love. It has to do, Ms. Penrose says, with alternating light frequencies."

Allison was unsure she felt any of the feelings George Tobias Lemon said she would feel, but, at least, she felt none of their opposites. "This must have taken a lot of thought."

"Hildegard Penrose is brilliant. She is a professor of Art at Bennington; got her MFA at Yale; studied in Paris, London, and Nairobi. She has participated in fifteen group exhibitions and has had seven one-person shows, including two here, of course, and she is a recipient of a MacArthur genius award."

Among the other artists introduced to Allison that day was a young ceramist who created highly polished images of diseased human organs and had just received his MFA from NYU. There was a conceptual neo-abstract (referential/reverential) expressionist who had gained her reputation recreating the works of Jackson Pollack in colored beads. But she was now moving on to recreate the works of Mark Rothko in colored felt. Allison also saw the creations of a "stone and dirt artist" who worked exclusively in "earth" and made what seemed at first to be abstracts but were actually long views and close-up portraits of plate tectonics. She had a BS and an MS in geology from the University of North Virginia and an MFA from Bennington and was well known for having been one of Hildegard Penrose's star protégés. Lastly, there was the wheelchair-bound artist who did miniature portraits of his friends and family on the caps of urine sample bottles, each filled with an actual urine sample from the appropriate friend or family member. He was a Ph.D. but was no longer teaching, having decided to devote one hundred percent of his time to his art.

Allison left the Hutchinson/Fordham Gallery in a state of nervous shock. It was not that she did not like the art that she saw. For example, she found the miniature portraits of friends and family to be quite charming, and what could better get at the essence of an individual than that individual's urine sample? Except maybe, of course, that individual's stool sample. Diseased human organs had a shocking honesty about them; they indeed did. Plate tectonics left her cold, but one could not deny the worldly-ness of the subject. And who could argue with peace, even if yellow was not your favorite color? No, it was not the type or tone of the art, which might not be a welcoming home for Frank's work, that made Allison uneasy. But rather the credentials of the artists. Especially when compared with Frank's lack of such credentials. How absurd she had been! A life-long academic, she should have foreseen this. Clubs can be exclusive, and membership can have stringent qualifications and might just be by invitation only.

Allison returned to the apartment long before the girls and sat in it alone as if she were sitting in a waiting room. She was becoming increasingly nervous in anticipation of their arrival, which led to anxiety, making it impossible to do what she might usually have done: explore the apartment and its unfamiliar things; pull out books and browse, even read whole sections of some; turn on the television for some news, or some diverting mindless programming. Instead, she just sat there feeling younger than she had felt in years, but not in a good way. It was the youth of frightened naiveté when the future seemed to be the other side of a vast chasm that one had to leap. It was the worst of all youthful feelings, far worse than the one that saw the future as a shear rock face to be scaled, for at least that was a future with solid handholds to grasp and footholds one could get a secure purchase of, even if the repetitive need to do so wore you down as you went up. You could miss a handhold, slip from a foothold, and fall at any time— halfway there; three-quarters of the way there; just about there.

Nevertheless, you were not powerless to try an ascent. But a chasm that one could never leap without the power of flight; therefore, any attempt to do so was futile, caused the kind of fear that led one to believe in the fantasy of sprouting wings and the comfort of eternal bliss. So Allison sat alone in this "waiting room," her Rubenton confidence smashed by Manhattan reality.

And yet...

After a while, she was kind enough to offer and make herself a cup of tea. Standing in the small and inefficient "urban" kitchen, waiting for the water in the kettle to boil, she found herself loving the kitchen. And as she moved from the kitchen with her hot mug of tea, back into the living room, over to the windows that she could look out of and down onto West 74th Street—narrow, yet busy with foot traffic and a yellow cab now and then—Allison felt a tingle in the pit of her stomach that she decided to adore. The trees planted along the street were fully leafed, causing abstract patterns of shadows to fall upon the sidewalk and street, which she found delightful. A horn honked; again; and again; and again. She found it amusing. Looking at the large monolith building across the street, she wondered what it had been. It was old. Close to a hundred years, she guessed. And it was temple-like. She looked up and saw a series of brightly covered Egyptian reliefs spaced along the top. Had this been the headquarters of the Masons? Or some mysterious Knights of Osiris, if there ever been such an organization? Possibly the builders had just been inspired by the first King Tut exhibit when Egyptomania had infected the country. Allison declared to herself that before she left this city, she would know the truth about this building.

By the time she had finished her tea, her youthful anxiety had gone away, but a slight nervousness remained and flared when she heard a key in the door and the door opening and knew that the girls were home.

Tilly and Bebe entered with Chinese take-out, laughing and chattering away about whatever they were laughing about. It was a chatter they soon engaged Allison in, for they had been laughing about Mary McFadden, the clumsiest girl in their school, who everybody had just loved, but who amused everybody because she was the personification of slapstick. Mary could do nothing without a slip, trip, bang, bump, crash, crush, or fall. She seemed to have been born with banana peels on the soles of her shoes, with the spatial faculty of a blind person, and with the coordination of a walrus out of water. They laughed as they put the food bag on the table in their small dining area next to the living room. They laughed as Bebe pulled out the little white boxes, and Tilly went to the kitchen and returned with plates and forks. They laughed as Allison did the honors and opened a bottle of wine. And they laughed between mouthfuls of cashew chicken, beef and broccoli in oyster sauce, sweet and sour shrimp, egg rolls, and steamed white rice. At the meal's end and their memories of Mary McFadden exhausted, all three were holding their stomachs and trying to catch their breaths. There was such a feeling of warm good fellowship— although what a Dickensian description to apply to three laughing women—that Allison was almost reluctant to bring up Frank. But she had to; she simply had to. So as they cleared plates, she said, "Let me tell you some more about this artist I've been telling you about, Frank."

"Oh, yeah," Bebe said, "sure, of course."

"Well, I told you, I met him at the hotel where I live and...."

"That's so romantic," Tilly said.

"What?" Allison was confused.

"Living at a hotel on a beach."

"Oh. Well, I find it convenient. Now, I told you, Frank's the waiter there, but that's truly the proverbial day job for him. He spends all his time off drawing."

"Is that his medium?"

"What?"

"Drawings."

"Well, he wants to turn them into paintings—large paintings."

"Oh."

There was a note of disappointment in Bebe's voice, but Allison continued. "Well, there was just something about Frank that was different. You could tell he was more than just a waiter."

"Mrs. Carr!" Tilly suddenly said.

"What?"

"Are you having an affair with this Frank?"

Allison blushed, probably for the first time in her adult life. The girls, well into their second bottle of wine, started to laugh, excused themselves, and hugged Allison. Allison would dearly have loved to become livid with anger, but she felt she couldn't and patiently explained that, yes, love had been made, but only after she had decided to patronize Frank.

"Do you mind if I ask how old he is?" Bebe said.

What would be more damning for them to take Frank seriously as an artist? That he was as old or older than Allison and so not young and hip? Or that he was ten years younger than Allison, making her a, what, a sugar momma? Therefore completely lacking any artistic discernment regarding Frank's work? "Oh, uh, the late forties, I would guess."

"Mrs. Carr!" Tilly said again. "A younger man! That's wonderful. Is he a good lover?"

"Tilly, that's none of our business," Bebe admonished.

"Didn't we always say that Mrs. Carr was pretty hot, and we wondered what she was doing with that bobo of a husband?"

"Tilly!"

"Listen, girls, take me seriously, okay."

"Okay, sorry, Mrs. Carr," Bebe sincerely said, sobering her demeanor, hoping her brain would catch up. "But we must be honest, we—we don't want to see you hurt. We talked a lot about this on the train today. You, see, one's not likely these days to 'discover' an unsung artist, some untrained natural genius out in the hinterlands. That's just not the system these days. Art takes a lot of training and mentorship, which, these days, is only available in the university system. People no longer starve in some garret, whatever that is, to do their art. Your Frank may be excellent; I don't know, but, I mean, what has he done?"

"He once earned an excellent living as an artist."

"He did? Well, I thought you said—. But doing what kind of art?"

"Illustrations."

"Illustrations for what?"

"Children's books."

"Oh, really, well, that's fine; we love children's books, and we love good illustrations, but that's not really what we—"

"You know, girls, do you remember me teaching you in the Introduction to Philosophy course?"

"Sure, of course," Bebe said.

"Do you remember me trying to explain the difference in the approaches to discovering truth between the Platonic and the

Aristotelian? How the one, the Platonic, was equivalent to a bunch of wise men sitting around in their togas debating the ideal number of teeth a horse should have in his mouth. And the other, the Aristotelian, was as simple as opening a horse's mouth and looking inside to count the teeth and find out how many teeth there were?"

"Oh, yeah, I remember that!" Tilly said.

"Well, girls, let's open up this horse's mouth and count the teeth, shall we?"

Allison retrieved several of Frank's drawings from her luggage that she had pleaded with him to let her take. He wanted her to take copies. She insisted on the originals. "Explain they are just drawings," Frank had said anxiously, "just plans; you must tell them that. You've got to explain my concept for each and what I'll do to realize them on big canvases. Here look, let me write everything down."

Allison brought out the drawings and a sheet of paper. She asked Bebe and Tilly to clear the few items left on the dining room table. As Allison laid the pictures out on the table, she made them promise to say nothing until she had explained the final form envisioned for each one. From Frank's notes, she presented each drawing and its proposed future as if she were giving a favorite child's proud particulars. Bebe and Tilly, true to their promise, said nothing. When finished, Allison backed away from the table, hoping the girls would take the opportunity to view them up close, get to know them, and even study them. They did, picking them up, sharing them, giving them due consideration, all dispassionately with no reactions, comments, and— this stung Allison the most—laughter. Allison had to assume or go mad that this was just their professional demeanors, their professional way of communicating with each other with faces Allison, once the teacher, the mentor, now the outsider, could not read.

Then, in concert, they turned and looked at her.

OH HOW HAPPY

Chapter the Seventh

"There are many things desirous about Los Angeles," Ben Alyn said to his friend Jackson Beck who had driven him to the airport. "Leaving it has always been at the top of my list."

The two friends sat in a bar at the Bob Hope Airport in Burbank, an incorporated city bordering Los Angeles and indistinguishable from it. They were waiting for the PA calling Ben's flight, which would take him on the first leg of a journey that would see him eventually arriving at The Briers Hotel situated on Leech Beach outside a town called Rubenton.

"For good, or just for an escape?" Jackson Beck asked.

Ben sighed a sigh he had sighed before and said, "Oh, well, for good has always been my dream. But I guess I'll take the occasional escape."

"You don't really mean that, Ben. I mean, what better place is there to live than LA? My God, the climate is wonderful. I'd never move back to Detroit."

"Whenever anyone defends Los Angeles," Ben said in the middle of sipping some malt whiskey, "they always bring up its climate, have you noticed? No one ever brings up its stunning beauty, its exciting culture, or its spectacular architecture. They always just bring up the climate. Surely other locations have climates, especially ones without a plethora of sun-drenched vitamin D, which, as you know, causes early onset mellowness."

"Ah, LA bashing is an old sport."

"Listen, Jackson, the truth is Los Angeles is a heap, and it is only worth living here if you are on the top of it."

"You're still bitter about that audition, aren't you?"

"Not bitter, Jackson; I dropped bitter a long time ago. It's a useless emotion in this business. Disappointed, yes. I really thought I had aced it. I knew I would get a call that night. I just knew it. How many nights has it been now?" Ben looked at Jackson as if he actually had the information.

"I'm sorry, Ben," Jackson said. And he indeed was, having known disappointment himself.

"No matter, Jack, no matter. The only thing fair about life is death."

"That's a harsh thought, Ben."

"Yes, but oddly enough, I find it consoling."

Ben took another sip of his drink and looked out of the large window before him at the various jets waiting on the tarmac. "You know, I like this little airport. I like it much more than LAX."

"What's to like about an airport?"

"Jackson, airports are the train stations of today, filled with the romance of comings and goings. I love airports."

"So why do you like this one better than LAX, which is like a major, you know, world-class airport?"

"Yeah, I know, but here—here, look, see those people getting on that plane. They have walked outside onto the tarmac, they're walking to the plane, and they get to board it by climbing that rolling stairway. It's real; it's essential; you can feel the experience of boarding this flying machine that will whisk you off to your romantic destination. Now, compare that with, you know, a big airport where you walk through this tunnel thing attached to the plane like a feeding tube. That's like going from one room to another; you never feel that you are actually getting onto a plane. You're just, you know, moving to another room that just happens to fly. It has all the romance of getting on an elevator. But every time I fly out of here, I feel like it's the Fifties again. You know what I mean? I mean, look out there; you can see the old newsreel now of stars walking up those stairs, or arriving, popping out of the side of the plane accompanied by the pops of flashbulbs. And here's Victor Mature, the handsome star of Demetrius and the Gladiators, just arriving home from location in Rome. Hey, Victor! Where are your sandals? Ah, if I had been here in the Forties and Fifties, Jack, I would have been a big star."

"You ain't done badly for yourself."

"Hell, I've hardly worked in seven years."

"You had a ten-year run in a hit series; that's more than anyone will ever say about me."

"Hey, you work consistently."

"Yeah, always for scale plus ten."

"Work is work, Jackson."

"But you had a series."

"Long gone now. And I was the second banana. And it was one of those weird series, you know. We were always in the top twenty, but it was like it never really made an impact on this town. It certainly didn't make me a star."

"It made you well-known."

"Yeah, in the hinterlands."

"Oh, so that's why you want to leave LA."

"Well...."

"Ahh-ha!"

"Listen, I'm going out to do this old war horse of a play for a guy I know who started a theater out there. He left L.A. because—well, the bastard can't act his way out of a paper bag, but, you know, nice guy. And he's dedicated to the theater, so he's started his own out there. So I'm going to go out there, and why not? This town completely ignores me. I can go out there for six weeks and be treated like something, like I matter, because, you know, let's face it; I'm going to be the biggest thing they've ever seen. And, you know—I'm being candid with you, Jack—I'm not a man fooled by my illusions. I'm an actor. An actor not only needs an audience; he needs an audience to applaud him. So look, nothing's happening here, so I go out there for six weeks, I get applauded, and people treat me like royalty. Think of it as going away to a health spa for your ego."

"Sounds good to me."

Ben took another drink. "If I had just gotten that damn series. I'm telling you, Jackson, it's the best thing I've ever read. I knew that character inside and out, not only what the writer put in, but, you know, what I could bring to it. But, I swear to God, if that series hits and the actor is right—and I would have been right—that series is going to go ten, maybe twenty years, it's just got something. Even if it only lasted five years, it's so special that your future stardom would be assured. In fact, you'd only want it to go five or seven years, milk it dry, then go on. That's probably the strategy the star should adopt."

"Whoever he might be."

"Yeah," Ben said sadly, "whoever he might be."

The PA announced Ben's flight, and he and his friend got up off their bar stools and gave each other a big hug with plenty of pats on each other's back, which was fulfilling for both, especially now for Ben. He needed the essentially human need for warm, physical contact with another mammal. There was nothing sensual about it; it was something far more critical than that.

"See you in six weeks, Jackson. If I ever return."

"Oh, you'll be back. You're an LA addict hooked on Hollywood heroin."

Ben smiled at the amusing truth. "Well, maybe I can detox on the shores of Leech Beach."

"Ain't going to happen, big boy, ain't going to happen."

"We'll see, Jack, we'll see."

And then Ben Alyn walked to his gate singing in a cracked voice that was once kind of famous:

Leaving on a jet plane

Don't know when I'll be back again.

If Ben Alyn had thought that the relatively small Bob Hope Airport, with its lack of boarding tunnels and its opportunity to plant your feet on its tarmac, was romantic, the Rubenton Airport should have thrilled him. However, it did not, for "airport" was a generous designation for what was just an airfield of one runway with a tarmac the size of the average mini-mart's parking lot. The terminal was not much larger than the average mini-mart itself, with amenities of comfort, refreshment, and nourishment reminiscent of such an establishment.

Ben had not very happily been waiting in the terminal "lounge" for twenty-five minutes, eating a Twinkie and sucking on the mini bottle of Jim Beam he had taken with him from one of the several airplanes he had flown to arrive here. Not the last, of course, for the previous had been a six-passenger turboprop that had not even offered a bag of peanuts and had hit a "bit of turbulence," as the pilot called it, on three separate occasions during a thirty-five-minute flight. If those were a "bit," Ben thought, I would hate to have seen a—what was larger than a bit? A bat? A bot? A butt? Well, whatever it was, they had tossed Ben around like a sock alone in a washing machine set on FULL LOAD. He plumbed the water in himself, spraying it out in an even flow from his pours.

He was now, via Jim Beam and Twinkies, trying to calm his nerves and restock his stomach, its previous contents having abandoned him on the last leg of his trip.

Where the hell was this Austin? Ben, annoyed, asked himself. Who the hell was this Austin, this Austin O'Brien that I find myself sitting in this dump at his entreaty? He had guested on a couple of episodes of Sgt. McKennen; I did a couple of Equity-waiver plays in North Hollywood with him. That's the kind of history we have together that I flew all the way to this dump for him? And where is this dump? Ben tried to remember—but he could not—in what state was Rubenton. All he knew was that there was supposed to be an ocean, but he had yet to see it. This Briers Hotel had better have room service; he threatened the universe. Hell, it had better have rooms!

"Ben!"

Austin came through the small glass door entrance to the terminal with a big smile and the aspect of a man who had been in an extreme rush for the last half hour. Probably the best performance he had ever achieved, Ben thought to himself. However, behind Austin came a rather attractive woman with a body worth thinking about, so Ben stood up even though he was unsure if his legs still resided beneath his hips.

"Ben, it is so good to see you, and I am so sorry for being late," Austin said as he grabbed Ben's hand and shook it.

"It's my fault, Mr. Alyn," the attractive woman said, "it is completely my fault. I was in a meeting that ran long, and I just couldn't get out of it, but I was determined to greet you at the airport."

"Is that what this is?" Ben said, looking around. "I thought it was a field for model airplane enthusiasts."

Pattie, who, of course, was the rather attractive woman, laughed heartily. "It is a mite small, isn't it? But, if my husband and I have anything to say about it, we will soon be voting on a bond to build a truly sufficient airport."

"This will not, I assume," Ben said, "be accomplished by the time I leave?"

Pattie laughed again, longer and louder than Austin had ever heard her laugh. "I'm afraid not."

"Maybe I'll take the QE2 back home," Ben said in defeat.

"What...?" Pattie was confused.

"Ben is a renowned wit," Austin had to explain.

"Oh," Pattie said in understanding and forgiveness. Whether it was forgiving Ben for his wit or Austin for pointing out her witlessness became clear when she continued her fawning of Ben. "Well, in any case, it is such an extreme, extreme pleasure to meet you."

"And I'm sure," Ben said, taking Pattie's offered hand, not for a shake but a hold, "it's extremely mutual. If I only knew who you were."

"Oh, Ben, I'm sorry, this is Pattie Heatherton, the principal of Rubenton High School, as I wrote you. She's the wonderful person who has put it all together to allow the Stafford Theatre to happen." Pattie broke into a shy, girlish smile. "She's our mainstay, our patron, and our angel."

"Oh, well, I had hope not to meet an actual angel," Ben said, now stroking Pattie's hand, "until shortly after my demise. But I must say, it would have been a shame to have waited."

"Why, thank you, Mr. Alyn." It was surprising that Pattie did not curtsy.

"Please, 'Mr. Alyn' was my grandfather. 'Benjamin' was my father. And I am but the humble Ben."

"And did you get your charm from your Grandfather and father?"

"No, only my testosterone. I'm afraid the charm I had to manufacture myself."

"Well, you've done an excellent job."

"Thank you, my—seraph. Yes, that's what I will refer to you as— my seraph."

"Well, we better go," Austin said, picking up Ben's suitcase. We're going to drop your seraph off at the high school first, and then I'll take you to the hotel and get you settled, and then, if you're up to it, I'll show you the theater."

"Let's go!" Ben said, taking Pattie by the arm and leading her out of the mini-mart terminal.

On the way to drop Pattie off, she dominated the time by waxing, not to mention polishing, enthusiastically about how thrilled they were that Ben was going to play such an important part in the inaugural production of the Stafford Theatre. And how happy she was that he had agreed to teach several "master classes" in acting for the students. Ben had made no such agreement. It was just an idea that Austin had mentioned to Pattie. But Ben was trouper enough not to put a damper on the idea. And, indeed, actor enough, through the subterfuge of grandiloquence, to convincingly portray how he had been excitingly looking forward to this opportunity that Austin, "...and my Seraph, of course," was affording him. "The molding of nubile young talent has always been one of my pleasures."

"Besides being a star in Hollywood," Austin said, "Ben is well known as a sought-after private acting coach."

"Really?" Pattie said. "Well, I'm beginning to understand that people in show business are very giving with each other."

"We're a community, that's for sure," Ben said with group identity pride. E did not mention that the private coaching started as just a supplement to his income but eventually became the bulk, managed from the closet-like actor's studio he maintained over a tux shop in Studio City. "You can't just be a taker; you have to give back."

Pattie also explained how they planned a special dinner in Ben's honor the next night at The Briers. She would be in attendance with her husband (she did not refer to him by either his well-known appellation or the private one she had shared only with Austin). And the members of the town council and the school board, Rubenton's head librarian, and, of course, the press, represented by the editor and chief reporter of the Rubenton Rubric, their weekly newspaper, the front page always printed in red ink. "It's just our simple way of welcoming you and showing our gratitude."

Ben did not doubt that it would be simple. "Well, it sounds delightful," he said, nevertheless.

After they had dropped Pattie off at the high school and Austin and Ben were heading out of town toward Leech Beach Road, Ben got out his cell phone, turned it on, and was displeased with it.

"Is there a problem in this area with cell phones?" Ben asked. "I couldn't get a signal out at that rinky-dink airport, and I still can't."

"Well, yeah, this is not a good area for cell phones. But they've got plans to build a microwave tower."

"Like the plan to build a new airport?"

"Yeah. The town has a lot of plans. This place is really burgeoning, and, quite frankly, the Stafford Theatre is not only going to be a big part of it; it's probably going to be the spearhead. The arts, and culture, once again, are leading the way. But will this country ever get it?"

"The Stafford Theatre?"

"Yeah."

"Where'd you get that from?"

"I named it after Jack Stafford."

"That old fart!"

"Hey, Jack Stafford has always been very kind to me. So I thought it was the right thing to do."

"Really? More likely just another reason for him to feel like a god on earth. But look, this cell phone problem, how will my agent get me at a moment's notice? You know agents, they're all about the moment."

"Relax, I've already taken care of it. I've alerted Mrs. Briers and the hotel's assistant manager that you might be getting calls from Hollywood and to get messages to you immediately. And I've told them you would provide them with a list of names they should look out for, and—"

"You have?"

"Sure."

"Shit! Now I've got to make up a bunch of names. I'll put down Spielberg, of course, and Redford, you know, people they've probably heard of."

"Ben, you don't have to—"

"But what about when we take a break and decide to go out on the town?"

"Ben, you were just there; there's not much town to go out on."

"Which is why the Stafford Theatre will be the spearhead?"

"Exactly."

"Well, maybe I'm overreacting. After all, I partly took this gig because I wanted to get away from there for a while. I guess Jackson was right."

"Jackson?"

"You know him, Jackson Beck."

"Oh, yeah, you did that Odets with him."

"Yeah, what a miserable experience that was! I got awfully tired of waiting for Lefty. Anyway, Jackson said I was addicted to Hollywood heroin."

"Well, it can be virulent, that's for sure."

Ben wanted to ask how the hell Austin would know, but of course, he did not. Instead, he fell into a silence that Austin respected, and they drove that way until they turned onto Leech Beach Road. Ben brightened up at the scenery, which he thought was beautiful. "Bucolic," Ben kept calling it and loved the twist and turns of the route. He was fascinated to see the little farms, and every time they passed small herd-letts of cows at pasture, he would stick his head out of the window and go, "Mooooooo! Mooooooo!"

"I used to do that when I was a kid. Grew up in Azusa. You know where that is? Out past Pasadena. It's right under the San Gabriel Mountains, you see, and whenever my dad took us up there to go to Crystal Lake or someplace, we'd pass by the huge Foothill Dairy, which was just at the foot of the mountain. No, don't ask me why they didn't call it Footmountain Dairy; I have no idea. Anyway, it stunk to high heaven with cow shit, but then, you know, you don't care about those things when you're a kid. So there was just this huge—I don't know what you want to call it, corral or pen or something—of cows. Black and white cows. And everybody in our family would go Mooooooo! Mooooooo! I cannot pass cows today without doing that, can't do it, physically impossible."

"Azusa, huh? Never been out there."

"Why would anybody ever go out there? Not the cultural highlight of Southern California, I can tell you. Probably one of the few cities in all of America where their hardtop movie theater closed for lack of business before their drive-in."

"You're kidding."

"No, I'm serious; they tore it down years ago. The drive-in is now a church—the First Church of Petting on the First Date or something. Azusa did have one of the first MacDonald's, though. That put them on the map! But, of course, that's been torn down too, so I guess Azusa is back off the map. Still, compared to Rubenton...."

Ben did not finish the thought as they suddenly came over the slight rise, revealing the ocean and Leech Beach.

"Oh, my God," Ben said. "This is cool; this is really kind of neat. Is that the hotel?"

"Yep."

"Crazy. You're right, what you said in your letter. It's like a little pocket in the world here; you're sort of isolated."

"Yeah, but everybody comes out here, from Rubenton and around. It's a well-known place. I mean to the locals."

"But it's not like a beach resort or anything?"

"Too foggy, too cold most of the time. But that's what we all like about it, I guess."

"Interesting. Well, Austin, maybe you've brought me out here not just on a trip but on a journey. Wouldn't that be fun!"

"Shit!"

Which was precisely what Dmitri had slipped on and fell into. Not chicken shit, but a few good fresh cow patties. Mr. Hendrickson saw this and laughed uproariously. In fact, in the time-honored tradition of a man of his ilk, he busted a gut while doubling over and may have even slapped his knee. Dmitri saw this as a slight to his honor, for some strange reason of possibly atavistic origin.

"Shut up!" Dmitri screamed. "Cut it out!"

Mr. Hendrickson did so immediately. There was something about the tenor of Dmitri's voice that he decided to take seriously.

"Okay, boy, don't get upset."

"Christ! Shit! Fuck!" Dmitri said, determined to be upset as he looked around at the shit where he now sat. And how much of it had adhered to his person. Especially right after he had plopped his patootie in the patties when he had lifted his hand in confusion and had run it through his hair, smearing shit through the strands.

"Now, come on, boy," Mr. Hendrickson said, walking over to Dmitri, offering him a hand up. "Don't take it so hard. Every farmer falls into some crap now and then."

"I'm not a farmer!" Dmitri said to Mr. Hendrickson's offered hand, again in a disturbing tone, and again Mr. Hendrickson noted but refused to acknowledge.

"Oh, I don't know," the farmer said calmly. "You've been doing pretty good." Then he reached down, grabbed the boy by the armpits, and gently pulled him up, receiving no resistance from Dmitri. "Let's get you into the house and into the tub and washed up. I've got some of my boys' old clothes that I think will fit ya."

Mr. Hendrickson led Dmitri to the back porch and told him to "Get out of them clothes."

"What! Here?"

"Well, I'm not going to let you track that shit all over the house."

"But then I'll be naked."

"Yes, that'll be the outcome of taking your clothes off, all right."

"Outside! I'll be naked outside!"

"Well, boy, there ain't nobody that can see you, and you won't be outside that long. Now just take your damn clothes off."

"You're a dumb piece of shit; you know that!"

Despite the anger in Dmitri's eyes, Mr. Hendrickson was sure he could see some sadness there. But maybe he had just wanted to or needed to, or perhaps he had spent too much of his life looking into the deep brown eyes of dumb cows. "Now, Dmitri, if you want to stand out here letting that shit dry on you while you draw all the local flies, go ahead. Me, I'm going inside and fix me some lunch." Mr. Hendrickson opened the screened back door and entered, saying as he passed, "Just don't stand by the door, don't want the smell to ruin my appetite."

"Oh, all right." Dmitri started to take his clothes off, then thought of something. "When I come through, don't look," he shouted through the door.

"Ain't nothing I haven't seen before," Mr. Hendrickson said from the kitchen.

"You haven't seen me before."

"Well, that's true. Is there something special about you that you don't want me to see?"

"No. It's just that, well, no one's ever seen me before except my dad and my grandma."

"You mean no girls have seen ya?"

"Well, yeah, sure, plenty of girls have seen me nude. I turn them on. They like my dick; I got a huge dick! But I don't want to show it to you."

"Hey, I don't want to see it. It might make me nostalgic for that bull I had back in '83. So, look, I'm gonna just stick my head in the refrigerator to look for some baloney, and you can streak through unobserved. Okay? So ya ready?"

Dmitri, standing nude on the back porch next to his pile of shitty clothes, feeling a strange freedom he had never felt before, yelled through the screen door, "Ready!"

"Okay, I am inserting my head in the refrigerator in five, okay? So get ready: Five-four-three-two-one—streak!"

Dmitri opened the screen door, ran through the kitchen into the back hall, and then dashed into the bathroom.

Later, sitting in the bathtub as the water steamed, so did Dmitri. He could hear Mr. Hendrickson in the kitchen, allowing himself a little laugh. "Fucking bastard!" Dmitri muttered. "Fucking son-of-a-bitch! I'll get him!"

"Hey, Jackson, how are you? It's Ben."

. . .

"Yeah, yeah, look, no, no, I just called to say hi, play catch-up, wanted to thank you again for sending on my Variety's."

. . .

"Sure, yeah, been receiving them fine."

. . .

"No, no, once a week is good; you shouldn't have to deal with them daily; no, that's too much to ask."

. . .

"No, really, the FedEx comes on Saturday, and I sit down and go through them in about an hour, less most of the time. Not much of interest in them, if you think about it, so I can just sit in my room and get them read. I got this great room; I told you about that, right? Anyway, I got this big window, and I just look out at the ocean—when you can see it—there's a lot of fog here all the time, and—"

. . .

"Yeah, no, this place is crazy, Jackson, it's really kind of crazy. But I'm getting kind of attached to it. The rehearsals are going okay. I mean, What Price Glory, it's kind of a no-brainer play to do. Yeah, sure, Austin's doing okay directing—surprisingly better than I expected. He's got some bright ideas and passion, Jesus Christ; he's got the passion for it. He's intensely riding this old warhorse. What I like about him—and don't we always like this about directors? —what I like is he's always open to suggestions. So I, well, I wouldn't say I'm co-directing with him, but I'm certainly adding my two cents now and then. Two cents? Hell, my valuable twenty-nine ninety-five worth now and then. And I'd say, at least fifty percent of the time, if not more, he's receptive to my ideas, especially on his performance, because you know how hard it is to direct yourself. So I'm just going along with that. And another good thing is, he's got this guy here, a guy who lives in the hotel, a retired Army major. Austin had him write up this amazing response to the play based on his own military experiences and, I guess, his father's, who was a career soldier or something, and Austin and I are studying this. We're trying to get some real verisimilitude—if I can thrill you with such lovely language, Jackson— some real verisimilitude about these characters, which ain't easy seeing how we are the only pros here. I mean, we are acting with a bunch of high school kids playing all the other roles, even some of the older soldiers. And as much as being around youth can invigorate one; I've had to do a couple quote-unquote master classes with the kids just to get them into our neighborhood. They're still several blocks away, of course, but being young, they are blessedly malleable. Except for this girl playing the one female role in the play, Charmaine De La Cognac. Got to love that name, right? Anyway, she's, I mean the actress, if I may abuse that appellation, is not from the high school, I mean, she, Trudy's her name, she went there before they started this new drama department, I explained all that to you before, right?"

. . .

"Anyway, now she's a waitress at the hotel—"

. . .

"Yeah, no, I'm not kidding. Anyway, Trudy really wants to be an actress, so Austin gave her the role. And, I have got to tell you, she's probably one of the worst actresses I've ever had to deal with in my career, okay? But, oddly enough, she's a good mimic—crappy actress but a great mimic. Austin says it comes from her worshipping Cissy McMann because she can do a dead-on Cissy McMann. I guess she's memorized every line Cissy had on that show and can do it exactly as Cissy did, including all the blocking and gestures. It's freaky, I can tell you. So Austin gets this brilliant idea. He has her study the old Cagney film version of the play; makes her watch it a hundred times or something, so she can mimic the actress who did the role in the movie. And it worked! I mean, that style is a little bit off from what we are doing otherwise, but it doesn't matter because, you know, she's just a little French slut, right? At first, Trudy didn't want to do this because she kept saying she would rather just play herself because she thought 'herself' to be damn neat—if you can imagine such a thing. 'Honey,' I told her, 'Maxwell Anderson did not write you into this play; he wrote a French slut into the play.' 'But-but,' she says. 'But shut the fuck up,' I say. 'Do you want to be an actress or not?' 'Yes,' she says. 'Well, have you ever noticed actresses tend to play a variety of parts, that they occupy many skins?' 'That doesn't matter,' she says. We almost had a knockdown, drag-out on that one. I mean, I have not been subtle in my criticisms of her acting abilities or lack thereof. But, damn it, I have some professional integrity. I mean, the play's the thing, Jackson, the play's the thing. But once, like I said, we got her to give us that mimic thing without bitching about it, well, you know, I guess she'll do okay. I mean, really, who cares? Who the hell's going to see this thing except the locals anyway? Still, she's pretty good-looking, and this place is not chock-a-block with sexual liaison possibilities outside of the under eighteen high school girls on the stage crew who all worship me. But I've never resorted to that bit of illegal passion, as you know, and I don't think I'll start in a place where shotguns might well be natural appendages of the paterfamilias around here. Of course, I have heard of a local bordello, but it seems to be frequented mainly by the men working on the oil drilling platforms, which burn brightly at night out on the ocean around here when you can see past the fog. That might be okay, but I have the feeling the ladies might have a slight smell of kerosene about them. I can't imagine they're great beauties, unlike the lovely Heidi and her crew, right? So, out of self-interest, I guess I should be kinder to the young-but-not-too-young Trudy. I mean, who knows, maybe in time if she improves...."

...

"Well, you see, I'm thinking Austin is so passionate about this theater that, you know, maybe I'll stick around. He needs some pros to form a real company; he obviously can't do it with just the local talent. So I'm already thinking about plays we could do together after this one. You know, The Front Page, The Odd Couple...."

...

"Well, hell, Jackson, why not?"

...

"No, I haven't heard from my agent. I've left three calls; he's never called back. Hell, I was off the map as far as he was concerned when I was home, so I've just, you know, taken myself off the map for real. Here, at least, I can act. Maybe we can get some of these kids up in quality, and we can do some good work."

. . .

"No, I'm afraid not; the surrounding area is not terribly exciting. Although there's sort of these farms that come up inland from the beach area before you get to any towns, and they're very—farm-y. I like them. The roll of the land, and all that. The animals and all that. It's quite charming to drive among them, this bucolic world of no overweening ambitions except to grow the crops and fatten the cattle. A man can breathe deep there, as I'm sure the farmers say."

. . .

"Of course, I'm being romantic about it, Jackson; what fun would there be if I weren't?"

. . .

"Well, you see, I'm not planning to work on the farms, so, yes, I can afford to be romantic, can't I, so why begrudge me as you sit in your little desperately-in-need-of-repairs-one-bedroom-Laurel Canyon-bungalow-waiting-for-either-a-fire-or-mudslide-to-destroy-it-so-you-can-collect-the-insurance-and-buy-a-condo-in-Westlake LA smugness."

. . .

"What? Are you kidding? One point three million for that dump?"

. . .

"Oh, of course, the land. Well, you're going to take it, right?"

. . .

"Well, I know your mother left it to you, Jackson, but still, sell the damn thing and get your condo in Westlake."

. . .

"Oxnard? That far out?"

. . .

"Well, yes, I know, but it sounds like something you would schnort out of your nose. You know, OX-SCHNARD! Well, in any case, sell the house, take the money, and God bless you. Oh! You know something I keep forgetting to tell you. Guess who the owner of the hotel is? Well, you know it's called The Briers, right? So do you remember a Briers in the business?"

. . .

"Come on, Jackson, give it some thought."

...

"Of course, you do. Think bad B movies desperate for cult status."

...

"Jackson, it's Duncan Briers!"

...

"Yeah, no, I'm not kidding, really, it's Duncan Briers!"

...

"No, I never did a film with him, but I remember the crap he used to do and that one, you know, that one weird one that kinda became famous. I forget its name. Although, you know, I think I auditioned for him once. Oh yeah, I remember now. I did! I'd completely forgotten. God, I'll have to tell him."

...

"Yeah, that's right, cracked up his car and almost died. That's when he came back here."

...

"No, he didn't start it; his parents owned it. He took it over when his father died and married—if you can imagine this—the woman managing the place for his dad, Emily. An interesting woman. She really runs the place. Duncan doesn't have much to do with it."

...

"Tools around in a wheelchair pushed by this strange idiot kid he hired, plays the stock market, and watches old movies."

...

"No, not his old movies, old old movies. You know, the classics, Thirties, Forties, Fifties, that sort of stuff. I sometimes go up to his room and watch some with him while I get politely smashed. Grand stuff, good stuff, what a star I could have been then."

...

"Well, I should let you go, Jackson. Take care; give no one my regards, as I'm sure no one misses me."

...

"Well, thank you, Ben, that's nice of you to say so. Enjoy OX-SCHNARD!"

Ben hung up the phone and fell into the quiet formed by the cessation of his voice. He looked out his window at an ocean, happy to be free this afternoon from its too familiar blanket of fog but still oppressed by the clouds above, which had put it into a gray mood. My mood as well, Ben thought. He hated breaks from rehearsals. What else was there to do? Should I drink, read, or masturbate? Or do all three? Drinking alone was just sad. Reading alone was natural, but the Cussler he had was just not doing it for him. Masturbating alone was also entirely natural, but he was afraid he would use it to spend too much mental time on the young-but-not-too-young Trudy, who had lately resided too much in his brain as it was. His confession to Jackson of a desire aimed at Trudy had been much lighter than the truth. The truth was he had become fixated on the girl.

First, because he couldn't believe that he had to act with such an incredibly bad amateur, it had pissed him off. It had driven him nuts. And he had felt it his duty to let her know in language unclouded, unfogged by any equivocation, that she not only had minuscule talents regarding the dramatic arts but was a living insult to those arts. It had been his duty as a performing artist of some note, merit, and integrity.

Second, because he couldn't believe how fresh her flesh seemed, how full of the essence of carnal delight it was as it beamed its light—yes, it had its own light—out into the world.

Third, because he could not get enough of the positive energy that she exuded, even when she was being difficult and just refused to understand.

But that was the energy that so attracted him, so thrilled him. The energy of pure ego, a bright, shining, innocent, glowing ego, unblemished, untouched by truth and reality, and yet not rank, not poisonous, not putrid along the edges like the egos he had dealt with daily in the splendid profession he had chosen. How could that be? He did not know. He did not care to know. He just found it so damn attractive.

Ben wanted some of that energy. He wanted her to smile and beam it at him; he wanted to hug her and soak it up; he wanted to kiss her and drink it in; he wanted to penetrate her and drill for it, like those derricks out on those platforms out on the ocean.

"Holy baloney," he said, reviving an original exclamation from his Azusa teenage years that he had created to set himself apart from the crowd. "What the hell am I supposed to do about this?"

Nothing for the moment, he knew. And it was a moment wherein he needed some diversion. Drink, read, or masturbate? Hell, no!

Ben picked up the phone and dialed another room. "Duncan, hi, Ben here. Are you, by any chance, watching some wonderful old movie and wouldn't mind a companion? The Maltese Falcon! Perfect! He sends the girl to the gallows, right? I'll be right up!"

When Frank listened to the message Allison had left on his voice mail, he could not decide if it was cryptic or just perfunctory.

Frank, I'll be in New York longer than I expected. I'll see you when I get home.

The message was maddening for several reasons. First, Allison had not said how long she would be in New York; she had only made a guess—a couple of days, a week or so maybe—and it had only been a couple of days, so why was she leaving this message? And second, if she took the time to leave a message, why didn't she say anything personal? Like:

Having a good time, wish you were here.

Or:

I miss you. Do you miss me?

Or:

I can't wait to have you in my arms again and be penetrated with your love rod.

Something along those lines would have been nice.

But she had gone to New York on business, so maybe, Frank thought, she's just being business-like. But then, what about the business? There was no:

Reactions to your work are incredible! They think you're a genius!

But then again, there was also no:

Sorry, Frank, they think your work is crap, so now I think your work is crap too. So I'm not coming home. I'm going to stay here in New York, where nothing is crap like you are crap.

It was just:

Frank, I'll be in New York longer than I expected. I'll see you when I get home.

Not that Frank minded the extra time to deal with the Trudy situation; Allison could take all the time she wanted. But then, again, if Frank was now officially designated by the big city, Big Apple, inner circle, high muckety-muck, oh-so-precious-and-powerful-cultural-Mafioso-arbitrators-of-art-as-crap, there was no reason to deal with the Trudy situation at all. And every reason to delight in it.

That was certainly a thought. But then Frank had another thought. The thought of someone flying excitedly to New York on his artistic/creative behalf, and that was better than sex, wasn't it? He had been tempted to believe so but had resisted that temptation. He concluded instead that the good feelings engendered by this thought were of a different kind and quality than sex and, therefore, did not need to be put into competition with it. But now, he was not so sure. Having a champion may well be better than having sex.

Now this champion had left him a perfunctory message that she did not need to, leaving him in a state of anxious perspiration. It would have been better to have stayed in glorious anticipation, assuming every day she remained in New York was a day she was succeeding in elevating his cause among the brilliant admirers of true talent. They who sat on their near celestial Manhattan thrones.

He played the message again, listening for the tone, timbre, pitch, and personality of the message, any one of which could be hiding the real message of the message, covering up the actual communication, deflecting the real into a surreal mundane:

Frank, I'll be in New York longer than I expected. I'll see you when I get home.

What the hell did that mean?

It could mean that things were going well, people were giving his work serious and due consideration, but nothing happens overnight. People always needed more time. Allison was persevering and staying the course and remaining true, so she needed more time herself. Still, as nothing was yet locked down, despite being positive, she didn't want to even leave a hint of possible success, for why build up hopes only to have them dashed?

How extremely loving and considerate that was of her.

And then, again, it might mean that now that she was in the center of the universe, she realized just how out on the fringe Frank was.

Or that while getting her education in the art market, she had met an extremely well-dressed, well-groomed, well-mannered, well-financed gallery owner. Who, with but the mere lifting of the merest finger on his left hand (assuming he was right-handed), could make Frank the most important artist of the decade. But as Allison had fallen in love with him at first sight, and he fell mutually as well, she was now too busy having a classic Manhattan romantic episode to deal with the annoying irritation of Frank's minuscule talent.

In either case, guilt—a deep, searing, nauseating guilt, Frank hoped—caused her to leave a message that communicated nothing.

And nothing, Frank finally decided, was what he could do about it. He almost, in fact, chose not to keep an appointment with the architect to go over preliminary drawings of the studio's interior. But he did and should have been excited by the architect's concept. But Frank could not feel it due to the deadening influence of his insecurity over whether the concept would ever become concrete.

It made him yearn for the days when he was a tremendous talent, a magnificent artist, infused with a stunning vision that reached revelatory heights. Yes, it was all in his mind, but at least enclosed therein, it was much more in his control.

He had always hated riding in the passenger seat.

When Allison did return a week and a half later, it was after a torturous trip that questioned the reality of whether we had indeed entered the 21st Century. Or the "Future" as it was known in her childhood. Does anyone still think the "Future" will be a perfect egalitarian paradise of technological marvels that will ease the burdens of life and see us all beautiful, smiling, and dressed in colorful and stylish jumpsuits? She did not think so. In one of the several waiting areas deemed "comfortable" by the airport management, where she uncomfortably waited during one of the many hours she had waited that day, Allison had tried to imagine the "Future." Not just tomorrow, next year, or even a decade hence, but a better future markedly different from the present that might be the adult reality for any child born today. She could not do it. Imaginative futures, she guessed, were a thing of the past. How sad.

There were several reasons why this trip home had been tortuous— mechanical failures; false alarms; a suspected terrorist; a fidgety seatmate of copious girth. But none had been worse than the moment when she had finished the last page of the only book she had brought for the flight. And the flight had not yet happened. Panic drove Allison to the gift shop and its rack of mass-market paperbacks, a hoped-for oasis in the middle of a desert. But the spinning rack had disappointed her as deeply as if it had been a mirage. Most of the books flashing by her hungry eyes were newly copyrighted and of no interest. There were several serial killer suspense novels and a couple of suspenseful True Crime books about serial killers. There were How-to-Become-Rich business books and one book on how to save your soul by becoming a rich Christian. There were three rising television star confessionals and two confessionals by political stars that had fallen. There were romance novels with no sex and sexy novels with no romance. There was a biography of a brilliant, consistently dirty comedian wherein he revealed that he had been buggered by a priest or two as a child. And there was a book by two priests blaming all the current moral depravity in the country on pop artists, especially brilliant, consistently dirty comedians. There was a How-to-Beat-the-Odds-in-Vegas book. A How-to-Beat-the-Uncertainties-of-Wall Street book. And a How-to-Beat-Your-Wife book. But the latter one, Allison assumed, was a satire. And then there was the current number one New York Times Best Seller that purported to reveal the secret writings of Jesus Christ. The writings indicated that Jesus was, in reality, a time traveler from our distant future sent back to start the world onto a non-pagan path. Otherwise, the Roman Empire would have spread across the globe and time, and we would never have had priests buggering and blaming. Allison wondered if Jesus had ever worn a jumpsuit. There were a few, just a few, books that one might call classics. But how often can one read Agatha Christie?

As sad as she had ever been, Allison returned to the waiting area with nothing but a Time magazine with a cover story on a subject that did not interest her. She sat down and opened the magazine to the "back of the book." She started to read a book review of a new memoir by a devout but progressive Islamic woman who had, dressed in an entirely traditional burka and Nikes, jogged in diminishing concentric circles every foot of her native theocracy as a protest over the subjugation of women. The book was entitled I Ran Iran. Allison suddenly got a brilliant and audacious idea in the middle of the glowing review. She stood up and quickly made her way to the lost luggage department.

"Do you only have lost luggage here?" Allison asked the official and officious custodian of the lost, a man of no great height, but as Allison had no height at all, it did not prevent him from looking down on her as he said:

"What?"

"I mean, do you have other items besides luggage that may have been inadvertently left in the waiting areas or on the planes," Allison said with clarity, something she now knew the custodian of the lost would be lost without.

"Yeah, sure, lots of junk."

"Books? Do you have any books?"

"Yeah, lots of that crap. Whatcha looking for?"

"What have you got?"

"I mean, what book did you lose?"

"I didn't lose a book. I just want to see what you've got."

"Why?"

"I might want to read one."

"Why?"

"Does it matter?"

"No, because I can't give you anything, but what you can prove is yours."

"Do you have books back there that have been there a long time?"

"Yeah."

"Think anybody's ever going to claim them?"

"No."

"So why can't I have one?"

"Because they ain't yours."

"Fifty dollars says at least one of them must be."

"You'd pay fifty dollars for some old lost book?"

"If it's the right book."

"Oh, I get it. Some collector's item, huh?"

"No. I just need something to read."

"You'd pay fifty dollars just for something to read?"

"In cash."

"Weird."

"Thank you for that insult. Should I report you to the management now, Mr.…." Allison looked at his nametag. "Mr. Johnston? Or should I wait and write a letter of complaint?"

"What are you going to complain about? That I wouldn't take a bribe?" the custodian of the lost asked, displaying more intelligence than Allison had credited him. "They got books at the gift shop."

"They've got nothing that I want."

"Pretty damn particular, aren't you?"

"Yes, I am proud to say," Allison declared, planting her petite body in such a way before Mr. Johnston that he knew that she had become, small though she was and with blue eyes as intense as they were, an immovable object.

"Well—fifty dollars, huh?"

"No. One hundred."

"Come into my library," the custodian of the lost said, opening the door to his domain.

Allison found a beat-up college edition paperback copy of Thackeray's Vanity Fair. "Bless those students going home on holidays," she thought, putting aside her usual disdain for used books.

So, for the rest of the tortuous trip, Allison had, at least, the amusing companionship of that little social climber, Becky Sharp. And when it finally ended—the trip, not Vanity Fair—she found herself back in Rubenton just after eleven-thirty at night on the day she was supposed to have been home just before one that afternoon.

Wearily, Allison got into her car—dirty from sitting at the airfield while she was away—and drove to The Briers. A certain amount of apprehension-boarding-on-fear kept her safely awake as she traveled the last leg of her epic journey along the intensely dark Leech Beach Road on this moonless night. However, as Allison drove over the final rise of the road, she experienced and embraced a lovely sense of relief when she spotted The Briers at the bottom of the road, illuminated by a few diffused lights breaking through a shroud of newly arrived fog. It was a sight more welcomed than she could ever have imagined. She happily entered the hotel's warmth, gladly received what she took to be the sincere greeting of the night desk clerk, and gratefully allowed him to relieve her of her luggage and escort her upstairs to her room. She did not unpack; she did not undress; she just collapsed onto her bed and quickly fell asleep.

The following day Allison did not wake up before dawn, as was usually her habit. So when she did wake up, she was famished but did not have the energy to make it downstairs for breakfast. She ordered room service instead and took a quick shower before it arrived.

Allison had imagined that when the kitchen got word that she was home and had ordered breakfast, Frank would be delivered it, which would be good because she had things to tell him. But Frank did not arrive with her Eggs Benedict and hot tea; Trudy did.

"Good morning, Mrs. Carr. Welcome back. Did you have a good trip?" Trudy said upon entering, carrying a room service tray and dispensing more cheer than Allison required.

"Thank you, Trudy. Yes, it was fine."

"Where was it you went again?" Trudy placed the tray on the desk in Allison's sitting room. She began to arrange Allison's meal, taking the metal lid off the plate of Eggs Benedict, unrolling the cloth napkin, taking out the silverware inside, and placing them in their proper positions beside the plate. And she put a little vase with a little carnation at the spot she thought most pleasant.

"To New York," Allison said.

"Oh really? That's great! I want to go to New York someday. Did you see any Broadway plays?"

"Actually, I was able to get to two of them."

"Really? Were there any stars in them?"

"Well, gee, I don't know. I don't pay attention to who are stars or not, dear. But I believe that in the revival I saw of Long Day's Journey into Night, Edmund was played by a young man best known for some TV show or other. But I couldn't tell you his name."

"Jordan Jones, he's on The Agony Factor. I saw his picture at the opening night party in People Magazine."

"Oh, was that his name? Well, he was very good."

"Yeah, he's neat. I would love to see him in the play. Well, here you go!" Trudy indicated Allison's breakfast, now beautifully laid out.

Allison approached the desk, sat down, grabbed a piece of wheat toast, and started to butter it.

"I don't mean to be rude, Trudy, but I'm quite hungry," Allison said just before she bit into the toast.

"No problem. Let me pour your tea."

Trudy did so as Allison, her mouth full nodded and gently grunted her thanks.

"Is it a good play?" Trudy asked as she put the pot down.

Allison swallowed and said, "Well, it's a classic"

"So I guess that means it's good, then, huh?"

Trudy surprised Allison by sitting down on the edge of the couch.

"Well, it's stood the test of time; continues to speak to people; remains relevant, all that sort of stuff." Allison bit off some more wheat toast and consciously decided to breach etiquette by continuing to speak while chewing. "Of course, as good and classic as a piece can be, the production could be bad, which this one, fortunately, was not."

"You know, I'm doing a play." Trudy sat back on the couch and made herself comfortable.

Allison began the process of cutting her Eggs Benedict into bite-size pieces. "Really?"

"Yeah, here at the new theater."

"Oh, yes, I heard something about that."

"I'm the only girl in the whole play."

"Well," Allison took a sip of tea to clear her palate, so the first taste of Hollandaise would be as potent and pleasing as possible, "that must be exciting for you."

"Well, it sort of is. We're just getting started, and it's already a lot of hard work. But I guess you got to do that hard work to make stardom, you know."

"That applies to just about anything in life, Trudy."

"Yeah, I know. It's a bitch."

Allison was going to render a few choice bits of Wisdom for Young Women, which she had developed over the years, but thought better of it. Besides, if Trudy seemed to want to stick around, Allison had other concerns. "Is, uh, is Frank at work today?" Allison asked, looking at her meal.

"Oh, yeah, sure, he's here."

"Oh. I have half thought Frank would have brought up my breakfast."

"Really? Frank never brings room service up. You know he's the head waiter."

"Oh, yes, I know, but, uh, he knew I was going to New York, and he asked me to check into something for him, so I thought that when he heard I was home, he would come up to find out about it."

"Oh, that's funny you should say that because he almost did, come to think about it, which sort of surprised me, but I said, No, Frank, I'll take it, and I brought it up for him."

"Oh." Damn nice of Trudy, damn it, Allison thought. "Well, listen, can you wait a moment? I want to write him a little note if you'll take it down"

"Sure, of course."

Allison pulled out some notepaper from the desk's middle drawer and wrote a short note with a sparse amount of precise information. When she finished, she folded the paper and inserted it into an envelope, licking the glue on the flap to seal it. She wrote Frank's name on the front, then got up and walked over to Trudy, who was still sitting on the couch and handed it to her.

As Trudy reached for the note, she looked up with pleading eyes that surprised Allison and said, "Frank's a really nice guy, don't you think?"

"Frank? Well, yes, I've always been pleased with his service."

"Oh, yeah, he's good at that, but I mean, as a person, don't you think he's really special?"

"Ah. Sure. I guess I wouldn't argue with you on that, Trudy."

Trudy's eyes continued to hold Allison's as she said, "Even though he's older, he's not, like, you know, old—you know what I'm saying?"

"Well, Trudy, from my perspective, of course, he's actually a little bit younger."

"Oh, yeah, I guess that's right. Sorry. Well—maybe he's ageless!"

"Yes, that's probably a good way of putting it."

"And, uh, and kind of attractive, don't you think?"

Allison had to break the eye lock at this point, suddenly realizing the traffic was not just one way. She walked back over to her breakfast. "Attractive? Well, sure, I suppose."

"Well, you know, look, um, can I talk to you about something?"

Allison returned to her Eggs Benedict, sad to now find them victims of the Second Law of Thermodynamics. "Don't you have duties downstairs, Trudy?"

"Oh, the rush is over, and anyway, I'm here with you, doing my job."

"Well, okay."

"I just, well, I don't have anyone to talk to about this, and I need someone to talk to, and you just always seemed like someone I could talk to."

"That probably comes from my years of listening to girls your age talk about all manner of things. I guess I developed a sympathetic demeanor to young women."

"Yeah, I guess that's it, I just, you know, I'm excited about something, and I have no one to share it with right now because I've been sort of sworn to secrecy."

"Oh. Sounds very mysterious and exciting. Does it have something to do with the play?"

"Oh, no, not really."

"Well, then, I suppose it's something romantic."

"Oh yeah, it's definitely romantic. And, you see, it's someone here at The Briers, so that's why it's secret."

"Oh. Well, Trudy, if you wish to confide in me, of course, I'll keep all your secrets. You don't mind if I continue eating, do you?"

"Oh, of course not. I like those Eggs Benedict too."

"Yes, they're excellent," Allison said, forking a bite and lowering her voice as she addressed it sadly. "Nice when they're warm, though."

"Isn't it interesting how Julio can make such great Eggs Benedict even though he's Mexican and all that?"

Allison needed to swallow—twice—before she could speak again. "Trudy, that's, uh, that's hardly a politically correct thing to say, you know."

"Oh, my dad said because I grew up on a farm, I don't have to be politically correct."

"Really? That's an interesting point of view."

"Farmers are elemental, you see; my dad says. You know, close to the soil and all that. They grow the food for everybody without which they could not live, so farmers are the most right of all human beings, my dad says."

"Well, I can certainly see where they are right, all right."

"Yeah, well, I don't know if all that's true or not, but, you know, he's my Dad and all. But, personally, I think, yeah, sure it's important to provide food for people, but entertainers, you know actors, and people like that, they provide something for, well, you know, for the soul, I guess, and that's just as important, don't you think?"

"Well, I've spent a lifetime trying to do just that, although probably not in a very entertaining manner. But, anyway, yes, I think it's very wise of you to have figured that out. That said, though, everybody has a place in this world, and I don't know if we should judge—"

"Yeah, we're all, kind of, sort of like equal, aren't we?"

"Well, that's always been the ideal."

"I mean, you know, I don't have anything against Julio because he's Mexican, you know, because I really, you know, I really like Julio!" Trudy said in her typically enthusiastic manner.

It was, though, a manner Allison did not know was so typical of Trudy despite the number of meals Trudy had enthusiastically served her. "Oh! Oh, I see. Then, back to this romance." A Shakespearean one, Allison was now guessing, "Is it Julio we're talking about?"

"What! Julio? Oh, no, of course not. I mean, I like him okay, but sexually he creeps me out."

"Oh. Well, I'm—"

"It's not Julio. It's Frank!"

In a most feminine, delicate, and subtle form of slapstick, Allison's transport from plate to mouth of a cold bite of Eggs Benedict wound up smearing her right cheek. She immediately repaired the situation with her cloth napkin as she tried to gather her thoughts and hide the shock of the revelation. Although not surprising given the content of a portion of their previous conversation, which now quickly replayed itself in one section of Allison's brain as another section found itself unable to quell an incredulous tone to the voice it had ordered to express:

"You're having a romance with, um, Frank, um, the waiter?"

As she was used to using her mental capacities, it was inevitable that Allison would immediately analyze the question she had just asked and the implications her manner of asking it indicated to determine its level of hypocrisy. Was she not also having a romance—is that really what it was?—with Frank, the waiter? But all thought of hypocrisy left her when she reminded herself that she was not having a romance with Frank the waiter, but Frank the artist.

"Yes, Frank's my honey! Isn't that awesome? But I haven't been able to tell anybody because we work together, and Frank says it would cause a problem with Mrs. Briers."

Allison put down her fork and took a sip of tea, not so much gathering her thoughts now as trying to find some. What kind of thought? The angry, jealous ones of a woman scorned? No, that was not a role she wanted to play. At least, not right now, for her—whatever—with Frank was also a secret. Should she have the thoughts of an older woman offended by the fact of yet another older man having an affair with yet another younger woman? Younger woman? Hell, an older girl more accurately! But, no, that would be a boring bourgeois reaction. And yet, as she grabbed for the thoughts of a mature counselor to this budding woman, she decided she could couch them in such terms as:

"Well, Trudy… My goodness, you know there is a disparity of ages there."

"Oh, Mrs. Carr, I know you're more sophisticated than that. Younger women hook up with older men all the time."

"Well, yes, Trudy, sadly, that is the case. But if I am sophisticated, I'm sophisticated enough to know that usually, in such cases, the older man is, at a minimum, rich and powerful, not a head waiter at a hotel."

"Mrs. Carr! How shallow is that?

Yes, Allison had to question herself, how shallow was that? Not very, she decided

"You know Frank is so much more than that," Trudy declared.

Oh, so she…. "You know about that?"

"About what?"

"About Frank being more than a waiter?"

"Well, of course, I'm his lover! I mean, he's kind, and he's gentle, and he's really taught me how to fuck good."

Oh. Well. What! "Really? Did you need to be taught?"

"Sure, it's not instinctive, you know. That's what I came to Frank for, to begin with, you see, because, well…."

Trudy explained how her original plan of seduction involved Austin and how she had felt some need for expert advice in achieving that goal. She laid it out as rationally as she had for Frank, and Allison found that she had no desire to argue the point. Instead, Allison only wanted to resolve a conflict that continued to rage within her between herself as Trudy's councilor, a role taken reluctantly, and herself as Trudy's competition, a position Allison found hard to imagine. Nevertheless, the councilor in her finally won out. She gave Trudy some standard cautionary advice, even as she sat there astonished over Trudy's ultimate goal to become a major television and/or movie star. While simultaneously making Frank a world-famous restaurateur with a cable television show, a best-selling book or two, and his name on packages gracing supermarket shelves.

Eventually, Allison scooted Trudy out with the urgency that she had an appointment in Rubenton to make, reminding Trudy as she passed the threshold, "Be sure to give my note to Frank."

"Oh, I won't forget," Trudy said with a lilt. "And thanks for listening. I feel so much better knowing someone knows. Secrets are such a burden, and I'm glad to get this one off my chest."

Allison felt a quick shame for her knee-jerk desire to offer an analogy to breast reduction and enduring pride in not succumbing to the reflex. "You're welcome, honey," was all she said.

Trudy smiled and then bounced down the hall towards the stairs.

When Trudy handed Frank Allison's note, he took it gingerly, handled it delicately, and stared at it as if he had acquired one of Superman's lesser powers, X-ray vision. But, unfortunately, he had not and so could not look beyond the thick, cream-colored envelope embossed with Allison's initials to discern the written contents within.

"Aren't you going to open it?" Trudy asked with a typical lover's attitude that she had a right to share in all things.

"Not right now; I'm working," Frank said as if Trudy had questioned his honor. He then slipped the envelope into his back pants pocket.

"Oh." Trudy did not seem fazed or impressed by Frank's sense of honor. She just smiled as she, in a lovely display of a lover's omniscience, stated, "Well, it has something to do with whatever she was checking on for you in New York,"

"So I figured." Frank started to move, desperate to find some duty to perform. Trudy moved in concert, her duty well defined.

"What are you interested in that's in New York?"

Frank impressed himself with a ready answer. "Cream Soda."

"Cream soda? What's that?"

"It's a soft drink you get in New York delis. Really good. They have a local brand in New York that I've been after Mrs. Briers to order. Mrs. Carr was just checking on their corporate address for me."

"Isn't that something you could check on the Internet about?"

"Yes, I suppose I could have if I actually had a computer."

"Well, my dad has one; I could have checked for you."

"Well, honey, I guess when I think of you, I don't think of computers. Mrs. Carr was going to New York, so I just thought—"

"Cream Soda, yech! Sounds horrible. Like fizzy milk or something."

"Why don't you check the dining room? There's a least one customer left, right?"

Trudy turned around and headed for the dining room, and Frank turned around and headed for Everyman's sanctuary. Once settled on the toilet seat, he took Allison's envelope, ripped it open, took out the note, and quickly read it.

MEET ME AT THE "STUDIO" AT 3 PM

It was hardly a satisfying missive. And what did Allison mean by the quote marks?

One often leaves a toilet dissatisfied, but rarely in the life of Man had there been such an emotional component to it.

When Allison got to the warehouse, Frank was already there. He came up to her as she was getting out of her car.

"Hi, welcome home!" he said with a big smile propped up at either end with solid apprehension.

"Thanks," Allison said with far more control of her smile.

"Was it a good trip?"

"Any trip you return from is a good trip."

What the hell did that mean?

Allison walked toward the building, looking around at the number of workmen carting away various debris left by Peterson Precision Parts, possibly even an abandoned putt-putt or two.

"I see they've started the clean-up to prepare for the renovation."

"Well, yes, the contractor called and asked if it was okay to get the clean-up out of the way. I didn't think it would be a problem."

"Sure, of course."

"Watch your step!"

Allison had almost stepped on a sharp piece of scrap metal. Frank's warning caused her to stop short, and she lost her balance and began to fall backward, but Frank was there, and Frank held her up. It was nice being momentarily in Frank's arms.

"So, Allison...."

Allison retook control and said, "Frank, we have to talk about something first."

"What is there to talk about but—"

"I think sex was a big mistake."

Frank looked at her, wondering where the purity of artistic considerations had gone.

"As a reproduction strategy," he asked, "for life on Earth, or—"

"You know what I mean. I blame myself. I'm sorry. It was ridiculous, and to be honest, I'm a little bit embarrassed."

There were a million bits of dialog, or so it seemed, that Frank could have called up at this moment. Dialog that had often been stated in such situations before. Whether in life, in novels, movies, TV shows, on the stage, among boys and girls; men and women; men and men; women and women; possibly even men and goats and women and donkeys. Hell, he didn't know. But among all sorts, at all times, in all mediums except, he assumed, video games. But he couldn't think of any, for all he was thinking was: What the hell did she find out in New York regarding my art—my art, damn it, damn your embarrassment, damn the sex, but don't damn my—

"I don't want you to feel like a kept man."

"A kept man? Well, I did have some momentary feelings along that—"

"It was unfair of me to turn my interest in you as a person, then as an artist, into something so—so carnal."

Yes, right, good, him as an artist! And yet he found himself saying:

"Carnal can be good. It's part of life."

"But there are so many emotions attached, and shouldn't our relationship be dispassionate?"

"Art is passion!"

"Yes, but I'm coming at it from a business point of view."

"No, you're not. You wanted to be involved in my story, wasn't that it? You wanted to be my champion."

"Well, yes. But after having gone to New York, I now realize how much stories, art—patronage, even—are all just elements of business."

"And yet you sound so sad about that."

"Not sad. Realistic."

"Oh shit!" Frank turned and walked away, then turned back and advanced. "I hate that word. I have always hated that word. I'll bet New York was one big fucking realistic apple for you, wasn't it? Were they condescending, these ex-students of yours? Haughty? Was that like a slap in the face? You talk about being embarrassed; I'll bet you were embarrassed to show my work to them once you saw their reaction, right? That must have been painful, running in there so—so enthusiastic in your championship just to realize that the reality is 'realistic.' And the most realistic thing we have in this world is this— this—these strains of elitism we have in this country, you know, in all fields, but especially in art. I'm not one of the crew, you know, I'm not one of the team. I don't have the history that those artists in New York have got. I know that. Don't you think I know that? Don't you think that's why I just do what I do? Because you do art just for the art of it. I know what I do, I know how good I am, I don't just follow fashion, you know. I can't do it to make other people happy. Why the hell do you think I do what I do? I gave up what I gave up? I've got to do what I do, that's all. And if those big-time, hoity-toity art mavens in New York don't like it, well, tough shit! So, fuck'em! And then if you fuck them then, you see, you can, yeah, you can—fuck me, you know, you can, you know, you can just—just be my girl. You know, give me some emotional support for the art, and let me just do the art. If you want to give me some financial support too, well, I would welcome that. Why wouldn't I? I'd be a damn fool not to. But, you know, this is too much, a whole studio and all that, maybe I just need—I mean—you know—maybe all I need is—well, hell—maybe all I need is you. I don't need no damn gallery in New York, and I don't need people trying to sell me, and I don't even need to sell the stuff because I know what I do, and I know it's good and that it brings me, you know, satisfaction. And, talking about satisfaction, didn't I satisfy you? And do you really want to give that up? I mean, art and sex, what the hell else is there in life? Let's not commercialize it! Let's not be business-like! Let's not be realistic! Hell, you know, you've got the money, I mean, I'll be a kept man, okay I can deal with that, let's just live in a fantasy world full of hugs and kisses and the excretion of sexual fluids and damn fine art and you and I, and we can be happy that way! Can you get out of buying this building? I mean, we don't need it; I'll make smaller—"

"Frank!"

"What!"

"My ex-students happen to think you are manifestly a genius."

Frank's mouth opened wide, as did his eyes, as did the moment. Finally, Frank said:

"You taught them really good, didn't you?"

It was not so much that Allison had taught Bebe and Tilly "really good," as she still knew how to exercise authority over them. "Manifestly a genius" was a bit of hyperbole that Allison had used simply to get Frank to shut up. Nothing will so grab one's attention as being told that one's self-esteem has a solid basis in reality. Not that Bebe and Tilly, after their silent but serious consideration of the drawings, did not express a liking of Frank's art, even admiration, for they did, and they were incredibly relieved and happy to say so. But after expressing their appreciation for the work, after lifting Allison's spirits, after she had breathed a sigh of her own relief, they brought her down by bringing up the ever-present BUT.

It is such a horrible thing, this nefarious BUT, that foulest of all single syllable words, that antidote to dreams, that spoiler of fantasies, that potent put-downer of aspirations. It is probably a truism missed by most grand philosophers that the single T BUT has mooned more people to far more devastating emotional effect than the double T BUTT ever has or could. For what is a bare ass in comparison to raw reality? Cruel and unrelenting, the horrible BUT goes about its merry way—for do not ever think it does not enjoy its role in life—sucking the joy out of hearts.

"These are fascinating, Mrs. Carr," Bebe had said. "Actually quite good."

"Yes, I agree," Tilly said.

"I congratulated you on your eye here," Bebe continued, "but...."

"But?"

"But I wouldn't know how to sell them," Bebe metaphorically dropped her pants and revealed the cracked reality.

"Me neither," Tilly thrust her tush out as well.

"Why?" Allison asked.

It was a simple question with no more syllables than the dreaded BUT. And yet it seemed to make Bebe uncomfortable as if it was an impolite question and that any answer she could offer would force her to express rude sounds that, even in this rude time we live in, would cause a diminution of her standing in society.

"Well, you see, I mean—" Bebe paused to take the time to grimace with psychic pain, "He has, you know, no real credentials to speak of."

"Credentials?" Allison pushed. "You mean degrees? Hopefully, from a major university? Or time spent under the mentoring of another artist of some agreed-upon good reputation?"

"That, certainly, or previous shows at reputable galleries, or inclusions in the collections of reputable collectors. You see, at the level of business that we do, our clientele demands to know that the artist is good."

"They can't tell that by looking at the art?"

"Of course not, Mrs. Carr," Tilly said with the precursor of a giggle in her throat, "Few of our buyers have any judgment whatsoever. If they did, we wouldn't be in business."

"So they don't buy works of art; they buy resumes."

"Sure, and why not?" Bebe put forth. "All collectors will pay lip service to the common cliché that you should only buy art you're in love with, but all but a few collectors want art whose value can be totaled up only on a calculator and with an exclusive use of the multiplication button."

"Do you hear what you're saying, Bebe?" Allison asked in a voice from a classroom from their shared past, wherein bright but not fully formed young women had debated the great questions of life. Bebe knew the voice well and knew what to expect."

"Well, now, Mrs. Carr—"

"Bebe! Do you hear what you are saying? Are you apprehending the illogic of what you have just iterated to me?"

"Mrs. Carr, I know my business."

"Is it knowledge, or is it opinion? Is it fact, or is it an assumption?"

"Mrs. Carr—"

"You are basically asking artists to be born fully formed out of the foreheads of gods!"

"Well, at our level, I suppose that's true."

"Well, that's ridiculous. Where's the fun in that? Where's the creativity? Where's the joy juice of life that I proselytized you to look for?"

"That's right, you did always use that term," Tilly said, delighted in the remembrance.

"Well, what do you think I meant by it?"

"I don't know. I just always thought it was one of those things that teachers say."

"But why do you think teachers say it, Tilly?"

"Because that's their job. But once you get out into the real world—"

"The real world! I hate the real world!"

"Well, of course," Tilly readily accepted Allison's declaration. "That's why you were a teacher."

"No, I mean, I hate the concept of the 'real world.' But, shouldn't the real world be what we make it?"

"In an ideal world, yes, but—"

"Shut up, Bebe. To say that we can only make the real world in an ideal world is a contradiction in terms. Now, do you agree with me that my artist is a hell of a talent?"

"Well, yes...."

"And what do you think of his concept that each of his paintings will reflect a different art style, either genre or period or materials, done in a huge format?"

"Interesting, but—"

"No buts while I'm talking. I went to your gallery today. What about this artist that's doing Jackson Pollock in beads? Who's going to be doing Rothko in felt?"

"Ah, yes, Westminster Abby."

"Westminster Abby?"

"It's a nom de plume."

"Shouldn't that be nom de pinceau?"

"Mrs. Carr, I thought you retired from teaching. In any case, Westminster is one of our leading conceptual artists. She has found a way to make the abstract concrete, bringing commentary into the realm of no comment. For example, her Pollocks are all about the illusionary nature of existence and that things may look solid, but they are reality made up of individual particles; therefore, a world that may seem calm is actually chaotic. And so Pollock, who seems to have made paintings that in no way reflect nature, painted the truest holdings up of the mirror to nature. And the Rothko's, well, I mean, the whole idea of using felt...."

Somehow Bebe thought this was self-explanatory.

"Yes?"

"Well, don't you see, Rothko was an abstract artist, a school of art considered by many to be cold and unfeeling, and yet his paintings are so intensely feeling. I mean, my god, they grace the inside of chapels! So the irony here of reproducing them in felt, not only a material that matches the look of his painting style, but a homonym of the past participle of to feel is absolutely delicious."

"Your buyers buy that crap?"

"Yes, certainly. If there is the resume to back it up."

"Well, it's time to make a change. What about thinking outside the box?"

"Oh, please, Mrs. Carr, that's a cliché that was but a passing fancy," Bebe said.

"I like the box," Tilly offered. "It's quite comfortable inside the box."

How could Allison argue with that?

"All right, then sell Frank on his—anti-resume."

The term was immediately appealing to Bebe. Like negative space or concrete abstraction, emotional intelligence, or selfish altruism. It was a simple term that spoke to the complexity of existence that may, after all, be nothing but an illusion. And thus had a depth, weight, and an essential, if not always obvious, obviousness in its closeness to the core. A core of great mass—of capital T Truth. Which, paradoxically, retained the elusiveness and ephemeral quality of a wisp of smoke that may, indeed, be nothing more than mist and so indicative not so much of that destroyed as of that changed.

"Anti-resume," Bebe said, interested and wanting to hear it again.

"Sell the outsider in Frank. The David to the Art Industry Goliath," Allison pushed with more clichés.

"Well, possibly...."

"Remember that—what was it? It was some catchphrase from something; I don't know what, that you girls were all using in school."

"Catchphrase?"

"It was something about badges, smelly badges, I think."

"Oh!" Tilly remembered and suddenly became a Mexican. "'Badges? I don't got to show you no stinking badges.'"

"That's it! That's the attitude. If there is the Law of the Fine Art Market, then sell Frank as an outlaw who don't got to show you no stinking badges—just his art. His art is his badge! America loves outlaws, right? At least it used to: Jesse James; Billy the Kid; Bonnie & Clyde, and all that. If it doesn't anymore, then let's rekindle the love. It's romantic; you can always sell romance, right?

"To hard-ass collectors putting up a lot of money?" Bebe was not so sure.

"That's the point, if they are putting up a lot of money for art, they've reached the point where their hard-asses have done their job, made their fortune for them, now they have time for romance. Listen...."

Allison was amazing herself. What a salesperson! And what fun it was to stand outside herself and watch her performance, the performance of a lifetime. Why here? Why now? Because it was her story, her new story, she knew that now. She would not be a supporting character after all; she would be the lead, the protagonist, the hero. And she was not going to let any fearful antagonistic BUTs butt into her story and derail it, stop it, hand it a premature death. This is not a short story; this is a novel! Maybe she was too old—No! Not too old, just not young enough—for it to be a long luxurious Nineteenth Century Novel of great expanse through time. But it damn well can at least be an entire modern novel, long enough to be satisfying without trying the patience of the short attention spans of the 21ST Century. So she sold, and sold hard, and, more importantly, took command, questioning Bebe and Tilly as to their best and most reliable big spenders who treated art as trophies indicative of First Places. She wanted a profile of all of them; she wanted the full details of their past stories, present conditions, and future prospects. She was looking for one, at least one, with a particular—she had to admit it—a specific resume.

"That's the one," Allison finally said.

"Why?" Bebe asked.

"What's his name again?"

"Mark Bayly," Tilly said.

"All right, Mark Bayly. He's wealthy, but not in a typical manner, right? He didn't inherit it."

"Hardly."

"And yet, he didn't get it through hard work and sacrifice."

"It was a pure fluke."

"He used to be a... What did you call him?"

"A voice-over actor. You know, voiced TV and radio commercials, cartoon characters, that sort of stuff."

"Out in California, right? Okay, so, you said he did—what?— narration for some start-up dot com company's commercial long before the bubble burst; took stock instead of a fee because that's all they could afford; the dot com took off in a big way, went public, he cashed out and got—what did you say? A hundred and thirty-two million? He immediately retires and moves to New York because that had always been his dream. He took his money and invested wisely, making more money. He really enjoys being rich but wants more than that; he wants to be accepted by others who are rich. Why? Because he had always been a—what did you call him? A closet snob? Not easy, though, because—because he has a lousy resume. That's important—make a note of it. So he started donating to charities, the arts, and doing other things the 'Rich' do, including collecting art and building himself a brand-new mansion. He's also a political contributor for the liberal side, right? It all helped; it opened some doors, he's somewhat accepted, but he's not, from what you tell me, fully there yet. Okay, now let's put it all together. A liberal nouveau riche parvenu—if that's not redundant—who still feels a bit of the outsider who's building a new home, presumably with some huge wall space, for what nouveau riche new home doesn't have a lot of expansive wall space? Frank's his boy! Frank can be his discovery. He can give Frank his first commission to fill that blank space with an incredible piece. One that will reflect not only Mark Bayly's sophisticated understanding of art and its history (which we'll give him if he doesn't have one) but also his left-leaning politics. We'll make sure it's very controversial, and you'll do the proper publicity, so everybody will want to see it. People who might have otherwise found a courteous excuse will accept his invitation to a private unveiling. The event will be hugely successful; Mark will be a made-man; Frank will be the hot new artist. And the three of us will be, I assume, not unhappy taking new commissions. Does any of this make sense, or am I just blowing smoke up my derriere?"

"Make sense?" Bebe said with genuine admiration saturating her voice. "Mrs. Carr, we should hire you as our business strategist."

"Thanks, but no thanks. That's not my story. I've found my story, and I'll stick with it. No sub-plots for me."

Allison and her ex-students were excited and started working on Allison's strategy the next day. That was also when Allison left Frank her cryptic phone message, saying she would be in New York longer than she thought. She had wanted to be in touch, not forgotten, but also to tell him nothing for fear that there was more smoke here than fire. Frank was in no position to be let down, if he had to be let down, in any manner but gently. As tough and independent as Frank thought he was—the lone gunman of artists—not caring what anybody thought, Allison knew him to be fragile. He was not a hard nut to crack; he was an eggshell, wonderfully strong top and bottom, easily crushed in the middle.

Bebe and Tilly took Frank's sketches, scanned them into a computer, and prepared them for projection. Then they set up a meeting with Mark Bayly at his new mansion, ninety percent completed, including, as they knew, a large wall or two. They allowed Allison to present Frank's anti-resume, his story. Whether it was the tale or the telling, Mark Bayly was intrigued. Then they projected Frank's sketches onto Mark's blank wall, asking him to imagine this period of art, that particular technique, some other manner of painting. Mark Bayly was hooked. He picked as his favorite the Dog of War.

"Timely yet classic," he called it. "How much?"

"Fifty thousand," Allison said, shocking everyone in the room but herself.

"Too much," Mark Bayly said.

"You can pay in installments," Allison said.

"Nevertheless...."

"The first payment will fall due January one, 2101."

Mark Bayly turned to Allison. "I'll be dead by then."

"Oh. Well, given the circumstances of your demise, I'm sure the debt will be forgiven."

Mark Bayly smiled. "Will I be held to a confidentiality agreement about the terms?"

"Only regarding the payment schedule. As to the price, you may be as free with the information as you would like."

Though they were shocked, Bebe and Tilly did not show it until the three women drove away from Mark Bayly's new home.

"Miss Fordham?" Bebe said.

"Yes, Miss Hutchinson?" Tilly responded.

"How will we write our invoice for our commission on this sale?"

"I don't quite know. In invisible ink?"

"Girls," Allison said, "you should be happy that Frank now has a resume."

None of this did Allison explain to Frank, for he was not the kind of person to appreciate the selling of the sizzle instead of the steak—especially when he was the steak. And that was fine; she liked that about him. Allison had once liked that about herself, in fact, and was amused (she refused to be appalled) that she now seemed to be quite appreciative of the power of the sizzle. It was, she had no doubt, due to all those years watching Big Jim's success selling sporting goods. After all, a baseball is a baseball is a baseball. But a baseball with the sizzle of an autograph on it, now that was something! Especially if it was the autograph of, of—. Allison suddenly could not remember the name of any Major League Baseball star whose John Hancock (a name she could never forget) on baseballs no rounder than any other baseball would make those balls sizzle. And she used to know them all. It had been a useless bit of memorized knowledge, like learning by heart the Periodic Table when the damn table, beautifully laid out, was available in any second-rate encyclopedia. But it had been more critical to Big Jim than her knowing Big Jim's cholesterol level. But now, she could not remember any of the names. How odd. How wonderful! She supposed the ability to tolerate sports had to move over to make room for her newfound ability to appreciate the power of the sizzle. Possibly there was only so much room she could allot the mundane in her mind, and right now, it had to be a practical sense of sneaky manipulation

Nature knows what it needs.

Frank now had confirmation that he was manifestly a genius and was happy. But only momentarily—Allison immediately burdened him with the responsibilities of being a genius.

The Dog of War had to be painted first, she said, and the dimensions had to be what Mark Bayly, his first commission, needed them to be to fill the space on the wall in his mansion where he planned to put it. There was absolutely no reason why Frank could not paint the Dog of War to those dimensions. Nevertheless, he allowed himself the protest that he had not planned to paint it quite that large, and besides, it was not the piece he wanted to do first; his mind was all wrapped up in the "Jesus Shut the Door" piece. He was dying to have the fun of doing that piece.

Nevertheless, Allison said, let's rent a space so you can get started on Dog of War while we wait for the studio to be finished.

Frank said he didn't want to start on it and then move it; he wanted to wait until he was in his studio—their studio—before he got started. Allison said she understood that but, nevertheless, Allison said again, staring up at Frank with her intense blue eyes, I'll rent the space, and you'll get started because Mark Bayly wants the painting by—she named a date—so he can have the unveiling before the height of the social season; otherwise he'll have a hard time getting positive RSVPs.

A deadline? Frank protested. Are you giving me a deadline?

No, Allison explained with the beginnings of patience to counter the beginnings of Frank's panic, I got you a commission. The deadline just comes with the territory.

But you can't; for Christ's sake, you can't rush Art, you can't put it on a deadline, Frank stated as if it was a truism that should not have to be said.

Are you that effete? Allison, quickly getting to the end of her patience, asked Frank the Waiter, although Frank the Artist was unaware of this. Are you that precious, that special that you can do your Art only—when?—only when you're in the throes of inspiration, I suppose? Only when your muse is active? I thought I was to be your muse.

No, No! Frank needed to explain. You misunderstand me. I've already had the inspiration; my inspiration is in the sketch, and that's done. I'm talking about the actual work, the handcraft of doing a painting of this size, scope, and complexity. What, do you think that's easy? Well, it's not; it's labor intensive. You know I'm not a machine; I'm only one man. But, Christ, you're like Pope Julius pushing Michelangelo back up that scaffold. Paint, Mikey, paint! Paint for the glory of God!

"You know," Allison said, suddenly a thinking individual of a rational bent of mind, "that's actually a good idea."

Frank was at a loss as to what would be a good idea: him becoming a machine or possibly using a machine? What device could he potentially use? Maybe it was Allison becoming the Pope or, at least, a religious leader or founding a new religion. She was certainly acting like she would appreciate some unquestioning apostles. And with those blue eyes, it might not be difficult.

"It's the way Michelangelo did it, isn't it?"

"Did what? Use a scaffold? I was just thinking of a big ladder."

"No, not just that."

Frank was alarmed. "You don't want me to paint 'Dog of War' on this guy's ceiling, do you?"

"No, of course not. But how did Michelangelo paint the ceiling?"

"Very carefully, I assume."

"No, with apprentices, right? With help, with students, we'll get you a bunch of students."

"What!"

"Your painting's going to be huge, right? It's like a production, an assembly, so we'll use an assembly line. You sketch it out and assign different areas to different students. It will be easy, like paint-by-numbers."

"Pain-by-numbers? But—but I wanted to do the painting myself."

Frank saw pictures of himself, the lone genius, high on the ladder—or scaffold that would look neat too—applying paint to canvas with care, precision, and a near-magical touch.

"Frank, there's no time. This is not that unusual of an idea, is it? I'll bet you other artists are doing it."

"Well, sure…."

"You've already done the real Art, right? You've had your inspiration; you've already gotten it down on paper. Now comes—you just said so yourself—the hard work, the intensive labor, the grunt stuff. You're the master; why shouldn't you have—grunts to do work?"

"Grunts? You can't just get grunts, you know. You can't even just get students; they have to be at least art students with some training and knowledge and—"

"I will take care of that."

"And pay for it?"

"I've committed to that, haven't I?"

"But—" Frank was going to protest some more, but he consented. Allison's blue eyes, which seemed to flare when he had said "but," were just too blue to relent, and you cannot fight that kind of blue. Besides, they were a joy to stare into. Frank decided he would hate not to have those blue eyes to stare into. So he consented.

"And speaking of money," Allison said

"Oh, yeah. See how pure I am? I hadn't even thought of that. I've always found it hard to make money the important thing. So how much did you get?"

"Fifty thousand."

"What!" It was not to be believed. But, of course, Frank could believe it because it was so amazing, so outrageous, but also so deserved, so right, so justified. "You're kidding; I hope not."

"No, I'm not. So, welcome to the big-time art market," Allison said with a smile as joyous as her blue eyes.

"That's—wow! —that's wonderful." Frank grabbed Allison and hugged her a Lennie kind of hug. Luckily, despite her size, Allison was no cute little furry puppy. "Oh, sorry," Frank said upon letting her go, realizing the hug may well have had a sexual component to it.

"That's okay, Frank. Keep up the enthusiasm."

"Well, of course, now, hell, I can pay for the students."

"No, not really. We're not going to make Mark Bayly pay it." Allison explained her rationale. Frank was fascinated by it.

"That was the quickest fortune I ever went through."

"Think of it as a loss leader."

"Sure. Still, it will be a lot of work for no money."

"Frank, this isn't waiting tables; this isn't punching a clock. Speaking of which, you can quit The Briers now."

Why was this frightening to Frank?

"But as I'm not getting paid—"

"Frank, I'm paying you."

"But—but now that you have to pay students—"

"Frank—"

"But—"

"Frank, do you love that job more than you've told me? Is it really that fulfilling? Are you looking forward to, I don't know, maybe meeting a cute waitress and marrying her?"

Allison made it clear by the tone in her voice that she was throwing out a wild supposition, not revealing secret knowledge. She was not going to do that. To do that would be to—here was the influence of Big Jim again—throw the ball into Frank's court. That would be a mistake, for he would probably drop it. Whereas she was not going to let go of the ball. For as long as she had the ball grasped firmly in her hand, she controlled its destiny. But there was nothing wrong with a little fake pitch. It was fun to see how fast Frank's reflexes were.

"Of course not," Frank said after a moment's confusion.

"Well then...?"

"Okay," Frank said, the experience of acquiescence making further acquiescence easier. "I guess I'll give two weeks' notice tomorrow."

And what kind of notice was he going to give Trudy? Allison guessed that he would not, not yet, due to several factors, youth, and beauty, not the least. Allison supposed Trudy was a situation she would also have to take care of, but that was okay. Allison was sure she was up to the challenge. And, besides, it was only proper that she should. Trudy was an unwelcome character in Allison's story, and it was up to Allison that she remains a minor one. Despite what she said about the sex being a mistake, she was determined to be in Frank's arms again. And why not? It was, after all, her story to tell.

WE WILL

Duncan was at the tattoo parlor showing "Poignant" Pete Peterson, an artist of the first rank as far as Duncan was concerned, the famous double headshot of Laurel and Hardy. What he wanted "Poignant" Pete Peterson to do was reproduce it in his brilliant tattoo art onto Frank's hairless chest. "Poignant," who was used to doing Chinese dragons and babes with big boobs and delicate filigree designs and Hard Rock Art and certain sayings such as DEATH NOW OR LATER or SEX SUCKS WHEN THERE IS NO SUCKING IN SEX and poems such as YOUR MAMA'S A WHORE/YOUR DAD'S A PIMP/YOUR SISTER'S A DYKE/AND YOUR BROTHER'S A WIMP/BUT YOU I LIKE and pastel flowers with ethereal fairies and bright green snakes and high flying eagles and national symbols and even corporate logos, wondered why anyone would be crazy enough to want a picture of Laurel and Hardy on their chest.

"You do Jesus, don't you?" Duncan asked him.

"Poignant" Pete Peterson could not deny it.

"And Buddha?"

That also had to be admitted.

"And how about Satan, Beelzebub, Mephistopheles, or as his friends call him, Dapper Damn the Devil?"

"Yeah, sure, all those guys too. But usually not for evil reasons, but just, you know, because the design's so cool."

"I don't suppose anyone's ever wanted Darwin?"

"No. But I've done a few of those fish with legs."

"Right. Well, there you are, 'Poignant,' all images of some meaning to your canvases of flesh."

"Poignant" Pete Peterson looked again at the picture of the fat guy with the happy cheeks and the skinny guy with the innocently dopey smile in their what-the-hell-do-you-call-them-again? hats.

"These guys mean that much to you?"

"I worship the very ground they're buried under."

"You're kidding?"

"In fact, I think I'll start a new religion with them as my icons."

"Wow, that's pretty crazy. What's it going to offer? I mean, every religion's got to offer you something."

"Salvation through lobotomies."

"You're kidding."

"But a special kind, a surgical procedure that will make you as sweetly stupid as the Boys here."

"Jeez, what kind of salvation is that? Those guys were really stupid, like, you know, they fucked up everything they touched."

"'Poignant' look around you. Aren't most people stupid?"

"You got that right."

"And you talk about fucked up – what isn't?"

"That's a point."

Now, how would you describe most people most of the time? Sweet or mean?"

"Most of the time?"

"Most of the time."

"Mean."

"And is mean good?"

"No, mean is crap."

"Right. So if the world's full of stupid mean fuckups, wouldn't the world be better off if they were stupid sweet fuckups instead?"

"Poignant" gave that point-of-view some pinpoint thought as he gave the picture of Laurel and Hardy some professional consideration.

"Well," "Poignant" finally said, "it's going to hurt."

"Pain, my dear 'Poignant,' is my friend."

"Take your shirt off, then, and let's get started."

With a swift flourish of his arm, Duncan removed his breakaway shirt and presented his canvas of flesh to "Poignant" Pete.

◆ ◆ ◆

THE MAJOR SAT IN HIS ROOM/WANTING TO CRY/FOR WHAT HE HAD JUST WROTE/COULD VERY WELL SMOTE/OLD FRIENDS AND FOES AWRY/BUT THAT WAS ALRIGHT/HE HAD BEEN TRAINED TO SMITE/BUT WITH SUCH SPITE?/VENGEANCE IS MINE SAITH THE LORD/BUT HE HAD BECOME SO BORED/WITH SOLDIERING FOR THE LORD/THE MAJOR SAT IN HIS ROOM/WANTING TO CRY/BUT TRY AS HE MIGHT/DESPITE SMITE AND SPITE/THE MAJOR COULD ONLY SIGH.

While Duncan was in the tattoo parlor having Laurel and Hardy applied to his hairless chest, Dmitri, who had wheeled him from The Briers on this mission, stood leaning forward on a railing on the boardwalk. Despite facing the vast and wondrous sea, he was only looking at and concentrating on the black Bic lighter in his hand. Dmitri would flick the Bic and watch the flame jump into existence and wiggle its nearly erotic wiggle to the slight scent of kerosene. Then he would release his thumb and kill the flame.

Flick, existence, wiggle, death/flick, existence, wiggle, death/flick, existence, wiggle, death.

If Dmitri had had a philosophical turn of mind—or any turn of mind for that matter—he might have seen an allegory for life in his creator's omnipotence over the little plastic wand of combustion. But all he saw was the little flame, and all he felt was its little heat, and all it meant to him was the slight diversion it offered at that moment when he was bored, just bored, nothing but bored, so God damn bored.

And tired. So God damn tired. What with working for crap-ass Mr. Briers—flick, existence, wiggle, death—going to piece-of-shit school—flick, existence, wiggle, death—having to spend the weekend in slave labor to Old Fart Hendrickson—flick, existence, wiggle, death—despite the nice hot chocolate, he was exhausted.

Flick, existence, wiggle, death.

Fucking Hendrickson had made him pump a big pill down a cow's throat.

Flick, existence, wiggle, death.

I'd like to pump a big pill down his throat.

Flick, existence, wiggle, death.

School sucks.

Flick, existence, wiggle, death.

Can't wait to get out, get my car, get the hell away from here.

Flick, existence, wiggle, death.

Mr. Briers is a pain in the ass. A PAIN IN THE ASS! The other day he said, "Dmitri, I wonder when young gits like you grow up do they become adult cretins?" Dmitri almost asked, What's a cretin? But for once, he thought better of it.

Flick, existence, wiggle, death.

The flame was both fascinating and funny. Dmitri liked looking at it. What was fire, exactly? Fucking hot, of course, but, you know, what is it? It's not solid, yet it's there, got color and—and—he did not know what to call it—roundness, he supposed. And yet...

"'No. You are such a lovely liar. You don't want to make me cry. So you lie a little—n'est-ce pas?'"

It was a tiny voice coming from far off to his left. Dmitri looked that way and saw Trudy at the end of the boardwalk, in front of the new theater, pacing back and forth, a small book in her hand. Again she said:

"'No. You are such a lovely liar. You don't want to make me cry. So you lie a little—n'est-ce pas?'"

Even at this distance, he liked her body. But it would be better to see it up close. So he went to the door of the tattoo parlor and poked in his head.

"Hey, Mr. Briers, shouldn't we be moving on? Let's go down to the theater."

Duncan, who was laid out on a table while "Poignant," in deep concentration, bent over his chest, said:

"Dmitri, for Christ's sake, don't disturb the artist; he might poke Laurel's eye out."

Dmitri walked in and saw what was going on.

"Holy shit, what are you doing?"

"What am I doing? What the hell do you think I'm doing? I'm having my nipples removed. They're no damn good to me anyway."

"No, you're not. You're getting a tattoo."

"What powers of observation!" Duncan exclaimed while grimacing with a pain unique even for him. "What depth of analysis!"

"Well—when you going to be done?"

"How the hell should I know? 'Poignant'?"

"Hell, I'm hardly done with Hardy here."

"Not for a while, Dmitri."

"Well, what the hell am I supposed to do?"

"Read a book."

"What?"

"Sorry, the pain is giving me delusions that you've got a mind."

"I'm bored."

"Do you masturbate?"

"What?"

"That's what I do when I'm bored."

"Here?"

"Well, no, not here; that would be completely inappropriate. Go to the bait shop."

"Mr. Briers—"

"I don't care what you do. Just stay on the boardwalk."

"Can I walk down to the theater?"

"Sure. Give Thespis my regards."

"Who?"

"Go, Dmitri. Just listen for my shout."

With enthusiasm somewhat alien to him, Dmitri walked abnormally quickly down the boardwalk, coming closer and closer to Trudy, who was completely unaware of this. He finally stopped in front of the theater and at a bench there. Trudy was concentrating on her text and mouthing a line over and over. It was fun to watch her, more fun than the flame. Dmitri thought she was really beautiful and had really great tits, you know, the kind you really want to, you know, flop your face into.

Dmitri flopped himself onto the bench, unseen by Trudy, who was facing the other way, her head still in the book. Then she raised her book and addressed the ocean:

"Le capitaine—il est parti?"

Then in a deep man's voice, she said:

"Just left. Don't cry, little one."

Then again, in her own, yet accented voice:

"Le nouveau sergeant. N'est-ce pas?"

"How come you're talking that language?" Dmitri asked in all profound innocence.

"Jesus Christ!" Trudy spun around. "Dmitri! You scared the shit out of me!"

This was of little concern to Dmitri. Indeed, the fact that the fright had caused Trudy to take in a sudden inhalation of breath, causing her breasts to gain even more prominence than they usually had, was a benefit of his action that he could not have predicted, certainly did not plan for, but was very pleased to perceive.

"How come you're talking that language?" Dmitri asked again in what could have been a perfect digital recording of the first time he asked it.

"I'm rehearsing," Trudy said as if not only Dmitri but the whole world should have been aware of this fact.

"What do you mean?"

"I'm trying to memorize my lines and get the accent right."

"What for?"

"Well, for the play!"

"What play?"

"Dmitri!" Trudy was frustrated and irritated with Dmitri in equal proportions. "What do you mean what play? Why the play we're going to do here."

"Well, what play is that?"

"What play is that?" Trudy seemed to ask this of some omniscient being above her as she sighed. "It's called What Price Glory. Just like it says on the poster you're sitting in front of."

Dmitri turned to look at the poster, which left little impression on him. Then, he turned back to Trudy.

"Oh. What's it about?"

"Well, it's about a bunch of soldiers in World War—ah—One or Two, I forget which one."

"Do you play a soldier?"

"No, I don't play a soldier. I play Charmaine."

"What kind of name is that?"

"Well, what kind of name is Dmitri?"

"Russian."

Well, Charmaine is French. It takes place in France during this war, and it's about a bunch of soldiers there, and I'm the only girl in the whole play, and everybody's in love with me."

"I could be in love with you."

"Gee, thanks, Dmitri. If I were depressed, that would drive me to suicide."

If the insult had an impact on Dmitri, he chose not to show it. But it was more likely that the barb had had no impact at all, Dmitri not being the best of listeners.

"So, how come you're talking that language?"

"It's French, Dmitri. I told you, Charmaine is French; it takes place in France!"

"Do you understand it?"

"Oh, sure. I mean, you know, I do now that someone told me what it means."

"What do you want to do a stupid play for?"

"Are you kidding? Acting's the greatest thing in the world. Although, it's a lot harder than I thought."

"Everything is hard," Dmitri said with a near philosophical depth of understanding.

"Yeah," Trudy agreed and sat on the bench next to Dmitri. "I'm tired. You see, I've got to not only memorize all these lines, because, you know, it's a play, and it's live in front of people, whereas, you know, in TV, Dmitri, in TV they put the lines on these big cards, they're called cue cards, and, you see, off camera, and the actors can see them, so as they're acting there are the lines there, so they don't have to memorize their lines, they can just concentrate on, you know, acting and being funny. But here, you know, here in the theater, you see, cue cards would pretty look stupid. At least that's what they told me when I asked. So I've not only got to memorize these lines, which I thought, at first, was going to be easy because they gave me an old film version of this play. I thought, well, that's great because I used to memorize, you know, Cissy McMann's lines—you know Cissy McMann, of course. I used to memorize all her lines by watching her shows over and over, so I thought, this is great, I'll watch this film over and over and memorize the lines, but then, you know what? The damn movie isn't like the play! It doesn't follow the play, it's not the same lines, and so, jeez, I can't do that. And they said, no, no, just watch it so you can get the accent, the French accent, and that's another thing I've got to do, I've got to try to do this all in a French accent, and, even the English, you see, not just the French words, I've got to do the English as if I was actually born in France. And I got to remember, and when we're rehearsing, you see, I keep slipping out of it and going into English, and this guy, you know, Ben Alyn, do you know Ben Alyn? Did you ever watch Sgt. McKennen? He was on Sgt. McKennen. He's here now, you know, he's going to be in the play, and I get to act with him on stage. Anyway, he's okay, I guess, he's kind of mean though sometimes, but he's okay, I guess. Anyway, he—I forgot what I was saying."

Dmitri, having to sit through the longest uninterrupted speech he had ever heard in his life, and thrilled that it was Trudy who was giving the speech, and more than thrilled that Trudy was giving the speech to him, found that he was listening to it, and, more surprisingly, understanding the bulk of it, so he found himself the possessor of precisely the information Trudy needed at this moment.

"You keep slipping into English."

"Yeah, yeah, I mean, not English, but, you know, my regular accent, and he yells at me this Ben Alyn. Anyway, so I'm trying hard to learn it because, you know, I want to do a good job, I really want to do a good job, but I keep telling them that, you know, who around here really cares if it's in the French accent anyway because, you know— this isn't France. But, and, you know, the meaning of the play is still there, she's still, you know, this kind of a slut girl, um—but if I could play it, you know, kind of just like myself, that would be cool, but, no, they want me to play it this way, so, and it's—yeah it's important so, you know, I'm trying hard, but it's hard."

Trudy suddenly stopped as if some universally mandated amount of time had expired. She took in a much-needed full breath of air, then let it out in a rush, giving animation to the focal point of at least half of Dmitri's brain, snapping some atavistic switch therein.

"Would you be my girlfriend?"

Neither surprised nor shocked nor thinking the request at all out of the ordinary, Trudy answered without letting a beat of time pass.

"No, I won't be your girlfriend, Dmitri. Don't be stupid! Besides, I have a boyfriend."

"No, you don't," Dmitri stated with utterly dense confidence.

"Yes, I do!"

"No, you don't. I've never seen you with anyone."

"What do you do? Follow me around? You only see me here at work, right?"

"Yeah."

"Well, how do you know what I do outside of work?"

"You never had a boyfriend in high school."

"I never had a steady boyfriend in high school, but I had a bunch of boyfriends."

"Who is he?"

"I'm not going to tell you."

"Why?"

"Because I don't want to."

"Okay." Dmitri could find no reason to reject her reason. "But, you know, I like you. I really think you're beautiful."

"Well, of course, you do, Dmitri. I mean, you've got two eyes, don't you?"

"But I mean, I also kind of like you because—because you're kind of funny."

"Funny?"

"I mean, you know, a good kind of funny."

"Well, okay. I'll pretend that's a compliment."

"Are we—are we friends even though I can't be your boyfriend?"

"Well, gee, I don't know, Dmitri. I mean, we see each other here at The Briers all the time, and we went to the same school. But then, who around here doesn't go to the same school? But, well, so, yeah, I, uh, I guess you can consider me a friend. But not a girlfriend, okay?"

"Okay."

"Doesn't mean I'm going come pick you up if you're drunk somewhere or anything like that, you know, I'm not that kind of friend."

"Okay."

"Just a 'Hi, how are?' friend here at The Briers."

"Okay."

"Trudy?"

It was Ben Alyn, the famous Ben Alyn, who had come out of the theater looking for Trudy because they were now ready for her to rehearse with him. He was unhappy to find her sitting on a bench talking to a dumb kid.

"I thought you were practicing your French accent?"

"Le capitaine; Le capitaine; Le capitaine; Le capitaine," Trudy said, standing up defiantly.

"Okay, not too bad. Now give me the whole line."

"Le capitaine—il est parti?"

"Okay, now read me an English line with the French accent. It's easy to have a French accent when speaking French."

"What line?"

"Any line, I don't care; pick it out."

Trudy looked down at her text and quickly read:

"I wanted to see the captain."

"No! No! Say 'captain' the way you said it before."

"But it's in English now."

"That doesn't matter; you're French. Again."

Trudy, puffing out a quick breath that gave her quick sensual lips, read the line again, which seemed to confirm something for Ben.

"More work, more study. But—I think you're getting close, Trudy. So we need to rehearse the scene now. But from now on, try not to get diverted when we send you out to study."

"Dmitri was helping me."

"Helping you?"

"He was coaching me."

"Oh." Ben turned to Dmitri. "I'm sorry, we haven't been introduced. Are you the local acting coach?"

"No, no, Dmitri's Russian."

"Well, how very Stanislavski of him. But what does that have to do with anything?"

"Well, that's foreign, and French is foreign, so I was having him listen to my line readings and—and grade me on it."

"I gave her an A," Dmitri was happy to report.

"All right, Trudy. Dmitri, it was a pleasure meeting you. Now get the fuck out of here!"

"Hey!"

"Well, don't be mean to him."

"Trudy, this play is going to be good. I didn't fly all the way out from Hollywood to this—beach—just to be in a crappy production. And one person can make a production crap. Do you understand that? Now Austin isn't going to be crap. And I am certainly not going to be crap. And if it kills either Austin or me—you will not be crap. So come on in, and let's rehearse and stop fooling around with the locals."

"The locals?" Dmitri asked. "What does that mean?"

Without answering Dmitri or bidding him a fond farewell, Ben grabbed Trudy by the wrist and dragged her away, leaving Dmitri alone outside the theater.

Dmitri looked out to the sea, which was, as it usually was, a somber gray that gave it a certain majesty. A majesty lost entirely on Dmitri. He saw, instead, out in the distance, the series of oil platforms. On one of them on this gray day, he could just make out the wiggle of a flame shooting out of a high pipe. He reached into his pocket and grabbed his Bic.

Flick, existence, wiggle, death.

"Fucking bastard!"

Flick, existence, wiggle, death.

"Fucking piece of shit!"

"DMIIITRIII!"

He heard the shout coming from outside the tattoo parlor. It was, of course, Duncan.

"DMITRI, I'M A MAN IN FUCKING PAIN. COME GET ME AND TAKE ME HOME!"

Pattie Heatherton found it both fascinating and frustrating to attend What Price Glory rehearsals. Of course, there was no real reason she should have come to rehearsals as she had no qualitative function to perform there. But that fact, and any logic attending to it, had not been strong enough to dissuade her from showing up for the rehearsals as often as her schedule permitted. And when her schedule did not allow it—Pattie often changed her schedule. Pattie had become this dedicated and diligent because she had decided that she had a proprietary interest. Not just in the theater—this building her school's money had helped to renovate. And not just in the Theatre, the institution that her school's money was helping to maintain. But in the contents therein. Not just in the funky reupholstered seats that her school's money partly purchased. And not just in any other inanimate objects that filled this now beautiful space. But—and here she had no shame even though it had been nearly 150 years since the abolition of slavery—she also felt a proprietary interest in the very animate Austin. And not just in Austin, but in his beautiful penis. For how could one, in one's consideration, be separated from the other?

Austin, not to mention his beautiful penis, was sitting three seats to Pattie's right. Whenever he directed in a theater, he demanded three empty seats on either side of him. Austin did this to create a cone of concentration around himself, protecting him from peripheral considerations. Also, he tended to gesture broadly and extravagantly when making a point. It saved others from unintended physical abuse, as one young assistant director, who had worked with Austin in Los Angeles before establishing his three-seat rule, could attest to, the evidence being her now slightly crooked nose.

Pattie would never have guessed it, but this imposed distance aided her fascination, giving her a broader perspective on the creative theatrical process. As tedious and boring as it sometimes seemed, it was also compelling and exciting to watch how, through a series of suggestions and demands, Austin directed the famous Ben Alyn and the ridiculous Trudy, shaping a palpable reality out of nothing but a sketchy rendering. Compelling because to witness this appealed to the mind that mused and wondered and even, on occasion, felt awe. Exciting because Ben Alyn was famous—not that Pattie had ever been a fan of or had even once watched Sgt.McKennen. But then, to be known even by those who have no idea who you are may well be the definition of Fame. And the idea that someone that famous, who you knew without really knowing, was someone you now actually knew, and whose flesh and, we presume, blood was actually something you could view unaided by recording devises and touch in more than your imagination, was like a big grab and tickle of your brain. And who does not enjoy a good grab and tickle now and then?

But Austin being three seats away also added to Pattie's frustration, for she would have preferred to have had him—and need we mention, the appendage of Pattie's affections—much closer to her, indeed, buried deep within her.

How long had it been? Oh, Lord, how long?

Somehow, she had never projected forward enough to realize that Austin's involvement in an endeavor of this kind would take up all his time, not to mention exhaust him, drain him of energy and, sad to say, sap him of stiff resolve. However, having no other choice, Pattie tried her best to allow her fascination to overrule her frustration. And so she concentrated on Austin's shaping of scenes for dramatic purposes, the accomplishment of which she had felt she could have made some pertinent contributions. But Austin's three-seat rule creating his cone of concentration was very effective. He never noticed Pattie's subtle little gestures indicating that she had something interesting to say.

◆ ◆ ◆

Emily Briers had to wonder about the shape her adult life had taken, especially regarding her relationships with men. For her relationships, which, of course, had only numbered two, had been kept to one family. She had been a father's lover and his son's wife. Unless life was stranger than she assumed it was, she thought this might just be an anomaly in modern times. But added to this—was it injury piled on insult, or the cherry on top?—she had also been a nurse to both of them.

The father, Fletcher Briers, had required the nursing that any elderly gentleman might, and as she had loved him dearly, she had been happy to provide it.

The son, Duncan Briers, had required the nursing that any victim of an unfortunate, debilitating accident might. As she, in a different but possibly equal manner, also loved him, she had also been happy to provide for his care. But is one ever obligated, no matter how much one loves someone, to nurse that someone's self-inflicted pain?

"Duncan, you're an idiot!"

"I've heard that before."

"Laurel and Hardy! On your chest!"

"I'm always either in bed or in the wheelchair; who would ever see it on my back?"

"You're an idiot."

"You said that."

"It bears repeating."

"It hurts!"

"No kidding!"

"But 'Poignant' said the pain won't last long, and then it will be fine."

"A fine mess, you mean."

"Oh, shit!"

"What? What's wrong?"

"I should have had him put the words 'Here's another fine mess' under Laurel and Hardy."

"Were you drunk?"

"I suppose I can go back and have him add it."

"Answer me, were you drunk?"

"I haven't had a drink since the night of the accident; you know that"

"You mean you were rational when you did this?"

"Rational? Rational? Who can be rational in this world?"

"Oh, for Christ's sake!"

After finishing her Nightingale ministrations, Emily left Duncan to soothe his pain via the caressing of his video remote. She went downstairs to find sanctuary in Fletcher's and the arms of her new lover, a Nineteenth Century Italian armchair in excellent condition and of elegant detail. As Emily laid her arms on the arms of this Latin lover, and as she rested her back against its splat and let her seat sink into Guido's seat (Guido Mancini 1794-1871), she started to laugh.

Emily had wanted to cry and had felt that she had every right to cry. Indeed, she would have died for a good cry, but she laughed instead. Because, really, what else could she do? For Duncan was incorrect in the implication of his rhetorical question, Who can be rational in this world? Some people can; of course, they can. She had always been. She had always looked at and accepted reality, making her choices based on a cold—no, temperature was not a factor—a simple, straightforward analysis of the known facts. So the world may not be rational, but she was. And the rational do not cry, knowing it does no good and has no effect. The rational can only laugh and, at least, derive some entertainment from the world, which was as reasonable a facsimile of happiness as she could imagine.

Frank had to quit his job at The Briers.

That was the mandate from Allison, who seemed to be in control here, a fact he wanted to embrace while pushing away, although hanging onto it so he could pull it back again and embrace it. Jesus! Contemplating this was like being a kid twirling around and around on the front lawn until you fell on your back onto the grass to watch the sky whirl above you. What the hell did he think about that? Well, it wasn't his art that Allison was controlling, despite the dimensions; despite the deadline, not really, they were just technical matters, right?

So he would quit his job at The Briers.

And how would his quitting affect Trudy? What would he tell her? The truth? Frank feared revealing the truth about himself to Trudy despite being a highly recommended option. Why?

Stupid question. It was the sex, of course.

No! Stupid answer. It can't just be about sex. The sex was great, of course—no, the sex was good, Trudy still had some problems with fellatio, and until she perfected that essential technique, she would never be great. Still, excellent or good, Frank figured that once Trudy found out the truth about him— that he was not just a nice guy and supportive teacher of sexual techniques destined to be a successful restaurateur enjoying fame with her in Hollywood, but an artist— well...

(You know, an artist-type artist. Not a neat artist like an actor or rock musician, but an actual artist that drew drawings. How could that make you famous? And what does that have to do with Hollywood?)

Well, that would be the end of the relationship and—it logically followed—the end of sex.

But it wouldn't be the end of sex, would it? It would just be the end of sex with Trudy, who was good but not great. There would be other sex, especially if he were "manifestly a genius." That would attract some other sex toward him, wouldn't it? Doesn't it work that way? And possibly some great sex. The sex with Allison, for example, had been damn great. So what was he afraid of losing?

Youth, you idiot!

Of course! Damn biology! It was his stupid, selfish genes wanting to replicate, looking for an excellent, young, healthy contributor and incubator to be the receptacle of their future existences. Why were his genes bugging him about this now? Didn't they know he had had a vasectomy? Am I to be a slave to my genes? He refused to believe so. He was, after all, a Homo sapiens, a conscious, thinking creature of prodigious mental abilities, especially compared to, say, an amoeba. We Homo sapiens have developed the mental strength to rise above our genes, haven't we? Or at least sidestep them?

Still—he could close his eyes and see the smoothness of Trudy's skin, that luminous quality it had, that sense that if you touched it, it would be silk, and so you felt it and—it was silk! My God, that was wonderful! And the tightness of the skin seemed to hold everything in near-perfect symmetry. And flowed with no divergence along all the sensual curves on her body: the two curves concaving to define her waist, of course; the domes of her buttocks, fun to run his hand over; her breasts, nothing but udders if Trudy had walked on all fours, but as she stood upright, young and beautiful, they were tight twin projectiles of fresh femininity. And the long slight curves on either side of her neck, coming down from either end of the jaw to the shoulders, flowed to end in curves giving birth to arms to hold you with. They were also curves upon which you could dwell.

And her clear and bright eyes, with their gravitational influence on either side of her mouth, formed her cheery smile. She always seemed such a happy kid.

How could he give that up?

How could he not? He was "manifestly a genius." How could he betray his genius, which had stuck with him for years, just for the allure of youth? But such youth! Such youth, though, should not go to waste. He would have to reverse his vasectomy if it could be reversed and have kids. But who knew how the little buggers would turn out? His art, within reason, he could control.

And control was everything.

Frank had not wanted to talk to Mrs. Briers in the middle of his workday, so he asked her if they could speak at noon after he got off work. Emily was curious. Frank rarely asked to talk with her, and she would have loved to have engaged in the conversation immediately. But, of course, Emily agreed to Frank's request and asked him to meet her in Fletcher's at noon. Probably he just wanted a raise, which she immediately decided she was more than prepared to give him.

Emily was calculating how much she could afford to raise his salary when Frank walked into Fletcher's at 12:03.

As Frank sat down at Mrs. Briers' request, he thought how odd it was that he had never been in Fletcher's before. Indeed, he had seldom been in any part of The Briers outside the dining room and kitchen since the day he started. Why was that? He certainly liked the hotel. He liked the ambiance, the welcoming quiet it always featured, and, as Frank looked around Fletcher's as Mrs. Briers finished up some paperwork, he enjoyed sitting among the antiques with the ticks of old clocks setting a rhymical beat of calm, like that of an untroubled heart.

Frank made a pact with himself to come back later and enjoy the hotel for its essence.

"There," Mrs. Briers said when she finished. "Sorry, but I wanted to know exactly how much of a raise I could give you."

"A raise?" Frank hated to admit it, but this pleased him.

"Well, that's what you wanted to talk to me about, wasn't it? And even if it wasn't, you are certainly deserving of one, so you're getting it even if you're not asking for one."

"Well ... uh ... That's great. I mean, I really want to thank you, but—"

"So, I was right. It's funny how you get to know your employees after a while, especially the good ones."

Frank felt like he was about to put a dagger into her. Not because he was leaving, but because he would disappoint her self-satisfaction, which seemed a not very nice thing to do, not to Mrs. Briers.

"I hope you will deem it an appropriate enough of a raise, Frank because the one thing I hate to do is haggle. So let me just say that this is the amount I can truly afford to give you."

She stated the amount, and it was fine, and Frank told her so.

"Good."

"Only, I'm sorry, but I didn't come in to ask for a raise but to give my two weeks' notice."

The surprise in Emily's eyes, possibly tinged with stammering wonderment, seemed so much like hurt that Frank wanted to take it back immediately.

"Notice? Why? I mean, is there something wrong?"

"No, I'm just—well, you see, I'm just, well, kind of a, you know, sort of an artist, and—"

"An artist?"

Frank was unsure she understood the word's meaning as the question lingered in Mrs. Briers' eyes.

"I draw. Pictures. And paint."

"Really?"

"Yeah, sure."

"And, so, did you get a job drawing somewhere?"

"Kind of."

"Kind of?"

"Well, you know Allison Carr?"

"Yes, of course."

"Well, you see, she's seen my stuff and likes it a lot, and—you know she went to New York for a while, well, she's got a gallery there to agree to show my stuff, and she's already got me a commission, and so she's, uh, fronting me, I guess you would say, and, uh, covering my expenses until the sales come in. She's the one who wants me to quit, you see. I wasn't going to at first, I figured—"

"Of course, you must quit. Frank, this is wonderful! What an opportunity!"

This was nice to hear. Frank was surprised by how nice it was to hear.

"Yeah, it really is. It's, you know, a dream come true and all that. Still, I don't want to cause you any—"

"Oh, to hell with me! I won't even let you give two weeks. Two days, that's all I need. Joe's been bugging me to let him take the morning shift, but I knew you preferred it, so I kept turning him down. He'll be thrilled. And Derek, in the afternoon, he's ready to be a headwaiter. So it will all work out." Mrs. Briers stood up and threw her arms out. "Come here!"

Frank stood up without thinking and walked into her arms. He got a big, warm hug for his trouble.

"Frank, I'm so happy for you."

That simple fact made Frank realize that he also was probably happy for himself.

Earlier in the day, Frank had also told Trudy that he needed to talk to her and he would wait around until her shift ended at two.

"I can't, Frank. I've got rehearsals; you know that."

"It won't take long."

"Frank, I've got to be there on time, or Austin and Ben will be pissed. Especially, Ben, he can really be a bastard. But, look, I know what you want to talk about; we haven't been getting together as much lately. But it's only because of the play, and you know how important it is to me. It's the beginning, you know. It's the beginning of everything that will be great for us, so don't be mad."

"I'm not mad, and that's not it. I just need to talk to you."

"But the rehearsal!"

"Look, I'll talk to Joe and tell him you came in fifteen minutes early, and I'll meet you on the boardwalk in front of the hotel at 1:45. Okay?"

"Well, okay. But it can't be a long discussion."

"Fine by me."

Which is what Frank said again when Trudy came up to him on the still fog-bound boardwalk and pushed her face up to his, and said:

"Kiss me, Frank. Kiss me now, even if we are by the hotel. Who cares? Yeah, I know, we work together; you're in a supervisory position over me, so what if people found out? But look, the fog's still here; who can see us? And even if they can, who cares?" Trudy took Frank's hands into hers. "Come on, be daring, we haven't fucked in days, and I've got to go to rehearsals and get yelled at because I haven't perfected a stupid French accent yet, and I need to know that somebody likes me. So kiss me, Frank, make it long and warm, don't argue with me, just do it."

In a flash of condensed thought, Frank realized that after he told Trudy what he was going to say to her, he would never get to kiss her again, and that would be a shame, but shame though it was, and as much as he might miss the kiss—Frank now knew he probably would not miss Trudy. "Fine by me."

Trudy smiled, and Frank kissed that smile. He made it long and warm, Trudy collaborating in kind. His hand went to her breast. Hers went to his buttocks. When they broke, Trudy said:

"That was great. I'm proud of you. Oh my God! What if somebody saw us?"

"Doesn't matter."

"It doesn't?"

"No. I just quit my job."

Trudy's eyes, her slightly exotic eyes, went wide. It was now time for an explanation. Frank did the best he could. Trudy listened with surprising patience. Frank was not sure the meaning of it all was sinking in, though, so he finally had to be blunt about it.

"So, you see, I don't want to be a restaurateur or, for that matter, go to Hollywood with you."

Trudy stood silent. Frank had expected tears, possibly screams, most likely both. Instead, he was getting silence. But not, it seemed, dumb silence. Trudy was thinking; he could see she was working it all out, somewhere deep inside her head. Frank was just about to call her back from there when she said:

"Well, of course not. I mean, why would you want to be a famous restaurateur when you could be a famous artist, right?"

"Well, I don't know if I'll be famous."

"Of course, you will!"

"Why?"

"Because I said so."

"Oh. But what about Hollywood? If I move anywhere, it'll more likely be New York."

"Frank, have you never heard of jet planes? Have you never heard of being bi-coastal? Besides, I can live anywhere I want when I'm a star. How cool it's going to be, me a star with an older boyfriend who's an internationally famous artist."

"Internationally?"

"Frank, haven't you heard of the global economy? I sometimes wonder who's the oldest around here. This is going to be so neat! When can I see your stuff?"

"Oh, well, now, I'm not sure you'll like it. It's—"

"Of course, I will; don't be stupid. Oh, shit! It's 2:10! I've got to run. I'll call you later!"

And run she did—toward the theater, into the fog, disappearing as if she had not been there at all.

Already Frank was not missing her.

He turned to walk to his car, and out of the fog came Allison.

"I hope you two will be happy together."

Frank was not at all surprised that Allison was there. There was little that was surprising him anymore.

"You heard all that?"

"Sure. Fog blankets vision, not sound."

"Look, it's a strange story; I didn't know how—"

"I know the story, and it's not strange at all. It's quite basic, in fact."

"How...?"

"Young women love to confide in me."

"I don't want her."

"Really? If she becomes a star, the publicity couldn't hurt, given the current state of the media in this country."

"I don't care. I don't want Trudy."

"Sounded like true love to me."

"It was only true lust."

"On your part."

"Allison, truly, I thought that once I told her I couldn't go to Hollywood with her and run a restaurant, that would be it."

"You want to get rid of her, then?"

"Yes!"

"And the lust?"

"No. I just want to focus it in another direction."

"Got a direction in mind?"

"I'm looking at it."

"Frank, I told you, we should stick to business,"

Frank grabbed Allison and kissed her. It was nicer, he figured than just telling her to shut up. After they parted, Allison said:

"Okay, I'll help you get rid of her."

"How?"

"I'll find a way."

The Major had not relented once on the physical fitness program he had designed for Austin and himself. Every morning they were scheduled to do so, they jogged along the beach and did the prescribed exercises. Even in the thickest of fogs, they ran, knowing, after a time, their route so intimately that only once did one of them miss a step and fall. It was Austin, of course. And between powerful breaths, he laughed with slapstick delight at himself stumbling amid the mist of foggy chaos. The Major stood over him, not laughing. But he smiled. It was a big smile, a smile of some pleasure. When Austin looked up and saw the smile, his delight shifted.

Running in the fog was amazing. When you run, the world recedes, and only the space you pass through seems real, a space very much collapsed within you. But running in a fog made that receding world alien and the collapse far more condensed. Austin often wondered if he had not been running with a companion, especially a companion as grounded as the Major, would he have run right out of this world and into some other.

Both looked forward to the sessions. The Major had insisted on silence during the runs, which Austin initially found hard. He was, after all, a man who liked to lob out language. But he soon discovered the beauty of that silence with only the crash of waves in his ears accompanied by the rhythm of their feet falling on the sand and their necessary breaths cycling through their lungs. There was still communication between the two men despite the lack of talk, and talk would never be able to describe the quality of that communication.

Talking commenced when the jog ended, and they walked slowly to cool down—instigated usually by Austin talking out his thoughts and concerns about What Price. He was trying to understand the military man. He would ply question upon question onto the Major, some of them seeming not truly pertinent to Anderson's play but more intimate regarding the Major's own experiences as a person who had fought and, he had admitted, killed an enemy. The Major did not mind. The questions brought out from him things he had wanted to say to himself for a long time. He listened to himself as intently as Austin did.

Always Austin wanted to know if the Major was keeping up his work on his play. "Yes," the Major would answer, offering no elaboration. Austin said he understood and encouraged the Major to keep the work close to himself for a while. "You don't want to dissipate the creative energy by talking about it," was the way he had put it, an idea he had gathered from several author interviews he had read. But eventually, the Major could no longer keep it to himself. He had written a speech for his main character, and it had scared him, sitting on the pages printed out from the computer. The Major looked at it and could see what it said, but, still, it was such a jumble of black letters signifying what? He tried to read it aloud but hated the sound of his voice reading these words. So he stuffed the pages into a pocket of his running sweats and brought them with him one day. After their run, he asked Austin to read them—to read them out loud.

Austin took the pages from the Major's offering hand and looked down at them. "You want me to do a cold reading?"

The Major, who did not understand the term, answered, "Well, um, I suppose the character might be perceived as—as, well, as a cool personality."

"No, no, I mean, should I read it right now without really studying it."

"Oh, certainly, yes. I would like to hear it now."

"Okay, sure. This is very exciting, Philip. But I'm going to need some background. Clue me in on who this character is and what's happening when he's giving this speech."

"Oh. Well, he's a Major."

"Like you."

"Uh, yes, like I was. And he's just resigned his commission."

"Like you."

"Yes. Like I did. And it takes place in a predominantly Islamic country where a war is going on."

"So your character is quitting in the middle of a war?"

The Major considered Austin's matter-of-fact statement. But then, it was a matter of fact.

"Yes. He's—quitting in the middle of a war."

"Okay. Got it. Let me give it a try."

They were standing on the beach quite a distance from the theater. The fog, as usual, was still in, although not as thick as it had been in previous mornings. Austin took another moment to look at the text, noting that the character's name was Macmillan, and then he began:

"You asked me, Sir, to give a satisfactory reason why I resigned my commission. I can give you an explanation, Sir, but I cannot guarantee that it will be satisfactory. I know you are disappointed in my decision, and I regret that as I believe it is probably the first time any superior officer has had cause to be disappointed in me. I have served my country in this uniform for over thirty years, Sir. I have worn it with pride. The Army has been my life as well, Sir. But unlike you, I cannot say with any honesty that the Army has ever been my family. I know you find that strange, as I have never taken the time to have any other family, but it is true.

Nevertheless, Sir, I have been faithful to my duty to the Army and have never once failed to carry out an order, even orders I might have questioned. I have never allowed myself such latitude. This includes the last order I received regarding the discharge of Corporal Bayati.

"Sir, Corporal Bayati was an exemplary soldier who served his country with loyalty and, if I may say so, Sir, with distinction. As a linguist and interpreter, Sir, there was none better. Not only regarding his Father's language. He took the time and made a concerted effort to gain a more than competent ability in several of the other languages spoken in this area of the world. He was a man of faith, Sir. It was not your faith, nor mine, but you can believe me when I say that he was no less reverent despite that fact. I can detail for you, Sir, numerous occasions when his abilities as an interpreter and translator saved lives. Precious, American lives. Lives of soldiers, Sir, who then continued to fight the enemy. I can name occasions when Corporal Bayati's abilities as a translator brought clarity out of confusion and order out of chaos and significantly helped us do our mandated job more successfully than might otherwise have happened. I can name occasions, Sir, when the upbeat, positive, can-do personality of Corporal Bayati lightened our load, brought smiles to our faces, and convinced us that this hell we were going through, we were going through not in vain.

"Corporal Bayati was a gentle man, Sir, with a sweetness of nature not very conducive to the military life. And yet when this current crisis came upon us, Sir—a crisis Corporal Bayati took somewhat personally—he did not hesitate to volunteer, did not hesitate to seek duty where he could best be utilized despite that duty placing him in harm's way. He was invaluable, Sir. To this Army, to the mission outlined by our Commander-in-Chief, to this country we have—become guests of. And yet, as ordered, I saw to it that he was discharged. And he got on a plane today for home. For America, Sir.

"It was an order I could have questioned, Sir. It was an order I should have questioned. But I did not. I did as I always have—I carried out your order with alacrity.

"But I will not carry out any more orders, Sir. Not for you. Not for this service. Not for my Commander-in-Chief. Not ever again.

"Given that, Sir, I must thank you for not invoking the stop-loss policy and preventing my retirement. Although I know you did not do it out of kindness. I'm glad you took me seriously and understood that I would have indeed ceased to obey orders, which would have led to a court-martial, which would have led to the publicity that you and I are both quite aware the Army does not need right now.

"The Army is a fine institution, Sir, and it will survive without me. The Army has turned me into a tough son-of-a-bitch, and I will survive without it. But I cannot leave without informing you that ex-Corporal Bayati will probably not survive. You see, Sir, not only did the Army not know that he was a homosexual when he enlisted but neither did his family or community. But now, I'm afraid, Sir, they do know. If you think America, or at least a portion of it, is intolerant towards homosexuals, you have no idea how—negative a situation Corporal Bayati will find upon his return home to his family and his—community. Hate will fall upon Corporal Bayati, Sir. A man who had never harmed any of his fellow creatures. A man who was universally liked by those who encountered him. A man who answered the call of duty from his country, adopted though it may have been—a man who has saved lives with no thought for his own. You and I, Sir, have condemned such a man to a hell I would not wish upon—well, even you, Sir. However, I might now wish it upon myself.

"That is all I can say, Sir. May I be dismissed?"

As Austin read and performed, he considered and assessed, and he came off the last words ready to declare:

"Wow. Okay. Interesting. I can do a better reading after some study, but I think I've got a feel for the character. I like the way you—"

In beginning to speak, Austin had kept his eyes on the text, addressing the words he had just read. When he raised his eyes to engage the author, he faced an odd sight. The Major was now sitting on the sand, shedding tears. Austin understood what he had only suspected before.

"You were in love with this boy, weren't you?"

The Major, who had relaxed his military bearing, recovered it.

"I don't think I'm familiar enough with the emotion to answer the question."

"Philip," was all Austin said in reply. But it was enough.

"I was—I was very fond of him—an excellent young man. He was so dedicated to the mission. Such a waste. And for such a—a stupid reason."

Austin sat down next to Philip. The sand was cold, but there was warmth from the nearness of Philip.

"Did you have—relations with him?"

"Of course not. He had a lover, a citizen working for one of the contractors. They belonged to two different—I guess you would say—denominations of their religion. They got into an argument, and in anger, his friend reported his activities to the Army. It must have been a hell of an argument."

"Philip—are you gay?"

There was a measure of hope in Austin's question.

"No. In all good conscience and honesty, I can declare to you that I am not a homosexual."

"Oh. Well, you know you can tell me if you are because—"

"You are gay. Yes, I had assumed so. Nevertheless, I am not a homosexual."

"Well, I can make assumptions too, and I assume you are not a heterosexual."

"I cannot make that claim either."

"Philip, what else is left?"

"I have amused myself for years considering the idea that if I was ever asked the question or had to fill it out on a form—something I have scrupulously avoided—I would, without hesitation, answer that I was an—autosexual."

"Oh. I understand. Exclusively?"

"It has been the only option open to me."

"I can't imagine that. But then, I can't truly know what your life was like in the Army."

"No. You never will, no matter how much I tell you about it."

"Autosexual, huh?"

"It was the only term I could think of."

"Interesting that you thought of it."

"We all strive to define ourselves."

"And when you are—handling the job, what, or who, do you think about?"

"For years, it was a Greek soldier. After a brutal battle during the Peloponnesian War, I would tend to his wounds. And then we would bathe together."

"Athenian? Or Spartan?"

"Athenian. I've had enough of Spartans in my real life."

"And who do you think about today?"

"Lately," Philip turned his head to look at Austin, "it has been you."

Austin smiled. He was afraid it was a girlish smile, which upset him, for he was not a girl; he was a man. So he tucked his smile in and brought his face up close to Philip's.

"Philip, have you never been kissed by a man?"

"Never."

"May I?"

"Please."

It was a gentle kiss. It was a kiss of sweet nature.

BE

Chapter the Ninth

Weeks passed. Whether just a few or more than many is a relative question, but whichever it was, Time operated as it always had and measured changes. Some of the changes were jarring and antithetical to what had been before. Some changes were small, subtle, incremental, and barely noticeable. Although which were which was, like Time itself, quite relative.

One change was the exit of Frank from the early morning atmosphere of The Briers' dining room. There were no more Salsa dances in the kitchen. Joe, the afternoon head waiter who had replaced Frank, was all business. Or "All asshole," as Julio had quietly declared, nicely indicating the morning staff's deep disappointment over the situation.

If any of the residents had noticed the change in the dining room, none of them had commented on it. As long as they got their food in a timely manner and well prepared for ingesting, what was there to complain about?

A noticeable change among the residents, though, was Allison Carr no longer coming down to the dining room for her breakfast. This would probably not have been noticed if she had been the same Allison she had seemed when she first moved to The Briers. Then she was taken to be a rather reserved, prim woman, possibly a widow, maybe even what used to be called an Old Maid, who preferred her own company or that only of a book. But now, as everyone had learned and gossiped about, she was a bright, energetic, rich divorcee who was out discovering artists (well, one, but one in their midst!) and running off to New York to make deals for him—and taking control of the renovation of the old Peterson warehouse into an artist's studio and spending most afternoons and many nights away from the hotel. Had they known that besides work on the renovation, hours of telephone calls to New York, London, Los Angeles, and other large art markets, and meetings with local suppliers of materials and services Frank needed, she was making physically demanding and passionate love to her discovery, they might have been even more impressed—or appalled—or, possibly bemused. Allison was no longer coming to the dining room in the morning, not because she was reserved and withdrawn, but because she was asleep. She rarely saw dawn anymore unless it was the last thing seen before sleep.

If, after waking and a quick shower, Allison did not take off immediately for Rubenton, she would have brunch in her room sometime between noon and two. She had requested that only Trudy bring her meal up and that she be allowed to stay with her for a while to keep Allison company as she ate it. Joe was not happy with this idea, but Mrs. Briers liked Allison and so had given her approval. It was as if Allison had adopted Trudy. She became interested in her life, loves, and plans for her future. She encouraged her to speak about them as she devoured her eggs benedict. Or Belgian waffles. Or mozzarella and mushroom omelets.

Trudy was grateful for the attention. Since Frank was off doing his art stuff (which she couldn't wait to see, she said, but Frank kept telling her it wasn't ready to be seen yet), and she was busy with the play, they rarely got to see each other to talk right now—let alone fuck—so she was lonely for a friend. And it was awesome that this neat older lady— this neat older, sophisticated lady—wanted to be her friend. Even more awesome was being paid to sit around on Allison's couch and talk about herself, a subject she had mastered.

Trudy talked about her dad and mom, and the farm. And Cissy McMann, of course, and how she knew just about everything there was to know about Cissy McMann, and what an influence she had been on her life, and how neat Frank really was, and how his maturity was helping her become more "woman" and less "girl," and how shocked she had been when she learned about his art stuff. She had also been a little bit upset that Frank had never shared his art with her, but she figured artists had to be sort of mysterious like that, and, you know,

310

unlike ordinary people, or they wouldn't really be artists, would they? Or at least really good artists. She made Allison tell her often how she thought Frank would be a major artist and, yes, possibly famous because of that; at least Allison would work very hard to make him so.

"I guess we both sort of love him!" Trudy said one day as if it was a bright idea she had just gotten.

"Yes," Allison said, who had come to like Trudy despite certain reservations. "In different ways, of course. My love is purely professional."

"And mine is purely pure. Except for the sex, of course. We try to make that purely dirty. I hope Frank hasn't been missing it too much."

"Well—he has his work to keep him busy."

"Yeah. And Frank can always masturbate, of course."

"Well—uh—yes—that is—that is an option."

"As long as he's thinking about me when he does it, I'm okay with it."

"Trudy, what a touching and romantic thought."

Another resident of The Briers who was going through a change, at first small and subtle but eventually quite apparent, was the Major. He was letting his hair grow. He had worn his hair short in a neat and precise military cut since his third birthday, when he had received one as a present from his father. But now—and not really at the behest of Austin, who had suggested it—he was letting it extend beyond his father's and Uncle Sam's perimeters. It was a fascinating natural process that he checked several times a day. Was he learning personal vanity? Something the uniformity of military life frowned upon. Or was it just a form of entertainment, the watching of a story slowly unfolding? What would be the end? Where was his natural part? Would he (and Austin) like it there? How full would his hair become? Would it be thick or thin? What direction would it take? What order should he force on it? Would he let it grow not just out—but long? Would it fundamentally change him, having the same old face under a new canopy? But then, again, was it the same face? Oh yes, in the main, certainly. Same eyes, same nose, same mouth, all older than even yesterday. But look, there was something new there. What was it? It was so damn elusive, he could not reach his hand up to touch it (but

Austin could, so Austin said), and he could not name it (but Austin could if Austin wanted to be mawkish), but it was there nevertheless, and he was not displeased over the fact. And neither was Austin.

Austin was also not displeased over Philip's play, now finished. He had comments, though, intelligent analyses. Each one seemed to open something up in Philip's head and excited him when he immediately saw how to change things to accommodate Austin's suggestions. It was fascinating; this shaping of a story, if, at times, also frustrating. But often fun, just plain fun. Fun was not a thing he had pursued in his life. He had not ever felt it was something he needed. Good times on occasions, yes—especially those celebrating a victory or, at least, the absence of defeat. And indeed, privately, it felt good to celebrate the continuation of his life when it had been, just recently, in question. But fun, just plain fun, no, he had not needed it. He had had Duty. To himself, to his country, to the memory of his father. But this fun, this fun in creation, it was a big, wonderful tickle. And he was beginning to like being tickled.

There was also a change in Austin, subtle to perceive but monumental in fact. He was in love. It was his first time. He was quite practiced in lust, truly having loved to lust, to lust after, to be the object of lust, and to use lust. But love had eluded him. Or he had side-stepped love. Who could tell in these matters? But now he was in love, joyfully in love, and he loved his love, despite being confused over the object of it: Major Philip McFadden, U.S. Army (Ret.). Hell, he was in love with G.I. Joe! It made Austin want to laugh. First over the situational slapstick of it, then in joyful celebration.

Austin had always assumed—and dreaded—that when he fell in love (he had never given up the hope), he would fall in love with another actor. Or possibly a ballet dancer, but that may have just been a physical thing. He had had dark fantasies about falling in love with a director (stage, never film, which was too horrible to contemplate), but he knew that to be slightly sick masochism on his part. Maybe he would find love with a novelist, which seemed somehow cerebrally right, but a playwright most definitely, which was the most romantic idea of all. In any case, knowing himself, he had assumed someone in the arts. He had, for a while, entertained the pragmatic notion of an investment banker, but in his life—an actor working for scale— he never encountered one. And he assumed he never would until he had something to invest, by which time the pragmatic necessity would no longer exist.

A soldier, though, had never appeared on the list. Why not? You would think a big, robust, and Someone-to-Watch-Over-Me kind of guy would be instantly appealing. But whenever Austin ran across that kind of guy—he remembered the military advisor on the set of Sgt. McKennen—he variously saw Nazis, or Southerners with red necks, killers of Bambi, men who would rather stroke the barrel of a gun than a penis. And all with voices tuned only to shout out orders to conform to their way of thinking and the God (spiritual or material) they worshipped.

When he first saw Philip, he was big and strong, of course, in his ramrod way, but Austin also perceived this to be a defensive stance, not an offensive one. There was a vulnerability there. Vulnerability in the big and strong, now that was appealing!

And now he was in love—crazy in love. But who in this community could tell? Austin was an actor from Hollywood; he was crazy, to begin with. And he wasn't going to announce it, as much as he felt the need to break out into song about it. Philip agreed. Not here, not now, neither one needed to deal with that as Austin had the responsibility to get the play mounted, and Philip had to let his hair grow out.

And write his play.

My God, Austin had said as he read a new draft based on his notes, I think it's becoming something extraordinary!

How about that? He had fallen in love with a playwright, after all.

Emily Briers never seemed to change, being the rock upon which The Briers rested. But Time cannot pass without change, and there was a change in Emily.

It was a change in the direction of her vision. After her youthful disappointments, the environment she had been forced to spend them in, and the further disappointment in not being able to extricate herself from that environment, her vision, aided and abetted by her discovery of The Briers, had turned inward. She had decided that all roads lead to The Briers. But now, with a trip to Europe in her future, the roads had turned around and were streaming outward. Was this changing her attitude towards The Briers itself? Yes, she thought. And she knew she should be disconcerted over the idea, but she was not. Not that she now hated The Briers where once she had loved it, but she was beginning to see it for what it truly was: a building, wonderfully odd, but just a building. It was a building that housed a hotel that catered not just to the passing trade but also people calling it their home, and that no longer seemed as sacred to her as it had once seemed, as Fletcher Briers had taught her to see it. The warmth of deep affection for The Briers that had always rested in the center of her being was not being replaced by the cold cash box considerations of income and outflow; the change was certainly not that radical. But Emily was beginning to realize that when she breathed in deep the atmosphere of The Briers, all she was filling her lungs with was air—a simple, plain mixture of nitrogen and oxygen. And that it was not as heady as it once was; it could no longer make her lightheaded. And as she liked being lightheaded and wanted to live for that purpose, she was happy to look outward and anticipate the new atmosphere of the Old World.

Would she not come back to The Briers? Of course, she would, lightheaded and with some of the Old World in tow. That was the plan. But what if she fell in love with it over there? And decided to fulfill her youthful desires full time? Well, she would cross that bridge—probably a wonderfully ornate bridge several hundred years old—when she came to it.

But what about her marriage? To whom? To Laurel and Hardy? Oh, who could tell? There were loves greater than that between a man and a woman, there really were, and one had to attend to them, they really had, or souls would shrivel, they would, they really would. Still, she loved the crazy, damn bastard, she supposed. If for no other reason than he carried some genes of Fletcher's; Fletcher, who had tried to get her to look outward and to go, as long as she always came back. What a dear man, a man who knew Emily better than she had known herself. And he was dead, damn it, he was dead, except for that which resided in Duncan, damn Duncan, the crazy bastard.

Duncan, damn Duncan, the crazy bastard had become an exhibitionist. He was so proud of the Laurel and Hardy on his chest that he would show it to anyone who asked to see it. And even people who had not. He hired a professional photographer to make a bare-chested portrait of himself. He sent it to all the tattoo magazines, what few friends he had left in Hollywood, distant relatives, and every Tent of the Sons of the Dessert, the official Laurel and Hardy fan organization. He also had a blow-up of it printed on poster board and forced Poignant Pete to display it in his tattoo shop. He tried to get the Rubenton Rubric to run the photo, threatening to pull The Briers' advertising if they did not, but Emily stepped in and stopped the blackmail.

Emily's action had upset Duncan, and he was angry with her for three and half days over her interference. Then, on the fourth day, as its second half was beginning, that anger was replaced with a fresh one when he found Emily, who never watched the TV, sitting in their room watching the TV. Duncan had just, three minutes before, decided that he wanted to see My Darling Clementine that afternoon because he really needed the legend, not the facts, of Wyatt Earp. And the good steady calm of Henry Fonda as he battled against the crotchety, conniving murderous mean of Walter Brennen, not yet limping, not yet funny.

"What the hell do you think you're doing?" he said to Emily, sitting in the easy chair, remote control in her hand.

"You're crippled, not blind, right?" Emily said as she pressed the pause button.

"You never watch TV."

"I've never been to Europe either, but I'm going."

"What's that got to do with this?"

"I just got in a whole collection of these DVD travelogues of Europe in the mail. So I'm checking them out."

"Why? You're going to Europe; you can see it then."

"I want to gawk now; I don't want to gawk when I'm there."

"What?"

"You're a cripple, right? Not deaf?"

"Emily, I want—"

"We all want, Duncan. And at the moment, my wants are being fulfilled. Which means you're going to have to do something else. It's sunny today; why don't you take Laurel and Hardy out and get them a tan?"

Duncan was as angry with Emily as he had ever been—except for the last three and a half days.

He did go outside, though, to let off steam. Once out, he decided to roll himself down to the theater to see how the rehearsals were going. He had done this several times, finding he liked being in the theater. He would roll himself into a section reserved for the disabled and sometimes watch what was happening on the stage, sometimes sleep, and sometimes get lost in his thoughts. Once, during a break, he had shown all the high school students his tattoo. Not one of them knew who Laurel and Hardy were, and that had pissed him off.

If he could only have told the little shits to sit, then snap his fingers and bring the house lights down, give the command and see a beam of light jump out from the back of the theater to hit a pure white screen and display, in a dance of black and white, the boys at Oxford, chumps though they were. Or as air raid wardens. Or in a near-apocalyptic battle with Jimmy Finlayson. Or, of course, doing their sweet dance way out west. Then they would have known and loved, he was sure, and then he would have been happy.

On this day, there was a break in rehearsals, so the theater was empty. So he sat alone, imagining My Darling Clementine projected before him. He smiled as he saw the broad vista of the vast Monument Valley tower above him.

He fell asleep.

He awoke to the horrible whine of Dmitri calling, "Mr. Briers! Mr. Briers!

Dmitri's voice carried from the boardwalk, then became louder as he entered the theater lobby, and was as irritating as Monument Valley was vast once he got into the theater proper.

"Shit, Mr. Briers, I've been here an hour already looking for you."

"So?" Duncan said, not at all concerned.

"So, I'm supposed to help you, not look for you."

"Well, if you can't find me, you can't help me until you look for me, so it's all the same thing."

"No, it's not."

"Yes, it is."

"No, it's not."

"Yes... Well, hell, you've found me, so roll me back to the hotel."

"Can I go home then?"

"You just got here."

"No, I told you, I've been here an hour already, maybe more."

"But maybe I've got things for you to do."

"But I'm tired, Mr. Briers, and I got to get up early tomorrow and go work at that old fart farm."

"You're lucky to be getting the experience."

"It's not an experience; it's a jail sentence. And shouldn't it be over soon?"

"Yeah, soon. I think you've just about paid your debt. Or you could keep working. Hendrickson tells me he's come to rely on you, that you're doing a pretty good job. So he'd be willing to start paying you."

"No way, I hate it there."

"Dmitri, you hate it everywhere. And what does that got to do with it? You'll earn more money and get that fast car faster."

That was a point. Dmitri almost thought about it.

"No, no way! I'm tired, and I'm tired of being a shit-kicker.

Duncan was disappointed. He had had his hopes.

"Okay, it's your choice. So wheel me back. And unless I can think of something in the meantime, you can go home when we get there."

Dmitri did not say thanks or acknowledge Duncan's generosity in any way. He just pushed, snorting each time he had to put out a little effort to get over an obstacle.

Hendrickson had not wanted to admit it, but he had begun to hate his weekdays of solitary farm labor. It was somewhat reminiscent of the time after his boys had left. The lack of their footsteps, the muting of their music, the cessation of their chatter to each other as they worked on some chore together had left a stillness within and about the house that he had found a too solid presence, one that he was constantly running into and having to push aside to get by. But, as irritating as that was, he had not hated that time because he knew it would do no good. The boys were gone. They would not be back except for the occasional visit, so get on with it, work, do the chores, tend to the cows, and deal with the chickens. Farm labor had become his refuge.

But now Mondays came, and he missed Dmitri. The dumb kid had grown on him. Yeah, like fungus, he said to himself. And unlike his sons, Dmitri would be back on the weekend. That fact should have consoled, but it did not, for it made Dmitri an anticipated presence that put into relief his current absence.

It was not that Dmitri was a joy to be around. The kid was a complainer and none too bright. But boy, was he amusing. Look, the kid was not all that bad, given his family, you know, Russian immigrants too busy just trying to get by, a motherless family, and his old Grandmother hardly spoke English. Hendrickson didn't know, but it just didn't seem a proper family to worry about how the kid was doing. But maybe they did, he didn't know; the kid just seemed like he needed something, that, despite having the family, he seemed like an orphan, or, better said, a stray.

Damn! This is why he refused to have more dogs after the boys left. He was a sucker for this kind of emotion.

He had once taken in a stray dog that had been kind of mean. With good reason, probably because he had been out loose in life, fending for himself, fending off those two-leggers who had hurt him when he was young, always chasing him off. But the easy access to food and Hendrickson's patience and attention had turned him around, and he had become a pretty good old dog.

Was Dmitri nothing but a two-legged dog? It was not very nice of him to think so.

Maybe he shouldn't have been so stubborn. Perhaps he should have gotten a dog when the boys had left.

Trudy could not believe it. COULD NOT BELIEVE IT! Cissy McMann had been linked romantically to an artist! It was in People Magazine. She had met him in London, where she was doing her play, at some party. It said he was a conceptual artist, but that was still an artist, right? They had a picture of something he had done. It was weird. He had done it on a barge in the middle of the Thames as it floated past the Houses of Parliament, that's what it said. He took a bunch of department store dummies and dressed them up like politicians, and judges—you know, the funny kind with the wigs—and even the Queen, and had them all hugging real, raw meat, skinned cow and pig and sheep carcasses, as they stood in a pile of dung. For what reason, People Magazine did not say, but the picture of him with Cissy McMann showed a tall, wildly-haired guy with bright red glasses holding hands with her in some park. He was, the magazine said, really famous, although Trudy had never heard of him before. He had only one name. It was Inyoface. Maybe Frank should change his name, she thought. Frank was a really dull name.

So Cissy McMann was her sister, her psychic sister, wasn't that obvious? If anything proved it, this did. She saw a time when they would all be at parties together, she and Frank and Cissy and Inyoface, best friends, all seen together in People Magazine. It was going to be so awesome!

But she would have to work on Frank. He needed a new name, maybe a new look. But she really couldn't think about all that right now; she was so tired. And yet so excited. She loved being at rehearsals, even when Austin or Ben shouted at her, which they were doing less and less. They even were very funny the day they first liked (finally!) her French accent. They did their version of "I Think She's Got It!" from, you know, My Fair Lady, and it was hilarious.

She liked being up on stage, saying her lines. She liked people looking at her as she did it. The other kids, the ones still in high school, were beginning to compliment her. That was neat. They were like her first fans! She already had one in mind to be the president of her fan club. He was a good organizer and knew computers and the Internet and all that. And, he had a crush on her—naturally—which was sweet. But she was the lover of an artist! Maybe not a conceptual artist, but he was an artist, and once she thought of the proper name for him, it will really be neat, everyone knowing it as they would know hers.

Life was going to be so damn good!

The most exciting recent change for the general population of Rubenton had been the installation of a microwave tower that finally allowed Rubenton and the surrounding area to receive decent cellular phone service. It had long been irritating for many in Rubenton, possibly to the point of psychological damage, to watch TV ad after TV ad after TV ad extolling the virtues of wireless communications. It was not so much living wired when the rest of the country was wireless; it was watching the cell phone evolve from a large, bulky, yet portable instrument of basic voice communications to a sleek, slim, indispensable electronic personal slave that catered to your every communal whim. Not being able to participate intimately in this evolution along the way was heart rendering. Not to have had the extreme post-modern pleasure of upgrading, then upgrading again and again and again in an ascendant flight toward (would it ever actually be reached?) some perfect Nirvana of cellular communications through voice, data, and pictures, both still and moving... Well, there was so much of the future now in their past; is it any wonder that many in Rubenton had felt cheated?

But that was all over now. Mainly thanks to the civic leadership of Harry Ogg and his wife, Pattie Heatherton. And it had come to fruition quicker than Ogg the Ogre and Pattie the Principal had initially anticipated, a fantastic feat in and of itself, as usually nothing in life ever came quicker than expected, save for male ejaculation and female menopause.

The commencement of cellular communications was a cause for celebration, so they had a ribbon cutting at the tower. Pattie asked Ben Alyn—the famous Hollywood actor best known for his role in Sgt. McKennen, and about to star in the inaugural production of the Rubenton Theatre Company at the new Stafford Theater—to do the honors. It was more than fitting. Ben Alyn's "feeling naked as hell without my cell phone" had given Pattie that extra burst of motivation to get the damn tower finally installed.

Ben had been happy to oblige and was wonderfully charming at the ribbon cutting, cracking everybody up with a quick patter of humor. He not only cut the ribbon but also made the first call on his phone, which was patched into a speaker system so that everybody could hear. And whom did he call but Tom Fowler, Sgt. McKennen himself, and currently starring in his third series since that show had gone off the air. The sitcom My Dead Dad had been ill-fated from the beginning, and the dramedy Detention Hall had been ahead of its time. But To Fit the Crime was currently the number one drama on TV, making it the sixth highest rated show in the country, right behind four unbelievable Reality shows and one sensationalist news magazine.

The people of Rubenton were thrilled to hear Tom Fowler's voice come out of the speakers. And what a nice guy he sounded like, apologizing for not being able to make the opening of What Price Glory but declaring that he knew that everybody would love the play, and especially Ben Alyn's performance. Ben could not help but beam at these words and be flattered, even though he hated Tom Fowler for consistently working when he did not. And for not getting him guest shots on any of his series. And for being an inferior actor to himself. But Tom Flower did not know this. Tom Flower was a dunce. And not only sounded like a nice guy, but actually was a nice guy, and so was incredibly easy to take advantage of, which Ben had decided to do because he had become convinced that his future lay in Rubenton at the Stafford Theatre.

Making a go of the theater would be a classic American success story that could rain glory upon Ben's head. Austin's, too, of course. But Austin could not do it alone. Although, of course, Austin got the gig first, what income there was from this venture was his. Fortunately, Ben had enough put aside that he could take a gamble. He had to do something to get a little glory and attention that he could turn into a real kick-in-the-pants for his career. Maybe this wasn't it, but it was worth cutting ribbons in Rubenton and calling impressive old friends to find out. Backdoor stardom was still stardom.

Pattie could not stop smiling as the ribbon-cutting ceremony went on. Her instincts about Austin, not to mention her lust for him, were paying off well. The whole town was beginning to get excited about the theater and having famous people among them, or even just on a speaker phone. Even Harry was starting to appreciate what good things were happening, spurred on by this crazy thing of having a legitimate, semi-professional theater associated with the town. Rubenton now had a Hollywood connection, and even Harry had to admit that that was a bit more glamorous than friction-proofing. And he and Pattie were getting the credit for it.

Only Pattie deserved the credit, of course, but she had been willing to share it with Hairy-butt Bastard because Hairy-butt Bastard had finally come around and was supportive. Part of this change, a not insubstantial one, might have been because she was fucking him more often now than she recently had been. (Austin was so busy; whom else could she turn to to keep her newly rekindled needs stoked?)

Pattie told Harry that the energy that she received from being around the creative process made her passionate. Had Harry but known, he said, he would have built a damn theater on the hill next to their house a long time ago. Nevertheless, Pattie determined that not much more time would pass before she had some lovely lust with Austin again. He was, after all, handsome, hot, a good lover, and the new star of the town. And Hairy-butt was but Harry.

But the most significant change in Rubenton and its environs was that which had happened in Frank's life. He was suddenly down by one skin.

His Frank the headwaiter skin now hung on a peg somewhere, a near weightless bag of no bulk, full of folds, the facemask collapsed in on itself, the two empty eye holes, brought together over a pushed-in nose, blankly staring at each other.

His artist skin, the something more comfortable he had slipped into after work, was now serving full-time duty. Was it still comfortable? Was it of fine enough material to take such full-time wear without getting worn? Or would getting worn, maybe a bit shabby, make it even more comfortable? Or would he wear holes in it, causing exposure?

Such questions and concerns were coming to Frank only at rare moments. He was too busy to dwell on them. Allison had found him an old, high-ceiling space in a building on Rubenton's main street to paint "Dog of War" during his studio's construction. It had once been a general store with a soda fountain. The soda fountain was still there, with everything in working order. The building faced east and an empty lot across the street, so nothing was preventing the morning sun from streaming through the two-story front windows the previous owner had installed. The light, then, for a good number of hours in the morning, was perfect.

Allison had asked Frank to list everything he would need to get started, and then she efficiently and quickly provided those needs. First, she had his original Dog of War sketch photographed and turned into a transparency. Then Allison got the proper projector for it. It light-splashed the transformed massive image of the president and the dog he had let loose onto the monster canvas now mounted on the back wall. She also draped the front windows with sections of black cloth, allowing the image to show clearly. And then Frank stood or sat on a tall ladder and began to trace the image onto the canvas.

During breaks, he interviewed art students Allison had found at the local community and State colleges. They were good kids, for the most part, eager and excited to be a part of art part-time that paid and kept them out of burger joints, gourmet coffee houses, and various other minimum wage-paying crap jobs. He looked at their portfolios, ascertained their understanding of art techniques throughout history, and picked the best for his crew of "assistants."

While he was finishing the tracing, which he insisted on doing all himself, Allison put his crew to work sorting and storing in an orderly fashion all the art materials she had purchased for the job. At times Frank would gather the gang together and discuss the painting style he wanted for this piece and how he wanted the brush strokes laid down. He showed examples from his art books; he did demonstrations on small pieces of canvas. The students were incredibly responsive, asking questions and looking for guidance. One, a very talented individual, well-spoken and precise in his language, suggested changes that were so monumentally stupid that Frank was dumb-struck and did not know what to do. He did not know whether to be angry and smite the son-of-a-bitch, or to be humble and accept the ideas for fear of not being liked. Allison could see Frank's dilemma and so simply separated the young man from the crew, gave him a week's pay, walked him to the door, and bid him farewell. When she returned to the others, she simply stated, "Art is not a democracy."

Allison was amazing. Frank loved to watch her. But it was diverting, and he felt the need for blinders, big ones, the kind made for a horse, that would prevent his peripheral vision from being invaded by her image, capturing his attention, taking it away from the creation emerging on the canvas by his hard work. Allison caught him now and then, sitting on top of the ladder, staring at her. She would chastise him firmly, mention the deadline imposed on him by his first commission, his first and only if he didn't meet that deadline. Still, Frank would sneak a glance now and then, for Allison was a wonder to watch.

If art was nothing but the self-expression of Homo sapiens, and Frank felt that that was what art was, then Allison was her own work of art. Her energy, command, and control over every situation she expressed when she walked, talked, questioned, exclaimed, mused, demanded, took delight, boosted, loved, kidded, turned, sat down with grace, or plopped down with fatigue. The music of her voice, the choreography of her dancing eyes, the image of the stances she took, the content of her mind, the form she gave it in expression, and the function she provided, were all an aesthetic delight to Frank. He wanted to frame her; he wanted to mount her (which, of course, he had); he wanted to present her to the world. No! He wanted to keep her to himself. He wanted to cry. Great Art always made him want to cry.

When Frank finished the tracing and his original sketch of Dog of War lived now on the huge canvas, everybody knew the actual work was about to begin. Work Frank now knew he needed the crew to accomplish in time. The crew felt that too.

Frank and that crew stood in front of the canvas, daunted together, just this side of defeated already.

It was late in the day. Allison told them to go home and get rested; they would start bright and early in the morning.

Frank wanted Allison to make love to him that night, but she refused. He needed to save up that energy for the task ahead, so he should go home alone, go to bed, and go to sleep. Besides, she had work to do. He was disappointed, but he agreed, and when he crawled into bed early, assuming he would lay there in apprehension most of the night, he fell asleep almost immediately. Such was the power of Allison's suggestion.

In the morning, they all showed up and stood once more in front of the huge canvas, no less daunted than the night before. Then Allison pulled the black cloth from the front window and the most glorious morning light rushed in to fill up the space and illuminate the canvas. The sketch lines now seemed faded, barely visible. It seemed as if Dog of War would vanish if they did not do something soon to capture it in light-loving oils. Still, following their leader Frank, they approached the task before them gingerly.

Suddenly there was a strange sloppy whoosh sound coming from the soda fountain. They turned and looked and were surprised to find Allison standing behind the counter pouring herself a cola from the fountain dispenser. She let it bubble up and flow over and laughed as the cold liquid ran down onto her hand.

Frank and the crew stood there disbelieving.

"I had it completely stocked last night," she said. "I got all kinds of sodas here; I can make Root Beer Floats, Malted Milks, Ice Cream Sundaes. So do a good job, guys, and there will be rewards."

They all laughed. It was perfect. And they turned back to their task at hand, now undaunted.

◆ ◆ ◆

One night while lying in Frank's arms, listening to his quiet breathing as he slept, and looking at a streak of blue oil paint that ran from his wrist to mid-forearm, Allison contemplated the change in her life. It was the second significant change since she had retired and left her husband. Or maybe it was just a continuation of that change, a change with chapters. Had she really thought she could retire to a fogged-in seaside hotel and a storage unit library and be happy? Maybe she hadn't been looking for happiness, just the absence of misery. But had she been miserable? If she had, it was a mundane misery; certainly not on the level so many—many being in the Third World—must feel day-to-day. Did they truly feel the misery, though? What other expectations did they have? Maybe they just got on with life, accepted their lot, and made the best of it. But in the civilized-industrialized-commercialized world, perhaps we are often too full of optimistic expectations and always too shocked over the disappointment when those expectations fail us.

But are our miseries frivolous just because they would look silly featured on a poster seeking aid?

Allison yawned. Frank's unconscious mind heard her, and his body responded, turning away from her.

Allison got up. It was time to leave and make that dark drive back to The Briers. Why didn't she stay? She didn't really know. There was, of course, the imposed secrecy caused by the lingering problem of Trudy. Neither she nor Frank wanted Frank just to dump Trudy. They both liked her too much to give her that kind of upset. So Trudy would have to dump Frank. How? Allison now had that figured out, but it would be a while before they could implement it. So it was still best for no one to know that her relationship with Frank was anything but professional and exploitative. Still, she could have always excused her not coming home by saying she had worked late in Rubenton and didn't want to make that dark drive. But she didn't mind the dark drive. In fact, she liked it. And she liked her room and The Briers; she liked her bed there. Who knows where the future was going to move her? She wanted to get as much of The Briers as she could, while she could.

But why move? She had paid rent ten years in advance for a reason. Frank had been drawn here for a reason. It was no time in either of their lives to set up house and become domesticated. The Briers could be as much of a home as they wanted. And for Frank to become a resident, where once he had served, could be an excellent point of interest in the resume Allison was building for him.

Rubenton was a good, calm place for Frank to work. She hoped to build an international clientele for his work—individuals and museums. But they could base anywhere in this shrinking world and travel to where they needed to travel when they needed to, which would be exciting. And yet, her recent trip to New York, a not unimportant element of this chapter, had given her energy, purpose, and guts. But also a fear of failure. All of which now drove her. Why would she not want to tap into that permanently? Overload? Words, it was all just words. The key was doing things. Where done was insubstantial, was it not?

She did not know right now and was too tired to figure it out. All she knew was that Frank, laying there asleep in his bed, was a vulnerable font of wonderful creation and needed her as no one ever really had before. And that giving to him would be giving to her. Commanding him would be commanding her.

"Christ!"

Allison looked at the time and realized she had a call to make. It was eight-thirty in the morning in London. She left Frank and went to her car. She got her brand-new cellular phone out of the glove compartment. How wonderful, how so right to her needs that they got that microwave tower up! She dialed and waited. Finally:

"Hello, yes, Adrian? Yes, It's Allison Carr. Have you looked through the slides? Yes? Good—good—excellent. Well, yes, of course, Adrian, you can wait until Frank finishes, but then you will be just one person in the line. Whereas, if you pre-buy, you'll have the London exclusive."

In any period of changes, there often comes one day crowded with them. In the weeks previously documented, that day came on a Sunday, the day scheduled for the first of four dress rehearsals for What Price Glory. Austin had ended rehearsals shortly after noon the day before and told everyone to go home and get plenty of rest, sleep late on Sunday morning, lie in a bit, and be leisurely. The call was for six p.m. for a performance at eight. Austin invited only a select few to attend and provide an audience: the Briers, Pattie Heatherton and her husband, Harry, Major Philip (as the high school kids had come to call him), and Allison Carr if she could make it.

Everyone was happy with the time off; they had been working incredibly hard, and not without anxiety and fear. The whole endeavor seemed at times to be a bunch of random, unrelated small parts out of control in a chaotic universe collapsing in on itself. Would it never make sense? Would it never expand? Then one day, a day very close to the first dress rehearsal, it did.

Austin could see it; Ben could see it; even Pattie, Major Philip, and Duncan Briers sitting quietly in the back could see it. And they were relieved. But they were adults and had all been thorough such experiences before, so their relief, while not unwelcome, was not unbounded. Trudy, however, and the high school kids (actors and crew) were giddy with relief and amazed to see a coherent whole before them, of which they were all recognizable parts. Not that the whole was perfect, Austin and Ben, and even Pattie and Duncan, could see that it was not perfect, but the kids did not know that. To them, it was a perfect miracle and one that may well become an experience that would change their lives forever.

But Austin gave them fair warning. "Trust me," he said as he excused them on Saturday, "the hard work is not done. The dress rehearsals are vital and will tell us a lot. Mistakes will be made, and there will be disappointments, anger, and depression. But it will all come together, I promise. So go home, get plenty of rest, sleep late tomorrow, lie a bit, and be leisurely."

Austin ignored half of his advice. He did not get much rest on Saturday night. Not because he was worried about What Price Glory, for there was nothing more to worry about. He had prepared the play, the players, and the stage as best as he knew how; what more he could do, he would do in the dress rehearsals, so what was going to be, was going to be. He had done all the creative work on the play, it was just the mechanics of execution, and they would take care of themselves with his competent oversight. To Austin, What Price Glory was already a thing of the past.

So he spent Saturday night on the future. He and Philip sat in Austin's room going over Philip's most recent draft of his play, which they had titled The Arabic Speaking World. It had become a play about translation and how when one speaks, one is always speaking in translation, as it is hard directly to communicate what is in one's mind, heart, and being. If it were easy, there would be no need for metaphors. This was true, of course, whenever one spoke to another. But The Arabic Speaking World also had something to say about speaking in translation to oneself.

They divided up the characters and read the play out loud. It was a thrill, a genuine, heart-quickening thrill. The work had become a thing they found a mutual love for, and they decided that night to dedicate themselves to it. What exactly that meant was not discussed; the feeling of the love was enough. Their making love late that night was the only expression needed.

On Sunday morning, Austin did take the other half of his advice—he had a leisurely lie-in. He spent most of it in a lovely languid mood, gently tickling Philip's ass.

Philip luxuriated in the particular pleasure of having his ass tickled. It was possibly better than sex, which he still had some problem acclimating to. Austin was a gentle lover, though, and made their sex, in contradiction to all reason, non-invasive. Part of this included simply running his fingers over Philip's bare skin. A pleasant sensation when it came to his face or arms, chest or back, but a damn wild trip to a high-pitch paradise when Austin's fingers came to Philip's buttocks.

"My God!" Philip had exclaimed the first time Austin's fingers had run over the rise. "My God, that's wonderful!"

"Your God has nothing to do with it," Austin said. "Or my God, for that matter. It's a pure human talent."

"Don't stop!"

"I won't."

Philip had never felt anything like it. No one had tickled him since his father when he was a very young boy, and his father had certainly never tickled his ass. He could remember laughing, laughing uncontrollably, and possibly never being happier than when his father worked his two hands under Philip's armpits. No one had tickled Phillip anywhere—anywhere in the world and anywhere on his body—since then. Nor had he tickled anyone. He had never had a child, of course, or a lover of any sex until Austin. What had he missed in his life? The first day Austin had tickled him, he was eager to reciprocate. But Austin was not ticklish.

"Sorry," Austin said.

Philip was sad and turned over onto his stomach again for more of Austin's fingers on his ass. In the middle of the delight, he asked:

"Do you have siblings?"

"A brother and two sisters," Austin answered.

"Do they have kids?"

"Yes, they all do."

"Ages?"

"Gee, I don't know. Tommy, Eric's boy, is about four, I guess. Mandy's twins are six, I suppose."

"Boys? Girls?"

"Girls. Identical. Mary's kid is ten, eleven, something like that."

"Are you close to them?"

"Sure."

"Do you visit them?"

"When I can."

"Do they know you're...?"

"Yes. Difficult at first. They've gotten used to it."

"Would you be willing to take me next time you go?"

Austin stopped the running of his fingers. He thought about this. He thought of Mandy's big two-story home in Vermont that was always golden with warmth because Mandy always was.

"Yes, actually, I would, I would be willing. And proud, Philip. Yeah, I think I would be proud to do that."

Pattie Heatherton wanted to give Austin a gift for completing the production of What Price Glory. She had considered many things. A trophy of appreciation from the same trophy shop where she ordered all the various high school trophies for sports, academics, and the band. An expensive sports coat. A fine leather-bound edition of Shakespeare or Neil Simon. These were just three of the ideas, all of which she finally discarded for the only idea that was just right, perfect, and would be, she was sure, the most welcomed. She decided to give him herself. After his self-enforced abstinence for the good of the play, the theater, and the drama program, he would certainly appreciate it. And possibly be moved by it. Moved—or thrust—into action, Pattie hoped.

At first, she thought she might sneak into his bed on Saturday night, but then she thought better of a better idea. He was, after all, exhausted; she could tell that. So why offer something he wouldn't be able to take full advantage of? No, Sunday morning was the time. He told everyone to sleep late on Sunday and lie in a bit. But she knew he was an early riser, and you can't break old habits, and getting a lay instead of a lie was not that much of a difference.

She needed to plan an account of her movements, though. Hairy-butt Bastard's regular golf game had been canceled, so that was a problem. He was probably going to suggest that they go out to breakfast, probably to the Lamplighter because he liked their Moby Dick Breakfast ("A Whale of a Meal!") consisting of a half-pound steak, four eggs, a large bowl of hash browns, a foot high stack of pancakes, and a small glass of orange juice. She thought of telling him that she was going to go to church, a place that sent chills up Harry's spine despite a professed belief in God, the existence of whom, he always said, was obvious to anyone with half a mind. She rarely went to church, but she thought she could say she promised some of her students that she would attend because they were performing in a special musical presentation. But as Harry could too easily discover later that this was not the case, she decided just to be honest and tell him that she had an early morning meeting with Austin to go over her plans for the opening night party. That Austin had left the plans for the party entirely in her hands, Harry could not and would not know, and that was good. So Pattie got up early and showered, then slipped into a devastatingly cute velour jogging outfit that she never jogged in but which would be easy to slip out of should the need arise—and she intended to make it rise. Underneath, she wore a lovely bra and a pair of crotch-less panties featured in a "Thrills for Him" catalog that she confiscated from a freshman's locker.

Hairy-butt Bastard was still asleep when Pattie left, blowing him a kiss.

When Pattie arrived at The Briers, she carried a briefcase and a business-like demeanor just in case she ran into Emily or Tom, the front desk guy, or any of the residents or guests. But it was very early, and the lobby was empty, the front desk was vacant, and the only sounds were those of preparation coming from the dining room. So she was unseen as she walked up the stairs.

When she got to Austin's door, Pattie took from her briefcase the key to his room he had given her. She quietly slipped it into the lock, turned it slowly, pushed the door open gently, and entered his sitting room. It was not that Allison did not want to disturb Austin, she wanted to disturb him quite a bit, but she did not want to disturb him quite yet, or in this manner. She planned to slip into his bedroom and, assuming he was asleep, slip the sheet off him—Austin always slept only with a sheet—slip down his briefs if he was wearing any, which he probably would not be, and slip her mouth around his penis. Assuming it was not already erect—a sleeping man's penis sometimes is—she was looking forward to giving him a gentle, warm, and moist mouth massage and feeling the indescribable pleasure and sense of accomplishment she always felt when an engorging penis grew in her mouth like an inflating balloon, like Jack's beanstalk, like swelling pride.

Quiet noises were coming from the bedroom. Damn! She thought, he's already up and watching the news on TV or has the radio on. Or maybe he fell asleep to the TV—that could be it. She did not give up her plan. But decided to alter it. She was going to allow Austin to gleefully pull her devastatingly cute velour jogging outfit off her post-fellatio. Instead, just in case he was wide awake and watching TV, she now would enter nude to present some exciting counter-programming. She slipped out of her outfit and started to slip off her crotch-less panties, but then decided, no, those she would keep on, so she pulled them back up. But she doffed her bra and fluffed her hair, and was ready.

In case Austin was asleep, she opened the door softly and slowly.

And revealed unto her was a deviate scene of depraved tickling.

Major Philip McFadden, US Army (Ret.), was lying in a prone position on the bed with a beaming smile. Austin O'Neil, Bachelor of Fine Arts, was propped up on one elbow, running the tips of his fingers over the Major's perfectly proportioned ass.

The gasp or cry or squeal or combination of all three that came out of Pattie's mouth was not only ungodly—it was inhuman.

Austin looked up. Philip looked up. Pattie instantly looked down.

"Holy Christ! You're a fucking faggot!"

Both Austin and Philip were in a relaxed enough state to forestall panic. Austin simply said.

"Faggot? I haven't heard that one in a long time."

"I don't believe it!"

"Well, at least Philip's butt ain't hairy."

"I'm going to kill you!"

"Now, Pattie, how would that go over? Nude High School Principal Kills Illicit Lover Found Tickling Ass Of War Hero."

That was when Pattie remembered that she was, indeed, nude, or nearly so. She struggled to cover herself up and fled to the sitting room.

Austin found her there hopping on one foot as she was frustrating her own goals in an uncontrolled effort to slip on her jogging pants.

"Pattie," Austin said, remaining calm.

Pattie, who had not yet attended to her top, got the bottom secured and turned to Austin, her breasts tagging along.

"Don't talk to me, you deviant asshole."

"What is that? An asshole that passes something besides shit?"

"Don't be clever. And don't be amusing. Nothing is amusing about this!"

Austin bent down, retrieved Pattie's bra and top, and handed them to her.

"Actually, it is nothing but amusing. But I can't expect you to see that."

"You're damn right you can't, you queer."

"Well, that's a little bit better than faggot, I suppose."

"You expect respect from me?"

"Of course. Look what we've accomplished. Look at what we've accomplished together. Why is that any less deserving of respect because I sleep with someone else? You sleep with someone else."

"He is my husband!"

"And Philip has become the most important person in my life. Surely you never thought you would be?"

Fully clothed, briefcase in hand, Pattie stood herself tall.

"You used me."

"It was mutual, don't you think?"

"I...."

"Did you not gain from it?"

"I...."

"Can you perceive any harm?"

Austin's calmness was infectious, and Pattie felt herself falling into a rational state of mind. But she did not want to be there.

"You bastard!"

"Yes, I suppose so. Will you refer to me now as Hairless-butt Bastard?"

A smile broke on Pattie's face, but the laugh she suppressed. Her anger, though, had been abated, and suddenly she needed to understand.

"Are you—are you, at least, bi-sexual?"

Austin shook his head—sadly for Pattie's benefit.

"No one is really bi-sexual," he said.

"But—but we had great sex," she said, taking a sad last glance at Austin's relaxed organ that had given her so much pleasure.

"Thank you. I'm not bi-sexual, but I am a damn good actor."

It seems to have been the wrong thing to say. Pattie hauled off and slapped Austin across the face, unfortunately forgetting to flatten her hand.

"Ow! That hurt."

"Good! I'm happy!" Pattie said as she rushed out of Austin's sitting room.

Austin cursed himself and went back into his bedroom. Philip was fully dressed and standing at attention.

Trudy was so happy that Austin had given them some time off. Mrs. Briers had also given her some time off, letting her take her one-week vacation two months before her anniversary date. And she gave her two weeks' leave after that so that during the three weeks of the "pilot" production of What Price Glory, she would not have to worry about work. And since Austin and Ben and even Mr. Briers, who used to work in Hollywood, had all invited "friends from the Industry" to come to Rubenton for the production (all expenses paid out of a "marketing" budget for important "word-of-mouth" generation), maybe she'll be discovered. Then she wouldn't have to go back to work at all. Snapped up and sent to Hollywood—was it that much of a dream?

But the chance to get some rest before dress rehearsals or to not tax herself too much during the run of the play was only part of the reason she was so happy. The more important reason was that Allison and Frank had finally invited her out to see Frank's work, and she thought it would be cool to see his work Sunday afternoon. Then she could leave from his temporary studio for the theater for her first dress rehearsal: Actress Visits Artist Boyfriend On Way To Play. It was so wonderfully real, so not being a kid, a waitress, a farm girl, or a resident of Rubenton who had never been anywhere else in her life.

If only she could drive to Frank's studio in something other than her dad's pick-up truck. At least her dad had washed it, which he rarely did, but he said he figured that a famous actress needed a clean set of wheels to tool around town. Her dad was so funny sometimes, and she loved him, she really did.

As she started to leave, her dad and mom stopped her and handed her a beautifully wrapped package with a big bow. She opened her mouth and widened her eyes, and wondered what for.

"We hear," her dad said, "that it is traditional to give an actress an opening night gift."

"But tonight is just a dress rehearsal."

"We know," her mom said, "but we couldn't wait. Plus, there's a practical reason."

"Really? Why?"

"Don't ask, just open," her father said.

It was a cell phone. Trudy was thrilled.

Her mom explained: "It's really worried me, you being out at night a lot, so tired from all that you're doing. Now, well, we can stay in touch, you know, in case of emergencies, there's even a special button there for calling 911."

"Not just emergencies; all the time. I want you to check in regularly."

"Dad, I am over eighteen."

"What's that got to do with our loving you?"

Trudy was moved, as a good daughter can be. She hugged her parents. Then she opened the box and took out the phone. It was neat and cool. It had a lavender cover. Her dad, who had read the instruction manual cover-to-cover, gave her a quick yet thorough tutorial on its use. Then they tested it. He called her cell phone from the home phone. To hear it ring made them laugh. Then Trudy called the home phone from the cell phone. When her dad answered, she simply said, "I love you," then ran for the truck, shouting out, "Bye!"

Trudy got in, put the cell phone on the seat next to her, gave it a loving look, and then took off for Rubenton.

When Trudy got to Frank's temporary studio, she was blown away—completely blown away. There was this huge plate glass window in front, and you could look through it and see the big painting Frank was working on! She could have come and seen this at any time! But, of course, home/The Briers/the Stafford Theatre had been her world of late; she had not even considered territory outside of it.

She entered to find Frank and Allison waiting for her.

"Wow!" Trudy said, approaching Dog of War. "It's really big!"

"Well," Frank said, "what do you think?"

"That's the President."

"It is."

"It's really neat you can make him look like him."

"Thanks."

"Where is he?"

"In a landscape of his own creation."

"Yeah, but where is it?"

"Ohio."

"Oh. It's a really big dog."

"True."

"He's not really cute."

"The President?"

'No, the dog."

"Well, he's one of the dogs of war."

"What does that mean?"

"It refers to a quote from Shakespeare."

"Oh. We read Romeo and Juliet in school."

"It's not from that one."

"Is the dog going to, like, bite him or something?"

"I sort of leave that up to the viewer's imagination."

"Well, that's not fair."

"What in life is?"

"Isn't this kind of illegal?"

"What?"

"I mean, you're threatening the President, aren't you?"

"Only with a metaphor."

"Oh. Boy, this must have taken a lot of work."

"It's labor intensive, all right."

"So you'll get a lot of money for it, right?"

Frank looked at Allison, then said, "Eventually."

"You got anything else I can see?"

"Just sketches of things I'm going to turn into large canvases like this. They're pinned up over there."

Trudy went over to a wall that had a wide corkboard mounted on it. There, pinned to the cork, were several pieces that Frank and Allison had decided would be first in the pipeline. Trudy looked them over. She did not know what to say. She only knew that Frank's work seemed "conceptual" in the sense of Inyoface's art as described by People Magazine. In other words, rude. But Trudy was not naive enough to be unaware that rude could sell and sell big, and rude could make you famous. So she quickly decided that she didn't have to like that fact but also didn't have to run away from it.

Suddenly she laughed.

"What?" Frank asked, very interested, very thrilled that he had finally gotten a gut reaction from Trudy.

"That's funny!"

"What? What?"

"'What, were you born in a barn?'" she quoted. "My mom says that all the time."

"So you like that one?"

"Yeah, I guess. So what's the Door to Irrationality?"

"You know, religion, superstition, that sort of stuff."

"But Jesus is a religion, right?"

"Uh...."

"So why wouldn't he be going through that door?"

"Well...."

"There's some more stacked over here," Allison said from a table by the soda fountain. Trudy looked over to Allison and then moved over to the table. One by one, she went through the stack of drawings. Allison moved away and joined Frank, gently taking his hand.

"Frank!" Trudy suddenly said in horror.

"What?"

"This is ... this is disgusting! Disgusting and horrible!"

"Really?"

"How could you?"

"Well, Trudy, it's just—"

"I never, ever want to see you again!"

Trudy ran, bumping the table, knocking a pile of drawings onto the floor. She was in tears by the time she reached the door. She opened it, turned, and looked at Frank and Allison. Both now seemed alien creatures of ugly demeanors.

"FUCK YOU!" Trudy screamed as she ran out the door to her Dad's pick-up truck.

"Well," Allison said with no note of triumph in her voice, although one would have been her due.

"Yeah," Frank said. Then he walked over to his drawings and started picking them up, including the one that had upset Trudy.

It was an extraordinarily accurate and lovely drawing of a nude Cissy McMann. She was sitting on a fancy Beverly Hills toilet wiping her ass while she smiled her trademark big glowing smile and looked right at you. A legend above her head in a typeface made famous by its use in the *Trial by Erin* logo said: DON'T BLAME ME! IT'S BIOLOGICAL!

"This was damn mean of us," Frank said.

"I know," Allison agreed.

Frank tore the drawing in half—then again—then again. He tossed the remains in a trashcan and then looked hard at Allison.

Allison looked back and gave Frank a weak smile. "Don't blame me. It's biological."

The call for six came, but none of the cast or crew did except for Austin, Ben, and Major Phillip. By six-thirty, Austin and Philip knew that the absence of "the kids" were a consequence of their discovery that morning by Pattie. At six-thirty-five, they explained the situation to Ben, who did not quite know what to think about it. He could only say, "I don't think we're in Hollywood anymore, Toto," which received a weak smile from Austin and no response from the Major, who did not understand the reference. Besides, Philip was dealing with some very mixed emotions, not the least being the one attendant to the fact that a second person in the world now knew that he was gay, the knowledge he was still trying to mix into a world view of some comfort for himself.

At six-forty-five, the Briers arrived. The lack of the expected activity was immediately apparent. Austin knew he owed an explanation. The one he offered alluded to a disagreement with Pattie Heatherton, but not the details.

At seven o'clock, the Oggs showed up. Neither looked happy as they walked down the center aisle, the overhead lights bouncing off Harry's shaved dome toward the stage where everyone gathered.

"I called all of my students and told them the rehearsal was off and not to come in," Pattie declared in a cold, business-like manner with a hint of the anger she was restraining.

"Yes," Austin said. "I rather figured that's what you did."

"Well, what did you expect?"

"Rational intelligence. But then I'm a sunny optimist."

"You're a fucking fag, is what you are!" Harry burst out.

"Hey!" Duncan said from his wheelchair, not liking the tone that had suddenly invaded the air.

"Well—" Harry started to say, but Pattie stopped him with a look.

"I see where you get your charming, archaic manner of speech," Austin said to Pattie.

"It doesn't matter what we call it, Austin; the fact is, you are a homosexual, and I, as principal of Rubenton High School, cannot allow my underage students to be exposed to you."

"You cannot discriminate against me on the basis of sexual orientation; you know that."

"I wasn't planning on it. But Mr. Ogg here, the school board's treasurer, informs me that we have a shortfall in this year's budget and there must be cuts. So I'm sorry, but we won't be able to fund a drama program after all."

"What about all the money you've already spent on this theater? Surely the other board members, the community, might be a bit upset that you're giving up the game after—"

"Regrettable, but I think the old stand-by about throwing good money after bad will placate the complainers. You must remember Austin, Harry and I run this town."

"The hell you do!" Duncan stated.

"Duncan, shut up!" Pattie shot down at Duncan.

"You can't talk to me that way; I'm a gimp, for God's sake."

"Duncan, this is none of your business!"

"Hey!" Emily shouted out. They were all shocked to hear it, as she had probably never shouted before in her life. "Everybody's going to calm down and explain to me the situation." It was a very commanding statement, and it made an impression.

Pattie turned to Emily.

"Emily, I arrived at your hotel early this morning to have a meeting with Austin in his room and found him in bed with the Major."

"And what were they doing?" Emily asked.

"What?"

"Were they sleeping or screwing?" Duncan asked.

"Quiet, Stanley," Emily said to her husband in a way that amused him. Then she turned her attention back to Pattie. "Okay, so Austin and Philip have an intimate relationship. What is the problem with that?"

"The problem is," Harry stepped in, "he's a deviate queer and faggot, and I'm not going to allow him to corrupt our youth. I don't care what the fucking liberals say. I don't care about anti-discrimination laws. I don't care about any of that shit! Hell, look at what he's doing. Look how fucking sneaky he is. He picks a play that seems all-American. Hell, it's about our honorable fighting men and all that, but it's just a cover so he can get a bunch of young high school boys spending all their spare time with him doing God knows what not—and in uniform! Hell, there's only one girl in the whole play, right? He even got a real military man to 'advise' him on the thing, and he turns out to be a fucking faggot too!"

Major Philip McFadden, US Army (Ret.), a fucking faggot in the view of some, slowly walked over to Harry, pushed his face kissing-close to Harry's, and said, very quietly:

"I think it's time for you to stop talking, sir."

Harry, known as Ogg the Ogre, who had never been intimidated in his life, was not on this occasion.

"Get the fuck out of my face," Harry said, pushing hard against the Major's chest.

No one in the room could explain how it happened—except for the Major, who felt no need to—but it happened, and Harry found himself sprawled out across the tops of several of the theater seats his wife had secured at substantial savings. He was now unconscious, which was not an ideal situation, but he was also now quiet, which was.

"Harry!" Pattie ran to her husband in shock over the incident—and the fact that she seemed to care. Austin came, too, as did Ben and Emily. Everybody's adrenaline was flowing. "Help me," Pattie pleaded, and they all worked to pull the large man off the tops of the seats, one badly broken, and lay him as gently as possible onto the aisle carpet.

Ben took his jacket off and made it into a pillow for Harry's hairless head.

As Harry breathed regularly and seemed peaceful, everybody's concern diminished.

"One wants to ask at this time," Duncan said, "what price glory?"

"Duncan!" Emily warned.

"Emily, I'm going to talk; you might as well accept it and stop talking yourself. Pattie, so you think none of this is my business? You forget that I own this theater and that Emily and I have made our financial contributions to its founding. Now, satisfy my curiosity, will you? If you had a scheduled meeting with Austin early this morning— in his room—why would he be stupid enough to be laying in his bed giving head to the Major?"

"Don't be disgusting. And Austin wasn't doing that."

"Doing what?"

"Giving head."

"Oh, I'm sorry, I just assumed, them being fucking faggots and all that. So what was Austin doing?"

"I ... I don't know."

"He wasn't butt-fucking him, was he?"

"Why do you insist on being disgusting?"

"I'm just trying to get at the facts here?"

"Why?"

"So I can understand why Austin would be so stupid to get caught doing what he was doing, whatever it was. Maybe it was perfectly innocent. Maybe the Major was just there having a meeting before you."

"In the nude?"

"It was Sunday morning; maybe they wanted to be comfortable."

"He was stroking his ass!"

Duncan laughed. Ben laughed. Emily hid her face.

"Actually, I was tickling it," Austin said.

"A form of Zen massage therapy, by any chance?" Duncan asked.

"No. Philip likes it after I give him head."

The Major reddened and went to sit way in the back of the theater.

"Oh," Duncan said. "So you are gay guys! Well, it was stupid of you gay guys to be doing that when you knew that Pattie would show up."

"We didn't know," Austin said.

"Oh."

"Pattie and I didn't have a meeting scheduled."

"We did too!" Pattie lied beautifully.

"No, you didn't, Pattie," Duncan said, "You were probably showing up to surprise Austin so you could give him a little head."

"That's—"

"Everybody knows you've been screwing the guy."

"I have not!"

"Sure you have. We all knew it. And as soon as the Ogre wakes up, he will know it too."

Pattie gave up—possibly because she was too proud of being secretly notorious.

"He won't believe you."

"Sure he will. A man like Harry loves to believe that kind of stuff. And if Harry knows, then the school board will know, and if they know, then the community will know. Why the hell should Rubenton have to go through all that?"

"Okay. So what am I supposed to do? I still don't want that man teaching at my high school."

Duncan turned to Austin.

"You don't really want to teach at that high school, do you? Unwelcome and all? Especially since I'm going to assume you and the Major are not just being casual about this thing, right?"

Austin smiled. "Well, yes, we are not just being casual. We've been discussing spending a lifetime together."

"Right, well, you're not going to do that here and call it a marriage. And Domestic Partnership is such an unromantic term. So you want to leave, right?"

"Philip's written a play. It's good. We were thinking of trying it out here, then moving it to New York. You know, off-Broadway or something."

"Got a gay theme?"

"Kind of."

"I don't think it's going to happen here."

"I guess you're right."

"So take it straight to New York."

"There's a money problem."

"No, there's not. I'm producing it."

"Duncan!" Emily was shocked.

341

"Emily, think of the fun you'll have when we transfer the play to London."

Austin was also a bit shocked and said, "But you don't even know if the play is any good."

"So you will make sure it is. Or I'll have to put you over my knee and spank you." Duncan turned to the principal of Rubenton High. "So, Pattie, let this production go forward. Why waste all this hard work? It's a pilot production anyway, right? Let it happen, then call it a failure, claim your shortfall, and get out."

"What about the money the school district has put up?"

"I'll reimburse it."

"Duncan!" Emily couldn't stand it any longer, "Who made you Santa Claus?"

"Don't worry about it, Emily; I have plans for this place."

"But—"

"HEY! HEY!"

It was Trudy, running into the theater, running down the aisle, upset, out-of-breath, disheveled, and dirty of face.

"I'm sorry I'm late, but ... but, there was a fire ... old man Hendrickson ... his farm ... it's all burned down ... he's ... he's real bad hurt ... he ... he almost died ... but ... but ... but Dmitri rescued him! Dmitri's a hero!"

Trudy had left Frank's storefront studio in tears and confusion. She ran to her dad's pickup truck and hurt herself as she opened the door, trying to squeeze in before it fully opened.

"Ow! Shit! Christ!" she said as she finally slid into the cab and onto the seat, pissed at the pain but not wanting to take the time to consider it. She got the key into the ignition; the truck started; she backed it and put it into gear to move forward, which she then did at speed not sanctioned by city ordinances.

She was in a state of shock but very much wanted to be in a state of denial, but it was all too fresh and awful to deny.

Why did Frank do it?

To hurt, that's all she could figure, to hurt.

Why would he want to hurt her?

And Allison?

They were holding hands. That was weird. When Trudy looked up at them, she saw that they were holding hands—holding hands in a conspiracy of hurt. Trudy was not so long out of high school that she did not see them as peers laughing at a prank at her expense, something she had never actually experienced in high school, except in empathy for the weak ones who had. So why was it now her turn?

That awful image of Cissy McMann was still in her head, and she wanted to shake it out, pound it out, and scream it out. So she screamed in the cab of her dad's pickup truck.

It was Allison. It must have been Allison. She thought back and confirmed, yes, she had never really talked to Frank about Cissy McMann. Why? Because it had never come up. But she talked about Cissy McMann all the time. But not to Frank because Frank was a man, her man, she had thought. See, that was important because most girls wanted a boy. No, not just in high school, of course, but even out of high school, into real life, girls all wanted just to have boys. She was not dumb; she could see that. Even her mom still thought of her dad as a boy. No one wanted a man anymore.

Movie stars were all boys, even the ones in their 40s now. Look at them all. Look how they dressed. Rock stars? Even the old ones, even the ones before when her mom and dad had been kids, Paul and Mick and those guys, they were all still just boys, weren't they? Every girl still just wanted a boy. And so had she, she guessed—until Frank. She had needed Frank to be a man when she needed Frank for what she first needed him for. A boy wouldn't have been right. Then she fell in love with him. She fell in love with a man. And somehow, you just didn't talk to a man about Cissy McMann.

But Allison, an older, neat, sophisticated woman though she was, Allison seemed to have wanted to be a girl with her, probably because she had worked with girls all her life. So, of course, she could talk about Cissy McMann to Allison, who must have told Frank, who must have told Frank to do that awful drawing as a prank so they could have a laugh at Trudy's expense. And Frank did it, for some reason, Frank did it, which meant he wasn't really a man after all, but just another dumb boy like all the rest.

Trudy, in tears and confusion and pain, had made no decisions about direction, she had not paid any attention at all to the road ahead of her as she drove, but soon, in a sudden moment of clarity, she found herself on Leech Beach Road heading out of town. She guessed she was going home. No! The play! She's got a dress rehearsal. She's expected; she's required; she's necessary. She can't be upset now. The show must go on, she said to herself, the show must go on; the show must go on.

She found the mantra surprisingly bracing.

She found the smoke billowing up ahead alarming.

After several curves, she could see it was coming from Mr. Hendrickson's farm; she could see that his house was on fire; she could see a car parked on the side of the road and an individual standing by the car looking at the fire.

Trudy pulled up behind Dmitri and his car and jumped out of the truck.

"Dmitri, what happened?" she yelled at the boy, who had not seemed to notice her presence.

"Huh!"

"Dmitri, look, Mr. Hendrickson's house is on fire. Where's Mr. Hendrickson?"

"I don't ... don't know, I just got here."

"We've got to help!"

"What?"

"Cell phone!"

"I don't have one."

"No, I've got one!"

Trudy ran for the truck and reached in to find the lavender-covered phone she had put on the seat next to her. She picked it up, still so new to her. The button, the 911 button, where? Oh here! She called, got the emergency operator, and reported the fire, the fact that Mr. Hendrickson was probably in the house. When she got off the phone, Dmitri was still standing there.

"You've got to go get Mr. Hendrickson!"

"What!"

"Dmitri! He's in there, maybe hurt or something! You've got to get him! Please, please, the fire trucks won't be here in time!"

Dmitri looked at Trudy. She was really beautiful. And he liked her breasts.

"Yeah, yeah, okay."

Dmitri ran across the field, past the chicken house, to the farmhouse, and disappeared into a wall of smoke.

When he emerged, he was carrying Mr. Hendrickson. Time spent picking up Mr. Briers and shoveling shit on the farm had made him a strong boy, and he carried Mr. Hendrickson easily across the field to the side of the road and set him down in front of Trudy as if the old man was an offering.

Trudy knelt to see if Mr. Hendrickson was okay. He was unconscious but breathing, if not breathing well. Then, they heard sirens in the distance. Trudy didn't know what to do, she didn't know if she should touch him, but she told him everything was going to be all right.

Dmitri stood above them.

"I'll bet you it was that ... that thing, you know, that space heater thing he has. It was frayed. I mean the wire. I kept telling him not to use it. My dad's an electrician, see, so I know. But he was stubborn; he kept using it. He was tired and going to bed early, so I was going home, but I forgot something, and I came back and—and—then, you know, you came."

Fire trucks, an ambulance, and the sheriff all arrived with the noise of their sirens, engines, doors slamming, and men shouting.

"Mr. Hendrickson," Trudy said to the old man, who she was not sure was breathing anymore, which really scared her. "It's okay now; they're here. Dmitri got you out of the house. He saved your life! Isn't that good?"

Going from breathless to an exhausted calm, Trudy explained all of this to everyone in the theater. They had sat her down on a seat in the front row and given her a glass of water.

"Did they take Mr. Hendrickson to the hospital?" Duncan asked her.

"Yeah. They put an oxygen mask thing on him and put him in the ambulance."

"Emily, take me to the hospital," Duncan said to his wife.

"Why, what can you do?"

"He's got no family here; we're neighbors, isn't that enough?"

"Sure, yeah, okay." Emily was sorry she had questioned the idea.

Everybody was quiet after the Briers had left, dampened by the drama overload. Harry Ogg had regained consciousness in the middle of Trudy's story, ready to re-engage, but Pattie had quieted him with a whispered, "There's been a fire." The Major had come back down to the front. Austin and Ben were concerned for Trudy.

Trudy finished a second glass of water and then looked around. "Where are the others? Aren't we having a rehearsal?"

"Uh," Austin said, "not tonight, there's—"

A soft, electronic musical rendition of The Pink Panther theme filled the theater. It was a slice of surreal that no one was prepared for, not even Ben, whose cell phone was playing the sound.

"Oh, that's me! It's been so long!"

Ben took his phone and looked to see who it was. It was the good and kind (he hoped) Eric Merryman, his agent, who rarely was one. "Hello, Eric, hi!" Ben said as he walked up the aisle to the back of the theater, hoping like hell Eric wasn't going to report that the agency was dropping him because he was stupid enough to do this little shit play in Nowheresville, which would not be out of the ordinary for an agency to do, as they loved giving terrible news just when you didn't need to hear any.

"So, why aren't we rehearsing?" Trudy asked.

"Oh," Austin said, "problems came up, but we'll do one tomorrow night and, you know, the other nights. Right, Pattie?"

"No, you're not!" Harry said.

"Yes, they are, Harry," Pattie informed her husband.

"What, but—"

"It's all been taken care of, don't worry about it."

"I don't—"

"They can do this play. But no more." Pattie said very emphatically for everyone's benefit.

"What? You mean there's not going to be a theater company?" Trudy asked, a million disappointments pushing down on her.

Austin smiled a gentle smile at Trudy. "Things aren't working out for that, but we'll do this play."

"And—and you're still bringing in your Hollywood friends?"

"Oh, sure."

"Oh, thank goodness. This has been a weird day; I don't think I could—"

"Don't worry then, we'll do What Price Glory, and you'll be great, and—"

"Nope, I'm afraid not," Ben said, coming back down the aisle. "That was my agent. I just got the lead in what will be the biggest hit in TV history; I swear to God! And I've got to be back in L.A. on Friday for wardrobe fittings. So I can't do the play, and you don't have an understudy."

Pattie bellowed out a loud, triumphant, "HA!"

"You bitch," Austin said.

"Hey!" Harry started towards Austin, but the Major stepped in his way, stopping him.

"Don't worry about it, Harry. Let's go home and have some great, normal, un-deviant sex!" Pattie took Harry by the arm and led him up the aisle, laughing all the way.

"What! What!" Trudy was looking to all who were left. "We're not going to do the play?"

"I guess not," Austin said, disgusted.

Trudy screamed and ran up the aisle, crying and wishing she were dead.

And why shouldn't she be dead? Why should such misery be allowed to exist in this world? Trudy had run outside, onto the boardwalk, and was going to run and run and run. But it was dark now. And there was fog. And the lights illuminating the outside of the theater were inviting and safe. So she plopped herself down on the bench by the theater and cried and cried and cried.

Life can't be this bad. She didn't want to believe that life could be this bad.

"Christ, you look horrible."

Trudy looked up. Ben Alyn was standing there. He looked at her face, which was not only tear streamed but snot smeared; her eyes were not only puffy but sad in a way he could tell they had never been sad before.

"Don't move," Ben said, "I'll be right back."

And he was, with a large roll of toilet paper from the Men's restroom. He sat down next to her.

"It was all I could find."

Trudy grabbed the roll and pulled a long ribbon of tissues off. She folded them over into a thick rectangular piece and blew her nose into it, a copious and nearly unbelievable amount of mucus pouring forth. Once the tissue was full, she stopped and held it out, not knowing what to do with it.

"Litter the boardwalk. We'll deal with it later," Ben said.

Trudy gratefully dropped the tissue. Then she pulled off another long ribbon and repeated herself, blowing until she was dry. That tissue hit the boardwalk as well. Then Trudy pulled off another ribbon, folded it, and used it to wipe the lower half of her face dry and clean. Then she made another one to wipe her tears dry. Only after all of this, and after taking a couple of deep breaths, did she thank Ben.

"No problem," Ben said. "I got a little concerned about you."

"Really?"

"Sure."

"Why?"

"Why not? Kind of happens when you work on a play with someone."

Trudy sobbed—a good old-fashioned one—tears flowed again, and she grabbed another ribbon of tissues to deal with them.

"There's not going to be a play now," Trudy lamented.

"Yeah. Sorry."

"Do you really have to go back and do this show right now?"

"Oh yeah. Right now is very important."

"But this was going to be so important to me. You guys were bringing in your friends, and I was going to be discovered."

"Are you so sure of that?"

"Of course! I've worked hard; I got the accent right, right? So they were going to see me up there on the stage, and, you know, really see me, and I would really impress them, and then, sure, why not? Why wouldn't I be discovered?"

"Well, probably because you're just not that good of an actress."

Trudy could not believe she had heard it. She looked at Ben with questions and accusations in her eyes; a key one flowed from her lips:

"Why is everyone being mean to me today!"

"I'm not being mean, Trudy, just accurate."

Trudy pulled violently from the tissue roll, setting loose a long stream that she grabbed at to gain control over. When she did, she gathered a lot of the tissues into a bunch, then cried into them.

"Look, Trudy, I don't mean to hurt you. In fact, it's the last thing I mean to do."

Trudy turned away from Ben to continue her crying.

"Look, you cry; I'm going to talk, okay? So don't say anything until I've finished."

"I don't want to talk to you anyway."

"Good. So stop talking. Look, this show that my agent just called about, it's a new sitcom. It's brilliant. I read for the lead months ago and thought that I had gotten it for sure. But I never heard back from the producers, so I figured I hadn't. I was really pissed. Not just disappointed, but pissed, monumentally pissed, because I knew the show would be a huge hit."

"Why?"

"You're talking."

"Sorry."

"I don't know why. Instinct. You can just tell. If I got it, I knew it would make me a star."

"I thought you were a star?"

"No, I'm a working actor with a small measure of fame due to a secondary role in a popular but hardly memorable TV series. You see, Trudy, one has to be realistic in life. I wasn't working much; my future did not seem bright. But this new series would change all that; I knew that. Not just a simple good change. A monumental, historical change! And I swore to myself that if I got it, I would take full advantage of it and set my career up to keep me on top for a very, very long time. So I really wanted it. But, unfortunately, I didn't get it. So I was pissed—and I came here."

"But now you got it."

"Now I got it."

"How come."

"You know Andy Scott?"

"Yeah, he's great."

"He got the role."

"Oh."

"It was a big deal. A major film actor going into TV. Except it rarely works. Nevertheless, the network wanted him, so he got the role, and I, who was perfect for it, didn't. The network was so confident they ordered the series without a pilot, poured a lot of money into it to get it on air as fast as possible, and at the last minute, the contract negotiations with Andy broke down, or he got cold feet or something, so he was out. But they had a series ready to go, and everybody knew it was too good for it not to. So they called me. I guess I was the producer's first choice anyway, so they were delighted and pushed hard for me. So it's Cinderella time for me, Trudy, and I've got to take full advantage of it."

"So that's why it's so important that you leave, okay, I get it."

"I'm not telling you this to explain why I'm leaving; I'm telling you this to explain why I want to take you with me."

Trudy turned to Ben. She did not question whether she had heard what she had heard this time. She knew she had heard what she had heard; she just needed to understand why it had been available for her to hear it.

"You want me to be in your show?"

"Trudy, stop being a fantasist. No, I don't want you to be in the show; you're a crappy actress."

"Stop being mean to me! Why is everybody being mean to me?"

"I'm not being mean, Trudy. I'm being honest because I don't have the time to be anything else."

"Well, why would you want to take me? You hate me!"

"No, I don't."

"Yes, you do!"

"No, I don't."

"Well, why have you treated me the way you have, then?"

"Well," Ben smiled, and that made Trudy interested. "Part of the reason is professional. I was dealing with a bad actress in what I wanted to be a good production. But the other part is, well—when you were a young girl, I mean young but not too young, weren't there boys who treated you kind of weird, kind of nice/mean, sticking your pigtails in inkwells and all that? Not that you ever had pigtails, not to mention inkwells."

"No." Trudy thought it was a stupid question. "Boys always liked me. Why wouldn't they? They were never mean to me, just stupid and immature."

"Well, yeah, I can see that."

"It's only been lately that people have been mean to me."

"Trudy, no one's being mean to you."

"Yeah, they are. You don't know all the facts."

"Well, I'm not being mean; I don't want to be mean. I mean, not anymore. Look, I've got plans, and I want you—I need you—to be a part of them."

"Why?"

"Because I probably ... you know ... uh ... love you ... I guess."

"But you think I'm a crappy actress!"

"Well, I'm not likely to fall in love with a good actress. I couldn't stand the competition! Don't talk again, okay? Just hear me out. This show is going to make me a big star. A big star, Trudy, and that's going to give me a lot of leverage; it's going to open a lot of doors throughout Hollywood. Not just the Hollywood of making films and TV, but the culture of Hollywood, the thing Hollywood is, the—the separate world unto itself that the rest of the world pays inordinate attention to. That gives it a lot of power. If you really want a long run in Hollywood these days, you can't just be a star; you've got to tap into that power. I want to do that. I don't want to be a star of a hit series and, three years after it's off the air, be forgotten already. Memories are short in Hollywood unless you weave yourself into the fabric of the place. That means not just acting, but producing too, and not just producing, but paying real attention to the social life, the community, the charities, that whole enchilada that is Hollywood. If I get this shot, I've got to do that, and I can't do it alone. I need a partner. That's what I want you to be, my partner."

"Partner?"

"As my wife."

"What?"

"Look, you've got to understand, even though you are a lousy actress, you're a wonderful character. You're a great person. You have this core of positive energy like I've never seen before. That's what makes you so damn attractive. Not your looks, which are okay, or your figure, or your breasts, or any other physical aspect of you, but that damn sunny bright smile and beaming eyes push ahead thing you've got. Christ, that's so refreshing. But, of course, it must be focused, developed, and matured. And I can help you do that. And then, quite frankly, I need to tap into it. You've got enough energy for the both of us, and I need it, honey; I need it to help sustain myself. And if that's not love, then I don't know what is. So what I'm telling you is, well, come back with me and just be yourself and share your positive energy with me, and as my stardom opens doors, I swear to God we can become Mr. and Mrs. Hollywood."

"By just being myself?"

"Look, some things are unexplainable; they just are. They become a phenomenon that knocks down barriers and conquers worlds. I think the two of us together can become one."

"So that would make me famous too, wouldn't it?"

"I guarantee it. It's the way the world works."

"So, maybe—so you think that means, you know, like, maybe later, I could get a reality TV show about me? I mean, I wouldn't have to act and—"

Ben laughed a good hearty laugh and took a chance and grabbed Trudy and gave her a big hug. It was a good hug, and she hugged back, and everything seemed to fit comfortably, and the energy that passed between the two was intoxicating. Then Trudy pulled back and looked at Ben closely.

"You are kind of cute," she said as she moved in to kiss him and test the waters.

It is wisdom as common as ignorance that people hate hospitals. Intimations of mortality undoubtedly underlie some people's disquiet when they walk down the wide corridors of a medical institution, as the brute fact of death overlies other people's unquiet fear and despair. There are those people, though, whose dislike of hospitals can rest on things trivial. The antiseptic smell some perceive, for example, or the sense, if not the smell, of decay. Some people just don't like doctors and their arrogance and the lectures they might give about diet and habits and other matters of good sense and life-altering efforts that are such pains in the ass to deal with. Nurses are not always popular, especially if they don't seem to care about your ills that, while unique to you, are quite commonplace to them. Sick people make certain people ill at ease. And being sick, of course, is no fun at all. A segment of visitors, or even patients, who come to hospitals seem to resent being outsiders, not a part of the culture, ineligible for membership in the club. These people hate the hard-to-refute evidence that they are dumb and that the doctors and nurses are smart. It is like being a tourist or business traveler in France: you don't speak the language, and you know the natives think less of you because of that fact. So the common wisdom is: Most people hate hospitals.

But not Duncan Briers. Duncan had always loved hospitals. Even during and after his extended stay in one in Los Angeles after his accident. Duncan loved the whole sense of the contained world that was a hospital. It was the drama, of course, or the potential for it. And also professionals who worked long hours to care for others, even if they did not always seem to care. But Duncan assumed this was tight control over sloppy emotions that, while they might display cute empathetic care, got in the way of acute pragmatic care. And it was all the tools of the trade, from the stethoscopes to the machines they hooked you up to that went beep-beep-beep or some such other mechanical sounds. It was, in fact, all those things that had helped make hospital shows on TV popular since TV became popular. There was an irony there, wasn't there? People hate hospitals, yet people love hospital shows. There must be a reason. After all, most people probably hate garbage dumps, but there were few garbage dumps shows.

When Duncan, powered by Emily, rushed into the large County Hospital that was, fortunately, located in Rubenton, he felt right at home and felt no compunction demanding satisfaction. He wanted to know how Mr. Hendrickson was, and he didn't give a damn that he wasn't a relative, which also had no bearing on the fact that he wanted to see the old farmer. In a big city hospital, of course, Duncan would not have gotten away with it, but this was a small community, he was well known, and he had always contributed to the hospital's various outbreaks of expansion as his father had before him. Mr. Hendrickson's doctor informed him that the old man was in critical but stable condition due to minor surface burns—he had been lucky there—and significant lung damage due to smoke inhalation. He was drugged but conscious, and, yes, he might appreciate a short visit from Duncan, as he had informed his sons, but they wouldn't arrive until late tomorrow.

Emily wheeled Duncan to the side of the hospital bed and excused herself. She was one of those who hated hospitals. Mr. Hendrickson had bandages on his arms and part of his face. He had a breathing tube in his nostrils. His eyes were open, and he smiled when he saw Duncan.

"'fraid I won't be able to deliver eggs for a while."

"Don't you worry about that, Mr.— You know, I've never known your first name."

"Leroy."

"Leroy."

"Wife called me Roy."

"Do you know what happened, Roy?"

"Damn house caught fire, I guess."

"Yes."

"Is it gone?"

"I'm afraid so."

"Good. Nothing but a drafty old barn."

"They say it was a space heater."

"What?"

"Dmitri said the wire was frayed; said he warned you about it."

Leroy Hendrickson very slowly shook his head.

"You don't think so?" Duncan asked.

Hendrickson shook his head again. His eyes, which had seemed to Duncan filled with awareness of his pain, now seemed less so, that awareness replaced by something sad and regretful.

"Tell me." Duncan gently commanded.

"Had been frayed ... Dmitri fixed ... wanted to because dad's electrician ... so he knew how."

"Oh."

"Anyway—"

There was sudden pain and discomfort.

"Okay, maybe I should go," Duncan said. "You shouldn't talk anymore." Duncan began to roll himself out.

"Water."

"Oh, sure."

Duncan rolled himself to the side table, took a cup with the straw, and positioned it so Hendrickson could sip. When the farmer finished, he continued:

"Anyway ... always unplugged it ... before going to bed ... always had ... wife taught me that ... she always afraid of fire."

"Dmitri said you went to bed early."

"Yeah. Unplugged it just the same."

"Dmitri?"

"Still there ... asked him to wash dishes ... never leave dirty dishes overnight ... but so tired ... so asked the kid to do 'em before he left."

"Bet he loved that."

"Not ... happy."

"Yeah, I bet. Leroy, get some rest. Tell your sons if there's anything I can do; they should call me."

"Okay ... thanks ... sorry 'bout the eggs."

One week later, Frank's studio was ready for occupancy, and Allison decided to have a studio warming. She decided to invite and fly in Bebe Hutchinson and Tilly Fordham of the Hutchinson/Fordham Gallery, soon to be the exclusive East Coast showcase for Frank's work, and Mark Bayly, of course, who would soon be the owner of Dog of War. This was the right thing to do, for they were the first and foremost cousins in a vast family of Frank supporters that Allison intended to build. The rest of the intended family—ex-students of Allison's, now well-to-do; gallery owners in Beverly Hills, London, Paris; serious collectors she had cold-called; all who had been responding well to Frank's work—would have to wait, though, until they were full members of the family. Which—as optimistic as Allison was about all this—Frank had to remind her they not yet were.

"I'm nervous enough meeting just these three who you've somehow conned into thinking I'm the next hot thing, I—"

"Frank! I didn't con anybody. Your work seduced them."

"Well, still, I'm nervous, apprehensive, anxious, and just plain damn scared. So let's make this thing as intimate as possible."

"Well, five people are far too intimate. We need to start this endeavor with something more celebratory than that. How about I invite the Briers."

"Yeah, sure, that's a great idea."

"And Austin O'Brien and his newfound friend, the Major. They're leaving for New York soon, going to have a play off-Broadway. If it's a hit, they would be good word-of-mouth people."

"Do you think an army major will like Dog of War?"

"I think this army major will."

And so, with the inclusion of the architect and the contractor, so that they may receive some applause for their work; "Poignant" Pete Peterson as the only other artist in the area; and, of course, Frank's student assistants, they held an intimate and—not to Allison's surprise but very much to Frank's—delightful studio warming catered by the Lamplighter Restaurant.

All were impressed with the studio. It had become a labor of love for the architect, and it showed. What was going to be Frank's living quarters instead became an office, a high-tech communications hub for what Allison intended to become Frank International. Frank, people now learned, would be moving to The Briers and living with Allison, making the studio warming an unintended—yet no less happy for that—engagement party. There were toasts to the architect and the contractor for a job well done; to the student assistants for their invaluable help; to the Briers for having been good and kind employers; to Austin and Philip for success in their artistic endeavors; and Allison and Frank for their newfound love.

But what about the art?

Dog of War overwhelmed them all, except maybe "Poignant" Pete for political reasons, him being the most conservative one there. But he liked Frank's graphic abilities and appreciated them as possibly only another artist could. Mark Bayly was in tears. He knew what impact the huge piece would have among his friends—he couldn't wait to see their reactions. Austin loved the drama of the work, the theatricality of it. Philip, standing at attention before the piece, shook his head. Frank at first thought this was disapproval until the Major said:

"They never understand."

"Who?" Allison, a courageous woman, ventured to ask.

"Leaders. Political leaders. We're but toys to them. Armies. Soldiers. Men. I hope the damn dog bites his head off."

Bebe and Tilly were delighted to hear it. Limited edition prints, they said, "Frank, we must consider limited edition prints."

Tilly and Bebe liked Frank. They had talked to him on the phone several times since Allison had come to New York, but that was all business, discussing which pieces he should do next to put in his first show. But now, especially after Frank got over his nervousness, apprehension, anxiousness, and just plain fear and was beginning to feel the high of being the center of attention, which brought out the core of his being and allowed it to fly, they found Frank charming in a wonderfully direct and humorously rude manner.

"Ah! Ah!" Tilly suddenly said.

"What, Miss Fordham?" Bebe asked.

"Miss Hutchinson, correct me if I am wrong, but would not the perfect title for Frank's show be, get this: The Frank Visions of Frank. No! The Perfectly Frank Visions of Frank.

Everybody loved it; everybody applauded.

"In fact, Frank," Bebe said, "Frank, that's all you should be, I mean, regarding your name. Frank. You get it? Just Frank, nothing else. I love it. Such a normal, mundane name, and yet, we will make it stand for something transcendent in its honest, forthright, brusque, and curt assessment of the world. No one should ever know your last name; we'll keep it a secret. Well, not a secret; you can never keep anything a secret. Still, we'll declare it irrelevant to understanding the nature of your work, which is universal, international, and non-national. So why use your last name? Why give people the chance to pigeonhole you, place you in a category, and make you represent something you don't truly represent? I mean, I assume that's right; I mean, you don't seem to be all that ethnic."

"No, I don't suppose I am. My mother was half English and half Irish."

"So you wouldn't take it as an insult if we dropped Cervantez?" Tilly asked.

"Well. It didn't seem to hurt Miguel too much. Although he spelled it with an S."

"And that's another thing," Bebe said. "We don't want people to think you're just tilting at windmills. We want people to think that you're so powerful in the points you are making that you're anything but ineffective."

"Maybe I should be Superfrank, then."

"No, that's ... well ... no, that would be going too far. You're Frank, just plain Frank, nothing but Frank, yet Frank is everything. Don't you think, Miss Fordham?"

"I certainly do, Miss Hutchinson."

"I don't know," Frank said. "It feels strange. It's like I'm nothing but a product."

"No! Don't think that!" Bebe and Tilly both said. Then Bebe said:

"You are a person, real, intelligent, flesh and blood, emotional, giving a damn about this world, so you lash out at all its stupidities, frankly calling things into question, as the best of humans should do. So, no, you are not a product."

"We're just going to sell you like one," Tilly added with a smile.

Later, as Frank settled down to spend his first night in his new home, a safe situation as Trudy no longer worked there, having left town with Ben Alyn, he fought to stay high, to keep the transcendent feeling he was now supposed to, frankly, represent. But the mundane crept in when he had to urinate, defecate, brush his teeth, and take care of a pimple on his shoulder. And stop being clumsy negotiating around a strange room with another person far more use to the space also moving around it, and get used to this new bed, not to mention the pillow he was given, which was far too fluffy.

Still, an unabated excitement held fast to him but suspiciously felt like fear.

Allison, an artist in her own right, could sense the confusion in Frank's head. She fitted herself into his arms in the bed and said:

"You're going to have to get used to this sometime."

"I know."

"Be generous with yourself. Be a good host."

"I could become very arrogant, you know."

"Good. How else are you going to do superlative work?"

"And I do want to. I want to do good work—great work."

"You will."

"But all this—product selling stuff."

"Don't worry about it. That's my job."

Frank looked at Allison. My God, he thought. Those eyes, those incredible blue eyes. If I could look at myself through those eyes, all would be well. He kissed her. The excitement intensified; there was renewed ascension.

"Is this a good story we're in?" Frank asked. "Are you enjoying it?"

"It's unputdownable," Allison said.

Rubenton had never had a hero before, so they decided to make a big deal out of it. They held an event at the high school to honor Dmitri for his quick thinking and bravery. Pattie Heatherton organized it all, inviting the community into the gym to attend what she intended to be a solemn yet life-affirming ceremony.

A Boy Scout honor guard marched the length of the gym—twice—carrying the national, state, city, and high school flags. The uniformed boys stood at earnest attention as they gave snappy three-fingered salutes while Tom Vaughn, the student body president, led the audience in the Pledge of Allegiance. The Rubenton High Band played not only the National Anthem but "The James Bond Theme" and accompanied the Rubenton High Choir as they sang "You Are the Wind Beneath my Wings." Annie Janis, a junior with literary ambitions, recited a poem she had written entitled "Hometown Hero," which the Rubenton Rubric printed within a border on the front page. And the school's World History teacher, Jack Stiller, recounted how the courageous and resourceful Russian people had, against overwhelming odds, beaten back two devastating invasions of their country, one by Napoleon and one by Hitler. Dmitri, he then postulated, had come by his bravery quite naturally.

As Pattie stood up on the makeshift stage, effortlessly directing the flow of these presentations and looking down upon the gathered community, she discovered something about herself: She was just where she should be. Vague thoughts that she might once have had about expanding her sphere of influence had left. And thank goodness because it would have just been the wrong move to make, a dilution of her true power to do good. She now knew that she was that most wonderful thing, that bedrock of American civilization: a civic leader; a bulwark of community boosterism; a local force, and Rubenton would have been so much poorer without her. Look what she had in hand: the shaping of the young minds of the community; a position as the wife of the leading manufacturer in the town; a powerful voice for improvements in the daily lives of her fellow Rubentonions.

She would run for mayor!

That decision hit her right in the heart—as she would later declare when declaring her candidacy—just as she called upon the current mayor of Rubenton, Harold Redding (a useless shit!), to present the first Rubenton Medal of Honor to the brave Dmitri.

As she sat on the stage listening to Redding drone on about the extreme risk to life and limb Dmitri had taken by a selfless act of true humanity, Pattie began to prepare her campaign.

PATRICIA HEATHERTON

A LEADER FOR OUR TOWN

A LEADER FOR OUR TIME.

Pattie smiled over how easily that slogan came to her.

Yes, she was where she should be. Pattie most certainly was where she should be.

How comfortable it was to know your place.

Sitting on the stage next to his wife, Harry Ogg took a quick look at her and saw her smiling. God only knows why, he thought, I'm fucking bored to death. But he supposed she had to smile, that it was part of her job, and he had often seen her smile in this official capacity. But there was something different about this smile—it just wasn't natural. Or, rather, it was natural; it just wasn't what should be natural for the occasion. It was a beautiful smile beaming out some inner glow. Pretty woman, Harry thought to himself while looking at her; I'm married to a pretty woman, all right. Life's damn good, all right. To think that Pattie started out meaning nothing more to me than a sweet little bit of snatch, and now she's my pretty wife, the excellent mother of my boys, a giving person important to this town that doesn't deserve her, and yet she's still—especially lately—a sweet little bit of snatch. Yeah, life's damn good—except for all the idiots there were. But I'm ogre enough to handle them.

Dmitri sat on the stage and wanted to giggle. It had been a strange time since he pulled old fart Hendrickson out of his burning farmhouse, receiving some minor burns himself. His father, sitting on the stage with him, had told Dmitri that he had been stupid to risk his life for an old man. But when the community started to make a fuss over Dmitri, he began to see his son in a different light. Maybe having a hero for a son could help him get more electrical work, and then he could quit his second job. Maybe if this had happened earlier, he could have gotten the job to do all the electrical work for that damn artist's studio they just did. That would have been a good job; that job would have paid well. Oh well, what's past is past; today is what's important. He quickly felt his coat's breast pocket again. Good, yes, he had remembered to bring plenty of business cards.

Dmitri's grandmother sat on the stage, not understanding most of what Mayor Redding was saying. But it didn't matter, she got to buy a new dress for the occasion, and she felt beautiful wearing it. She didn't know what to think about what her grandson had done, or, rather, when she did think about it, her thoughts were slightly dark, so she kept them to herself for amusement. Like Dmitri, she wanted to giggle.

Mayor Redding continued to drone on, and Pattie hoped like hell that he would run again because it was going to be easy, very easy, to beat the idiot.

Emily and Duncan were in the gym, at the back of the audience. Duncan was not thinking of local politics. Nor was he amused. Nor was he there to worship Rubenton's first and only hero. He was not sure why he was there. But he knew he needed to be there. Not to say anything, not to do anything, maybe just to witness something awful, as humans occasionally find themselves fascinated to do. Look at that wreckage, that carnage, that reminder that life is chaotic, random, unfair, and mean. And yet, of course, it is the only plane of existence we have sure knowledge of despite what certain materialistic (in the sense of cold hard cash) spiritual institutions would have you believe. So we're stuck with it. So we live with it. So we get on with it. But wouldn't it be grand—oh, so damn grand—to find the tiller and sail the boat in some exciting direction?

One of Leroy Hendrickson's boys came in the door at the back of the gym. He came right over to Duncan, who had spent much time with him and his brother since they arrived home. Duncan had given him and his brother a room at The Briers gratis and a significant discount on their meals. Duncan was not surprised, but he was saddened to see him. The son squatted down to face Duncan.

"Hi," he said in a breathless whisper as the ceremony continued on the stage.

"Is he?" Duncan asked.

"Yes, he's gone."

"Oh, I'm so sorry," Emily said.

"Doctor said it was his heart. Just couldn't take the trauma."

"What about the funeral?" Duncan asked.

"He said he didn't want a fuss."

"Well, he's going to get one," Duncan insisted. "They're having one, aren't they?" Duncan indicated the stage.

"Yeah," the son said. "Should I tell them?"

"No. Why spoil it for them? You go back to your brother. I'll take care of things here."

"Okay. You know, really, Dad didn't want a fuss."

"Well, you got to do what you got to do. But if you would like a memorial, we'll do it at the hotel. Costs on me. Ate a hell of a lot of his eggs, you know."

"You're awfully kind."

"Yeah, I know. It's been the bane of my existence."

The son did not quite know what to make of that, so he simply said goodbye and quietly slipped out of the gym.

On stage, Dmitri received his medal to thunderous applause. Then he was made an honorary member of the fire department's rescue squad, and they gave him a helmet to signify that fact. The Rubenton Merchant's Association gave him a hundred-dollar gift certificate good at any one of seven downtown stores. And the Lamplighter Restaurant gave him a coupon book good for ten two-for-one meals any day of the week except Friday and Saturday.

Mr. Mayor!" Duncan suddenly called out and started wheeling himself up towards the stage. "I would like to add to Dmitri's bounty. As his employer, I've gotten to know him quite well, and I think I know what he really wants." Duncan brought himself right up to the stage and looked up at Dmitri, who loomed above him with a weak smile. Dmitri had learned to be apprehensive when it came to Duncan. "Dmitri, you've worked awfully hard for me with one real goal in mind—that fast, powerful sports car you've dreamed of for so long. Well, as no one has been so—affected—by your act of heroism as I have, I don't want you to have to wait one more moment for your dream to come true. So you go out first thing in the morning to any car dealer in town, pick out the fastest, most powerful, coolest car you can find, and tell them to send me the bill!"

The audience and everyone on stage were thunderstruck with surprise in a deliciously old-fashioned way. Not only applause, as loud and aggressive as before, but cheers broke out. Dmitri's weak smile became an unbelievably broad and somewhat stupid grin.

Many people came up to Duncan, and each slapped him on the back—a not comfortable series of blows—and congratulated him for his generosity. Duncan, of course, knew better. But he took their painful enthusiasm like a man and accepted their sudden waves of admiration with a certain grace, adding substantially to the overall good feeling of the evening.

HAPPY ENDINGS

No one was shocked that Trudy had "run-off" with Ben Alyn to Hollywood. If any girl in town had seemed too—too—too something for the town, it was Trudy. And she did not really run off. Ben went to her home and charmed her parents, and not just because he had a measure of fame. He declared his love for Trudy with sincerity they found quite moving, and they could not find the desire to protest the situation.

Everything worked out pretty much as Ben had predicted. He jumped right into the show and was intensely busy at it. But he still made the time to give Trudy plenty of attention and play Pygmalion to her Galatea. It was no sacrifice; it was all part of his plan. The show debuted and soon became the phenomenon of the season, then the number one hit show, then the measure of artistic and financial success in TV for years to come, then an American entertainment institution. Ben Alyn became one of the most famous celebrities in the nation.

He did not marry Trudy when he first brought her to Hollywood. Instead, he waited until the end of his show's second stunningly successful season. Then, in a wedding covered by media more mass than mass media had ever been before, Ben and Trudy took their vows in front of the elite of Hollywood. Timing, Ben well knew, was everything.

Trudy loved it all. She adapted to Hollywood without a hitch, maintaining a true fan's adoration while gaining industry savvy and social sophistication. Soon, without pissing people off, which was an amazing feat in Hollywood, Trudy was advising Ben on his career. She seemed to have an inborn sense of what the audience would want, which some attributed to the fact that she never gave up being a member of the audience herself. Indeed, one of her most attractive qualities was that, without diminishing her role as Ben's number one fan, she was a sincere and enthusiastic, yet never sycophantic, fan of so many other talents in Hollywood, many of whom became friends. Like Ben, they came to rely on her amazingly positive attitudes to get them over Hollywood's amazingly negative attributes.

And yes, she got to know and become close to Cissy McMann. They became like the sisters Trudy had always felt they were, and she gave one of the eulogies when Cissy McMann tragically died young.

Trudy did not get her Reality TV series. The form became passé just before it was the proper time for such exploitation. But she got three children: Ben Jr., Cissy, and Frank.

She forgave Frank. He had written a letter explaining things, and he and Allison came to Hollywood to see her and explain how they had to hurt her to help her. Trudy had gained enough sophistication by that time to understand. Trudy, Ben, Frank, and Allison had a wonderful dinner after one of Frank's gallery shows in Beverly Hills. Ben and Allison that evening were very mysterious, seeming to share an old secret.

Trudy and Ben became collectors of Frank's work and prominent promoters of his talents. Trudy even told Cissy McMann about the horrible drawing Frank had done of her, detailing it with some embarrassment. Cissy roared with laughter and wondered if she could get her hands on the picture. Regrettably, they told her, Frank destroyed it. Not to be put off by that unfortunate fact, she asked Frank to recreate the work in oil, and, oddly for him, he did. Cissy hung it with pride above the toilet in one of her guest bathrooms in her 27-room Hollywood Hills mansion. It hung there until the day of her death, her husband, understandably, having never liked the piece.

Some called Trudy's life a fairy tale. She knew that was not true. It was just a rare incidence of a person being allowed by those around her, and by the unfeeling universe, to just be herself and not to have herself compromised by the awful struggle that life can be for most of us. Every day Trudy thanked the oddities of life for her good fortune, usually by training her sight on something beautiful: A tree, the ocean, a running horse, one of her children asleep, Ben when he was laughing. Every day she acknowledged that there was the possibility that it could all go away. But Trudy never really believed it. She had a simple attitude: Her life was wonderful. Why shouldn't it be? How could it not be? And why, you know, wouldn't it always be?

Austin and Philip did not go to New York, not immediately. Instead, they went to Canada and married, renouncing their U.S. Citizenship. It caused quite a stir. They were accepted for Canadian residency and citizenship so readily because Major Philip McFadden, U.S. Army(ret.), became an outspoken opponent of America's current war and America's continuing slide into pockets of homophobia. And the current liberal government in Canada found it convenient to highlight the issue. As a result, the U.S. Congress passed a special Act rescinding Major McFadden's military pension despite his years of loyal service. The Canadian government committed to making up the loss.

The Arabic Speaking World was produced in Toronto first, funded by Duncan Briers, as he had promised. They wanted Frank to design their sets, but he refused, much to their dismay. But when Allison explained why they understood. However, upon reading the play, Frank became inspired and dashed off a drawing and gave it to Austin and Philip as a wedding present. With Frank's permission, they used it as the poster art for the play. The play, directed by Austin, was an immediate success. Austin decided not to star in the play because he was now happy enough in his life to admit to himself that he was not that good of an actor. It was quite a relief, a relief that only added to his happiness.

The Arabic Speaking World ran for three years in Toronto, its success fueled by a near underground railroad of Americans traveling up north to see it. Broadway called, and conservative columnists, cable commentators, Internet bloggers, and street protesters threw a collective and very coordinated fit. Duncan did not care; controversy sells, he said. But Emily put her foot down. Besides, she said, let's milk Europe first. Duncan, of course, refused to travel, but Emily was happy to take on his duties. They premiered at the Edinburgh Festival, causing a sensation. They transferred to the West End in London and grossed more than any non-musical play had in twenty-seven years. Soon there were translations, and The Arabic Speaking World played in every European capital to great acclaim and lucrative box office receipts. It was not just the controversy; the play was incredibly moving. Soon, a company was performing the play in Japan, and even one in China, although to smallish crowds of the elite. Australia, New Zealand, and South Africa all supported runs of the play from one to three years. The one place in the world The Arabic Speaking World would not appear was the Arabic-speaking world. For understandable reasons.

Austin became an in-demand directorial talent. Major Philip continued to write, receiving a book contract not only for his memoirs but also for novels. And he continued to write plays. Austin and Philip became very rich.

Finally, New York could wait no longer. The Arabic Speaking World opened on Broadway and, with its quality and controversy making it a sensation, completely revitalized the fabulous invalid. That year's Tony Awards surprised everyone by tripling its usually dismal TV ratings.

The one thing they did not do was sell The Arabic Speaking World to Hollywood. They did not need to for any financial reason, and, fearing a dilution of the true power of the play, they certainly did not need to for creative reasons. It's a play, Philip said; with military discipline, it will always be a play and nothing but a play. How stupid, people said; how admirable, people thought.

Austin did, though, become a film director. During the shooting of his first movie, they had a wonderful reunion with Trudy and Ben Alyn. They all toasted each other and had many laughs. Trudy—who was truly beautiful that night and delighted Austin with her maturity—gave Austin a big, wet, tongue-intensive kiss on the mouth in parting.

"Anything?" She asked.

"Sorry," Austin said, shaking his head.

"Good," Trudy said, then gave him the warmest of hugs as Ben and Philip laughed.

◆ ◆ ◆

Pattie Heatherton became the mayor of Rubenton. She was later indicted for embezzlement of city funds. She beat the rap. Some attributed it to jury tampering by her husband Harry, but it was never proven. Nevertheless, her political career was over. It hardly mattered; she and Ogg the Ogre still ran the town and were perfectly happy to do so.

A curious effect under the greenhouse roof of the continuing global warming of the Earth was a slight degree change in climate which caused the perennial fog along Leech Beach to—suddenly, it seemed—become a more normal now-and-then visitor. Duncan was not sure global warming caused this. Not that he doubted the fact of global warming, as so many government and corporate officials officially did; it was just that he thought it was far more likely that Emily had ordered it. For sunshine having a more prominent role to play on Leech Beach and at The Briers now seem so right, what with the place gaining a particular prominence due to the controversy over Austin and Philip's play, and the residence of Frank, just Frank, the art phenomenon everyone was talking about.

Tourism became a far more important factor in the life of The Briers than it had been, and it fit nicely into everything Emily and Duncan wanted to do. They had wanted to upgrade the boardwalk, and so they did, building it up, extending it, and putting in certain attractions. Duncan and Emily wanted to retain the residence aspect of The Briers, as that, they felt, was its soul, so they built a new building, Briers Suites Beach Hotel, especially for transitory visitors. It was as architecturally odd as, and complimentary to, the original building. Duncan and Emily had great fun overseeing its design, planning, and construction. With her new and growing contacts in Europe, Emily wanted to build up Fletcher's, so she did. Most of this growth, of course, was paid for by the immense profits they had received from producing The Arabic Speaking World.

As Duncan never traveled, he never saw a performance of The Arabic Speaking World until they videotaped one and sent it to him on DVD. He enjoyed it, wasn't crazy about it, but he enjoyed it. It gave him more of a taste for the theater, though, which Duncan indulged by bringing in road companies of various plays to play at the Stafford Theater. His method was simply to pick the plays he wanted to see and book them. With the new tourism packing the new Briers Suites Beach Hotel, the runs were always successful.

But what Duncan most enjoyed doing was putting on a Classic Movie Film Festival four times a year at the Stafford Theatre. He had decided to do this the night What Price Glory crashed in a blaze of none. At that time, Duncan assumed he would get little, if any, audience, but he did not care; he just wanted to see the movies he wanted to see on the big screen. He would sit in the theater alone if he had to, although he thought of making attendance a condition of employment at the hotel. However, due to climate change, the new tourism, Emily's marketing skills, and possibly, just possibly, the movies themselves, the festivals became successful and, soon, nationally famous. The festival's logo, a shot of Duncan's Laurel and Hardy chest, became nearly iconic.

Duncan MCed each festival, told amusing stories about the selected films, and hosted the celebrities that started coming regularly. Most importantly, though, he was the number one audience member. As he emotionally responded to a film flickering so beautifully onto the screen he had installed, the audience responded the same. It was as if they were tapped into Duncan, and Duncan fed them. And they fed back a love, a simple, unadulterated love, as they occasionally took their eyes off the moving illusions to sneak a glance at Duncan sitting in his special place, dead center in the theater, bathed in a living, flickering light, looking up towards incomparable giants moving across the screen, sometimes sitting on the edge of his seat, sometimes laughing uproariously, sometimes crying unashamedly. It was quite a wonderful sight to see.

Frank became highly successful. Or, rather, Frank and Allison. His art, her energy; his arrogance, her determination; his humor, her seriousness; his heart, her mind; their story—their love.

The Perfectly Frank Visions of Frank was an art show that became legendary within weeks of its opening. And it did so in an unusually organic way for the times, and not just in a more hype-induced claim to fame. Not that Allison, with the aid of Bebe and Tilly, had not hyped the show and hyped it in the best of current coldly calculating calls for attention. But the warm heartbeat of people moved by Frank's work, and moved to want to spread the word, seeped deeply into likely consciousnesses far more effectively than even key-wording "Frank," "Perfectly Frank," and "Visions of Frank" into the search engines of the World Wide Web. Allison, Bebe, and Tilly wondered why this should be so, looking somewhat stupidly into the horse's mouth. Content and craftsmanship, intelligence and integrity were the simple answer they arrived at after a long night of pondering the subject. The outrageousness of some of Frank's images didn't hurt either.

Every one of the pieces on exhibit sold, and Frank made bold to be happy about that.

Allison and Frank decided, despite this dream-like success in the dream-like New York, to remain in Rubenton, eventually taking over the whole third floor of The Briers and building onto his studio, which became a tourist destination. Frank continued to employ art students as assistants to complete his huge canvases, but now they came from all over the country and eventually the world. He even had Allison find a few not very friendly but talented urban graffiti taggers with police records to be court-ordered to work with him in a program he called "Say it, don't spray it." Frank was surprised that he could teach—such an irony, as he never could be taught. Some of his assistants, the ones he especially mentored, became quite good, building successes and reputations he enjoyed. The main thing he taught them was that the joy of art is in the doing. Every good thing that might happen after doing was just an added-on benefit. But even if nothing good comes— at least you had the joy of doing.

His students loved him not just because he taught them but also because he could make them laugh.

Allison began representing some of Frank's students, building a stable of artists. Frank never once became jealous—he encouraged it. He said it was because he had found success relatively late in life. So what could ever threaten him?

He did become incredibly arrogant, but that was part of his charm because he was so amusing about it. Because of the nature of his work, Frank's opinion was sought by the world at large on a wide range of subjects. Of course, he had a standard answer: "I think my work makes my opinions clear." Nevertheless, they sought after him to elaborate, which he would in an amusing, arrogant way, which, of course, made him even more of a celebrity.

"I don't have to sell you any more," Allison told him one day. "You're pretty good at selling yourself."

Despite all this, deep down inside, Frank was humble. Not that he ever took the wimp's way out and attributed his talent to something "greater than himself," a god or universal mind or some such silliness. But Frank was happy to be in awe that humans—essentially just hunks of clay after all—could be so creative. Not all humans, of course, but enough of them that he felt humble in the face of the fact that he seemed to be one of the elect.

One day, after he and Allison had returned from a trip for a show in Bonn and an unveiling in New York, they sat in the sunshine on Leech Beach, missing the fog, but feeling fine, nevertheless. After some time staring at the ocean, Frank turned to Allison and asked:

"Does your sea creature ever show up anymore?"

Allison thought about that for a moment. The sea creature, in a way, was always with her, as Frank's drawing of it, which still hung on the wall, was her favorite of all he had ever done. But she had to answer:

"No. No, I guess he's gone back down beneath the waves."

"Why is that?"

"You're the only behemoth I can handle now."

"No, really, why do you think?"

"I don't need him anymore, I guess."

"Was he a need?"

"Sure."

"A need for what?"

"If I could have put it into words, I probably wouldn't have needed it."

"Ah."

"Nebulous enough for you?"

"Yes. Nice and murky."

They got up and headed back to The Briers.

"You excite me, you know," Allison said.

"Oh, God, sex again? Isn't ten times already today enough?"

Allison laughed and punched him.

"You know what I mean."

"Do I?"

"In a big, broad, expansive, all-encompassing way."

"Wow. I'm impressed. And I didn't think I could impress myself any more than I already have."

"Idiot. Take me seriously. Do you know how rare this feeling I have may be?"

"Oh, don't say that. That would be too sad for the world."

"But it is, don't you think?"

"I don't know. I don't even want to think about it."

"Why?"

"Might curse what we have."

"No! Do you think?"

"I have been called an iconoclast. But our love is one icon I'll never throw mud at."

"Promise?"

Frank stopped and turned to Allison. He looked at her, into her blue eyes. He ran his hand through her hair, now more gray than blonde and destined to remain that way as he had refused to allow her to color it.

"Knowing you as I do—and I do—you no longer need promises."

Allison smiled and placed her head on Frank's chest to hear his heart.

Dmitri had done Duncan proud. He had picked out the world's fastest, most powerful, most expensive sports car. They had to order it, especially from Los Angeles. The salesman had called Duncan to make sure he was serious, for he could not believe it, and he could not believe the commission he was going to make. Duncan told him: Do it. And get it here fast. Fly the damn thing in if you must. Duncan had made the salesman very, very happy.

Dmitri was incredibly proud of the car. A stupid and unwarranted emotion, of course, as Dmitri had had nothing to do with the design, engineering, construction, or even purchase of the vehicle. He was just the passive receiver. Nevertheless, Dmitri was extremely proud of the car, as if he was the car. Which he probably would not have minded being.

Dmitri and his car became a common sight around town. Duncan had told Dmitri he no longer needed him and let him go but forced one of the hotel's vendors to give him a job. It was an easy, part-time, well-paid job, and once Dmitri had barely graduated from Rubenton High, he had plenty of time to drive his car around town as he tried to decide what to do with his life. A struggle of mental effort that he was not likely to win. But he didn't care. He had a hell of a lot of savings because now he did not have to buy a car. And an easy job bringing in more money, so what was the motivation to think of the future? Now was now and now was really neat. He found that sophomore girls in high school really liked him now. He impregnated two of them but didn't get caught as they had plenty of other suitors to lay blame on for the laying. Dmitri began to realize what a fortunate guy he was, which he took credit for in a monumental misunderstanding of the random nature of the universe.

Life was good; that's all he knew. He could afford the best video games, was getting laid all the time and had a car that made every other car in Rubenton look like shit on wheels.

His favorite thing to do, of course, was to drive Leech Beach Road. Drive? Fly! He would hit 100 a 110 and manfully handle the curves, his *music blasting in a decibel competition with the speed of the car,* **the** landscape whizzing by in a blur, his heart racing, his adrenaline pumping, his brain as focused as it was possible for it to be focused—

Oh, look! That's where old fart Hendrickson's farm used to be. Abandoned now, a big FOR SALE planted into the field. But no one had bought it yet. Who would? Who would want to be a stupid, shit-kicking, egg-plucking, cocoa-making—

Oh—the cocoa—he had liked the cocoa.

But not as much as he liked this! This was fun and fast! This was great and loud! This was happiness as intense, as high, as giddy as— as—as a never-ending, super-powerful ejaculation!

How fortunate it would be if we could all die so happy.

THE END

Before publishing ten critically acclaimed novels, award-winning and Amazon Bestselling author Steven Paul Leiva spent over twenty years in the entertainment industry as a writer and producer. He worked with such talent as Academy Award-winning producer Richard Zanuck; director Ivan Reitman; literary legend and screenwriter Ray Bradbury, and Star Wars producer Gary Kurtz; He even lent his voice to the Academy Award shortlisted (placing in the top ten) animated short, "The Indescribable Nth." https://vimeo.com/14857442

Leiva produced the animation for Space Jam, putting together an ad hoc animation studio for Warner Bros in three days over the phone. During this time, he wrote novels and a play, Made on the Moon, which premiered at the 1996 Edinburgh Festival Fringe, receiving a four-star review from The Scotsman. writing novels. Since 2003, he has published ten novels, a novella, and a book of essays.

His work has been praised by literary great Ray Bradbury, Oscar-winning film producer Richard Zanuck, NY Times bestselling author and Pulitzer Prize finalist Diane Ackerman, and Star Trek actor John Billingsley, the greatest bookworm in Hollywood. He has received the Scribe Award from the International Association of Media Tie-in Writers.
You can find more about Leiva and read his blogs at https://tinyurl.com/ydgpkps8

Blood is Pretty
The First Fixxer Adventure

Meet the Fixxer—with wit and aplomb, he works the fruitful fields of Hollywood, fixing the sins and correcting the stupidities of the denizens therein. In *Blood is Pretty,* he comes to the rescue of "the most beautiful woman I have ever seen" to extricate her from the grip of the soul-sucking sexual desires of a producer born in slime and takes on the task of buying off with money and muscle a film geek who won't cooperate with a director of minuscule talent who simply wants to claim "V"—the geek's "Holy Grail" of a film treatment—as his own.

Hollywood is an All-Volunteer Army
The Second Fixxer Adventure

What those in the know in Hollywood really know is that if they need a dark deed done, if they need a sticky personal or professional problem "fixed," they can call upon the mysterious and dangerous Fixxer. Whether you are a successful comedy film director whose "art" has never truly been appreciated because the country's most important film critic has held a grudge against you since college, or you are a neophyte and naïve screenwriter who resents the professional blackmail she has just suffered, you call upon the Fixxer.

Traveling in Space

A unique first contact novel from the aliens' point-of-view.

The last thing the factfinders—who call themselves Life—expected to find while traveling in space in "The Curious" on a mission from their planet, The Living World, was other life. But one day, they stumble upon the third planet out from a backwater sun and find it teeming with a vast diversity of life, including one sentient and cognizant—if primitive—species that they dub: Otherlife.

Being not only from "The Curious" but inherently curious themselves, they begin to study the Otherlife and their alien culture, discovering such strange things as marriage, intoxicating drinks, weapons of minor and mass destruction, the gleeful inhaling of toxic substances, two-parent families, layered language, genocide, non-nude bathing, and—the strangest thing of all—religion.

This first contact between Life and Otherlife, disconcerting for both, has moments of humor and moments of horror—and neither escapes the encounter unchanged.

12 Dogs of Christmas

A Novelization

Winner of the Scribe Award from the International Association of Media Tie-in Authors.

Based on the beloved independent family film.

12-year-old Emma O'Connor is sent to live with her "aunt" in the small town of Doverville. Emma soon finds herself in the middle of a "dogfight" with the mayor and town dogcatcher. In order to strike down their "no-dogs" law, Emma must bring together a group of schoolmates, grown-ups, and adorable dogs of all shapes and sizes in a spectacular holiday pageant. The 12 Dogs of Christmas is a fun, heartwarming story featuring a diverse canine cast and is perfect for all those who love dogs, kids, and Christmas.

By the Sea
A Comic Novel

A modern comic adult fairy tale with an ensemble cast of Cinderellas. Instead of a kingdom by the sea, our story takes place in and around a residential hotel by the sea. The architecturally eclectic Briers Hotel is situated on Leech Beach, a not particularly inviting beach, being often fog-bound and always scruffy. But it's the perfect setting for our Cinderellas, male and female, who put up with the scruffiness of life while striving to make it through their various personal seaside fogs. Theater; art; antiques; old movies; sex; more sex; death; fast and slow cars, chicken shit and cow poop; military bearing and erotic emissions—not to mention the wicked witch, the sea serpent by the sea shore, the village ogre, the village idiot, and several Prince Charmings—all figure into this merry tale with a multitude of happy endings.

IMP
A Political Fantasia

Thomas P. Powell's ascension in politics was both unusual and yet very American. From traffic cop to Vice President of the United States, his climb up the ladder of public service was often due to the push of random acts and not-so-happy accidents—although Thomas held the opinion that it was due solely to his singular innate moral authority. What matters is what's within; that's the Powell political philosophy. Then, on the cusp of his grasping the last rung of the American political ladder, something truly within suddenly appears. A horrible homunculus, an impetuous imp, climbs out of Thomas's right ear to bedevil his nights and confuse his days and take him on a crazy, wild, nauseating, and nuclear journey.

It's as if *The West Wing* was done as a *Twilight Zone* episode.

And you thought our last political nightmare was surreal.

Journey to Where
A Contemporary Scientific Romance

When a radical experiment into the nature of time is sabotaged, the scientific team finds themselves in an alternate universe, where humans never became the dominant life force. Instead, dinosaurs evolved into intelligent bipeds, developing language and societal structures.

The scientists have to learn to communicate with this alien species, who view them as unusual pets, and figure out how to recreate the original experiment in a non-industrialized world, so they can go back home—assuming there's a home, or even a universe, to return to.

But the scientist who sabotaged them is trapped in this new world with them. And he's looking to rise to power, even if his quest means the death of his traveling companions. A contemporary scientific romance in the tradition of H. G. Wells and Jules Verne

Creature Feature
A Horrid Comedy

THERE IS SOMETHING STRANGE HAPPENING IN PLACIDVILLE!

It is 1962. Kathy Anderson, a serious actress who took her training at the Actors Studio in New York, is stuck playing Vivacia, the Vampire Woman on Vivacia's House of Horrors for a local Chicago TV station. Finally fed up showing old monster movies to creature feature fans, she quits and heads to New York and the fame and footlights of Broadway.

She stops off to visit her parents and old friends in Placidville, the all-American, middle-class, blissfully normal Midwest small town she grew up in. But she finds things strange in Placidville. Kathy's parents, her best friend from high school, the local druggist, and even the Oberhausen twins are all acting curiously creepy, odiously odd, and wholly weird. Especially the town's super geeky nerd, Gerald, who warns of dark days ahead.

Has Kathy entered a zone in the twilight? Did she reach the limits that are outer? Has she fallen through a mirror that is black? Or is it just—just—politics as usual?

Bully 4 Love
A Rather Odd Love Story

Adolphus Seruya is a happy, middle-aged, unambitious bachelor and professor of History at a prominent community college. Then suddenly, SHE walks into his classroom. Lavinia Carson is beautiful in a unique yet compelling way. And radiant almost beyond description. Thus begins a rather odd story of love rejected, love ignored, love found—and cuttlefish pizza.

Extraordinary Voyages

What if a man wanted to go to the moon from the time he was an infant? Not a toddler, not a child, not a young man, but a babe in his mother's arms? What if Baron Munchausen traveled from 1790 to 1641 to take Cyrano de Bergerac to Mars? What if the man who wanted to go to the moon from the time he was an infant wrote some rude poems? What if the author of this book wrote his own Wikipedia page that he was sure Wikipedia would never publish? What if you bought this book and found out?

Includes the critically acclaimed novella *Made on the Moon*.

The Reluctant Heterosexual
A Tragicomedy In Four Movements A Prelude And An Interlude

With *The Reluctant Heterosexual,* Steven Paul Leiva concludes his thematic trilogy: **The Love, Sex and Pursuit of Happiness Novels**. All three novels look at these essential aspects of the human condition, with each novel focusing on one of the three. *By the Sea: A Comic Novel* looks at our unease when unhappy. *Bully 4 Love: A Rather Odd Love Story* takes a skewed view of this most revered emotion. And now, *The Reluctant Heterosexual,* as the title predicts, concerns sex, which is not always the same as love, nor is it always a happy situation. Subtitled *A Tragicomedy in Four Movements A Prelude And An Interlude,* each section of the novel, as in a musical composition, has its own tempo, mood, and form as it tells the story—and stories—of Robert Leslie Cromwell and Sandy Smith. Two *Homo sapiens sapiens* surviving and striving in the late 20th-Century.

Robert and Sandy are intelligent, creative, not unattractive, wealthy, married to each other, and in love. And yet their procreating bodies might as well be standing naked on a savanna in Africa in the late Pliocene Era. It's the sometimes comic conflict between ancient bodies and modern culture. Can there possibly be a happy ending?

The Definition of Luck or The Post-Modern Prometheus

Khadambi Kinyanjui, a 6-foot-five Kenyan who grew up in London, is from a wealthy family. Joe Smith, quite a bit shorter, is a red-headed orphan who grew up with his Aunt Liz in a hole in the California desert. Both are brilliant scientists. One is a neurobiologist, the other an astronomer, who first meet in 2049 under the Tommy Trojan statue at the University of Southern California. They become the best of friends but a very odd couple. And yet, their brotherhood is more robust than most actual brothers.

Then tragedy strikes the pair. Death is near for one of them. What can fend it off? Can the mind, the *self*, be uploaded to some digital realm? Can one become more than a human and far less than an animal? Or will the fix be something unexpected and mysterious? Can this human survive? Can humanity? Can friendship?

Searching for Ray Bradbury
Writings about the Writer and the Man

Includes the title piece written for the *Los Angeles Times* and "The Man Who Was Himself," Leiva's memorial appreciation of Bradbury commissioned by the Science Fiction & Fantasy Writers of America for the Winter 2012/13 edition of their quarterly magazine, *The Bulletin*. Other pieces were originally written for *Neworld Review*, KCET.org, and his personal blog. **With a special foreword by Hugo and Nebula Award-winning author David Brin.**

**"Steven Leiva not only promises but delivers. Bravo!"
— Ray Bradbury, Author of Fahrenheit 451**

"Steven Paul Leiva is a master wordsmith able to take on any genre or blend them. **— Jean Rabe, *USA Today* Bestselling Author**

"(Steven Paul Leiva has a) genuine flair for originality and a distinctive kind of narrative storytelling that quickly captures the reader's total attention." **— *Midwest Book Review***

"Leiva writes…with a great deal of depth and perception." **— Stuart Nulman, Montreal Times**

"Leiva deftly interweaves characters' past and present to create a vibrant ensemble that is immediately engaging." **— *Literary Fiction Book Review***

"Leiva is witty and engaging." **— Areyon Jolivette, *The Daily Californian***

"I hung on to Steven Paul Leiva's every word" **— Joanie Chevalierm, *Readers' Favorite Book Reviews.***

"The author's true strength is in storytelling." **— *Ricky L. Brown, Amazing Stories Magazine.***

www.ingramcontent.com/pod-product-compliance
Lightning Source LLC
Chambersburg PA
CBHW051315250626
47155CB00007B/2332